When you came into my life

— Blanca Moore —

iUniverse, Inc.
New York   Bloomington

When you came into my life

iUniverse books may be ordered through booksellers or by contacting:

iUniverse
1663 Liberty Drive
Bloomington, IN 47403
www.iuniverse.com
1-800-Authors (1-800-288-4677)

ISBN: 978-1-4401-7494-0 (pbk)
ISBN: 978-1-4401-7495-7 (ebook)

Printed in the United States of America

iUniverse rev. date: 10/29/09

For James, my inspiration.....

Acknowledgments:

Sandra Hancock Stark	editing with A Serenade for Reyna and When you came into my life.
Karen Williamson,	for helping me with her knowledge on San Juan, Puerto Rico
Silvia Muir Sigcha	for her help with her knowledge on Costa Rica
Alexys Flowers	for her constant support throughout my work
James M. Moore	for his advice with sailing boats
Miss Lucille	thank you for allowing me to use your anecdote
Lorene Brown	thank you for allowing me to use your anecdote

My sincere thank you, I would not have been able to complete my work without their help.

List of Characters

Charles Hamilton	Father	
Kate Hamilton	Mother	
Irene Hamilton	Daughter	The Hamilton's
Sarah Hamilton	Daughter	
Laura Hamilton	Daughter	
Clare	Housekeeper and friends of the family	
Joanna	Maid	
Lorenzo	Chauffer and gardener	
Cindy	Nanny	
Inez	Apprentice cook	
Dr. Brent Miller	Cardiologist	The clinic
Dr. Darrell Moore	Cardiologist	
Lourdes	Accountant	
Christina Findley Long	Nurse	
Maureen	Nurse	
Betty	Office helper	
Mr. Betancourt	Chief of Police	
Toni Betancourt	Mr. Betancourt's wife	The Betancourt's
Benny Betancourt	Son	
Cristobal Lopez	Father	The Lopez's
Angelita Lopez	Mother	
Dr. Carlos Lopez	Surgeon, son	
Martin Lopez	Son	
Alvaro Lopez	Son	
Kelly	Dr. Lopez Accountant	
Luis Moran	Christina's body guard	
Pete Findley	Christina's father	The Findley's
Theresa Findley	Christina's mother	
Dr. Keith Simon	Partner with Carlos	The Simon's
Cary Simon	wife	
Linda Long	Christina's daughter	
Amy Long	Christina's daughter	
Lisa Tyler	Brent's fiancée	
Carl Smith	Sarah's boyfriend	
Sean	Irene's boyfriend	
Isabel Saldaňa	girl in the Island	
Juan	man from the jetty	

Chapter One

Irene was waiting for her sisters to leave school, they were late, "Father will be upset if we don't get home on time for dinner," Irene thought while she waited for her sisters, Laura and Sarah.

"Oh, you're finally here, what kept you?" Irene asked her sisters.

"The turmoil in the halls. You have no idea how many kids come out from the class rooms at the same time," Laura told her sister.

"Do you remember I used to attend this school?" Irene replied.

"Start the car. Or are we going to argue in here?"

"Let's go."

As usual they were late for dinner. Their father, Charles Hamilton, liked to have an early dinner.

"We're waiting; I hope Clare kept dinner hot for us." Charles said. Charles and Kate had been married for almost twenty five years and they knew nothing would be dull with their three daughters around.

"Did you have a good day, girls?" Kate asked.

"Some of the same, a lot of running around."

"Sarah, you're not saying anything, dear," Kate said. "Is everything all right, sweetie? Oh, here is Clare now with dinner."

"Clare, it looks delicious, and it tastes better." Kate told Clare.

"Irene, today is Friday, do you think Dad would let us go to the Mall?"

"All we can do is ask Sarah. Who are you going with?" Irene asked.

"I thought the three of us could go together, isn't Sean going?"

"If I went, Sarah, I wouldn't care if he came along," Irene said.

"Laura, would you like to go?"

"Yes, I was waiting to see if you got around to asking me."

"Oh, you know I was only securing the trip, if Irene doesn't go, neither are we."

"All right, we can all go if Dad lets us go. Who is doing the asking?"

"You're acting as if we're not allowed to go anywhere. I'll ask," said Irene.

"They're drinking their coffee in the garden," said Laura.

"Dad, Mama, is it all right if we go to the Mall this afternoon?" Irene asked.

"Are the three of you going together?" Charles asked their daughters.

"Yes, we're going together." Sarah answered.

"You mean when you get there you won't split up?" Charles asked with sarcasm.

"Dad, sometimes we want to see something the others won't care for."

"All right, you can go."

"Oh, thank you Dad."

On the way to the Mall, Irene lectured them.

"Sarah, don't leave the Mall, I know how Carl is."

"I won't get out of the Mall, Irene."

"Laura, how about you?"

"Irene, you know how Benny is," she said

"I know, I was teasing you."

"Okay, let me park before you run. One hour. I'll see you right here in one hour."

"Irene, please, we can't go around the Mall in one hour; two hours, okay?"

"I don't know what I have in my head today, but okay, two hours it is."

They all split to where they were to meet their respective boyfriends.

Irene found Sean by one of the stores and started walking with him. In the meantime Laura couldn't find Benny anywhere, she went to one of the coffee shops and sat there to wait for him.

Carl met Sarah, he tried to kiss her. "No Carl, not in public."

"What's a little kiss?" he said. "Okay, if we can't kiss here let's go for a ride."

"No, that's the first thing Irene warned us about. We can't leave the Mall."

"I'm not taking you out of town, just to get a little privacy. Come on, just for a little while."

"Okay, but we can't stay long, all right?"

"Sounds fine to me." Carl told her as he led her to one of the exits.

Carl and Sarah left the Mall. "I don't know why I'm feeling so guilty about leaving; I guess because I promised Irene I wouldn't leave the Mall."

"Oh, we'll be right back, what's the harm in wanting to kiss your girl?"

"Let me find a lonely street so we can neck a little bit," Carl told Sarah. "You know, I want to marry you. Let's elope tonight."

"I can't do that Carl; besides that, I'm only seventeen years old."

"We can tell them you're eighteen; we can go out-of-state and get married."

"Carl, I'm not doing that, don't ask me again," Sarah told him.

He found a remote street and started to kiss Sarah. He started getting too rough with her and she began to pull away from him, telling him to stop. When she did, he started hitting her and telling her he had the right to kiss her, and the more she pulled away from him the more he hit her and pulled on her clothes. He slapped her face with both hands with a rage unknown to Sarah; and then he opened the car door and with both feet he kicked her. He pushed her out of the car and left her there in the middle of the street and took off fast.

Sarah laid there, motionless; then she began to move ever so slowly; at first to find out where she was. She found herself in the middle of a dirty street. She looked around and started to crawl off of the street and towards the sidewalk; . . .crying.

Sarah stayed there on the street sobbing. A car stopped. "***Oh my God***," she thought "***he is back!***" The car stopped in front of her, and she saw Benny getting out of his car.

He stopped when he saw her. **"Sarah, is that you?"** he said when he recognized her.

"Benny! What are you doing here? Laura is waiting for you at the Mall."

"Get in my car. What happened to you, anyway?" he asked helping her. "Do you know where Laura is waiting for me?" Benny helped Sarah up and into his car.

"No, we split up when we got there and I don't know where she was supposed to be waiting for you. I was stupid enough to go for a ride with Carl."

"I had to run an errand for my Dad at the last minute, now I'm glad."

"Yes, me too, I don't know how I would have gotten home otherwise. Benny, I can't go to the Mall looking like this; I'll stay in the car."

"Okay, don't worry; I have some magazines there, just cover your face in them." Benny parked the car away from the Mall entrance and started to run in.

He was running looking everywhere, when he finally saw Laura.

"Laura, I'm so sorry I'm late, but I had to run an errand for my Dad and on the way back I found Sarah in the middle of the street. Carl beat her up and pushed her out of his car and left her there." he told Laura.

"Oh my God! Where is she?"

"She's in my car waiting for us. Let's find Irene."

"No, Benny, you find Irene and tell her what has happened; I'll go to Sarah and stay with her. Where is your car?"

"I'm parked by the fountain. I'm sorry I was late, Laura, but that is the reason I found Sarah."

Laura left the Mall and Benny started looking for Irene and Sean.

"Oh good! There is Irene," Benny told himself.

"Irene, I've been looking for you. Something happened to Sarah; she is in my car, I think you better come with me. Laura is already there with Sarah."

"What's happened to Sarah, Benny?"

"I'll tell you once we're outside of the Mall, Irene." Benny said.

Once they were outside, Benny explained to Irene what had happened with Sarah. "And that is how I found her, Irene."

"I knew he was no good, but I couldn't tell her. I didn't want to wait until he showed her what he could do to her." Tears rolled down Irene's face. Irene got in the car and hugged Sarah. "Baby," she said, "look at yourself, let's go to a gas station and get your face washed. You can't go home looking like this."

"Oh, Irene! What are we going to tell Dad and Mama?"

"And look! Your dress is torn and soiled. How are we going to explain that?"

"We can't claim an accident because Laura and I are not dirty."

"We can say a bicycle ran over you," Laura said.

"Not bad, but if we start making up stories it will never end. I say we tell Mama and we can spare Dad from this kind of news. Mama can tell Dad on her own time,"

"I guess so." Sarah said.

Benny said, "I think you should press charges against Carl, Sarah."

"He made sure there were no witnesses, it's his word against mine."

"Well, there are ways to take care of him. For example, a court order to prevent Carl to get close to Sarah again. If he does, he can be put in jail," Benny said.

"Yes, that's a restraining order, is that correct, Benny?" Laura asked.

"That's right, it can be done very discretely, you can make an appointment with my Dad. You know my Dad is the Chief of Police, right? I can let him know you're going to call, and you don't need to talk with anyone else."

"First things first, let's go in this gas station so you can wash your face, Sarah."

"Are you coming with me, Irene?"

"Of course I am, baby." (Irene was several years older than her sisters and she treated them like her own children.)

Irene combed Sarah's hair and gave her, her compact and her lipstick; Sarah did her best to fix up her face and said, "Let's go."

Clare had worked for the Hamilton's since Charles and Kate first got married and Kate treated Clare more as a friend than a maid.

"Charles, you look a bit pale today, is there anything wrong with you?" Clare asked.

"That's just what I told him when we were coming downstairs," Kate said.

"What is this, a conspiracy? I'm going to lay down for a bit," he said.

Kate looked at him leaving the dining room table. She looked at Clare and got up herself and followed Charles to the living room.

When she arrived, Charles was unconscious. "CHARLES! CHARLES!"

The girls were walking in from the Mall at the time.

"What happened?" Everybody rushed to the living room. "Mama, what is it? What happened to Daddy?"

"Irene, get help, I think your father had a heart attack!"

Irene rushed to the phone to make the call.

The Ambulance arrived and the Medics started to work on Charles. "Miss, call Dr. Miller, he is not in the phone book yet, he is the new Cardiologist. You have to call the operator to get his phone number; you want him there for your father," The medic told Irene.

"Do you know his full name?" Irene asked.

"Brent Miller, I'm sure."

They gave Charles some medication in the IV they had just placed in his arm.

"Dr. Miller works out of the Doctors Hospital, and it's a great facility."

"Take him there, we'll follow you," Kate said.

"Irene, did you get in touch with the Doctor?" Kate asked

"Yes, Mama, he is on his way. Do you want me to drive?"

"Of course, baby. I think I'm too nervous to drive myself." Kate told Irene.

Sarah said, "I'll be right back." She had changed her dress by the time she went back downstairs.

Kate, her daughters, and Clare were all there. They sat quietly in the waiting room.

Dr. Miller came out to speak with them. "Mrs. Hamilton?" he asked.

"Yes, Dr. Miller, how is my husband?" Kate asked Dr. Miller.

"He is resting comfortable now, he had a mild heart attack. I'm going to put him on a low fat diet; be careful what he eats, he needs to eat, but not to indulge himself, only food that is good for him. I'm going to keep him in the hospital for a few days to rest and run some tests and start him on his new diet, but when you take him home you have to be careful with him."

"Yes Doctor, we were just telling him how pale he looked. He got up from the dining room table and I followed him to the living room to check up on him and he had already passed out. He only had time to walk there before he collapsed."

"That's good information, Mrs. Hamilton." Dr. Miller told Kate. As he looked at the girls surrounding their mother he asked, "Are they your daughters?"

"Yes, Dr. Miller, this is Irene, Sarah and Laura, and Clare is a family friend."

"I'll give you a copy of that diet tomorrow; I think I have a copy in my office; if I go to my office I'll bring it in, otherwise it'll have to wait unless one of you would come there and pick it up. My office is on Maple St."

"All right. Good night Dr. Miller, thank you for coming in tonight."

Kate woke up all covered up with a blanket.

"Oh, I don't think I'll be able to straighten out again," she said.

"Me either," Clare said.

"Clare, what on earth are you doing here?"

"You didn't think I was going to leave you here by yourself, did you?"

"I told the girls last night to take care of themselves the best way they could," Clare said.

"Good for you, but I don't remember them leaving."

"You got pretty sleepy very soon."

"Did you go in to check on Charles?"

"Yes, but he was out all night, just like you were,"

"I didn't sleep well the night before last, so last night caught me by surprise."

"I guess," Clare said.

"What time is it anyway?"

"It's not eight yet."

"Good morning, Mama. Clare."

"Irene, you got up early!" Kate said.

"Mama, how is Daddy," Irene asked ahead of her sisters.

"He is still sleep."

"Let's go have a look; he might be awake by now."

As they were going in, Dr. Miller met them at the door.

"Good morning, everybody," he said.

"Good morning, Doctor Miller," the girls said

"Everybody is up so early this morning," he said to them.

"We came to visit Papa."

Dr. Miller addressed his next question to Irene. "Are you still in school?"

"I'm in my last year of Financial School at the University," she said.

"Impressive," Dr. Miller said.

"It is not like being a Doctor, but then, I didn't want to be a Doctor."

"Listen, I didn't go by my office to get your father's diet. Would you mind coming by to pick it up?"

"Is your office open on Saturday?" Irene asked him.

"Sorry, no. I guess at this point, I need to visit with my patient," he said smiling.

When they got back in the car, Sarah asked Irene, "What was all that about?"

"Nothing, he wants me to go by his office and pick up a diet for Dad."

"Really? And what else?" Sarah played her sarcastic game.

"Nothing." Irene said.

Irene was looking for Dr. Miller's name somewhere on the street; she finally found it, she parked the car and walked to the office. Irene found Dr. Miller working the office window.

"Dr. Miller, what are you doing at the window?" I thought you were the Doctor."

"I'm just opening my office, and I don't have a Secretary, do you want the job?"

"I might, you know, since this is my last year and I don't have any more credits left to do. I just took a chance to come by after you told me you're not open."

"No, we're not, but there is so much to do. Well, walk around to the inside and start working."

"No, not this minute! I have to pick up my sisters from school; they had their SAT test today. I have to ask my parents if they approve of me working."

"Really? Can't you make your own decisions?"

"Dr. Miller, I'm still in school; not looking for a job."

"You're right. I'm just eager. My personnel consist of my Accountant," he said.

"Well, I'll ask Mama this afternoon. We have to ask my Father later, are you going to give me my father's diet, Dr. Miller?"

"Where is my head? Let me see, here are the diets," He said giving Irene one.

When Irene arrived at the school everybody had left, and Sarah and Laura were waiting alone.

"Was this a joke?" Sarah said.

"No, did the school close earlier today?"

"No, Irene, we've been standing here for thirty minutes waiting for you. By the way, where were you?" an aggravated Sarah asked Irene.

"I went to Dr. Miller's office to get father's diet, but I couldn't have been there that long." she said surprised at the events.

"All right, there is no need of bickering." Laura said, "We forgot to tell Irene to pick us up earlier today since we only came for our SAT test. No one knew at what time we were getting out of school."

"By the way," Irene said, "Dr. Miller wants me to work in his office. He doesn't have a secretary, and he was working the window when I arrived."

"Oh, now we know what you were doing, you were looking for a job."

Irene just looked at Sarah and shook her head and went on.

"Sarah, did you have any problems at school today?"

"I did, but I went to the Principal's office and Carl left me alone."

"How is your face?"

"I needed a thicker layer of make up this morning."

When they arrived at the Intensive Care Unit, Kate was there and of course, Clare at her side.

"Mama, haven't you been home?"

"I tried to tell her to go rest a bit, but she won't listen to me." Clare told them.

"What did the Doctor say?" Irene asked

"We're still waiting for test results," Kate said.

"Mama, let me stay here now. I don't have to go back to school; you know I don't have any more credits to complete. Go home. If there is any news I'll call you."

"I think I'll do it, Irene, because I'm getting so tired."

Kate addressed Dr. Miller saying, "Dr. Miller, I'm glad you came back."

"I received the results I was waiting for, Mrs. Hamilton, I recommend a triple by-pass for your husband, it's the safest way to repair the damage he has."

"Who will perform the surgery, Dr. Miller?"

"I am the surgeon, Mrs. Hamilton." he said. "I can give you my credentials. I am capable to do the surgery."

"Oh, I only meant, I didn't know who the surgeon was," Kate said.

"I want everybody here before seven in the morning so you can talk to your husband before we start giving him any kind of anesthetics," he said.

"I was going to leave, but now I think I'll stay," Kate said.

"Mrs. Hamilton, I believe you need to rest tonight, so you can stay here tomorrow night. I saw you last night, there is just so much you can take." he said.

"Mama, let me stay as we had planned, you can all go home," Irene said.

A few minutes after six in the morning, Kate and her daughters, accompanied by Clare were all there.

"How is everything, Irene?"

"The same, Mama, I went in to see Papa, but he was asleep every time," she said.

"I'm going in to see him; maybe he's awakened by now," Kate said.

"Charles, I was hoping you would be awake, how are you feeling this morning?"

"Great, Kate, I wish you didn't worry so much about me."

"How can I not, Charles? You're on your way to heart surgery," Kate told him swallowing her tears.

Charles held her hand. "Kate, we all know we're here on borrowed time."

"But we all want to borrow as much time as possible," she said trying to smile at him.

"All right, it's true, but I feel it's not my time yet, okay?"

His voice was absolutely emotionless and it frightened her.

She replied in a low and terrified voice. "I'll be here waiting for you, Charles." Kate told him as she leaned over to kiss him good bye. "The girls are outside the door." she told him.

The nurses were there to take him to the Operating Theater.

"See you later, Dad."

"The Lord will be with you." they said to their father.

"Girls, I think there is a Chapel around here somewhere," Kate said.

"I know where it is, Mama, let's go," Irene told her mother.

It seemed they had waited for hours. Kate must have gone to the main doors dozens of times. Finally, Dr. Miller opened the double doors hard as he came out fast. It startled Kate, "Dr. Miller!" Kate said in a fainted voice.

"I'm sorry, Mrs. Hamilton; I guess I must have been coming out faster than I thought." She dismissed it with her hand.

"How is Charles, Dr. Miller?"

"He is doing fine; you can see him in a few minutes. By that time all the girls were there waiting to hear about their father.

"I don't want everybody going in at once, and I don't want anyone crying or that looks as if they have been crying. That is not good for him," Dr. Miller advised. "Mrs. Hamilton, you look very frail to me. I'd like for you to eat three full meals every day, and get plenty of rest, because if you don't, you'll be in a lot of trouble, Mrs. Hamilton."

When they were coming out of the ICU Room, Kate almost collapsed as soon as they reached the hall.

"Mother! Please. Don't do that," Irene said.

"Oh, Irene, he looks so bad, he has a tube inside of his mouth."

"Yes, Mama, you were told about it, when you went to learn about the surgery."

"Well, I had forgotten about it; it's terrible."

Clare helped Kate to a nice easy chair.

"Kate, let me get you something to eat."

"I can't eat anything, Clare."

"Do I have to remind you what Dr. Miller said about you?"

"Okay, get something, but very small Clare;

"Did the girls go to school?"

"Today is Sunday; they went home for a little while, Kate. Irene was talking about staying with Charles tonight, but I think you should let me stay and she can relieve me after school tomorrow."

"Yes, I don't think they need to stay here overnight; you and I can manage."

"And you, only if you go home and take a nap."

"You need a nap as much as I do."

"I'm a tough woman, Kate, I can take anything."

"Clare, you're just getting over having all your teeth pulled and having your plates set. Are the plates bothering you any?"

"Oh no, they did a very good job."

"When can we go back in to see Charles?"

"Every two hours, Kate."

When Clare went back to the waiting room, she found Kate sound asleep. She shook her head and tried to cover Kate up with a blanket she had brought from home.

She went to sit down on another couch and put her feet up and went to sleep herself. When Irene and her sisters came back to the hospital, that's how they found them both. It was time to go in. Irene started to go in and had second thoughts; her Mama would kill her if she didn't wake her up when it was time to visit her father.

"Come on Mama, it's time to visit Papa." But she couldn't wake her up. She tried again; "I didn't know Mama could sleep so deep," she thought. But she called her again and again, then she called Clare, "Call somebody, Clare; something is going on here with Mama."

She knelt in front of her mother and held her hands. Dr. Miller was there in no time; "What happened to your mother?"

"I was hoping you could tell me, Doctor." Irene said with a shaking voice.

"Let me see," he picked her up easily. Kate was a very small woman and Brent was a muscular man without having obvious muscles. He took her into E.R.; Irene followed them. "Clare, stay here, don't tell the girls yet." Irene asked Clare.

Brent listened to her heart, "Irene, your mother is extremely exhausted, and she passed out from exhaustion."

"Mother! She couldn't stay away from Dad, she almost collapsed coming out of the ICU room earlier."

"Irene, she is not eating or sleeping, she is under a lot of stress. Not a good combination. Your father probably will stay one more day in ICU. When he gets out of there, your mother will feel a lot better," Brent told Irene. "Do you want to sit here with her? It might make her feel better when she wakes up."

"What do I say to her when she does Dr. Miller?"

"Tell her she needed a good rest, it's the truth. But after that; I'll have a talk with your mother. She has to do a better job taking care of herself."

"I'll appreciate that very much Dr. Miller. She doesn't listen to us." Dr. Miller left and Irene leaned her head on the back of the chair and went to sleep.

Laura and Sarah woke Irene up, "Irene, why is Mama sleeping here?" Irene put her finger over her mouth to ask them to be silent and motioned them outside of the room, once there, she told them what had happened.

"Poor, Mama, as always; she just couldn't stay away from Dad."

"Yes, but we're all going to have to watch out for her and make sure she eats well and gets proper rest."

"By the way, Benny, told his father about what happened the other day with Carl, and we're letting time pass." He thinks Sarah needs to go to the Police Station and file her complaint," Laura told them.

"I know that; but we can hardly do it without letting our parents know, I don't see how we can tell Mama now," said Irene.

"Can we at least get a restraining order?" Laura asked.

"I think I want to do that, Irene. If you come with me, I do want to try to keep Carl from approaching me at school," Sarah said.

"I'll come with you Sarah. Laura and Clare can stay here. Is that all right with both of you?"

"Of course, but what do I tell Mama?"

"About her sleeping here?"

"Tell her the truth. She collapsed from exhaustion. Dr. Miller brought her here, she needed to rest."

Irene and Sarah arrived at the Police Station. Once inside Irene asked for Mr. Betancourt; they were immediately ushered into his office.

"Miss Hamilton, come in. My son Benny told me you might be coming in. What may I help you with?"

"This is my sister Sarah, she is seventeen years old, and my father had an open heart surgery yesterday, that's the reason our parents couldn't be here with her."

"All right, tell me anything you think I need to know."

"Last Friday, after school, I went for a ride with Carl Smith. He promised me we would be back to the Mall in a few minutes, where my sisters were waiting for me. But instead, he parked the car and started kissing me; I protested. I told him to take me back at once. It made him mad and he started slapping me, punched me hard; he tore my clothes. The more I protested, the harder he hit me, then he kicked me with his feet until he pushed me out of the car where he left me. I crawled from the middle of the street where Benny found me and took me to my sisters."

"Did you know that Carl has a Police record, Miss Hamilton?"

"No, he was always demanding, but other than that; I had no reason to suspect."

"Well, he does. Do your bruises still show? And what do you want me to do about Carl?"

"I was hoping to get a restraining order, so he won't approach me at school" said Sarah.

"That won't be a problem. Also, stop by the investigation department and let them take a couple of pictures; they might want to clean your make up."

"Of course. If Carl approaches me, what am I supposed to do?"

"Call us, you call us <u>immediately</u>."

"Thank you for your help, Mr. Betancourt," Irene told him.

"You need to sign some forms before you leave," he told Sarah.

On the way back to the hospital Sarah told Irene, "I was so scared, thank you for coming with me, Irene."

"It was better because he knew we were coming. Let's hurry up so we don't have much explaining to do."

"I think if Mama is up to it, I want to go ahead and tell her, Irene."

"I'm glad you feel that way Sarah, she'll understand why she wasn't told sooner."

When they arrived at the hospital; their Mother, Laura and Clare were still visiting with Charles.

"Papa, they took the tube out of your mouth! I'm so glad."

"Well," said Charles, "to what do we owe the honor of your presence?"

"Should I ask Dr. Miller to place the tube in your throat again?" Irene told Charles laughingly. "Oh Dad, we had some errands to run, but we have been outside most of the time."

"I know baby, I only wanted to tease you a little bit."

"Okay, in that case, I forgive you."

"Sarah, what in the world do you have on your face?" Charles asked unexpectedly.

"I was running at school and I didn't see a boy on a bicycle Dad."

"He really threw you, didn't he?"

"Yes, but he fell as well."

"Well, that's one of the hazards of going to school."

Kate walked to the hall, and Irene knew it meant for her to follow her, so she followed her mother, and Sarah followed them as well.

"What do you mean Sarah was run over by a bicycle and I wasn't told?" She was livid, trembling, she was infuriated.

"Mama, sit down please; we need to talk," Irene told her.

"Sarah told Daddy that to calm him down, but that was not what really happened. What happened was, and you understand that because with Dad's heart attack first, and then the surgery we couldn't come out and tell you any of it before now. It was Carl who beat Sarah up, Mama."

Kate stood up. "What? What are you saying?"

"He left her in the middle of the street, and it was fortunate that Benny just happened to come by because he had an errand to run for his father, and he was coming that way, he picked her up literally from the street and brought her to the Mall where we were."

"And why were you not at the Mall like you were supposed to have been, Sarah?"

"It was my fault Mama, I shouldn't have gotten out of the mall, but the fact is; I did, Carl convinced me."

"Anyway, Mama," Irene told her, "Sarah and I were at the Police Station this afternoon to file a complaint against Carl. Mr. Betancourt, the Police Chief, filed a restraining order against Carl so he won't approach Sarah in school or anywhere else."

"All right Sarah, I hope this taught you a lesson you won't soon forget. When we tell you something, there is a reason; you know that."

"Yes Mama, I knew that, but now more than ever, I'm sorry." Sarah said with her face buried in her hands, sobbing.

Kate put her hands on Sarah's shoulders. "All right, we won't speak of this again. I don't think anyone has eaten, how about if we have a bite to eat at the Cafeteria?"

"I love you, Mama." Sarah told her.

Irene went to call Laura and Clare so they could eat dinner together. When she got back to her mother; two Policemen were talking with Sarah. She put her hands over her face and began to cry.

"What happened?" asked Irene.

"We were attempting to deliver the restraining order against Carl Smith, and he began to run. It's customary to ask the person to stop or we shoot. And when he began to run, he was shot and killed; he had a record, so obviously he thought it was regarding something about it, he never knew it was only for a restraining order."

"Oh, Irene, it's all my fault Carl is dead," Sarah said sobbing.

"No Sarah, if he hadn't done what he did, you wouldn't have had to send him a restraining order. You couldn't have allowed him to hit you like that again." Irene stayed behind to console her sister who was blaming herself for Carl's death.

Chapter Two

"It feels so good to be at home again." Charles said.

"Charles, we're all going to be on your diet so you won't have an excuse."

"But you don't need to lose weight."

"Your diet is not for that, it's only a healthy diet."

"Well then, I'm glad I'm the reason no one is going to have a heart attack in our family," Charles said smiling. "Let's go for a walk, darling. I want to go to the garden. You know? I saw our garden when I was at the hospital," he said.

"What do you mean?"

"I think my eyes were closed most of the time after surgery and I imagined I was in the garden sitting on that swing with you; that kept my mind occupied."

"How nice, I'm glad you told me that Charles. Are you sure you're up for a walk that far?"

"Kate, it's not far."

"It's far for you." She told him.

"We'll ask Dr. Miller next time we see him, okay?"

"By the way, he asked Irene to work in his office."

"Doing what?"

"Running the office, I think."

"Has Irene finished school?"

"She said she doesn't have any more classes."

"Well, if she wants to work there, I think it'll be all right."

"Okay, I'll tell her, are you ready to walk back to the house, Charles?"

"Yes, I guess Clare has breakfast ready by now. By the way, how is her mouth?"

"She is eating all right."

Clare met them at the dining room door.

"I was going to call you. The girls are here and I don't want them to disappear."

"They won't. Let's eat, Kate." Charles told her.

When they sat, Kate said, "Let's say a special prayer today that your father is home, let's join hands," They joined hands and Kate said a beautiful prayer.

"Clare, this is a beautiful lunch, are you sure it is part of the diet?" Charles asked Clare.

"It's just decorated," Clare told him. Kate smiled and shook her head.

"Irene, I talked to your father, he said if you want to work at Dr. Miller's office it's okay with him."

"Thank you, Dad. I was trying to think about what to do with my free time."

Irene got dressed and quickly went to Dr. Miller's office.

"Dr. Miller, is your offer still open?" she asked him as she walked in.

"You still see me behind the window, don't you? But I hired a new employee, a Nurse. Come in and I'll introduce you. Christina Long, meet Irene Hamilton." They both smiled and hugged.

"What is this, don't I get to introduce you?" he asked smiling.

"No, you don't. We went to school together, but we had lost touch with each other."

"We were best friends; haven't seen each other since she got married." Irene said.

"Okay, now we have someone for billing, a Nurse and you Irene will run the office and the patients, is that too much?"

"We'll try it and see how it goes, don't you think?"

"Also, I've in mind to enlarge my practice and bring in another Doctor; I might as well let you know now."

"Yes, we need to know any plans you may have, when the new Doctor arrives."

"I'm sure we'll need another nurse, and another person to do a little from each desk.

'How many patients do you have now?" Irene asked.

"You'll have to ask Lourdes that; I'm sure she can tell you."

"Lourdes," Irene began....

"One hundred and twenty seven patients," she said

"And you have been handling everything by yourself?"

"No, I hired someone from the "Office for Hire" Agency. I just haven't been able to find anyone who wanted the position on a permanent basis. I was getting desperate."

"Who wouldn't be?"

"All right, when did you start working here, Christina?"

"Today." she answered.

"Well, Lourdes, we'll both need your help," Irene told Lourdes.

"It's very simple," she said. And she proceeded to explain the job to them. They were all very involved with their instructions when someone came in. A beautiful young woman; Irene looked outside. There was a convertible parked by the door that wasn't there earlier; hers, she was sure.

"My name is Lisa Tyler. Is Dr. Brent Miller in?" her voice was despotic. She added, "My things are on the back seat, bring them in," she told Irene in a very authoritarian voice.

Irene couldn't believe her ears. "Really?" She said. "Bring them in yourself if you want them; someone might steal them." she said in an amused voice.

"Don't you work here?" she asked Irene.

"Not as a doorman, I run the office. We have a Nurse and an Accountant. Sorry, you're out of luck, no doorman," she said smiling at her.

Lisa was furious when she walked to the door to get "her things;" Brent came in.

"Brent, darling." She told him throwing herself at him. "No one wants to bring my things from the car," she said kissing him.

"Lisa, this is my office, not your Hotel," he said disgusted with her. "What are you doing here anyway?"

"I came to see you, I haven't heard from you, so I thought it was high time I came myself."

"I didn't call because our engagement is over."

"No, did you believe that?" She said acting amused.

"Yes, I did, we are through."

She looked around. "Shhh" she said putting a finger over his mouth, "they'll hear you."

"Let them hear me, it's the truth; it's over between us and you know it."

"But I already booked a room at the hotel."

"Spend one night here, and leave tomorrow, I don't want to see you again."

"Do you have another girlfriend?"

"No, but I'm not looking for one either, not one like you anyway."

"I brought you a gift."

"No, thank you Lisa, I don't want any of your gifts."

"But you did before."

"I have them all packed, you can take them all back."

Lisa had fire in her eyes when she walked out, "You'll never hear from me again." she told him.

"Is that a promise?" Brent asked her.

"Dr. Miller," Irene told him. "You saved yourself a bad headache for the rest of your life."

"I know; I wanted to finish that relationship for a long time. I kept waiting for her to do it, and she did because I moved over here. She even gave me a ring back I was stupid enough to give her, so I wasn't about to take her back. I want to apologize to all of you for what she said to you."

"She wasn't talking to Christina or I, she was talking to Irene," Lourdes told Brent.

"Do you mean....?" Brent pointed to Irene.

"Yes, I had the honor all by myself."

"I'm sorry Irene; don't ask me why, she doesn't need a reason to do what she does best: insult people." Brent said. "I tell you what; go to lunch with me as a peace gesture."

"Oh no, you don't have to take me to lunch, I'm fine, really."

"If you don't go to lunch with me, I'll assume you're mad at me."

"Lunch it is, I don't want anyone to accuse me of anything," she said smiling at Brent.

As soon as Brent left, Christina and Lourdes approached Irene. "I see you're flirting with the boss."

"He started it, didn't you see him?"

"And why didn't you stop him?" Christina asked Irene.

"Have you noticed how cute he is?"

"I was sure you have a boyfriend. You used to always have one."

"A boyfriend? Even engagements get broken. Didn't you witness one that was broken only a few minutes ago?" Irene said being ironic.

"Oh, you're the same as you were in school." Christina told her.

Brent came out of his office. "Are you ready to go to lunch, Irene?"

"Yes, Dr. Miller."

"Irene, while we visit and no one is around, please call me, Brent."

"All right Brent, I'll be glad to. Where do you want to eat lunch?"

"I'm not really familiar with restaurants around here, why don't you lead the way and make a suggestion?"

"Well, what do you feel like eating for lunch today?"

"I would like a good lunch because I didn't have time for breakfast."

"Okay that's a good start, how about a steak house? They have everything."

"Tell me how to get there."

Irene explained to Brent the way to the restaurant and he parked.

They were seated by the window; Irene turned her face toward Brent and smiled. That's when she saw Christina and her husband Mike eating lunch.

"Look Brent, there is Christina and her husband, Mike. I didn't like him for her. I don't know what she saw in him."

Their waitress came over with the menus, "What would you like to eat?"

"I want a ham and cheese sandwich and the soup of the day," Irene ordered.

"And you, Sir?"

"I want a medium-well sirloin steak, baked potato and a green salad."

"Yes, you must have been hungry," Irene teased him.

Christina stopped at their table and Mike was forced to do the same.

"Irene, Dr. Miller, how nice it's seeing you here. Meet my husband, Mike Long."

Brent stood up and shook Mike's hand, "its nice meeting you Mike."

"How are you Mike?" Irene asked him.

"Excuse us, we need to leave," Mike said as he pushed Christina out of his way.

Brent looked at them as they walked away.

"I see what you mean, who can like him?"

"Unfortunately for Christina, she did. We better hurry up; I know it's your office, but we still have to be there on time for the patients."

"When you're right, you're right." He finished up his steak and they left.

When they arrived at the office, she noticed Christina had been crying. She didn't say anything to her, but she watched her, and when she knew no one was around she approached her.

"Christina, what's the matter with you, you were fine earlier."

She looked down and tears started to roll down her face. Irene put her arm around her. "How did you get like this so quickly?"

"She lifted her sleeve and showed her a big bruise."

"Christina, was it Mike?"

"Who else, Irene? My back and my legs are in the same shape."

"He beat you up that fast? You were just with us not more than twenty minutes ago."

"He has practice."

"Why do you allow him to do that to you?

"I don't know what to do; I can't earn enough money to support my children and rent an apartment somewhere, he knows that."

"Christina, you're coming to my house, leave that good-for-nothing, you know my parents would love to have you staying with us."

"I have to plan to leave him, Irene. I tried it before and he told me if I tried it again, he'll kill me, and I believe him."

"We'll see about that. You can put a restraining order against him, if he gets within a certain distance from you, you can call the police and they put him in jail.

"If I could believe he'll stay in jail, but overnight won't do. He'll come after me with more fury."

"Now that we found each other you're no longer alone, Christina." Christina hugged Irene, "Let's go to work or I'll be without a job."

Irene went into Brent's office. She was fuming. "Do you know what just happened?"

"No, but I think I'm going to find out."

"Mike beat up Christina when they left the restaurant, she is covered with bruises."

"What do you mean, he beat her up?"

"She showed me her arm, but she said her back and her legs were in the same shape."

"She is my employee now; get her to go to the examination room please."

"Christina, Dr. Miller said for you to go to the examination room."

"Whatever for?"

"Because like I told you earlier; you're no longer alone, Christina."

"Would you come in with me, Irene?

"Of course, Christina."

"My God! Christina, what kind of man is he?" Brent asked Christina.

"Not a good one, Dr. Miller."

"You need to go to the Police Station and press charges against him. Ask for a restraining order, and move away from that house, do you have anywhere to go?"

"Yes," Irene said, "she can go to my house."

"You are good friends, aren't you?"

"Only the best," Irene answered.

"I have to pick up the children at Day Care, and then I'll go home and pack."

"Christina, may I suggest to go to the Police Station first?"

"You're right."

"It's been slow this afternoon, why don't you go ahead and leave so you don't waste time."

"Thank you Dr. Miller, thank you Irene. I'll come to your house tomorrow."

"That is a good thing you're doing Irene, offering her shelter, just like that."

"Not really, we have been best friends all our lives, until she married Mike."

Christina went to the Police Station and waited to talk to someone about pressing charges against Mike. When she was waited on, she was asked so many questions, she was uncomfortable. Then she was asked to go to another room and take her clothes off.

"Is there a Police Woman in this Department, Sir?"

"Not at this time, we need to take photographs of your body to confirm what you said happened to you."

She raised her sleeve and showed the Policeman her arm. He laughed.

"Could I use your phone please?" Christina asked the Policeman.

"Of course."

She called the office and told Irene she needed her there at once. Then she went outside and told the Policeman she was going to wait for her friend. When Irene arrived, she didn't arrive alone, Brent was with her.

"Is there a problem Christina?"

"They wanted me to disrobe, Dr. Miller; I just couldn't do it without a woman present."

"Sir, I thought you had to be more professional than that at a Police Station." The Policeman just looked at Brent and shrunk his shoulders. "Coming?" Christina and Irene went into the room where they took photos of Christina.

"Thank you for coming, both of you. It felt so good to have someone to call for a change."

"I should have come with you to begin with, but I didn't think they were going to act like that."

"I guess I'm just lucky, Irene," she said trying to smile.

"Do you want to go ahead and come home with me now, Christina?"

"I'm so scared Irene."

"Okay, you'll come with me. We'll get the children and then go to my house. You can pack some other time. In the meantime, you can wear my clothes."

Irene and Christina and both of her children walked into Irene's house.

It was a very spacious mansion with ample beautiful gardens. The home was larger than Christina remembered. A large chandelier adorned the living room; the dining room also had a chandelier somewhat smaller; large paintings hung in different locations. Large vases with beautiful silk flowers were located everywhere. The furniture looked to Christina like French decor. Heavy drapes coordinated with the rest of the house.

It startled her at first. "Oh Irene, I didn't remember you're so rich."

"Christina, how can you say that?"

"You're so nice; I've forgotten that you came with money."

Irene just shook her head smiling at Christina.

"Mama, Papa, look who I have here with me."

"Christina! How nice it is seeing you again. And look who we have here?"

"This is Linda, she is seven years old, and she goes to second grade. Amy is only two years old, and she goes to Day Care."

"Mama, I invited them to stay with us."

"Of course, Christina, it's high time we have some little ones in this house."

"Thank you, Mrs. Hamilton, I appreciate you so much."

"None of that, you know you have always been welcome in our home."

"Irene, I think the back bedroom looking onto the garden will be the best bedroom for them; its larger so she can have the children with her. They need to find their way around in this big house. I'll get Clare to get smaller beds for the children."

"Oh Mrs. Hamilton, I wish I didn't have to be so much trouble for you."

"You're not, we love to have you and the children, and you know that."

Irene went upstairs with Christina to show her the way to her bedroom and to give her some of her wardrobe.

In the morning; Christina came out early with the children ready for school,

"Good morning," she said.

"Good morning, did you sleep well? Christina, let's have breakfast." Irene told her.

"We have to rush or we'll be late for work. Thank you for letting me wear your clothes."

"I'll tell Brent you'll be along in a few minutes; he might not be there himself."

"Yes, but he is the boss." she said smiling. "Look at this, I'm actually smiling."

"You have a lot more where that smile came from Christina, you'll see."

"I want to thank everybody for welcoming me with my children."

"Irene told me last night why you are here. If she hadn't invited you I would have been very disappointed in my daughter."

Sarah and Laura came by running, "We're late; good bye."

"How are they going to school?" Kate asked

"Mama, Clare is going to take them; have you forgotten?"

"Yes, I knew, I just didn't remember."

"Mr. Hamilton, how are you feeling this morning?" Christina asked Charles.

"I'm as healthy as a bull." he said.

Everybody laughed and left to go to their respective duties.

Irene was visiting with Lourdes.

"I don't know why I have a bad feeling with Christina not showing up by now. She has had plenty of time. There is Brent now, she didn't want to come to work after he did."

"Irene, would you come to my office please?" Brent asked Irene. As she walked in, she said jokingly, "Am I fired?"

"Irene, sit down please." He was so somber that it scared her.

"What has happened Brent?"

"Irene, Christina went to drop Amy at the Day Care, Mike was waiting outside for her. He shot her Irene…. in the stomach. There were a lot of people outside, it's a wonder he didn't hit a child. He has been arrested, some men there held him until the Police came for him. But Christina might not make it. She is in surgery as we speak. We can manage at the office, Irene, go and stay with her. She doesn't have anyone else but you. Do you know where her family is?" Irene shook her head; she was sitting with her hands over her face crying.

"Yes, if you think I can leave, I'd like to be with her; let me call Mama first. I knew he was a piece of scum but I never thought he would shoot her."

"Mama, Mike shot Christina; we have to pick up the children. Do you know where they are? I'm going to the hospital now. Brent said she might not make it."

"Don't worry about the children, Irene; we'll take care of them."

"I'll tell Christina not to worry about them. If I'm able to talk to her."

Irene drove to the hospital; she didn't know how she got there until she noticed she was in front of the building. She went in and asked where Christina was, she was still in surgery.

She hadn't been sitting there too long when a Doctor in green scrubs from surgery came out asking for the family of Christina Long. Irene stood up and walked to the Doctor.

"My name is Irene Hamilton, I am with Christina."

"Are you her family?"

"I'm the closest she has to a family; she and her children live in my home."

'I'm sorry, but I can only speak to someone who is family to her."

"Well, you can go to jail and speak to her husband who just shot her or else you can speak to her seven year old daughter, shall I go fetch her?"

"All right, I understand, I'm Dr. Carlos Lopez; I just did surgery on Mrs. Long, she is in critical condition. One of the bullets hit her pancreas; another one went to her liver and one just above the liver. As you know, she was shot three times; all was very meticulous work, she had other injuries that were not as bad, but they had to be repaired and it took time. I didn't want to keep her under anesthesia as long as I did, but I had to. I've done all I could but she has to bring herself out of that, she has to be very strong. Maybe, if she is lucid enough, you can talk to her."

"Could I go in now, Dr. Lopez?

"Yes, she might not be able to speak, but she can hear you."

Irene ran in, looking for Christina.

There she is, she thought to herself.

"Christina; it's Irene. Your children are all right, they're home with Mama." She cleaned her face; tears didn't let her see anything. Christina was still under the effects of the anesthesia and didn't respond to Irene's words. She sat at her side holding her hand, mumbling to herself, "I tried to tell you about Mike, but you didn't listen. Why didn't you listen to me?"

Christina started to move and tried to talk to Irene, "Don't talk, save your strength. Mama is taking care of the children; you don't have to worry about them."

With great difficulty, Christina started trying to say something with a very low and broken down voice; she said, "Take care of my children, Irene."

"We'll take care of them while you are in the hospital; but then, you can take care of your own children, do you hear me? You're coming out of this to take care of your children; you are not going anywhere but home with us." Irene said .

Chapter Three

Dr. Brent Miller walked in. "Brent," Irene said in a low voice, "She looks so bad."

"Dr. Lopez is a brilliant surgeon, she is very lucky he happened to be in the emergency room when she was brought in. If anyone can save her life; it's him."

"I'd like to stay with her until she wakes up Brent. She tried to speak, but I know she wasn't lucid enough."

"Of course. I told Lourdes to re-schedule the afternoon appointments."

"Thank you, Brent."

"The only thing, now we're going to need a nurse again."

"I thought about it; let me speak with my sister, Sarah. She took nursing in school as part of her curriculum. She is in her last high school year so she has only very few credits to do; in fact, they might consider her working in a Doctor's office as part of her classes and let her go now. I'll talk to her."

"That would be great, Irene. We could do that until we can find a nurse or until Christina is well enough to go back to work, whichever comes first. Something else I need to tell you, I put an advertisement for a partner in a special magazine for doctors, so you're going to be getting some phone calls."

"You were not joking when you mentioned it the other day, were you?"

"I can see the need for another cardiologist in this town, and I can't do it all alone. When Christina gets better, and she will, Irene, I'd like for you to decorate the office. You can get together with Lourdes for the financial part. She can tell you what I can afford. And I trust your taste to decorate the office. We'll leave the extra office until the new doctor arrives."

"Lourdes, Brent wants me to decorate the office; he said to wait until Christina gets better. It has been about ten days. I think she is safe now, but he told me to consult with you about how much he can afford."

"He said that? That man can afford anything you want to buy, Irene."

"Really?"

"He sees all the patients he can handle, plus he does at least three surgeries per week. I tell you he is raking in the money; I guess he doesn't know it."

"Do you have the time now to go around the office with me and make a list of what is going to be needed here?"

"Of course, the way I see it, we make the time," she said laughing.

So they both went around the whole office and Irene made a long list.

"Can you come with me to town after work, Lourdes?"

"Yes, I was thinking about visiting Christina, but I'm sure you're going as well."

"We can go there first so we're not too tired after shopping and make an excuse."

Irene and Lourdes arrived at the hospital and found Christina sitting on a comfortable chair next to her bed.

"What do we have here?" Irene jokingly asked Christina. "I'm so glad you're sitting up, Christina. It's been only ten days."

"Just barely. They wanted me to walk a few steps," speaking with difficulty, she said, "It made me so tired."

"Don't try to answer, Mrs. Long. Your friends don't mind, I'm sure."

"Please, call me Christina; I have to do something about that name, Irene."

"In time, Christina, everything in time," she told her squeezing her hand.

Then, speaking to the nurse, she said, "Do you have a form Christina can sign so the Doctor can talk to me? I have you to know, Christina, I have to fight everybody for information because we're not blood relatives. I told Dr. Lopez, he would have to go to jail to speak to the man who shot you or else I could bring your seven year old daughter. I guess he got my message," Irene said smiling.

"I guess you weren't laughing when you were talking to him." Lourdes said.

"Nurse, do you think they can bring my children over here?" Christina asked.

"I'll talk to Dr. Lopez, but I have the feeling he'll give you permission."

"Irene, do you think someone could bring the children? I know I'm already asking too much of all of you, but I don't know what else to do."

"I'll talk to Mama, Christina; someone will bring the children to you."

"Well, Lourdes and I are about to do some shopping to re-decorate the office, so we had better leave."

They left the hospital in a hurry to accomplish what they had to do.

"Where are we going to do our shopping, Irene?"

"Where do you prefer to go, Lourdes?"

"Why don't we go to the World's Department Store?"

"Honestly?"

"Yes, I love to go there, why? Don't you like it?

"Lourdes, don't you know that store belongs to my family?"

"It does? No, I didn't know that. It seems to me you'd be taking me there."

"That's why I told you we didn't have to go there."

"Well, that's where we can find the best selection and the best quality."

"I think so myself, but I'm not shopping there to bring business."

"I would," Lourdes replied.

Irene smiled and shook her head. "There is my car, let's go."

"Okay, here we are."

"I feel funny coming in with the owner," Lourdes told Irene.

"Please, Lourdes, I mentioned only because I thought you knew."

"Do you have the list with you?"

"Yes, let's go to the furniture Department first."

"Miss Hamilton; how nice seeing you around here."

"Hi, Bonny, how are you? We're looking for office furniture."

"Come this way, please."

"We're going to need a special discount for this purchase, we're buying a lot; you know. I'd like to see a big desk and a big comfortable chair for a Doctor's office, corner tables, and coffee tables. Do you have silk flowers here? We also need chairs for the patients," Irene said as she walked along the room looking around.

"Let's select the desk and chair first. What do you think about this one, Lourdes?"

"I think it is quite majestic, Irene."

"We have some silk flowers here, Miss. Hamilton, but if you don't like them, you can go to the interior decorator department. There is a big selection there."

"We're also going to need carpeting and Venetian blinds."

"If you want me to, I'll walk you to the carpeting department; you might want to choose the carpet first before you select the flowers so you can base your colors on something."

"Let me see some swatches, please. Let's sit down to look at some colors and at the different kind of carpets. I think for an office we need a solid color thick carpet; the color is more intense, maybe honey. Beige or brown are too dull. What do you think Lourdes?"

"I think you're right. I like honey; I think beige or brown are too dull." Lourdes repeated.

"Bonny, when can you send people to measure the office? We need the work done on a Saturday. Do you have to look at the men's scheduling book?"

"No, I'll tell them to work you in. They'll be there tomorrow to take measurements."

"That's great Bonny; I know we'll be back because we're going to need something else. Besides that, we're getting another doctor very soon."

"We'll see you soon, Miss Hamilton."

"Thank you for all your help, Bonny."

"Lourdes, I am going to ask you a favor: not a word to Brent about my family owning that department store, please."

"I won't say anything, Irene, but why?"

"It makes me feel uncomfortable; he'll find out whenever, not before. I am sorry I told you, but for some reason I thought you knew. Something else about the old furniture, was it rented?"

"Yes, Dr. Miller's desk and mine, the waiting room chairs, coffee tables and corner tables."

"Well, I'm going to try to send the new furniture over the weekend. So, please call that place and have them pick up their furniture Friday evening after closing time so it won't be in the way."

Irene went into the dining room in a rush. "I'm running late, Mama."

"Good morning to you, too," Kate told her smiling.

"I'm sorry, good morning. How are you feeling Dad?"

"I'm fine, the question is, how are you?"

"Last night I went to the hospital to visit with Christina. By the way, they have given her permission for the children to visit her. Could Clare take them today?"

"Lourdes and I went to our Store and bought the furniture and carpeting Brent needs for the office. They're coming today to measure the office so they can do the work on Saturday."

"I know today is going to be a long day, we don't have a nurse. Do you think Sarah could work at the office as a nurse's aide until we can find a nurse? I know she had two courses in nurses' aid in high school."

"I don't know if she can, Irene, does she know how?"

"Like I said; she had a training course at school and she has finished school. I didn't know there was a shortage of nurses; ask her when she comes home. Mama, we really need her."

"Be careful Irene, don't drive too fast."

Irene arrived to the office just as Lourdes did.

"Lourdes, when you go to lunch will you have a key made for me please? If Mama hadn't held me up so long I would have been here earlier with no key."

"Yeah, I thought about it and then forgot to have a key made for you."

"Have several keys made; my sister is going to be the new nurse, and the new Doctor will need a key also."

"That's good," Lourdes said, "I was giving myself courage for the new day."

"I don't know if Sarah will be able to come today, we'll find out."

'The workers are supposed to come sometime today, so it's a waiting game."

"What do you know? Here are the workers now."

"It pays to know someone, that's what I always say," Lourdes said blinking an eye to Irene.

Irene smiled and put her finger over her mouth and went "Sshhh."

"Good morning, Miss Hamilton, my name is David and we're here from 'World Department Store' to measure the rooms you want us to carpet. This is Roland."

"Come in, please. This is the waiting room; and Doctor Miller's office. You can measure that other office but that will be carpeted later on."

The men started to measure the waiting room. When they went inside, they saw the examining rooms, don't you want them carpeted?"

"No, it is more hygienic with linoleum," Irene told the man.

"But you can measure Dr. Miller's office; right in there."

"How long does it take you to put the carpet down?"

"If we have the carpet that you choose, I'll be here tomorrow."

"Do you work on Saturday?" Irene asked the man.

"Yes, ma'am, all day."

"If you would, we would rather you come on Saturday because the office is closed."

"I'll be here, ma'am; at what time do you want us here?"

"You give us the time and we'll be here."

"Is nine o'clock too early for you?"

"Not at all, I'll be here at nine o'clock sharp."

"Irene, do you want me to come Saturday?"

"No, Lourdes, thanks; there is nothing to do, but be here and kill time."

"Well, if you change your mind, give me a call; do you have my number?"

"I don't, but it's a good idea to exchange our home numbers."

"Brent should have been here by now, don't you think so?"

"We don't book any patients until 9:30 a.m. because Dr. Miller likes to spend time with his patients at the hospital."

"I know. When my Dad had his surgery he was very attentive with both of my parents. My mother had a bad time when my Dad had his surgery."

"Ever since I met him, he has always been a caring Doctor, and that is a quality you don't always find."

"That's because they don't teach that at school, you are born with it."

"Let me count the patients we have booked for this morning." Irene started to count: ten this morning and ten this afternoon."

"Good Lord, you're going to have to be his nurse and I take care of the window, Irene. How many patients are here now?"

"Only five."

"Okay, as soon as you see Dr. Miller arrive, take the first patient to the examination room."

"Lourdes, it seems to me you know a whole lot more about it than I do; I'll take care of the window, you'll be the nurse."

"Okay, chicken," she said smiling.

Irene swatted her with a file she had in her hand.

Lourdes escorted the first patient to the back examination room and prepared him for Dr. Miller's arrival.

At noon, Brent walked to the window, "Irene, would you go to lunch with me?"

"Dr. Miller, what will people say? They'll think we're an item?" she said winking at him.

"That'll be all right with me, but the fact is, we don't have time to talk in the office and there are a few things I'd like to discuss with you."

"All right, I thought I'll have a little fun with you but if we must talk business I'll sacrifice myself," she said laughing.

"Are you always teasing people?"

"Oh no, only the chosen ones."

He laughed and told her, "Let's go before someone else comes in."

"Do you want to go to the same restaurant?"

"It was good, wasn't it?

"Yes, let's go there." Irene said. "Did you have time to visit Christina today?"

"Yes, that's one of the things I wanted to tell you; when I was there, someone from your house came over with her children. What a pair of precious children! I can't for the life of me, comprehend how that man could beat up his wife and look those children in their faces." said Brent.

"Because he only looks like a man, but he is not one. He is a beast."

"You know, I know Dr. Lopez very well, I'm going to tell you something very confidential, Dr. Lopez told me he could hardly work on Christina because of the bruises on her body and the bullets; because there were three bullets Irene, they were surrounded by the bruises. He was so mad, so disgusted that a man could do that to his wife."

"Now, you understand why I was so mad?"

"Yes, I do, and I admire you and your family for welcoming her the way you did."

"We all loved Christina from the time we were in school. I was devastated when I saw her bruises; I knew my family wouldn't have a problem with Christina or with the children living in our home."

"In any case, let's eat." They ordered and had a very good time; they felt at ease with each other. Brent looked at Irene and smiled.

"Lourdes and I ordered the furniture and the carpeting for the office only your Office. When the other doctor comes, we'll do his office. They're coming Saturday to put the carpet down, then it needs to be shampooed before they bring the furniture; I hope you'll like your desk."

"Can I afford it?" he said smiling and pretending he was scared of the bill.

"I took your accountant, she approved what I spent."

"How about your sister? Is she going to work for us?"

"Yes, but I wasn't able to talk to her yesterday, I left her a message with Mama."

"All right, are you ready to leave, Irene?" He said taking her by the arm.

"Where are you taking me?" she said acting alarmed at where he would take her. Brent just shook his head and smiled. "You're a delightful person, Irene."

"Thank you, Dr. Miller." She said with a bow. "But outside of my joking mode, I have to be here on Saturday for the workers to be able to come in and lay the carpet down. They promised me it'll be ready on the same day."

"Irene, it's going to take all day. It's your day off! I'll come when I leave the hospital."

"Brent, you don't know how long you have to be at the hospital, the men are coming at nine."

"Well, when I'm able to, I'll be there."

When they arrived to the office, Lourdes was there talking to Sarah.

"Sarah, what a pleasant surprise, did you decide to work here?"

"I thought I would come, I need to know what's expected of me, and if I'm able to do it."

Brent started asking her questions, "Do you know how to take blood pressure? Can you take the pulse, give injections? Help people sometimes to change into their gowns because some elderly people are not able to change by themselves."

"Yes, to everything." Sarah said smiling.

"Have you finished school?"

"Working here will give me enough credits to stop going to school before graduation."

"We have a full house today, can you stay?"

"Of course, I'll tell the driver I'm staying; but I don't have a nurses' uniform."

"I have enough coats, wear one of my coats," Brent told her.

Irene interrupted, "Dr. Miller, you have a call from New York."

"Do you have a name?"

"Oh, I'm sorry, Dr. Darrell Moore."

"Oh my God, DARRELL! I'll take it in my office, Irene."

"Darrell, how in the world did you find me?"

"I saw your ad for a partner in your Practice, I'm very interested."

"Are you in New York now?"

"Yes, I am, but its wearing thin very fast. I thought I wanted to live here. If you remember, for a while, that's all I talked about."

"You don't have to tell me, I know. I have to tell you this is nothing like New York. It is rather a small town in comparison with New York. It's about two hundred thousand people, I guess. There are several hospitals, I like it here; but then, I never wanted to live in New York."

"Could I come see your Practice?"

"Of course you can, can you invest in my Practice?

"Do you mean to say, our Practice?"

Brent laughed. "It will be good to work together again; do you behave yourself these days, Darrell?"

"What do you mean? I'm a respectable Doctor."

"I know, I heard that before. When can you be here?"

"I might want to drive my car; but I may fly. If I do, where do I fly to?"

"You can fly to Los Angeles. Once there; you can catch a flight to 'Los Caminos.'

"Irene, you're going to have to go back to the store and furnish Darrell's office; he is coming in a couple of days to see our office. He is a good friend of mine; we went to school together, I had no idea he wanted to get out of New York."

"Let me call Bonny, the lady who waited on us, I know her very well, she might save me a trip to the store."

"Bonny, Irene Hamilton here. Do you remember I told you we're expecting another Doctor? Well he will be here in a couple of days, so I'm wondering if we could do his office by phone, Yes, same desk but a lighter color, same carpet, same everything else,. Just the desk a little different so they don't get confused. Don't forget our end tables and more flower arrangements. What we can't use I'll send back; Is that all right with you, Bonny? Also, don't forget the Venetian blinds for the other office. They are the same size as the one we're doing now."

"Do you want the same pattern on the second desk, Miss Hamilton?"

"The only difference will be the color."

"I think it will be fine that way, Bonny. Are we getting all the furniture tomorrow? Because we can only do this on a Saturday. If they don't finish, they're going to have to come back the following Saturday and that means we'll have to wait all week with the office half done. Are the same men going to shampoo the carpet? In that case, by the time they go back for the furniture, the carpet, should be dry. Yes, Bonny, I'll give them time to eat lunch."

When Irene turned around, Brent was laughing, with his unmistakable masculine laugh Irene had learned to love.

"What? What did I do?" Irene asked Brent.

"You 'Shanghaied' that poor woman; she didn't stand a chance with you, and the men, you were prepared not to give them their lunch time." Brent couldn't stop laughing.

"But they're going to finish our office tomorrow, and your friend's office as well."

"Well, that means we can go eat lunch ourselves," he said.

"I'll bring lunch because I don't know if we're going to be able to go out."

"Do I have to eat lunch by myself?" Brent asked her with a sad face.

"Oh, I thought you would be here; I'll bring lunch for you too."

"In that case I won't get mad at you."

"Look, I'm shaking."

"Come on, what are we having for lunch?"

"It's just ten o'clock in the morning Brent!"

"Oops! I guess I haven't eaten breakfast yet."

"Well, maybe I can find you an old doughnut from yesterday."

"Do you intend to poison me?"

"You can go out and get something to eat."

"I'll eat the old doughnut."

Irene was sitting on one of the counters trying to stay out of the men's way. That is where Brent found her when he got back from the hospital.

"I think we should go sit in the car while they shampoo the carpet."

"That's very nice of you, Miss Hamilton," Brent told Irene.

"If you were not my boss, I'd hit you with something."

"And she's violent too."

"Okay, time out."

"Why? Don't you have a comeback?"

"Yes, but I don't dare."

"We're not working, there are no patients around, you can tell me anything."

"I'd rather not, then you'll be looking for something to say to me; besides that, they're coming with the furniture. I have to go in and make sure the carpet has dried. I'm anxious to find out if you're going to like what I bought."

"I'm sure I will," Said Brent.

"Seriously, do you think it has been enough time for the carpet to have dried?"

"It's almost three o'clock."

"Okay, bring the furniture in. Let's go, Brent, they don't know which furniture to put in each office. They're bringing the waiting room furniture first."

As they walked in, they both stopped at the entrance.

"Irene, it looks beautiful; I love the furniture!"

"Well, the rest is going to be easy," Irene said as she walked into Brent's office. Irene was placing some of the silk flowers in one of the vases.

"Well, what do you think Brent?"

"I think it's absolutely beautiful, Irene. You outdid yourself. Now; we are a first class Practice."

"Let's go to your friend's office."

"Irene, don't you think you should learn his name? Doctor Darrell Moore."

"I know; I'll be more careful."

"Would you go out to dinner with me tonight?"

"It depends if Dad is not in one of his moods."

"What do you mean?"

"Since the surgery he has been very touchy; he believes we don't want to spend time with him. After all, I've been gone all day."

"If I came a little earlier and spent some time with him, he might forget about you not staying with him all day."

"We can try if you want to, but if he acts sore, I'm staying with him."

"Okay, Daddy's girl."

"We're all like that."

"Competition, competition."

Brent came in dressed in a light summer suit. He looked utterly handsome.

"Clare, is Mr. Hamilton downstairs?"

"Yes Dr. Miller, come in, please. Please, follow me," said Clare.

"Mr. and Mrs. Hamilton, Dr. Miller is here."

"Dr. Miller! What a surprise." Charles said standing and shaking his hand.

"How do you feel? And you Mrs. Hamilton?" Brent asked them.

"May I ask what are you doing here?" Charles asked Brent very abruptly.

Kate gave him a reprehensive and surprised look.

"I went to the hospital and looked in Christina's room. So, I thought I would come over, because I know Irene didn't have time to visit with her today."

"How is she doing?" Kate asked Brent.

"She is doing much better than anyone anticipated she would do."

"The will to live, Dr. Miller; she has two small children."

"I know; I met them a few days ago when I visited her."

"Do you go to visit her every day, Dr. Miller?" Charles asked him.

"I try to, Mr. Hamilton. Don't forget, she was working for me when she was attacked."

"True, excuse me; I couldn't remember you have a reason to want to see her. We have known her since she was a child."

At that time, Irene walked in. "Hello Dr. Miller, how are you?"

"I came to let you know I visited with Christina a moment ago, she sent her regards to all of you and kisses to her daughters."

"Is she doing better?'

"Much better; as well as we all hoped she would do."

"That is so incredible, especially after I was told she might not recover."

"You understand that when we have a patient with a very small chance for survival, you can't give the family a false sense of hope."

"You're right, I haven't thought about it that way."

"Have you eaten dinner yet, Irene?"

"No, I just dressed to eat dinner with my parents."

"Mr. and Mrs. Hamilton; could I invite Irene to have dinner with me?"

"Why don't you ask her, Dr. Miller?"

"Irene, would you like to have dinner with me tonight?"

"Papa, is that all right with you?"

"It's all right with me, if you want to go."

They left. Brent told Irene. "You made me sweat for nothing; your father was very friendly, after he found out what I was doing in his home."

"I say you made an impression on him."

"Where do you want to go?"

"Would you mind eating at 'our' restaurant where we had lunch?"

"I was thinking about that place, I really like eating there; without being in a rush, will be a new experience. By the way Irene, you look wonderful."

"So do you, Dr. Miller." He looked at her smiling, and shook his head.

"What?" She said. "You paid me a compliment; I thought I'd do the same."

"Okay, here we are. What do you think you feel like eating?"

"To tell you the truth, I have no idea. That's why I like this place they have absolutely everything."

"I feel guilty not visiting Christina today."

"If it makes you feel better, I told her about you spending your day off at the office with the decorators. I also told her she'll be happy to see the results when she goes back to work."

"I bet she was very happy to hear she still has a job."

"That she was, she was happy when I mentioned to her. She said she didn't know what she was going to do."

"I guess I better reassure her she can stay at our home as long as she wants to stay there, forever if that's how things work out."

Chapter Four

Brent and Irene were seated and they were reading their Menu.

"Roast beef in red wine sauce sounds so good."

"You're not going to believe it, but I was looking at the same thing."

"Well then, let's try that tonight. Would you like to try some wine as well?"

"I don't ever drink. I wonder if it'll make me feel tipsy."

"I promise not to take advantage of you; I'll take you home at once."

"Do you know what? I'm not going to chance it; I'll try that at home sometime."

"I have to say, that was a very wise decision."

"Yeah, I'll drink water."

"Me too." The waiter had arrived to take their order and they continued chatting.

"Irene, this is absolutely the best roast beef I have ever eaten."

"I have to agree with you, it is delicious."

"I think we have found 'our' restaurant."

"Yes, we have."

"Irene, I'm sure you noticed we are very compatible. I would like to see you on a regular basis, to know you better. What do you say?"

"You took me by surprise, but yes, I feel the same way, I have been seeing someone Brent, I have to see Sean to break up with him. It has never been serious, just a school friendship, but it has always been more his idea than mine."

"I didn't know you were seeing someone. I'm sorry, Irene."

"I didn't even have to mention it to you because, like I said it has never been serious. But I feel obligated to talk to him just the same. Do you still want to see me?"

"I do, Irene." And when he said it; he held her hand. She smiled.

He drove her home. "Is it too late to go in, Irene?"

"What time is it?"

"A few minutes after ten."

"Yes, I think so. When you're on more friendly terms it will be all right."

"All right, I'll leave you by the door. Can I kiss you before we get out?" She didn't answer. She got closer to him and they kissed. She had dreamed of being crushed by his embrace. His kiss lasted forever. Then, they stayed together in an endless embrace.

"We're going to go slow Brent; I feel a cascade of feelings coming out of me. I've never felt this way before. It's different. With Sean, I knew I wasn't in love with him, I only went out with him for company."

"I understand, Irene, I have never felt this way before about any one. I was supposed to have been engaged, but you witnessed the outcome. Love wasn't included in the deal."

Irene went in; most of the lights were already out, but in the study, there was a lamp still on. "Mama, what in the world are you doing here? Were you waiting for me?"

"No, I came back downstairs, I wasn't sleepy. How was your date?"

"It was great Mama; Brent wants to see me on a regular basis."

"How about Sean? Do you remember him?"

"You know about Sean, Mama. From the beginning it has only been for dances; occasionally we would meet for coffee or to go to the Mall.

But I told Brent I have to talk to him. I'll give him a call tomorrow. Let's go to bed, Mama. Have you talked to Sarah about Carl?"

"Yes, she said she's all right, but I know she is not."

"I hope someone comes along that is good, like she deserves."

"She is not even eighteen years old and already has a heavy load in her heart."

"Good night, Mama."

"Good night, Irene."

When Irene went into the dining room, everybody else was there already.

"Good morning, did I sleep in?"

"No, we were just early this morning."

"How was your date last night?" Sarah asked Irene.

"Who said it was a date? What happened was that; on Saturday, I spent the day at the office working with the decorators and didn't visit Christina."

"Well, it looked like a date to me."

"Really? How do you know what it looked like, you were not even there."

"I was upstairs, I have eyes."

"Okay, Brent asked me to see him so we can get to know each other."

Charles cleared his throat and looked towards Irene.

Irene looked at Sarah furious she had to say something about Brent before she was ready for it.

"Irene, can I ride to work with you?"

"I'm happy you need a ride, Sarah."

When they were in the car; Irene said to Sarah. "I hope you know I didn't appreciate your comments about Brent and me at breakfast."

"I'm sorry Irene, I didn't realize about what I was saying until you answered me."

"Well, I didn't want to say anything yet. I don't know how it's going to turn out."

"I think he is a very nice person and gorgeous."

Irene smiled. "Yes, I agree with you."

"Here we are." said Irene.

When they walked in, Sarah said. "Wow, it's beautiful Irene!"

"Wait until you see the offices."

"What do you mean the offices? Did you fix more than one?"

"We're expecting another Doctor, Brent wanted me to go ahead and remodel his office as well."

"Do you know who is coming?"

"As a matter of fact, I do. It's a friend of Brent. They went to college together."

"When is he coming?

"That, I don't know, I think he is driving from New York."

"The whole office is beautiful, Irene. You deserve a lot of credit for this."

"Lourdes! I didn't know you were in already."

"Yes, after the tour through the office, I went to work so we can pay for it."

"I only bought what you approved, Lourdes."

"The new Doctors office? Funny, I don't remember that."

"Well, you're right, but when Brent talked to Darrell, (he is the new Doctor), he asked me if we couldn't go ahead and decorate his office since he'll be here this week."

"Well, they're going to send the bill; I'll have it covered by then."

"I didn't know we were that close with the expenses."

"We weren't Irene, until the decoration bit happened. Dr. Miller has bought a lot of expensive equipment; there are monthly notes for that."

"Well, Brent has three surgeries this week."

"Also, Dr. Miller wants me to keep paying Christina. Could you get her information? She didn't work long enough for me to get it."

"I will, I'll try to go to the hospital on my lunch hour. I couldn't go to the hospital Saturday because I stayed in here all day long."

Irene arrived at the hospital and went into Christina's room. She found her sitting on a chair eating her lunch.

"Christina, you look so good." She walked to her and kissed her.

"I'm so sorry I didn't get to come Saturday, but Brent told me he saw you and that you're looking great. Sunday after Church, I came, but you were asleep."

"How are my children Irene?"

"They're fine, Christina; Amy asks for you all the time, but Linda knows you're in the hospital. They're home now, school is out you know."

"Oh Irene, and here I sit doing nothing for my children."

"And it is not your fault. By the way, I need the information to deposit your check Christina."

"I worked only a few days, Irene."

"Brent is going to keep paying you, so give me the information."

"Oh, Irene, I can't accept that. Then your parents are giving me shelter."

"And we all love you; you only need to get better, that's all the pay we want.

By the way, I haven't seen Dr. Lopez, is he still your Doctor?"

"Yes, Irene, and he is so nice. When he makes his rounds, he just visits with me and encourages me that I can do better and not to think about Mike. He is a very kind man."

"Sounds like it, Christina. I think you need to think about starting divorce proceedings against Mike; so when you get out of the hospital, the divorce will be in motion."

"When I was able to speak after the surgery, an attorney came over to see me. He knew about Mike shooting me at the school; I think his wife was a witness. Anyway, he was pretty mad about my case. He wants to handle my divorce."

"I think that's great, Christina. I imagine Mike is still in jail."

"I have no idea, Irene."

"I think I'm going to pay a visit to Mr. Betancourt, the Police Chief."

Irene was late for work. Sarah was at the window. "Thank you Sarah."

"Did you know you brought me to work? I couldn't eat lunch Irene."

"Oh Sarah, I'm sorry. I rushed to see Christina, and forgot about you."

"There is a lunch diner around the corner. I ate there."

"I thought you said you couldn't eat, Sarah."

"I didn't know where to eat; I had to look around for a place."

"Poor baby."

On the other side of the window, there was a very handsome man smiling.

"I'm sorry, Sir, may I help you?" Sarah asked the newcomer.

"I'm Dr. Darrell Moore. Is Brent here?"

"I'm sorry, no. I think he is still at the hospital."Irene told him. "But you can come in, Dr. Moore. While Dr. Miller comes back to the office you can see your office, we just finished decorating it."

"Are you, Irene?" Darrell asked.

"Yes, how do you know my name?"

"I talked to Brent at a great length," he told Irene.

"Here is your office, Dr. Moore."

"Wow! It's great, I like it."

"Good, I'm glad you do."

"Here is Dr. Miller now, Dr. Moore."

"Hey, Buddy, how in the world are you?" They greeted each other. "Has Irene given you the grand tour?"

"No, I only arrived; she only had time to show me my office," Darrell said. Irene left them and went back to work.

"Well, how do you like things so far?"

"I think things are getting better by the minute," he said rubbing his hands, with his eyes looking towards Sarah.

"Heeeyy! You just stop it right there. Sarah is Irene's sister and you stay away from her, buddy."

"What's the matter with you Brent? I was just making an observation."

"I'm familiar with your observations. You stay away from her or there is no deal."

"I was only kidding; we haven't seen each other for a long time; I felt like playing around, you know."

"I know, Darrell, but you have to know that it can't involve Sarah. Something else: this is <u>not</u> New York. It's a pretty small town in comparison; be careful how you treat women around here; you might get in trouble. You'll be well known as a Doctor pretty soon, and fooling around with women is not taken lightly here."

"How do you expect me to act?"

"Respect everybody if you want to have a place in their society. If you start by being the playboy you have been in the past, no one is going to take you seriously. You need to think about it; if you want to stay here."

"Playboy is getting old, all right; I'll play it your way."

"Shake on it?" Brent asked him extending his hand.

"Of course," Darrell replied shaking Brent's hand.

"Okay, can you invest in the Practice?"

"I told you I'm able to, how much do I need to put in?"

"I have put in the firm $ 250,000.00 . Half of it puts you in, equal share.

"All right, I'll open an account over here and transfer my money to the bank. I had one of the Doctors in my Practice there, to take care of my patients."

"Tomorrow, we'll go to the hospital together, I'll introduce you around to everybody, then we put an advertisement in the newspaper announcing you have joined the Practice. I guess Irene can do that today."

Brent called Irene on the intercom. She came immediately.

"Did you call, Dr. Miller?"

"Yes, Irene, place an ad in the paper announcing Darrell is joining our Practice. Darrell, give Irene your credentials, colleges, Master Degrees, Doctorate, the works."

"Irene, start interviewing another person for office work, and a nurse, since Sarah is only an aide. Hopefully we'll be getting more patients and we need another pair of hands around here."

"Do you want another ad in the newspaper for that as well?"

"No, I'd rather have word of mouth for that."

"Dr. Moore, can you give me your information now, or do you want to give a copy of your resume?"

"Yes, Irene, I think I'll give it to you later."

"Is that all, Dr. Miller?"

"Yes, Irene, thank you."

Irene went back to her desk. Lourdes asked her, "What was that all about?"

"Advertising for Dr. Moore and we need to get another nurse and a clerk for us."

"Irene, I have a sister who is looking for a job, she is a good worker, but her Company left town."

"Do you think she can be here tomorrow?"

"I'm sure."

"What's her name? Is she married? And does she have any children?"

"Her name is Maureen, she is divorced and she has no children. And she is an excellent nurse."

"All right, we're growing, I like that. Do you know something? I don't know if you're married or if you have children yourself."

"I have never been married, Irene, and I have no children either."

"I'm going to the hospital after work to visit Christina."

"Don't forget Dr. Moore's advertising."

"Yes, but I have to wait for the information, he said he'll give it to me later."

"Christina, you're walking in the hall! I didn't expect you out of the room."

"I want to get out of here as soon as possible. They told me the more I walk, the sooner I'll get stronger so they can discharge me."

"I hope you're not worried about the children, because they're fine."

"I know they are, Irene, but you know I want to be with them."

"I do," Mama said. "Tiger, he's our dog, has taken up with them so much. I don't think he has ever seen a child at home. He doesn't even lie down by Dad any longer when the children are playing in the garden; he likes to play with them."

"How does your father take that?"

"Are you kidding? He is enjoying the children so much. Both of my parents think of your children as their grandchildren, you know."

"Let's change the subject, how about your divorce Lawyer?"

"He came over and he wants me to list my conditions for the divorce, he said I can ask for everything he has, which is nothing."

"What are you going to ask for, Christina?"

"For my children, Irene."

"Of course, but not just like that, Christina. Make him sign unconditional custody, he is never to try to see the children or you ever again. If he refuses, he can go to jail for attempted murder. That's what you can bargain with, his freedom. He has to leave this area, Christina."

"Yes, that is a great idea, Irene, thank you. And Irene, Dr. Lopez has asked me if when my divorce is final, he wants me to consider seeing him so we can get to know each other."

"Christina! That is wonderful news; Brent said he is a good person, and he is great looking too! And a great surgeon as well. We can see that with the results of your surgery."

"I told him yes, I want to see him outside of the hospital, but we have to wait for this business with Mike. Mike might try to kill Carlos as soon as he finds out."

"Yes, it will be better to wait some time. I have to run, I have a million things to do, I haven't had the time to tell you, Brent has a new partner for the office."

"A new Doctor?"

"Yes, and we hired a new clerk and a new nurse. He expects a lot more patients."

"I won't be able to recognize the office when I come back. You told me I can have my job back, is that still true?"

"Of course; bye, I have to run." And Irene left in a hurry to go back to work.

When Irene got back, she found a paper with a long list of medical hieroglyphics she couldn't possible read. She took the paper to Brent.

"Brent, am I expected to read this?" and she put the paper on his desk. Brent looked at the paper and let out a loud laugh. And yelled out "**Darrell.**"

Irene told him, "He might hear you if you use the intercom."

"He heard me; he was waiting for me to call him." The door opened up and there stood a smiling Darrell.

"Darrell, why did you write this?" Brent asked him showing him the note Irene had given him.

"You know I don't like to brag." Brent started to cough as to tell Irene that's what he likes to do.

"Dr. Moore, I'm trying to do my job, and you're keeping me from it."

"You can announce I'm here, I don't need to let them know which schools I have attended."

"Perhaps you don't, but people need to know if they can trust you."

"You tell him, Irene." Brent said.

"Okay, Brent and I went to the same schools. Harvard, Oxford, Mayo Clinic, I have worked with heart patients for over eight years. Same as Brent."

"Not exactly, we went to Harvard together, but I didn't go to Oxford although I was at the Mayo Clinic three years. I have worked with patients longer because I didn't go to Oxford. How long were you at the Mayo Clinic?"

"About three years as well. From there, I went to Oxford." Darrell said.

"Very impressive, Darrell."

"You see? That's why I didn't write it down."

"If you went, people need to know. We need a copy of your diplomas; unless there're already framed. I'll get them framed and hang them up on your wall. I need to rush this to the newspaper. Both of you are still too young for this kind of resume. How old were you when you went to the University?"

"I was wondering when that was coming."

"Why?" Irene asked.

"Well, we were what people call, Bookworms. We were always competing with each other. We started the University at fifteen, Irene."

Irene sat on the first available chair she found. "My God, Brent! Why haven't you ever mentioned it to me? This is grand."

"Because I got where I didn't want anyone to know, Irene. Didn't you, Darrell?"

"Not me, I always enjoyed seeing their eyes grow large in disbelief."

"You would say that," Brent said laughing.

It was closing time; Brent called Irene to his office. When she got there, He asked her: "I still have a couple of patients I have to see, Irene, would you have dinner with me?"

"Is Sarah staying late with you?"

"Yes, Irene, I'm sorry but the nurse has to stay."

"I have to stay myself, Brent; she rode to work with me. And yes, I'll have dinner with you."

"I'll call Christina while Sarah is busy."

"Christina," Irene said, "it's Irene, how are you feeling today?"

"Much better, I think I'm going to be discharged this week."

"That'll be great, have you heard from your Attorney?"

"Yes, in fact I'm waiting for him now; with the divorce papers."

"Please, call me with more news about it, Christina. Listen, Sarah is ready to leave; I'll be talking with you."

She put the receiver down; she looked in the telephone directory. When she found her number, she began to dial it. "Mr. Betancourt? Irene Hamilton, how are you doing, Sir? I'm calling regarding my friend Christina Long. She is about to be discharged from the hospital and frankly, I am very nervous about Mike being let out of prison."

"And why are you afraid he'll be released from prison?"

"Because in order to get full custody of her children, and for Mike to lose all his paternal rights, she agreed to give him his freedom in exchange for her children. He is not supposed to ever get in contact with them or ask to see the children."

"But you don't trust him, is that right?"

"You got it, Mr. Betancourt, he is supposed to leave town, but I'm afraid he is not going to leave for long."

"All we can do, Miss. Hamilton is to send him outside of our county."

"Doesn't he have to report to anyone?"

"If his wife gave him full freedom, no one can touch him now."

"How about the attempted murder charges?"

"I have to see his release papers to answer all your questions."

"I'm sorry, Mr. Betancourt, but you understand, she almost died."

"I understand. I'll do what I can."

When Brent approached Irene, he found her with teary eyes and didn't even notice he was there standing next to her.

"Irene, what's wrong?"

"Christina signed her divorce papers today. She didn't press attempted murder charges against Mike in order to obtain full custody of her children. He is not supposed to ever approach them again; never see the children again. But now, I'm scared for her. That evil man is going try to kill her again. I just called Mr. Betancourt about Christina."

"We can't let that happen. We'll get a body guard for her."

"She won't let us do that, but we don't have to tell her. If she notices the man following her, we will tell her it's a Policeman."

"I think we better introduce her to her body guard before she gets scared"

"Where can we get a body guard?"

"I think we can start by asking the Chief of Police for advice."

"But of course! Why didn't I think about that?"

"Nothing like the present." Irene called Mr. Betancourt again. Irene explained their plans to Mr. Betancourt. "What do you think?"

"Yes; I can recommend a couple of people to you."

"No, just give me one name, that way no one else will know."

"Brent, could you talk to Dr. Lopez? Explain the situation to him; tell him to wait until Mike is out of town before he discharges Christina."

"I'll talk to him, baby. Don't worry. He'll understand."

"I'm so scared for her, Brent, I was fine; and then I began to think about Mike being released from prison and kept seeing him coming towards her with a gun."

"That's because of what's already happened to her, Irene. It brings it back to your mind; your imagination is running away with you. But I will speak with Carlos and I'm sure he'll agree with you."

"Thank you Brent, I plan to go see her as soon as I can. I'll give the investigator's office a call; maybe he can come over to see me here at the office."

"Do you want me to make the call, Irene?"

"It might be a good idea, I'm so nervous."

"Okay, where is the number?"

"It's in my purse, I'll get it; be back in a minute."

"Well Irene, I only spoke with the secretary. She said she'll give Mr. Moran my message, he'll call back soon."

"Did she say when she expects him back?"

"She said he shouldn't be too long."

"Well, I guess it's nothing else we can do but wait."

"Irene, how many patients did we have today?"

"I can't say by memory, Brent. Let me bring the appointment book."

When Irene came back she said, "Twenty-two today. Brent, we have booked thirty-two patients for every day of the week for the next two weeks. That's thirty minutes for each patient for each one of you, Brent."

"Can we do that, Irene?"

"I think if both of you try to be here by nine o'clock we'll be fine."

"Irene, I do surgeries. On those days, you can't book patients in the morning."

"Okay, I'll re-schedule the ones that are coming when you're doing surgery, we don't schedule your surgeries, so I don't know when you and Darrell are in surgery. We have to know that, so we can write them in the schedule book. That way one of you is always here. I'll reschedule some of the appointments; I'll tell people you have to do surgery that day. It won't be a lie, Brent."

"As long as you don't let people come without a warning, Irene. We have to be careful about it."

"I'm sorry, Brent; we all have been making appointments, what I think I'll do is find out when you're doing surgeries and I'll write it in the book."

"Yes, I would think that should have been done all along."

"It was my fault, Brent. I guess I got confused between Darrell coming in and at the same time that Christina was attacked. Besides that, you know this is the first time I worked in something like this, Brent."

"Okay, no harm done. All I'm saying is that we have to be very careful with the appointments, all right? Have all the patients been called, Irene?"

"Let me check, Brent."

When she came back she told Brent. "Yes, the waiting room is empty"

"Do you want to have dinner tonight?"

"Do you still want to have dinner with me?"

"What are you talking about? Why not?"

"You're so unhappy with me; I thought I was getting fired."

Brent got up and walked to her and hugged and kissed her. "Irene, don't you think we have to talk about what happens at the office? And if there is something that needs to be corrected, it has to be corrected, Irene."

"Don't pay any attention to me, I'm so crazy."

"Come on; let's go eat dinner, all right?"

"But first, let's go visit Christina."

As they were leaving, the phone rang and Irene answered it. "Dr. Miller's office?"

"This is Luis Moran; my secretary gave me this number Miss."

"Yes, Sir, we're looking for an investigator or rather a body guard for a lady who was attacked by her husband. She is about to divorce him and we prefer to know that she is protected by a professional person."

"Who gave you my name?"

"Mr. Betancourt, from the Police Station."

"All right, we can talk, where can we meet?

"Just a minute, please."

"Brent he wants to meet us, where can I tell him?"

"We're going to the hospital, Irene."

"Mr. Moran, we're going to the hospital. The one on Main Street."

"Okay, I'll leave now. Which entrance are you going to use Miss Hamilton?"

"Main entrance, I'm going to be with Dr. Miller." When she hung up, she asked Brent, "Should we tell Christina about it?"

"I think when she starts to leave the hospital; she is going to be apprehensive, that will be the time to tell her." She nodded.

When they arrived, they sat near the entrance, and a tall, hefty man approached them. "Miss Hamilton and Dr. Miller?"

"Mr. Moran?"

"At your service."

"I told you most of it, her name is Christina Long, and the man who shot her is Mike Long."

"I was afraid you were going to say that."

"Why?"

"Because he is bad news, he has a long record and he is a dangerous man."

"My friend found that out the hard way. He shot her in the stomach three times. She almost died and she has two small, little girls."

"Well, I'm going to take the case because of the circumstances, and because Mr. Betancourt recommended me. When do I meet the lady?"

"We were thinking when she is ready to leave the hospital."

"And when will that be?"

"After he is released from prison. That was the deal she made with him through her attorney, in order to get complete custody of the children. He is not supposed to try to see the children again. But I believe when the Police send him out of town, he'll come back again."

"You're right; the deal was not to try to see the children again. Was anything said that he is not going to try to see her either?"

"I don't know, you would think her attorney would know."

"You'll be surprised how many things attorneys forget. At any rate, I would like to meet the lady."

Irene looked at Brent. "What do you think?"

"He is the expert; I think we need to start by following his advice."

"Let's go Mr. Moran."

When they arrived at Christina's room. They found her sitting on a chair having dinner.

"Christina, you look so good. Meet Mr. Moran."

"It's very nice meeting you, Mrs. Long."

"I'm not Mrs. Long for much longer, so I want to start by giving my maiden name: Findley. My name is Christina Findley." She looked at Irene. "Who is he?"

"Christina, I have been very worried about you and everyone agrees with me. When the Police release Mike, he might come back. Mr. Moran is your bodyguard."

"Irene! Why?"

"You're asking why, Christina? In one word, Mike."

"If I may, Miss Christina," said Mr. Moran, "Miss Hamilton is right. For a length of time you'll be in great danger. Unfortunately, the Police only come after-the-fact; you need to be protected while he wants to get even with you. I won't be next to you, but I'll be close enough, I know what Mike looks like, I have done surveillance on him before, mark my words, he'll be back."

By that time, Christina was crying, "My God what am I going to do?"

"Do what your friend wants to do for you, Miss Christina. Let her protect you for your children. She tells me you have two small children and you want to live for them, don't you?"

"Irene, how can I repay you for all that you're doing for me?"

"By living, Christina; by staying alive for Amy and Linda."

"Dr. Lopez is going to wait several days after Mike is released from prison before he discharges you from the hospital, Christina; we're trying to take all the precautions to protect you."

Christina couldn't contain herself she was sobbing uncontrollably by now. Irene knelt in front of her. "Christina, please, you're just weak from all that has happened to you, you'll be all right, you'll see."

Dr. Lopez walked in "What are you doing to my favorite patient, Irene?"

Irene stood up also with teary eyes.

"What's happening here?" he asked.

Brent explained the whole thing to Dr. Lopez.

"Christina, I think everything is very sensible, no reason for tears."

"Dr. Lopez, you know my situation, they have spent so much money on me. It's hard to let them spend more money. How do I repay all that kindness?"

"Christina, we only want you to raise your own kids, don't you want the same?"

Christina looked at Irene. "You know there is nothing I want more."

"Okay, Mr. Moran, you are hired."

Chapter Five

Kate and Clare arrived at the hospital with Linda and Amy and their Nanny, Cindy. When they tried to go to the elevator, they were stopped because the children were not allowed to go upstairs.

Kate told the receptionist, "These children have already been upstairs once before, how come they can't do it now?"

"I think it was a special permit, that is not for every time they come to the hospital."

"Clare, please go to the nurse's station on Christina's floor and ask the head Nurse what we can do about it. Could Christina come down stairs to see her children?"

When Clare arrived at the nurse's station on the third floor, she made the inquires Kate asked her to do. The nurse said, "Let me see her chart. Yes, that lady is allowed to go downstairs if she wishes to." Clare went to Christina's room with the good news she could see her children who were waiting for her in the front Lobby.

As Christina left her room with Clare, Luis Moran followed them. When they entered the elevator; Luis Moran ran downstairs.

He saw the elevator opening and the children ran to their mother. Clare was pushing Christina's wheelchair and embraced both of her children. She kissed them both and hugged them for a long time.

"Thank you, Mrs. Hamilton for bringing them to see me."

"We're too close to the door, Christina," Kate told her. "Why don't we walk to the Cafeteria and get something to drink?"

When they got up and started walking to the cafeteria, a man grabbed Christina and started to drag her to the main door. She screamed, Luis Moran was ready for him and placed himself behind Mike and put a gun in Mike's ribs. "I'll kill her if you don't let me go," Mike told Moran. Moran didn't move a muscle.

"Where do you think you are going dead? Because you might hurt Miss Christina again, but you won't know it because I am going to make sure you'll be *just as dead*." Moran told Mike. He chewed his words, his eyes were lethal. "Let her go, you signed papers that you won't bother her or the children again. You'll fry in prison!"

Mike dropped his knife, a police car pulled in and two policemen got out and went in running, "okay men, he is all yours. Don't lose him again; he was trying to take the same woman he almost killed a few weeks ago."

The nurses took the wheelchair Christina was in and started trying to take her upstairs. Several doctors came out of Emergency. One of the doctors was Carlos Lopez. "What's happening here?" He asked, Kate told him "They wouldn't let the children go upstairs, so Christina came out to the Lobby in order to see her children."

"And who authorized that?" Dr. Lopez asked.

Clare answered him, "The head nurse on the third floor; she checked her chart and told me Christina was allowed to come downstairs. Carlos was visibly angry; he pushed Christina to the elevator, "Mrs. Hamilton, please come to Christina's room and bring the children."

Kate signaled Clare and Cindy into the elevator. Christina kept crying, Linda, her oldest child kept caressing her mother's hair. When they arrived to Christina's room, Carlos helped her into her bed and checked her blood pressure, he kept shaking his head. Then he finally remembered something: He asked Kate, "Mrs. Hamilton, could I speak with you in private? Maybe the ladies who came with you could stay in here with Christina and the children and you and I can go into my office."

"Of course, Dr. Lopez."

When they stepped outside, Dr. Lopez asked Kate, "Mrs. Hamilton, since Christina's life is going to be in jeopardy and I can't get her blood pressure to go down because she is afraid every time the door is being opened, Mike is going to walk in. My parents live on a Ranch outside of Los Caminos. There is no way Mike could guess she is at my parent's home. I think that is the best hiding place for Christina."

"Dr. Lopez, I think that is a marvelous idea, but Christina wants to be with her children, I don't think she would consider leaving them again."

"I agree with you Mrs. Hamilton, I meant with the children. Also, Mr. Moran."

"Well, you can ask Mr. Moran and then Christina."

Irene walked in with Brent. "Hey, what's new?" she asked. Everyone laughed.

"What did I say that was so funny?" Irene asked.

"Well," Christina said. "Let me tell you in a word, Mike happened again."

"What did he do?"

"They wouldn't let the children come upstairs to see me when your mother brought them, so Clare came upstairs to ask the head nurse what we could do?"

She related the whole story to Irene and Brent.

"Good God," said Irene. "I'm thankful Mr. Moran was here with you."

"Yes, I was thanking God when I saw Mike, if it hadn't been for Mr. Moran; there is no telling what would have happened."

"Yes, let's not speculate about that."

Dr. Lopez and Kate walked in. Dr. Lopez said. "I was in a conference with your Mother, Irene."

"Hello, Dr. Lopez."

"Yes, hello."

"Well, I had a thought after what happened earlier," and he went into detail about his idea. "Where is Mr. Moran anyway?"

"He might had gone to the Police Station since he is the one who made the arrest." Kate said.

"Yes, it sounds right. I have the feeling Mike will try to come back. But since he was freed, I just don't know how they will handle this."

"I think this is a new offense, they have to handle it as such."

"Christina, what do you think?" Irene asked Christina.

"I think I will do what Mr. Moran says, I hate to go to Dr. Lopez parent's home. I don't know them; they have never heard of me, and I'm going over there after a surgery half crippled with two children and with a man after me trying to kill me, not a very desirable guest."

"Christina, if I didn't think my parents will be concerned for your welfare, I wouldn't have offered. But believe me when I tell you, they will love for you and your children to stay at 'Las Palmas,' that's the name of their Ranch. Something else that just popped into my mind. You shouldn't get visitors, because I know we're going to try to find out about Mike, but sometimes, Police don't let people know the whereabouts of their assailant."

Irene said, "Could I visit or speak to Christina?"

"No, I think it is the best way to protect Christina, Irene; but we'll consult Mr. Moran as soon as he comes back and ask for his expert advice."

"Whose expert advice are you seeking?" Mr. Moran asked as he walked in.

"Yours, that's whose," Dr. Lopez answered him. And he went into detail with his plan.

"Miss Christina, you are a lucky lady to have so many people in-you-corner, I think Dr. Lopez has a master plan; it's something I would've put together. I will go with you. Whatever clothing you need from your house will be brought here, the children, luggage, etc. We'll leave for the Ranch straight from here in an ambulance; you won't go to see your parents for at least two weeks Dr. Lopez. We're going to make sure where Mike is before we make a trail for him to find."

Irene walked to Christina and hugged her, "Well, we agreed we would do whatever Mr. Moran advised, so we better do it, we can't even talk on the phone."

"I will miss all of you, but hopefully it won't be a long time," Christina said. "Mrs. Hamilton, I don't have words to express myself to thank you for all of you have done for me and my children."

"Just stay well, Christina, that's what we want from you."

"Well, let's go so we can bring the clothing. I guess it's safe to do that now, huh?"

"Do you know what? No, thank you, Mrs. Hamilton, somebody can go to town from the Ranch and buy the most necessary things for them. Let's not risk it."

Kate looked into her purse and pulled out three hundred dollars, it's all I have in my purse, Christina."

"Just a minute," said Brent, "we're still paying Christina until she can go back to work. Christina, we'll refund the money to Mrs. Hamilton out of your check, okay?"

"You know?" Christina said, "For years, all the luck I had was bad; I'm thankful that page has been turned and now, I see good luck coming my way, thank you everybody."

Irene said, "Yes, all you had to do was leave Mike." Everyone laughed.

"When is Christina leaving, Dr. Lopez?" Irene asked Carlos.

"Since she is not going to be getting medical care, I would like to give her a good check up before she leaves; maybe within one hour. Is that okay with you Mr. Moran?"

"Of course, Dr Lopez, I don't want a sick lady on my hands."

"Okay, Irene, to answer your question: probably late tomorrow."

"In the meantime, I'll go back to the Police Station and open my ears," Moran said.

Irene was trying to work, but she couldn't get past the thought of Christina in so much danger. "Lady, good morning, good morning," then a tap on the window.

"Oh my God, I'm so sorry, I wasn't all here."

"No, I can see that, what happened to you? Did your boyfriend leave you?"

"Not yet, but he will if I don't wake up. I'm sorry Mrs. Wilde."

"Oh, don't worry about me, nothing like being young again."

Sarah came over and told Irene, "I saw that, what's going on Irene?"

"I'm worried about Christina, Sarah."

"But you're doing all that can be done Irene. You should be thankful you thought about hiring that investigator. Christina would be history by now if you hadn't done for her what you did, think about that."

"Thank you, Sarah, I will think about that."

"Yes, you need to watch out for our patients."

"No kidding."

Brent walked behind Irene, "Hey beautiful, are you free for lunch?"

"Let me look in my pink book if I have any openings for lunch. Yes, you're in luck, I'm free today."

"I think I'm finished with my last patient Irene."

"Could I ask Sarah if she has any plans, because she is riding with me?"

"Of course, go ahead. I'll be happy for her to come along."

"Sarah, do you have any plans for lunch?"

"As a matter of fact I do, Dr. Moore invited me to lunch."

Brent was listening; he took off to Darrell's office.

"Darrell, I thought we made a deal! Hands off with Sarah."

"What are you talking about? It's just lunch."

"I know how your lunches end. Don't forget she is not eighteen yet."

"**She is not?**" he said very surprised

"I think I told you her age before Darrell, take it easy with her."

"Don't sweat it, Brent, we're fine."

"I want it to stay that way."

Darrell thought to himself. "I know she's twenty three. I'm a good judge in pretty girls' ages." And Darrell convinced himself Sarah was older.

Irene asked Brent. "What was all that about, Brent?"

I went to tell Darrell that Sarah is not eighteen years old yet."

"Really Brent?"

"I know my friend, or I wouldn't have said anything; I'm telling you, he has always been a lady's man."

"Thank you Brent, you know she is just coming out of that situation with Carl and she is very vulnerable."

"I know, Irene, why do you think I ran to his office as soon as I heard Sarah telling you her plans to have lunch with Darrell?"

"Well, I lectured her, that's all I could do; she'll be eighteen years old soon."

"If we don't leave pretty soon, we won't have time to eat," Brent said.

"At least we don't have to decide where we want to eat, let's park."

"I wonder how Christina is."

"She is fine, Irene; she is safe."

"I'll try not to be a nuisance to you with my worries."

"Come on; loosen up, let's order lunch."

When they arrived back to the office Darrell and Sarah were coming in themselves. "Here, delivered to you in one piece." Darrell said laughing.

"I'm not laughing, Dr. Moore," Irene told him.

"When you get to know me better; you will. I'm a happy man with a good sense of humor."

"We'll see," Irene replied. Then she turned to Sarah and asked her. "Did you have a good lunch dear?"

'I did, Irene; Dr. Moore is a very polite gentleman."

"You see? I told you." She saw the amusement in his eyes, she smiled. "Okay," she said and she stretched her hand to him, "Friends." they both said.

As Irene turned around Brent was behind her, so she faced him.

"I knew he would get you on his side." Brent said smiling.

"Well, we work together, to stay mad at him; he has to 'trip' first. So I'll be watching him," Irene told Brent.

Brent called Irene to his office. "Brent? Do you need anything?"

"I just received a call from Carlos Lopez. He called his parents home from the hospital's main office. He didn't think Mike would be so well acquainted inside of the hospital, anyway she is doing fine. He spoke with Christina and with Moran."

"Oh Brent, how nice, did Moran say she needs to stay there longer?"

"She has only been there a couple of days, Irene, but maybe we need to speak to Mr. Betancourt and ask him if things have changed because he attacked her again."

"I hope so; this was after the deal she made with him."

"Do you want me to call him, or do you want to make the call?"

"Please call him, Brent."

"All right."

"Mr. Betancourt, how are you? Dr. Miller here, inquiring about Christina Long's case. Since Mike attacked her again after he was out of prison, doesn't that change the case? After all, he attacked her in the middle of the hospital with a knife."

"He is in prison Dr. Miller, but I can't tell you anything else, you know these lawyers come up with new laws we haven't heard of yet."

"Should we have a lawyer for Christina?"

"No, Dr. Miller, the District Attorney will handle that this time."

"When they sentence him, can they put a clause to be sent out of state?"

"I don't really know, Dr. Miller, but I promise I'll talk to the District Attorney." Brent hung up and looked at Irene. "Okay, you heard my side of the conversation; now let me tell you about his side. How about if I tell you over dinner?"

"That's an offer I can't refuse. How about Sarah?"

"We can take her with us or we can take her home."

"Sarah, sweetie, do you want to go to dinner with Brent and I? or if that is not appealing to you, we can take you home."

"Actually, Dr. Moore asked me to dinner earlier, do you want to make a foursome?"

"Yes, I think I prefer that to wondering where you are."

Sarah knocked at Darrell's office, "Dr. Moore, are you ready to leave?"

"Any time Sarah, I told you to quit calling me Dr. Moore. My name is Darrell."

"But I'm your nurse, how can I call you anything else?"

"Irene calls Brent by his name."

"But they're engaged, Dr. Moore. I forgot to tell you, we're a foursome."

"We are a what?"

"A foursome, we are going with Dr. Miller and Irene."

"Lovely." he said with a humorous smile, as usual.

"Well, where are we dining this evening?" Darrell asked Brent.

"We have a restaurant we go to on a regular basis, I hope you like it."

"Come on Sarah, you can ride with me to the restaurant." Darrell said.

"Irene, is that all right?"

"I guess so, go ahead."

Darrell blew Irene a kiss.

"Has he always been like that, Brent?"

"Ever since I have known him; and it have been many years"

"Here we are, I'm so hungry Brent, aren't you?"

"Yes, I can eat. There is that new couple."

They all went into the restaurant, Irene walked with Sarah ahead of the guys.

Darrell helped Sarah sit down, "Are you all right?"

"I have an idea! Sarah refuses to call me by my name, how about if both of you call me 'Tyke' that's my family nickname for me; no one else will know you're talking to me if they over hear you, how about that?"

"Why is it so important to you that we call you by you given name or nickname?"

"You call Brent by his name, I'm jealous."

Irene couldn't help herself, she laughed out loud.

Brent was surprised and asked her: "Irene, I have never heard you laugh like that."

"That's because you're not funny." Darrell told Brent. "How about it? Will you call me Tyke?"

"All right, but if you get out of line with my sister, I'll punch you on the nose."

"And I believe you would."

"I am not smiling." Irene said with a very straight face.

"Okay, let's eat."

"To eat, we're going to have to order first."

"Call our waiter."

"Irene, may I take Sarah home?"

"I don't know, Tyke, I don't know if I can trust you."

"You can, Irene, you can trust me. Tell her, Brent."

"Oh no, I'm not going to be in the middle of this; you make your own decision."

"All right, she can go with you this time." Sarah smiled and shook her head.

"What are you smiling about?" Irene asked her.

"That I wasn't asked by either one of you," Sarah responded.

Darrell said. "Because I invited you to dinner, I thought I should take you home."

Darrell took Sarah by her arm and left with her.

"Did I do right, Brent?"

"I think you did, he did invite her to dinner."

"Irene, I heard Sarah tell Darrell that you can call me by my name because we are engaged, I want to make that statement right, what do you say?"

"Are you sure you love me, Brent?"

"I do Irene, very much."

"Me too Brent, I love you very much."

They had just arrived to the car; Brent pulled a small box out of the glove compartment.

Irene's eyes were wide and full of surprise.

"Is this the ring you gave Lisa?" she asked him.

"This is my mother's ring, Irene; look at the inscription."

It read, 'Love forever Peter.' "Oh Brent, it's beautiful, thank you." He smiled and they embraced, and then Brent pulled his face away from hers and kissed her.

"Irene it is not too late; could I come in and talk to your parents tonight?"

"Yes, darling, they'll be happy for us, they both like you very much."

When they arrived at Irene's house, Darrell and Sarah were parked in front of their house. "Oh, look who was late." Darrell told them in a jesting quip.

"Sarah, look what Brent just gave me, "And she showed her the engagement ring.

"Oh Irene, it's beautiful! Congratulations, both of you!" She said.

"Yes, congratulations are in order." Darrell said.

"Let's go in before Mama starts asking what we are doing out here so long."

"Good evening, Mr. and Mrs. Hamilton, how are you doing this evening? Meet our new addition to our office, Dr. Darrell Moore."

"Very nice meeting you, Dr. Moore, how do you like our town?"

"I like it very much, Sir."

"Well, sit down everybody." Charles said.

Brent spoke up. "Mr. and Mrs. Hamilton, I would like to ask you for Irene's hand in marriage. We have fallen in love, we have been going together and tonight we made the decision that we want to get married."

Kate and Charles looked at each other. "Well, we feel like we know you better because of my surgery. That made us realize the kind of person you are, and we like what we have seen. Yes, Dr. Miller. We'll be happy to oblige."

"Sarah, please ask Clare to bring us a bottle of wine to make a toast."

"Yes, Papa."

Clare came back with a bottle of champagne. Joanne followed her with a tray of wine glasses. Once everybody had a glass, Charles raised his glass and said:

"For the happy couple, may they always be as happy as they are today." Everybody raised their glass, Brent and Irene kissed briefly.

Darrell asked Charles, "Is Irene your first daughter who marries, Mr. Hamilton?"

"Yes, she is, we have two other daughters, Sarah and Laura. But they're much younger than Irene. They haven't started college yet."

Darrell turned around and asked Sarah point blank. "How old are you Sarah?"

"I'll be eighteen next month," she said shyly.

"Eighteen".... "I thought you were at least twenty-three!" he said alarmed with his findings.

No one noticed, but Brent could hardly hold his own, he was about to explode in laughter, he knew Darrell was already getting ready to court Sarah. They stayed a little longer and then Darrell and Brent left.

On the way out, Darrell told Brent, "I might just kill you for this."

"For what?" Bent answered him.

"Sarah told me she is going to be eighteen next month!"

"Darrell, I told you several days ago she is under age, don't you remember? I was blue in the face trying to tell you."

"Yes, I remember, but I thought you were kidding me."

"That's what you get for thinking."

Charles said. "I think we startled the new Doctor with Sarah's age."

"I think you did, Papa."

"Well, he has to get over her."

"Mama, have you seen my ring?"

"No, let me see it. It's beautiful, Irene."

"Yes Mama, it was his Mother's ring. I thought at first it was the ring Lisa gave back to him. He said he has always had this ring with him ever since his mother passed away. His mother told him to give it to the woman he would marry one day."

"Where is Laura, Mama?"

"She is in her bedroom."

"I'm going upstairs and show her the ring. But first, I have something to tell you."

"My God! Something else?"

"Dr. Lopez called Brent this afternoon and told him he had called his parents house from the hospital and spoke with Christina and Moran."

"How is she feeling, Irene?"

"Much better. Being with the children has something to do with it, I'm sure."

"And then Brent called Mr. Betancourt and had a talk with him about Christina."

"Of course Mike is in prison, but he really couldn't give Brent any other news."

"Well, that's a lot more than we knew earlier."

"Mama, I'm going to shower and talk to Laura. Good night."

Chapter Six

After showering, Irene walked to Laura's bedroom, she found her at her desk working on something. "What are you doing? School is out. Haven't you heard?"

"I'm just killing time, I'm writing about us."

"Really? That's grand; will you let me read it sometime? I came to show you my engagement ring, Brent gave it to me this evening."

"Oh Irene, I'm so happy for you, I think he is a wonderful man."

"I think so, Laura, we love each other very much. But I also want to tell you we know something about Christina. She is doing well, but she needs to stay where she is a little longer."

"I don't know why, but I believe that Dr. Lopez has fallen in love with Christina."

Irene smiled. "That's very observant for a kid your age, I think so myself but I have been with them a lot, Laura, and you haven't. How did you get an idea like that into your head?"

"I really don't know, Irene, it's more like a feeling, you know."

"Humm, I hope you're right. Christina needs a man like Dr. Lopez. He is good and kind, and loves children. Well, good night, I have to go to work tomorrow."

Sarah rode with Irene to work, "I wish I didn't have to depend on you for transportation, Irene."

"I don't mind, Sarah, why should you?"

"If you want to go somewhere I have to go with you, I need my own wheels."

"It'll happen soon enough, you'll be eighteen in a couple of weeks."

"When I say it, it sounds so long. . . two long weeks."

"Did you take drivers Ed at school?"

"Sure, I can drive; I just don't have anything to drive."

Irene pulled off the road, got out of the car and went around it.

"Move over, kiddo," she told Sarah. "Don't start too fast."

"Oh Irene, I could kiss you."

"Today, at our lunch hour, we'll drive to the Department of Motor Vehicles and apply for your learners permit. From now on, you're my Chauffer."

"Oh Irene, I love you."

"I love you too, but don't get emotional; you have to watch the road."

Sarah ran into the office, "Lourdes! Lourdes! I drove to work! I'll get my learners license at lunch time." Sarah said all excited. Darrell was coming in;

"Isn't that something? She can't even drive." He said in passing.

Irene was being very amused by the events. She was sure Darrell had fallen in love with Sarah, and Sarah didn't even notice it; it was very funny.

When lunch time came around, Sarah was ready to leave. "Sarah," Irene told her. "There are still two people in both Doctors offices, you can't leave yet."

"Oh," she said all disappointed. "Okay, I'll wait."

When the patients left, Sarah went where Irene was, "I'm ready, Irene."

"Okay baby, let's go," Irene told Sarah.

Darrell was leaning by his door, he shook his head. "The least that you can do is, don't call her baby."

"I was six years old when she was born Darrell, she has always been my baby."

Darrell was looking at the door lost in his thoughts, Brent asked him

"A penny for your thoughts."

"Oh brother, I don't think you want to know."

"Try me." Brent replied.

"I have fallen for Sarah like a school boy."

"You what? Oh Darrell, you're about to pay for your sins," Brent said laughing.

"I'm afraid so, I don't think I can even say anything to her, she is not old enough!"

"Oh Darrell, you don't know how funny that is."

"I can tell you, it is not funny," he said aggravated at himself. He turned around and left.

Irene told Sarah, "Why don't you and I have lunch today, just the two of us?"

"I'd like that, Irene. I'm so happy! I didn't think I'd ever be happy again."

"Why, sweetheart? You need to try to get that image out of your mind."

"I'm beginning to, Irene; things are getting easier these days."

"I'm glad, Sarah, I know it was a trying time for you, but you have to realize that Carl wasn't a good person and what happened; was his fault. You didn't know he had a record, but he did, that's why he ran, Sarah."

"I know, I have to repeat that so my hard head listens to me."

"Here we are Sarah; let's go in and sign yourself up for your license."

"I'm so nervous."

"Today it's nothing; leave your nerves for later, when you come back for your test."

Sarah and Irene went back to the office. "Lourdes, do you want to see my learner's permit?"

"I guess I'd better say, yes."

"It's just temporary you know. Irene is going to train me so I can get my real license."

"When are you going to be eighteen?" Lourdes asked Sarah.

"Almost two weeks, I can't wait."

"What are you planning to do then?"

"I'm going to college."

"What are you going to study?"

"I haven't decided yet. Can you imagine?"

"Surely, you have an idea."

"Not really."

"Lots of people take a year off because they can't decide, Sarah."

"Not me, I don't know what I'm going to be, but I know I want to go to college next year."

Darrell entered the building. With a very serious look, he bowed his head to Sarah and went by.

"I wonder what happened to Dr. Moore," she said

"Maybe he got jilted today." Irene told her.

"You think?" was Sarah's reply.

Lourdes looked at Irene. Irene was trying very hard not to laugh.

Brent called Irene to his office.

"Irene, do I have many patients for today?"

"I was looking at the schedule; we had a couple of cancellations."

"Good, maybe we can leave early."

"Brent, you know that Sarah rides with me."

"Do you think Lourdes could take her home for you?"

"I'm sure; what's going on Brent?"

"I'd like to go somewhere and just talk to you, darling."

"I'd like that, Brent."

"Lourdes, is your house too far from mine? You know where I live don't you?"

"It's not far. No, why?"

"Brent wants to talk to me and I want to know if you can take Sarah home."

"But of course, I'll be glad to, Irene."

"Now, for the hard part, I hope she wants to go. And I just thought about something. My car is here; she can drive but not alone. Never mind Lourdes, thank you but I have to take her home myself."

She went to Brent and told him she had to go home. "Can you pick me up?"

"I'll leave the office right after you do, I won't be long."

Irene and Sarah left. Sarah drove; Irene thought that would keep her from being so mad at Irene for wanting to send her with Lourdes.

Irene ran upstairs and changed clothes. Then, she went back downstairs and waited for Brent.

In about forty five minutes, Brent pulled into the driveway.

"What happened?" She asked him when he came in.

"Darrell happened. He is so unhappy, Irene. You don't know the half of it."

"I wouldn't tell Sarah if I were you, but he said he is so in love with Sarah, he feels like a school boy."

"I guessed it Brent, but I thought it was funny."

"Yes, I made fun of him, and I told him it was funny. He said; it is not a bit funny.

But he has always played around with many girls, that's why I went into his office the other day and had a talk with him about Sarah. He has it bad."

"Well, I'm sorry Brent, but Sarah is too young for him or anybody else."

"Yes, but I didn't want to come here and talk about Darrell. Irene, how about if we set a date for our wedding?"

"Don't you think it's too soon, Brent?"

"Not if we're ready to be married, and I am, Irene. Aren't you?"

Irene looked at him and said. "Yes, Brent, I want to be your wife as soon as we can put the wedding together." He drove to the shore where he parked. They embraced for a long time and kissed. Her feelings for him were intensifying; his touch was both soft and caressing.

She pulled back and asked him. "When do you think you want us to be married?"

"This is July, before Thanksgiving. That will give us four months."

"I was hoping you'd say that. It's still early. Why don't we go back to my house and we can talk to my parents tonight."

"We can buy a house, Irene, but I have my apartment."

"But isn't Darrell living there?"

"Yes, he is. But he can find himself his own apartment; he is there until he can find his own place."

"To tell you the truth, I think I would prefer to look for a house first."

"Okay, we can try that. We're almost at your house. We haven't eaten yet, Irene."

"Are you hungry?"

"I could eat."

"I'll fix you something to eat, nothing fancy you know."

He smiled. "Am I going to be your guinea pig?"

"No, I cook sometimes."

They went into the house, they were all eating dinner.

"Sit down," Charles said. "Have you had dinner yet?"

"Mr. Hamilton, you have saved me from being Irene's guinea pig."

"Do you mean, she offered to cook?"

"Well, we came back in a rush to talk to you and your wife."

"Okay, fork it over, I can smell it already."

"We would like to get married in November, before Thanksgiving."

Charles looked at Kate. "Four months, what do you think Kate?"

"I think if that's what they want to do, we can get it done."

"Thank you, both of you, now we have to plan."

Brent told Irene. "I think the first thing to do is: go to the Church and find out what date they have available, then pick out invitations, my dress, and Bride Maids dresses, and oh! a place where we are having the reception. We could have the reception at the Club, but I think our garden will be a beautiful setting for it."

"November is a beautiful season in California," Kate remarked.

"Who are going to be your bride maids?" Kate asked Irene.

"I thought Sarah, Laura and Christina; and Linda will be my flower girl."

"Yes, Amy is too young."

"Who is going to be your best man, Brent?"

"I guess I better ask Darrell or he'll have his feelings hurt."

"He is your only friend over here."

"To tell you the truth, I have thought about asking you, Mr. Hamilton."

"Thank you for the thought, Brent." Charles said.

"We have to check about the cake, and catering, decorating the Church and our garden."

"Good Lord," said Brent. "Why don't we elope?"

"Brent, what is the matter with you?"

"He has my vote," Charles teased.

"Charles!" Kate said scandalized at her husband's remark.

Both men laughed out loud at the women.

Sarah said, "What can we do to help; Irene?"

"Get yourselves one of those long note pads, and start with the guest list."

"Hey, can I invite all my friends?"

"Family friends and family, kids. We're not having a big wedding."

"Have you thought what your colors are going to be?"

"No, we just decided to get married this evening."

Kate said: "Let's get serious; we have to reserve a caterer because if the wedding is going to be before Thanksgiving, we're going to have a lot of competition around that date."

Irene said. "Mama, why don't you meet me at Connie's Flower Shop at my lunch hour? We can do that much before we talk to the Priest; we could see Father Gabriel after work. Brent, we have not talked about Church at all, which Church denomination do you attend?"

"I haven't been to a Church since I was a child Irene, where ever you go is fine with me."

"Papa, you're probably going to have to buy yourself a tuxedo, whatever you have is too old for my wedding; Mama, I thought we could buy a dress for Clare and she can sit with the family, not be with the servants. She could sit by the guest book when people come in."

"Irene, that's a wonderful idea, I'll tell her."

"To answer your question about a tuxedo for me Irene, I was planning to wear a suit."

"Papa, how can you wear a suit for my wedding?"

"For one thing, it's going to be in our garden, I'll feel silly to dress up in a tuxedo to go the back yard."

"Mama, are we going to have to hold the wedding reception at the country club for Dad to wear a tuxedo?"

"Ask him if he prefers to hold the wedding at the country club?"

"Brent, are you taking notes? They gang up on you to get what they want."

"Yes, I have my book out," he told Charles jokingly.

"Changing the subject, Laura, I haven't seen Benny, are you mad at each other?"

"Oh no, Irene, he is working two jobs because school is out."

"You know? He can be an usher."

"He'll like that Irene, thank you."

"Okay, that's enough planning for the first day. After we talk to Father Gabriel, we can do a lot more like order the invitations. We don't have a list yet."

"Brent, how about if you and I walk to the garden and you can see firsthand how big it is."

"I think I'm going upstairs and read some before I go to sleep," Sarah said.

"And I think I'll follow your steps," Laura replied.

"Charles, why don't you and I do the same?"

"Is that your way to let me know I over stayed my welcome?" Brent asked.

"Oh no, you stay and visit all you want," Charles told him.

"Sarah, are you ready to leave?" Irene asked Sarah on her way out.

"Yes, I'm ready. Are you telling Lourdes, Betty and Maureen you and Brent are getting married?"

"Yes, I don't see why not. I only wish I could tell Christina."

"It would be nice, maybe you can talk to Dr. Lopez."

"At the same time, that might make her want to come back sooner than she should."

"I know, that wouldn't be a good idea."

"Anyway, I need to speak to Mr. Betancourt and ask him about Mike's case."

"Here we are Irene, don't you think I'm a good driver?"

"You're a very good driver, Sarah; you have my vote for your license."

"I'm glad I have a key, the office is still closed. Lourdes will be upset she wasn't the first to be here today."

"Lourdes, did you sleep here last night? At what time did you come in?"

"I had to come earlier because there is a lot of paperwork to do, Irene."

"Lourdes, have Betty work the window today and I'll help you with billing, I have a degree in Finance, I can do that, don't put the entire load on you."

"Thank you Irene, I appreciate that."

"It makes me feel bad that you didn't say anything about it, you know we can help each other."

"I know, I know."

"Do you know how many patients we have today, Irene?"

"I haven't seen the schedule, Lourdes. Let me have a look."

Irene walked to the window to read the schedule and went back to Lourdes.

"We have a full house, but there is no surgery this morning or afternoon either."

"That's good. Well, Irene, these are some of the bills that need to be mailed."

"Do I have to make invoices for them?"

"Yes, all of them, and I get on the other side and pay the incoming bills."

"Sarah, can you manage all right with both Doctors?"

"I do it every day, Irene. And don't forget Maureen is here now."

"I know, but today, there is no breathing time, we have a full house."

"Good, that's the way I like it."

'The Doctors are coming in now."

"Good morning, Ladies, how are you doing this morning?"

"Good morning, Dr. Miller, Dr. Moore."

"Can I take the first patient to the examination room?"

"Is it lunch time yet?" Sarah asked. Darrell answered her.

"Yes, are you inviting today?"

"Not really, I'm hungry and I was wishing for it."

"Would you like to come to lunch with me today?"

"Dr. Moore, you haven't been talking to me, I thought I had offended you."

"No, no, I had something that was worrying me, but it has passed."

"I'm glad, I have to ask Irene because I ride with her, you know." Darrell made a big breathing sound of resignation.

"Irene, may I go to lunch with Dr. Moore?"

"Did he ask you?"

"Yes, did you think, I did?"

"No, I was surprised because I thought he wasn't talking to you all that much other than at work."

"That's what I asked him, he told me he had something worrying him, but it has passed now."

"Okay, but keep your guard up at all times."

"Irene, what is he going to do to me at lunch time?" she said dismissing Irene's fears.

Brent and Irene were having lunch at their favorite restaurant, they had just ordered and they were chatting while waiting for their lunch.

"Brent, I don't know if I did right by allowing Sarah to go with Darrell."

"Of course you did right, Irene; you know I haven't been at ease with him and Sarah, but the way he feels for her now, she can't be in better hands."

"That bothers me Brent. She is not quite eighteen years old and how old is he?"

"Thirty three, but I'm also thirty-three, Irene. Do you think I'm too old for you?"

"I'm twenty-four years old, Brent."

"That's even better; I thought you told me you're twenty-three."

"I might have, I had a birthday recently, and my mind probably is not used to it."

"Oh, here is lunch. Good, I'm starved."

"Brent, do you think I could send a message to Christina through Dr. Lopez?"

"About us getting hitched?"

"Is that what we're going to do?"

"I remember my Dad using that terminology. Yes, I can give him a call."

"I would love to tell Christina in person, but I'm afraid we would be followed."

"Have you talked to Mr. Betancourt?"

"The other day, but I haven't called back. I don't want to tire him with my questions."

"He is aware that you're concerned, it's not curiosity that makes you ask him questions, Irene, he understands that."

"When I talked to him the other day, he told me he didn't know anything about the case, other than he was in prison."

"Ask him if he is still in prison and if he is going to stay there."

"Yes, I believe as soon as we go back to the office I'll give him a call."

"Mr. Betancourt, this is Irene Hamilton. I hate to bother you again, but I need to know about Mike Long. Do you know if he is going to stay in prison for a long time?"

"I spoke with someone here; he said that they're considering charging him with attempted murder again because it was a different offense."

"Oh, that would be such a blessing, Mr. Betancourt. Thank you for talking to me and for being so patient with me."

"Not at all, Miss Hamilton."

"Brent, they're going to charge Mike with attempted murder again."

"I'm glad Irene; I know Christina will be relieved as well."

"You can tell Moran when you talk to him, and let him know about it."

"I will later, but now, I have a few patients to take care of."

"I'm sorry; you should have told me I was taking too long in here."

"Never mind; Ask Sarah to bring in the first patient."

"Sarah, how was lunch?"

"It was fine Irene; he was very nice to me."

"How nice?"

"You're impossible, you know. Mama called, she said she made an appointment with Father Gabriel for six o'clock."

"Great, that gives me time to go home after work."

"She said Brent has to be there as well."

"I'll let him know. We have to leave in a hurry today, okay?"

"Irene, Dr. Moore invited me for dinner tonight, is that all right?"

"You have to go home first and ask Mama and Dad."

"I'd like to change clothes if I go with him; any way."

"Sarah, don't forget that he is much older than you baby."

"Yes, especially if you keep calling me baby. But it's nothing like that; he just doesn't know anyone yet," she said.

Irene looked at her sister, "I'm glad she is so naive." she thought.

"Okay sweetheart, just keep an eye on him and don't let on I have warned you."

"No, I imagine he would be mad at you and I don't want that."

"Thank you, little sister."

"Here we are. Home in one piece."

"Thank you, I have to run and get dressed to go out with Brent."

"Irene, please don't tell me you've forgotten you and Brent need to go to Church with Mother to talk to Father Gabriel."

"I won't tell you, but it was not in my mind at all, thank you. In fact, I don't remember telling Brent at all."

"Brent and I talked about sending Christina a message. Then I called Mr. Betancourt and you know how busy we were today."

"Brent, did I tell you we have an appointment to see Father Gabriel?"

"I don't think so, Irene, but we're ready to go, so we can just stop there on the way to our favorite restaurant."

"Not really, Mama is coming with us, maybe Dad but I'm not sure about him."

"It's almost six, Mama, it's time to leave or we're going to be late."

"I'm here Irene; Charles decided to go at the last minute."

"That's great; are we riding in the same car, Mama?"

"No, you go ahead and leave, and I will wait for your Father."

"Let's go Brent; at least we might be on time."

"Good evening, Father, how are you? May I introduce you to my fiancé?"

"Brent Miller." Brent said shaking the Priest's hand.

"Very nice meeting you, Brent, are you the Doctor who did surgery on Charles?"

"Guilty as charged," Brent said.

"Sit down please, are your parents coming, Irene?"

"Yes, Father, Mama was waiting for Dad when we left."

"Well Brent, are you Catholic?"

"No, but I haven't been to a Church since my childhood, so I can't claim a church at all; only that I believe in God."

"That's a good start, but you have to start coming to church and follow instructions about the Catholic Church if you intend to marry Irene in her church."

"Yes, I intend to marry Irene in her church and I will do whatever is required of me; sometimes, because of my profession, I might not be able to be at one of the Masses or a meeting I'm suppose to attend. Emergencies happen all the time."

"I understand," Father Gabriel told Brent, "I'll give you a book for you to read, and if you read it thoughtfully, you can find out what Irene is all about. Because this is what she believes."

"Thank you for giving me the opportunity to learn your religion, Father."

"Charles, Kate, it is good seeing you, come in and sit down. We have been talking about the wedding but I haven't asked them when they want to get married."

"Saturday before Thanksgiving." Irene said.

"Good Lord, Irene, you couldn't have found a busier time."

"I know, but maybe it's possible; I had to try for that date."

"I have to check my book, but I can tell you there're going to be more weddings that weekend than I can count."

Father Gabriel got up and went to another office and came back with a book.

"I have a noon Mass, Irene, how about that time?"

"Mama? Do you think it's a good time?"

"Personally, I think it's perfect, it's going to be in our garden."

"Brent, what do you think about the time? And you Papa?"

"Just give us a map and we'll find it; huh Brent?" Charles said.

"Then, I'll put you down for that time and date, Irene and Brent."

"Thank you, Father."

"Brent, I expect to see you and Irene in church every Sunday."

"I'll be here unless I have an emergency."

When they were leaving, Kate asked Irene, "Do you want me to make an appointment with the caterer? You heard what Father Gabriel said about the weddings for Thanksgiving."

"I was thinking about that Mama, maybe they could also handle the cake."

"If you want me to, I can do that tomorrow, and you take care of the flowers and your dress."

"Are we not having lunch together tomorrow, Irene?" Brent asked her

"If you want to, we can pick something up and eat it on the way. You can come with me."

"To help you pick out your dress, Irene?" Kate asked her. "I don't think so."

"You're right Mama, I wasn't thinking."

"We'll have dinner tomorrow night, all right?"

"We can also have dinner tonight." he told her.

"Okay, we can leave now, we'll see you later, Papa, behave yourself."

"That's my line, you behave yourself."

"Did Sarah ask you if she could go out to dinner with Dr. Moore?"

"Yes, he came in as we were leaving, that's what took us a little longer to leave for the Church."

"Did they say where they're going for dinner?"

"No, do you want to meet them, Irene?"

"No Mama, I was only curious. Let's go Brent."

"Are we going to our restaurant? Or do you want to go elsewhere?"

"Let's go there. I'm going to try to forget about Sarah and Darrell."

"I vote for that. Sweetheart, I think if I know Darrell a little bit, and I do, he is going to wait for her to grow up a little bit more."

"I believe you; it's just that she just came out of that situation with Carl. She is so vulnerable, she has no idea what's in Darrell's mind."

"I know, but we're here for her, and I'll be watching Darrell, Irene, I promise you. But I repeat, he is not going to harm Sarah."

"Enough of that Brent, I'm going to get off of that, what do you want to eat?"

"I never heard anything sweeter in my life. How about if we order wine while we wait?"

"It sounds great. Do you remember when we ate dinner the first time? We ordered roast beef in wine sauce; I'd love to have that tonight."

"You read my mind, Miss Hamilton, I'll have the same."

"Make sure you'll be able to drive when we leave," she said smiling with a wink in her eye. Brent leaned over and kissed Irene.

"Hey, none of that," They heard a voice behind them. It was Dr. Lopez.

"Carlos, sit down. Join us." Brent told him.

"No, I don't want to interrupt anything."

"You already did that, so you might as well sit down," Brent told him.

"Do you have any news about Christina?" Irene asked Carlos.

"Yes, Moran thinks it's safe enough for her to come back; and she needs to be checked. She is a nurse so that helps somewhat."

"When is she going to be able to come home, Carlos?," Irene asked.

"First day I'm free to go to my parents' ranch."

"Oh, if she is able to come home, I can send someone after her, Carlos."

"But, can they find the place? It's quite a complicated road."

"You can draw me a map, can't you?"

"You better draw it, Carlos, I can tell you, you are not going to win this one," Brent told Carlos laughing. Carlos pulled out a pen and started to draw.

"I can't wait to have Christina back with us," Irene said smiling.

"She is very lucky to have a friend such as you are, Irene." Carlos told her.

"She is a great person, Carlos; all she did wrong; was put her trust in a man like Mike, then she stayed because of the children."

"I know, she told me a lot of what has happened to her with him. I don't think she would get mad at me for telling you both, but we're waiting for her divorce to become final to announce that we love each other."

Irene put her hand on Carlos' hand and said to him "You have never made a better decision Carlos; she is going to be a blessing in your life."

"I know, but thank you for telling me that. I love the children too, and she knows that."

Irene's eyes were tearful but she smiled. "I'm so happy." she said.

Brent said, "Congratulations Buddy, welcome to the family."

"Thank you, I'll see you sometime tomorrow Brent. Irene, I'll tell Christina you're getting married soon."

"I wish you would stay and have dinner with us, Carlos," Irene told Dr. Lopez.

"No, I have never liked to be the third wheel," he said waving his hand to them.

"I'm so happy for Christina and the children, they deserve someone good in their life, and Christina suffered too long with that....man."

"The best part of it is, that you won't be blaming yourself for whatever happens to Christina."

"Now, don't make fun of me," she said kidding Brent.

"You know I'm not, baby. They're coming with our food, let's eat."

"Sarah's birthday is next week; I'm going to talk to my parents about throwing her a birthday party."

"If I can do something sweetheart, let me know," Brent told her.

"I'm thinking about convincing my father to buy Sarah a car. She wouldn't expect that at all, but she'll be going to the University next semester, she'll need a car."

"That's a great idea, Irene, but maybe not for your father," he said laughing.

"He might resist in the beginning, but he'll understand it is the most practical gift they can give her, and she will love it."

"Yes, but now I'm thinking what can I give her for her birthday?" Brent asked Irene.

"I imagine some costume jewelry, they're very pretty and Sarah loves them."

"I hope you take time to go with me, I'm hopeless when it comes to choosing a gift for anyone, you'll see."

"You can learn. I'll be happy to teach you." she said squeezing his hand.

"And it's time to eat sweetheart, it has taken them so long to serve us tonight, I have forgotten what we've ordered."

"Me too." Brent replied.

"Irene, I was thinking we shouldn't rush into buying a house, we can live in my apartment and when we find a house we like, we can buy it at that time."

"Yes, I thought about that too, but I keep thinking about Darrell living in your place; I don't want to start our married life with your school buddy between us."

"That's not going to happen, Irene. When I get home tonight, I'll tell him to start looking for an apartment now to make sure he'll have one when we get ready to move in. Besides that, there are several things we need to buy, like a larger bed, a new living room set and a dining room set, as well."

"Yes, I'd like to go to the kitchen and see how big it is and what we might need in there."

"Of course." Brent replied.

"Oh, Brent, we're going to be so happy!"

"I know Irene, but let's not spend so much on the apartment if we're going to be looking for a house. I don't want us to get so comfortable there that we don't want to move out."

"You're right darling; I just get carried away with the arrangements. I get so excited!"

"When are you going to look for your wedding gown?"

"I had to make an appointment for next week, also for Sarah, Laura and Christina; they're going to be my Bride Maids. You know, I have a thought to dress up Linda like a small bride for a flower girl, what do you think?"

"I think it's a wonderful idea, we should have asked Carlos earlier; in any case, it shouldn't be more than a couple of days until Christina comes back."

Chapter Seven

Irene and Sarah got home after work and Irene asked Sarah, "Are you going anywhere tonight?"

"Dr. Moore invited me out to dinner again but I told him I needed to be home tonight to take care of something I've been neglecting to do."

"What in the world do you need to do?"

"Nothing," she said smiling, "I'm just following your advice."

"Good girl. Brent and I are going out for a while."

As they were walking in, Christina and her children met them.

"Christina!" They hugged and then Irene knelt down and kissed the children.

"What a wonderful surprise!" she said.

Sarah hugged and kissed her and the children as well.

"How long have you been back?"

"Not too long really, we have been trying to unpack and get ourselves re-acquainted with the house again. The children get lost every time they are by themselves."

"How about at Carlos's house, how did you get along over there?"

"Mr. and Mrs. Lopez could not have being nicer, Irene, they made me feel so at home even if I didn't know either one of them. They are such wonderful people; they inspire love with their presence, their hospitality surpasses anything I have ever seen, except here at your house, but here all of you have known me all my life."

"Well, I'm glad you had a good time over there. How big is their ranch?"

"I couldn't see it all, they took me for rides sometimes, but of course, most of their land has no roads because they ride their horses. But their home is absolutely majestic, its old Spanish style."

"Christina, let me go change clothes, Brent is coming in a few minutes and I need to be ready."

"Of course, what is that I hear you're going to get married?"

"Yes, believe it or not, we plan to on Saturday before Thanksgiving," she said while she started to run upstairs.

Christina held Sarah by the hand, and said "Well, tell me what you are doing these days Sarah?"

"I'm working at Dr. Miller's office as a nurse' aide, but as soon as school starts, I'm going to register at the University."

"Do you know what you're going to do?"

"Not yet, I have lots of thoughts in my head, but that's all."

"Good evening," Brent announced himself.

"Hello, Dr. Miller, it's nice seeing outside of the hospital?" Christina said shaking his hand.

"These are my children, Linda and Amy."

"I visited you lots of times, but you're always 'out'," Brent told her smiling.

"How are you ladies, I remember you!" Brent said petting their heads.

Charles and Kate came down, "What is this? Do we have a party? Charles said shaking Brent's hand.

"Where is Irene? I didn't think she would leave Christina the day she arrived."

"She wanted to be ready when you came over, Dr. Miller." Christina said.

"We're about to be family, so call me Brent."

"Okay, Brent it is, unless I'm at work, if I still have a job."

"You do. You can't imagine how many more patients we have since Dr. Moore arrived to our office."

"Whenever Carlos discharges you, you're welcome to come back."

"Hi, stranger." Irene told Brent kissing him briefly on the lips.

"Hi yourself, I was visiting with Christina. Listen, if you prefer to stay I understand, we can go to dinner tomorrow."

"Christina wouldn't let me do that, would you Christina?"

"Oh no, I couldn't enjoy the visit if she misses a date with you."

"Good evening!" They all looked around, and there was Dr. Lopez, all smiles.

"You see? I have a date myself." Christina said smiling at Carlos; Clare came and announced dinner was served.

Irene looked at Brent with inquisitive eyes, "Of course we're staying, Irene." So they all walked to the dining room; Carlos picked up Amy, and held Linda by the hand, Christina clinched to Carlos's arm. Irene put her hand over her mouth in a moment of intense emotion to see that picture; Brent squeezed her hand and led her into the dining room.

Charles stood up with a glass of wine, "I want to offer a toast in honor of Christina coming back home, and to Carlos and the children that are a new family; I know it is in the foundation stage, but I know in my heart that this is a very strong kind of foundation that will never collapse."

Everyone applauded. Carlos stood up. "Thank you, Mr. Hamilton, I think everybody here knows how I feel about Christina and her children and I hope the next time I speak in public, I can say 'our children'." Christina was sobbing,

Carlos sat down, embraced her, took his handkerchief and dried her tears.

Kate said "let's pray, but after everything that was said here, I think it was sort of a prayer in itself."

"Christina or Carlos, do you want to say the prayer?" Kate asked

"You do it, Carlos; I'm too emotional and I couldn't do it right now."

After Carlos said the prayer, platters started circling around the table.

"By the way Mama, where is Laura?" Irene asked

"Benny came over to take her to a movie and to dinner."

"I heard he is working," she replied.

"Yes, I believe Laura said he is working for a construction company."

"Good, I know Benny will save his money for college."

"After a movie and dinner," Charles said.

"Christina; do you plan to see the attorney who contacted you at the hospital?"

"You could call and make the appointment for the same day that you have your check up." Carlos suggested.

Kate offered, "You know that our driver can take you anywhere you want Christina; just try to give him some warning so he won't have other plans."

"Thank you, that's very kind of you." Christina said.

"Nonsense, I just don't want you to try to get transportation elsewhere when we have it here at home."

"Excuse me," said Brent," but what is this dish we're eating? It's delicious. I don't remember eating anything so exquisite."

"I don't know, Brent. But I'll ask Clare. As long as she has been with us, she always surprises me with new dishes."

"Irene, make sure you get her recipe," Brent told Irene.

"Hey, don't think I'm going to cook when we get married."

"Not every day, but every once in a while."

"Yeah, I love her biscuits; I'll get that recipe as well." Charles looked at Kate with amusing eyes, Kate ignored him.

Christina excused herself to put the children to bed. Carlos asked her if he could go along. So, they all got up from the table and went upstairs.

"That is just marvelous," Irene said. "I just love to see them together." Clare came over to ask if they needed something else. Kate asked her,

"Will you ask Cindy to stay with the children? That way Christina and Carlos will be able to come back for dessert."

"That's a good idea, Mama," Irene said. "In fact, when Christina goes for her check-up Cindy could keep the children for her."

"You're right, Irene; I'm going assign Cindy to the children." Christina and Carlos walked back into the dining room. "Thank you for sending Cindy to keep the children company, Mrs. Hamilton."

"Christina, I'm going to assign Cindy for the children, do you like her?"

"What's not to like? But I feel I'm abusing your hospitality."

"You know we have always counted you as one of our children, Christina."

"Well, I think Cindy would be a blessing for me, especially when I bathe the children."

"Christina, haven't you been helped on that?

"I didn't ask anyone, Mrs. Hamilton, but Linda helped me with Amy."

"I'm so sorry, Christina; Cindy will be at your disposal from now on."

"It was only today, and I'm out of practice."

"Yes, I'm sure Carlos's parents didn't let you do anything."

"Well, when I arrived there, it was soon after my surgery, so I was really an invalid and they treated me like one."

"Where is Mr. Moran?" Irene asked.

"He told me yesterday he was going to talk with Mr. Betancourt and after that he'll have me under surveillance,"

"That's good to know," Irene replied.

"Someone ask Lorenzo to come talk to me, please." Charles said.

Kate said, "Lorenzo is our gardener. He's also our chauffeur when needed."

"Do you want him to come right now, Charles?"

"Yes, I don't want anyone to get up from the table, but as soon as possible."

"Clare, I'm glad you came, could you ask Lorenzo to come over, please?"

"Yes Kate."

"Charles, may I ask you why you want Lorenzo?"

"Yes, dear, I just learned Mr. Moran will be sleeping in his car, I think we can make better arrangements for him."

"That's great thinking, Charles."

"It's very thoughtful, Charles," Brent said.

"Lorenzo, I'm glad you were close by."

"Christina, do you remember what kind of car Mr. Moran drives?"

"It's a dark blue Chevy, I believe," she said.

"Lorenzo; there is a man inside of that car. Go to it and ask him if his name is Luis Moran; tell him Mrs. Christina needs to speak with him."

"What should I say when he comes in; Mr. Hamilton?" Christina asked him.

"I'll speak to him, but he doesn't know me so I sent your name."

Charles stood up, "Mr. Moran? Charles Hamilton. Welcome. What can we offer you; have you had dinner yet?"

"Well no, Mr. Hamilton."

Charles looked up and Clare was waiting for him to tell her what he wanted.

"Clare, please bring a setting for Mr. Moran and full dinner for him."

"Thank you very much, Mr. Hamilton, what can I do for you?"

"I just heard you have Christina under surveillance, do you have to be in your car?"

"That's customary."

"May I ask how do you manage your simple daily routines?" Luis Moran smiled at Charles.

"Well, I have an idea; you can stay inside of the house, the main issue is to protect Christina, you can be here where she is, you don't have to do it from the street, do you?"

"I have never done it another way, Mr. Hamilton. If the subject I'm waiting for comes by; I'll see him."

"Call Mr. Betancourt and ask him to let you know if your subject has been turned loose or if he has escaped. Does anyone have anything against Mr. Moran staying in here?"

"No, it's a surprise, Mr. Hamilton, but I think it should be okay," Christina said.

"When you take a bath, you let Lorenzo know, and he can take over for you."

"I have to give that a thought, Mr. Hamilton; I have never been treated so well."

"Tonight, you can think about it in the house; in fact, you can put your car in the garage, anyone who knows your car will think you are off the job."

"Now, that is a thought. Yes, that is a very good idea, Mr. Hamilton. I could be here incognito, Mr. Hamilton. I'm going to take you up with your idea; I think it is a very good strategy. In the morning, I'll call Mr. Betancourt.

Irene went downstairs after her shower; singing and walking into the kitchen. Clare turned around surprised to see her.

"Irene, what in the world are you doing up so early in the morning, don't you know it's Saturday?"

"Of course I do, you don't see me dressed for work, do you? I'm ready to learn how to make biscuits; Brent loves your biscuits."

"Okay Irene, let me get everything, you write it in your recipe book."

"I don't have a recipe book, Clare."

"You're going to need one, Irene, every time you like to keep a recipe, you write it down in your book."

"Let me go to Dad's office, I'll be right back."

As soon as she left, she told Inez, a young kitchen apprentice, "You either leave the kitchen and no matter what Irene does, you do not laugh, understand?"

"Why would I laugh?"

"Because Irene has never been in the kitchen before, I'm surprised she found it."

"Well, I'm glad you warned me, Clare. Now I know and I will prepare for it."

"Prepare for what?" Irene asked coming back to the kitchen.

"Inez also wants to learn how to make biscuits, so we make two batches."

"I have put all the ingredients on the table, Irene. Do you want me to make the biscuits and you watch the first time?"

"No, I want to make them while you give me instructions."

"Do you want to watch, Inez?"

"Come to think about it, today is not a good time for me. Bye."

"Well, it's just you and me, baby."

"Clare, Brent doesn't like for you to call me baby; he likes to call me Baby."

"Okay, okay, what shall I call you?"

"How about, Irene?"

"Oh, we're going to be smart, huh?"

"Let's start Clare. Brent is coming over this morning, to eat my biscuits."

"**Oh God!**" Clare thought.

"Let's begin with two cups of flour, sift the flour well."

"How do I sift?" Irene asked Clare.

"Do you know what it means?"

"I think so, but I have never done it."

"Why don't you let me fix the biscuits the first time, then you can do it next time Irene?"

"Because Brent is coming over to eat my biscuits; not yours."

Clare began to explain everything to Irene, but she didn't even know the name of the kitchen utensils and Clare was running out of patience.

"Okay, but I think the dough looks kind of firm, Irene."

"Oh no, I put plenty of milk."

"Okay, if you think you put in everything I told you....."

"I did, we can bake them now, I can't wait." Irene said.

Clare said a silent prayer when she put the biscuits in the oven.

"I'm going to change before Brent comes over Clare; you can just bring the biscuits to the table when they're ready."

"I hate to take credit for your baking, Irene; why don't you come back to the kitchen and you take them to the dining room."

"Hey, yes. That's a better idea; I won't be too long, Clare. Thanks." As soon as Irene left, Clare cleaned the table and started another batch of biscuits; she worked as fast as she possibly could, but Irene came back before she could take the second batch out of the oven.

"Clare, why are you making more biscuits?"

"Just in case there are not enough, Irene. I always make two batches."

"Are mine ready?"

"I'll check Irene." Clare went to the oven and pulled them out.

"They don't look the same as yours, Clare, Why?"

"Let me see, Irene," She tried to break it with her hands as she always did, and the biscuit didn't do anything to the touch; Clare knew they weren't any good, they were very hard.

Irene grabbed it out of Clare's hands and threw it on the white kitchen wall. The biscuit broke; Irene went to the wall and said; "It cracked the paint!"

Irene was furious; she was so mad that tears were rolling down her face. Clare said, "Irene, wait, you're going to learn, Baby, let's use my biscuits today. You take those biscuits and then you learn how to make them."

"No Clare, I can't lie to Brent. I can't tell him these are my biscuits."

"It's not like you killed somebody, it's just a little white lie, please. Your Dad would think its funny and pretty soon, they'll be laughing."

"You're very convincing; I'll do it, trash the others."

Irene walked into the dining room with a tray of hot biscuits.

"Irene, did you bake these biscuits?" Charles, Brent and Kate asked.

"I had to change clothes because my clothes were full of flour."

"They're delicious Baby." Brent said.

"I'm impressed," Charles said.

Irene looked up, and then she dropped her head, "I can't do it," she said.

"Yes, you can, Irene; these biscuits are out of this world," Brent told her.

"Brent, Papa, Mama, I'm sorry, Clare told me to bring her biscuits because mine turned out terrible," Irene said trying to swallow her tears. Brent got up, "I appreciate you trying to do it for me, Irene." He kissed her.

"What happened, Baby?" Charles asked

"Do you promise not to laugh?" Irene asked them "Clare was right there with me the whole time; I don't know what I did wrong. But even before I put them in the oven she told me the dough was too firm and I didn't listen to her. When my biscuits were done they were as hard as a rock, I was so angry I threw a biscuit at the kitchen wall, and it cracked the paint!" Irene said.

Brent, Charles and Kate looked at each other, then looked at Irene, neither of them wanted to laugh, they tried not to....but couldn't, Charles was the first to let a huge laugh out loud. Irene got up, "Papa, you promised!"

"Irene, how can I not laugh? It's so funny!"

"Mama and Brent didn't laugh," she said.

Charles looked Brent's way, and he had disappeared; Kate hid her face between her hands; her face was scarlet red and she was trying so hard not to laugh, but in fact, she was…laughing…

Irene sat back down, "Well, I guess it is funny if it didn't happen to you." Brent walked back in, "Sorry, he said, I had to go to the wash room."

"That's all right Brent, I just don't want to be made fun of again." Brent hugged Irene, "I love you, Baby, and the biscuits has nothing to do with it."

"It happens to all of us when we are learning. When Charles and I first got married, he came back from the store one day with three of his brothers who were here visiting, and wanted a cheese omelet;

Clare had gone to the market, so I thought, I can do it. And I started putting my ingredients together, I served the omelet to Charles and his brothers, and they started to eat, but didn't pay me any compliments, so I ventured, and asked him, Well, what do you think of your omelet?" And he answered, "Well, it would've been better if it had something in it!" "I had forgotten the onions and cheese on the board! They all laughed at me! Remember, Charles?"

"Oh, yes, every time I eat an omelet, I make sure Clare cooked it."

Brent and Irene were walking to the garden, Brent said, "Irene, when we go out later on, let's go buy a gift for Sarah. By the way, I know Darrell is buying something for Sarah; he went to a jewelry store yesterday. He didn't mean to tell me it just slipped out and he finally admitted it was Sarah's gift. I said to him; "I hope it's not an engagement ring." He said, "No."

"I hope not, she thinks he invites her out because he doesn't know anyone. She feels sorry for him."

Brent put both of his hands on his head and laughed out loud, "I won't tell Darrell; it's too good; I'll wait until he gives her his gift."

"Her birthday is Wednesday. I have to go to the dealership with Dad so we can have her car at home when she gets home from work."

"How is Sarah going to get home?"

"She is eighteen years old that day; she can drive by herself on Wednesday."

"And what are you going to tell her that you're not going home?"

"I'll tell her I'm going to get her birthday present."

"You have it all figured out, huh?"

"I have to; Papa is coming over to pick me up."

"Why don't you let me take you? Sarah might see him."

"Yes, you're right; I'll tell Papa I'll meet him at the dealership. Thanks"

"Papa, it's almost six o'clock I didn't want to be so late getting back home."

"They'll wait for us, Irene. Who is going to be there for the birthday party?"

"Just us, Brent, Dr. Moore; I invited Lourdes and her sister, and Betty because we work together, Christina and Laura; Laura might have invited Benny."

"Here they come with the car now, it looks good, doesn't it?"

"Sarah is going to be so happy; this is the car she wanted."

"Let's go."

Irene drove in blowing the horn in Sarah's fancy red sports car. As she was stepping out of the car, she heard a yell that pierced her ears.

"**Oh my God**," Sarah said, "I thought Dad would get me a car, I thought he might consider getting me a car, but not *my car.*" Sarah got into the car not believing it was hers. It was so incredible!

"Thank you Papa, Mama, thank you, thank you!"

There stood Darrell smiling, Brent and Irene, Kate and all the others.

"I'm glad you like it, Sarah." Charles said.

"Well let's go in, we can't take the car in Sarah, but we have a cake inside."

"Do we do the gifts first?" Kate asked.

Irene said, "I'd like that, don't you Sarah?"

"Yes, let's open them while I'm in the mood." Everybody laughed.

Charles said, "Your mother and I were first."

Irene gave her a watch; Brent a set of beautiful earrings, Christina gave earrings as well, then it was Darrell's turn. He gave her a jewelry case, and when she opened it, it was the most beautiful set of pearl necklace and earrings, very expensive looking. She looked at Darrell, "Dr. Moore, this is too much, this is too expensive, I can't accept this gift," Sarah said.

"Why not? I bought it because I wanted you to have it, please take it," he begged. Sarah looked at Kate looking for help; Kate nodded her head with a smile.

Sarah looked at Darrell and said, "Thank you, Dr. Moore, you're very kind."

"May I put the necklace on you Sarah?" Darrell asked.

"Yes, please," she said.

Kate said, "Let's eat dinner, then you can cut the cake."

Darrell managed to sit next to Sarah; he was very happy to be there, and everybody knew his secret by now, only Sarah didn't know it, and he didn't care.

It was a very happy table, Sarah was elated, and Darrell was beyond that. After dinner, the table was cleaned up and they brought a beautiful cake. Aunt Clare, did you bake the cake for me?"

"Of course, baby, who else? I know that's the kind of cake you like."

"Aunt Clare, I'm eighteen today, no more calling me Baby, okay?"

"I forgot baby ...well, I'll keep trying."

Sarah told Darrell, "She came to work for Mama before I was born."

"Yes, I understand. My mother had a servant who took care of us and she treated us kids like we were hers. Thinking back, it's kind of funny now." Her name was Cesarine," Darrell continued, "she said because she was a product of a cesarean section."

"Oh Darrell, how funny." Sarah said laughing and looking at Darrell, She put her hand on his; he felt his heart went right to his feet. He looked down. "What happened Dr. Moore, did I say something wrong? I only laughed because I thought it was so funny." Sarah told him holding his hand. Darrell couldn't take her touch without saying something to her, but his better judgment told him to wait; it was too soon, still too soon.

"Do you have any siblings Dr. Moore?"

"Do I ever! We are six brothers, Sarah."

"My world, all men? Not even one girl?"

"The only one that mother had; died when she was a toddler."

"How sad, how did she die?"

"I heard there was an epidemic of some kind and it took her."

"It's so sad when a child dies," Sarah said.

"Well, this is a party, time to be happy."

"Here are the matches, Sarah," Clare told her coming back with them. Darrell stood up, "Let me light the candles." And he proceeded to light them.

They started to sing out "Happy Birthday" to Sarah, and then they all applauded.

Sarah stood up and blew the candles, "Did you make a wish, Sarah?"

"Of course, don't I always?" she responded.

Clare, Inez and Joanna came back with dessert plates and the cake started to circulate around the table.

"Who would like coffee with this delicious cake?" Charles asked.

"Hold your horses; coffee is coming, Charles," Kate said

"Thank you everybody, all of you for having made this birthday the best ever," Sarah said.

"I'm glad baby, we tried hard. I guess you know by now, you'll always be our baby, all of you girls," Kate told her.

When they started getting up from the table, Darrell asked Sarah if she would walk with him to the garden. "Of course, Dr. Moore," she replied.

"Sarah, do you think you could try to call me Tyke?" He asked her as they started their walk.

"I'm so used to calling you Dr. Moore, it won't be easy for me to do it, but I'll try."

"That's enough for now Sarah."

"Dr. Moore, *sorry*, Tyke. I've been getting a feeling that you are treating me somewhat differently than you were before, am I right?"

"Sarah, I wish you wouldn't have asked me a question like that, because I can't lie to you. When I first saw you, I thought you were much older. You looked older than your years, and before I knew, I had fallen in love with you. That's when I stopped talking to you. I didn't know what to do when I found out how young you really were. I planned to wait a little longer and the only reason I'm telling you now is because you asked me 'why' so directly."

Sarah was too startled to speak; she was caught off guard by the vibrancy of his voice. She stood there, blank, amazed and extremely shaken.

"Sarah," Darrell said, "I'm sorry, I hope I didn't scare you."

"No, oh no, it's just that it was so unexpected, I never thought you liked me like that," she said shyly.

"That's why I planned to wait longer, but besides the truth, I didn't know how to reply, when you asked me why I treated you differently; I didn't know I was. I have to tell you, I'm very aware of the difference in our ages, and that worries me."

"I believe it is too premature to even think about that. I didn't know you felt that way about me, so my feelings toward you right now are just friends. If you want to just continue the way we have been treating each other, its fine with me; if in the future I feel differently about you, I'll let you know," said Sarah.

"Sarah, you're very mature for your years."

"I think I better tell you the reason why," she said." I had a school boyfriend, who was very aggressive and demanding of me and it was very hard for me to be his girlfriend. But because he was always so insistent, I kept dating him, and then one day not too long ago we went to the Mall. Irene, Laura and I went together and we met the boys there. He insisted we go out of the Mall. I didn't want to, but again I gave in and he took me to an isolated street, and started to kiss me. I began to push him away; it infuriated him, he said I never let him kiss me, and he began to hit me, and hit me," By this time tears were rolling down her face."He pulled my hair, tore my clothes, slapped me many times and then kicked me out of his car and into the street where he left me. I crawled to the edge of the street, I don't know how long I was there, and then I heard a voice. It was Benny, Laura's boyfriend, He saw this woman lying on the street and he was offering help before he recognized me." By now Sarah was sobbing. "He helped me into his car and took me to the Mall. He went in to find my sisters."

Darrell held her hand. "I'm so sorry you had such a bad experience, Sarah, I promise, if you have me, I will always love you and protect you."

"That's not all, Tyke; I want to tell you how it ended. Because I knew I would see Carl in school, Irene took me to the Police Station to obtain a restraining order so Carl couldn't approach me anywhere. When they went to his house to give him the order, unknown to me, he had several other charges with the Police. The Police said he must have thought he was being arrested and he ran. They ordered him to stop and he kept running; they fired at him, and he was killed. I blamed myself for his death for a long time. But Irene made me understand he did that to himself by living the way he lived."

"That's right, from what I hear, you didn't even know he had a record against him. You were only protecting yourself from any more harm," Darrell said. Sarah rested her head on his chest and held his hand; she looked more delicate than ever. Darrell closed his eyes; she felt the power within him as he held her in his arms.

"Tyke, I think I'm also feeling differently about you. But you have to be patient with me; that episode in my life has left me shaken for a long time."

"I will be patient, Sarah; we'll go at your own pace. You'll mark the path."

"And about our age difference, my father is fourteen years older than Mama."

"That's the best news I heard in a long time," he said smiling.

As they started back to the house, they met Brent and Irene.

"What is this? We were looking for you," Irene said.

"She speaks for herself; I thought we had gone for a walk," Brent replied.

Irene noticed they were holding hands.

"Is there something I need to know?"

"Not a thing." Sarah replied.

Darrell and Brent looked at each other and smiled.

Sarah and Darrell kept walking to the house. "You're growing up Sarah."

"It was about time, Tyke." she said smiling at him.

Irene watched them leave. "Brent, what did she mean?"

"She has grown up, Irene."

"That's what I was afraid of."

"Don't be, we can't always stay as children, there comes a time when we all have to grow up; it was her time, Irene."

Irene bowed her head, "My *baby.*" she said.

"She is everybody's baby, Irene; you'll get over it when you have your own babies."

"I guess," she told him.

"Irene, sweetheart, shake that feeling and let's talk about our wedding, we have so many things to decide."

"Of course, you're right; do you know I haven't talked to Christina about her being my Maid of Honor and Linda my flower girl?"

"Let's go, maybe Carlos is still there."

Brent was right, Carlos was there with Christina. "Well, hello?" "With you arriving in Sarah's car I haven't had the time to tell you, my divorce has gone through; I'm officially free of that jerk I was married to."

Irene went to Christina and hugged her, "I'm so happy for you." she said.

"Not half as happy as we are, I just proposed to Christina, we'll be married as soon as the proper papers are filed. Show them your engagement ring."

"Oh, you were ready, weren't you? What a beautiful ring Christina!"

"Are you going to get married here, Christina?" Irene asked her.

"Carlos wants us to be married at his parents Ranch; I think under the circumstances, it's safer."

"I can hardly wait until Mr. Moran comes back from the prison. Maybe he'll really have some good news this time about Mike."

"Good news for whom him or me?" Christina asked.

"Let's focus on what we're trying to do. Christina why don't you try to gather all the documentation you'll need in order to get married. Irene, could you make time to go with Christina to get whatever she wants for our wedding?"

"Of course, but first, I have to ask my boss." She said looking at Brent.

"Just let me know when you plan to take off." Brent replied.

"We already talked about it," Christina said, "all we want is to get married. We are going to have a small reception with Carlos's family and all of you who are able to attend. Mr. Hamilton, would you give me away, please?"

"I'll be honored, Christina." Charles responded.

"Mr. Moran, I'm so glad to see you, did you find out anything?"

"Yes, Mike has been held on a one million dollars bail, no one has offered to pay it for him; he'll be there for a very long time, Mrs. Christina."

"Thanks the Lord," Everybody said.

When Carlos left with Brent and Darrell, Christina and Irene started making their own plans.

"When can we go shopping, Irene? I'd like to go soon in case something has to be ordered."

"You heard Brent, I have to let him know ahead of time and he is right. We can plan our shopping trip for the day after tomorrow."

"Okay, do you have any color in mind?"

"I'm thinking a soft cream color. Do you think that would be all right? Asked Christina.

"Anything you want to wear is all right, Christina. How about the Maid of Honor?"

"I think I leave that up to your, Mother. I chose her, Irene, because she has gone above being nice to me. In my mother's absence, she has been one to me."

"What about the banquet, Christina."

"Carlos said his family will kill a couple of cows and grill hundreds of steaks."

"How about the cake? We can make that here at home, Christina."

"Irene, they have a lot of servants at Carlos's home, let them do it all. They want to do it."

"I think we need to give a dinner for them to come and meet us, don't you think so? Before the wedding."

"It would be very nice, Irene; you are all the family I have."

"Well, we'll do it. But what happened with your parents, Christina?"

"After I married Mike, I lost contact with them. Mike didn't want me to be in touch with them, and they moved around so much, I have no idea where they are."

"Well, that's too bad; maybe sometime they'll remember how close you and I were in school and get in touch with us. I'm tired Christina, I'm going to bed. Good night."

"Good night, Irene"

"I'm so glad Brent let you leave the office today, Irene."

"He didn't mind me coming with you, Christina; he just wanted me to leave things organized at the office."

"I know, I wish we didn't have to drag Mr. Moran with us."

"I like Mr. Moran; I learned how indispensable he is, didn't you?"

"Okay, I know, I know. He has saved my life several times, I just wish I didn't have that over my head," Christina said.

"I can imagine, but it's better than the alternative."

"Let's get busy; where are we going, Irene?"

"To the same shop where I'm getting my own dress. Don't forget Carlos said, "whatever you want when he gave you his credit card."

"Maybe he doesn't expect me to clean him out," She said laughing.

"No, but you can get a pretty nice outfit and everything that goes with it, and maybe something for Linda as well."

"I don't want anything too fancy, Irene; it's going to be a very casual wedding, don't forget."

As they walked in at the Bridal Boutique, there was a dress for every occasion. Christina stopped to admire everything on her way.

Irene stopped with her. "You don't have to stick to a color just because you chose it earlier. If you like a dress, try it on."

Doris came over to wait on them. "Miss Hamilton, are you here for your dress? I don't think it is here yet." She said to Irene.

"No, Doris, I brought you another customer, she is getting married next week."

"Wow! She is going to have to get something from the floor."

"I intend to. My name is Christina Findley."

"It's very nice to meet you. Do you know what kind of dress you want?"

"It's not the first time I am getting married, so I need something casual."

"But not too casual," Irene ended Christina's sentence. Irene continued, "Do you have something in a cream color, calf length, very elegant."

Doris thought for a moment and said, "I believe I have just what you want."

In a few minutes, she came back along with a smart smile.

"Okay, is this what you have in mind?" Doris asked Christina.

And then they saw this beautiful model wearing Christina's dream dress.

"I think this model is your size, Christina."

The model paraded in front of them, one direction then the other.

"Well, what do you think?"

"Oh, it's exquisite," Christina said, her eyes misty and wishful longing to wear the dress herself.

"Christina, go ahead and try the dress on," Irene told her, with a mischievous look in her face.

"May I?" Christina asked shyly.

"Of course," Doris told her, "and if you don't like that one, we'll keep looking."

Christina went behind the curtains and the model followed her.

Doris asked Irene, "Why is she so shy? We're here to serve her."

"She has gone through a lot; she'll shake that off soon enough." Christina came out from behind the curtains wearing the cream dress. Irene stood up and faced the incredible sight of Christina wearing the beautiful cream gown, she smiled at Irene. "Do you like it on me?"

Christina was tall and graceful, her hips tapered into the long regal gown.

"This gown was made for you, Christina. No one else could wear that gown like you do, Christina, you look absolutely stunning."

"Do you really think so? Do you think Carlos will like me in it?"

"I know he will, he would be crazy not to."

"Doris, while she has the dress on, how about if we try on some head pieces? Maybe a small hat or maybe something with a big brim. That really might look more elegant on Christina since she is so tall."

Doris disappeared behind the big curtain and later on came back with several hats and helpers carrying a number of accessories."

"Sit over here, Miss Christina," Doris asked her, "Which one do you want to try first?"

"How about the hat with the big brim?"

"That's the one I would have chosen," Doris said.

"Irene, it's the same shade as the dress. Don't you think so, Christina?"

"If it's not, its close enough, why don't you stand up and walk towards the mirror, we'll have a better look"

Christina stood up and walked to the mirror.

"I wouldn't change a thing Christina, what do you think Doris?"

"I never sold a dress with accessories like this; usually they try everything in the store, even if they go back to the first thing they tried on."

"Do you carry shoes to compliment her attire, Doris?"

"We do, what size do you wear Miss Christina?"

"I think seven narrow, the last time I bought shoes."

"Carlos is going to be so proud when he sees you," Irene said.

"Irene, let's go eat lunch, I haven't done that in such a long time."

"I guess it'll be all right, let's tell Mr. Moran where we're going."

"Tell him to come inside the restaurant, but not to the same table."

"He wouldn't sit with us, Christina."

"I'd like to get a dress for the children and then we can leave."

Mr. Moran was in the car when they arrived to go home.

"Did you get bored, Mr. Moran." Irene asked him.

"Not really. This is the kind of work I do. Believe it or not, I find it's very interesting. It helps me study people, and I study everyone who goes by," He said smiling. "Did you get everything you needed, Miss Christina?"

"I've been meaning to tell you Mr. Moran, my name is Christina Findley, I think you should know I go by that name now, it's my maiden name."

"I knew some Findley's a long time ago, but I lost track of them, Pete and Theresa, I wonder where they are?"

Christina got very quiet; she straightened her body and leaned towards Mr. Moran. "How do you know those people, Mr. Moran?"

"Pete and I went to school together; I was his best man when he married Theresa."

Christina franticly looked in her purse; her hand came out with an old photo. "Are these the people you're referring to?"

Mr. Moran took the photo, looked at it, then looked at Christina with inquisitive eyes. "Yes, who are they to you, Miss Christina?"

Christina's eyes were full of tears when she answered him. "They are my parents, Mr. Moran; and they have disappeared from my life, I haven't heard from them for almost eight years."

"We have to talk about that, Miss Christina."

Christina nodded and closed her eyes in prayer.

Chapter Eight

When Carlos went to visit Christina, he found her lying on a sofa just outside of the living room near the garden. Her eyes were closed.

"Christina, sweetheart, is there something wrong?" He asked; kissing her.

"Carlos," She said hugging him and falling into his arms crying.

"What is it, Baby? What is the matter?" He asked her anxiously.

"Mr. Moran knows my parents; this is the first time that I actually spoke with someone who has known them after so many years."

"Well, does he have any idea where they can be?"

"No, but he is very interested in finding out what has happened to them."

"Thank God, maybe we can find out something, now that we know someone who is actually interested in the case."

"I had lost all hope I would ever see my parents again, it has been so long."

"You won't be alone any longer Christina, we'll face this together."

"I don't know how to thank you for loving me."

"Haven't you ever heard you don't 'thank for love'? We can <u>thank the Lord,</u> for putting us together, but we don't thank each other. Did you get everything you wanted Christina?"

"I think so."

"Well, I want you to keep that card, anything your heart desires, get it."

"I'm afraid to open my eyes, and all of this will have disappeared. I have never been so happy, Carlos."

He kissed her. "That's what I want for you, just be happy."

Irene and Brent walked in, "Hey, hey, that's enough for one day," they said laughing.

"I was telling Carlos about Mr. Moran knowing my parents," Christina said.

"Yes, isn't that something? And he was Christina's Dads, Best Man."

"Christina, what else do we need to do to get married?" asked Carlos.

"We need to get the rings, and who is going to marry us?"

"My uncle is a Priest; Mama's brother. He doesn't live too far from the Villa."

"A Villa?" Irene asked.

"It's the Ranch. We have always called it a Villa, old name for it, you know."

"I guess it is, it's a magnificent Mansion," Christina said looking at Irene.

"My God, I can't wait to go. Carlos, we would like to have a dinner to invite your parents to come over and meet us one day next week."

"Let me know when, and I'll send word to them."

"Do you know exactly when you're getting married? It has to be before the wedding."

"Let's count the chores we have to do, maybe I can tell my secretary not to schedule anybody one day so we can do something together, Christina," said Carlos.

Charles and Kate walked in. "Good evening, everybody," they said.

"Mama, Papa, I was just telling Carlos we need to have a dinner for his parents, one day next week because it has to be before the wedding."

"Today is Friday, how about Wednesday? That'll give us time to plan our dinner and we give them time to plan to come to town."

"Mama, where is Sarah?" Irene asked Kate.

"She called from work and asked me if she could go to dinner with Dr. Moore."

"She didn't even want to come home to change clothes?"

"That's what I asked her; she said, no, they weren't going to dress up."

Irene looked at Brent and looked down in despair. Brent squeezed her hand, but said nothing.

"Irene, when are we going to look at that living room set we saw the other day in that store window?" Do you want to go in before they close?"

"I guess so; we need to know how much it is. Do you mind Mama?"

"Of course not, you have to get ready too."

Carlos said. "So do we, Christina, I have my apartment, but you have to go in to see it and find out what you want changed."

"We better get out of here before they close. Bye."

They left in Brent's car. "What was all that about, Brent?"

"I saw your face Irene; you want to see if you can find out where Sarah is."

"Do you know where they are?"

"No, Darrell didn't tell me anything. Besides that, it was probably planned at the last moment."

"Brent, why are you driving to your apartment?"

"Just habit, Irene, but in case he might have brought her there."

"That's his car, Brent. What did they do with her car?"

"Maybe they're in her car. But let's go upstairs any way."

Irene had trouble breathing; she didn't want to find Sarah in Darrell's apartment.

Brent carefully opened the door. They both stood there motionless. Darrell and Sarah were kissing; her face was buried in his neck. They never knew Brent and Irene were standing there. Irene cleared her throat, they both stood up fast and very surprised.

"I can't say I'm sorry we disturbed you," Irene said.

"We stopped here for a minute before we went to dinner," Sarah said.

"And was this part of your plan, Darrell?" Irene asked him

"Irene, you know I love Sarah, I'm not trying anything underhanded with her."

"Sarah, do you feel the same way about Dr. Moore?"

"I think I do, Irene."

"You mean you don't know and you let him kiss you like that?"

"He wasn't doing the kissing by himself, you know," Sarah answered.

"If it's all right with you, Sarah, I'd like to ask your parents for your hand in marriage tonight, when I take you home," Darrell responded.

Sarah looked at him. "I would like that very much, Darrell," she said kissing him.

Darrell smiled; "I never thought getting married would make me so happy."

Irene went to Sarah and kissed her, "I hope you will always be happy, Sarah."

"So do I, Irene, I wish the same for you," she said smiling.

"Why don't we go to dinner together, kind of a celebration?" Darrell said.

"I think it's a good idea." Brent said. "We always told people we were brothers; now it's going to be true; kind of."

Carlos went in looking for Christina and found her in the living room waiting for him. She stood up smiling when she saw him.

"Sweetheart, I was about to give up on you, what happened?"

"There was an emergency and I had to take it."

"Are you ready to leave?" Carlos asked her.

"Let me let someone know we're leaving."

While Christina went in, Mr. Moran came out to speak to Carlos.

"Dr. Lopez, I want you to know I'll be behind you when you leave."

"Is there any reason you should do that, Mr. Moran?"

"Everything I do is for safety. We know Mike is in prison but he has friends on the outside that owe him favors, that's how those people work, you know."

"Okay Mr. Moran, we are going to the jewelry store on Main Street."

"When are we leaving, sweetheart?" Christina asked.

"I thought we had made an appointment to get our wedding bands."

"Is that today? Since I haven't been going to work I don't know which day I live in. When are you going to let me go back to work?"

Carlos looked at her. "Christina, we're getting married; I don't think you need to go back to work."

"Carlos, Brent had been paying me all along, I have been paid the whole time since Mike shot me."

"I didn't know, but I'll talk to him and refund the money you received. I would like for you to stay at home and take care of the children."

She looked at Carlos and said. "Do you know how beautiful that sounds to me darling?"

He smiled and held her hand. "Here we are, let me park."

When they entered the jewelry store, they were approached by a very proper and expensive looking sales man offering his services to Carlos.

"Sir, may I be of some assistance?"

"Of course; we're getting married, we want to see wedding bands."

"This way please," and he showed them the way to a private show room.

Once there; he came out with several covered trays and proceeded to show them all kind of rings for the occasion.

"Which one do you like, Christina?" Carlos asked her.

"They're all beautiful, are we going to get them engraved?

"Of course baby, which ring do you think you like?"

"Just a simple band, Carlos."

"No, let's get one with diamonds."

"I'm not a diamond person, Carlos."

"You are now, my dear."

She looked at him and kissed him briefly on the lips.

The gentleman that was waiting on them said, "I think you have made a decision, have you?"

"Yes, I believe we have," Carlos replied. "Let's try them for size first."

"What do you want engraved on them, Christina?"

"Our name, the date of our wedding, is there room for the word "always?"

"It will be room." Carlos leaned over and kissed Christina.

"When is the wedding date?"

"Let me call home, Mama might have the date for us now."

"Mama, its Carlos, how are you and Papa? Listen, Christina and I are at the jewelry store getting our wedding bands, but we need the wedding date engraved, have you talked to Father Francis yet?"

"Yes Carlos, he said whenever you want to get married he'll open any date for you, so you can set the date."

"Christina, its Saturday all right? Do you think everything else will be ready in four days? Today is Tuesday."

"We'll be ready, darling." Christina responded all emotional at the thought of getting married in four days.

"Mama, tell Father Francis Saturday at noon, I love you, I'll call you soon." Carlos turned his attention to their attendant, "When can I pick up the rings?"

"Tomorrow, how are you going to pay for the rings Sir?"

"With plastic, how else?" Carlos said smiling. "Let's go, Baby."

"If I'm dreaming don't wake me up, Carlos." she told him on the way out.

"It's real, Christina, don't doubt it, I'll love you, baby," he said.

"Do you want to go back to the house or do you want to go eat dinner first."

"Can we be selfish today and go out to eat dinner?" she asked Carlos.

"It's not being selfish baby; we need to be alone sometimes."

Carlos drove slowly by the seashore; Christina rested her head on his shoulder.

He drove to the end of the pier and parked, and then he put his arms around Christina and kissed her with all the passion he could grasp. She could feel his heart thudding against her own. They remained in each other arms for a long time. Slowly he disengaged himself from her embrace and said to her:

"I think we better think about dinner my dear."

"I always thought you're a very smart man, I was right." she said smiling.

Carlos started the car and asked her. "Do you have any favorite restaurant you want to go tonight?"

"I wish we didn't have to go to a restaurant, Carlos."

"Me too, but we must. There, that one looks nice, let's go in there, okay, Baby?"

"It's going to be the longest four days of my life," Christina said smiling.

"For me too, Baby." Carlos responded.

Arriving at the Hamilton's home, Christina and Carlos went in.

"Mrs. Hamilton, we have the date for our wedding. Saturday, four days from today."

"Oh my God, I better go shopping tomorrow."

"Please, don't go into any big expense for us, our wedding is small."

"It's not about how many people are coming to the wedding; it's who is getting married. And I couldn't be happier, Christina."

"Make sure you draw a map to the Ranch, Carlos. We called your parents today, they're coming for dinner tomorrow. So, somebody better draw them a map or they'll get lost on the way into the city."

"Let me go talk to Cindy for a minute, Carlos." Christina left. When she came back she asked Kate. "Do you have any idea when Irene and Brent are coming back home?"

"No dear, they left, I'm sure they're having dinner somewhere."

"How about Sarah and Darrell?"

"No idea either, I'm sorry."

"Why don't you call your mother and confirm that our dinner in their honor is tomorrow; also, give them our address."

"Thank you, Mrs. Hamilton."

"Our pleasure, Carlos, I guess by now you know that Christina is part of our family."

"Yes, I know, and soon, she'll have my family as her own."

"Clare, what do you have for Saturdays' menu?" Kate asked Clare.

"Since you're having beef for the wedding, I thought we'll have turkey, dressing, several vegetables, green salad, hot bread and cake."

"Wow! Clare; that is a banquet."

"I thought that's what you wanted."

"Of course, I know it's going to be delicious."

Brent and Irene, Darrell and Sarah walked in holding hands.

Charles and Kate were in the living room sipping a cup of coffee.

Mr. and Mrs. Hamilton, good evening, Darrell said initiating their greetings. "I would like to talk to you, please."

"Go ahead, Darrell." Charles replied.

"I think you know that I love Sarah, I would like to ask you for her hand in marriage." Charles and Kate looked at each other.

"I know you know how young Sarah is, Darrell, she hasn't started college yet, and you've not only finished, you have experience in your field. We like you, but I'm not sure we like you for Sarah."

Darrell was holding Sarah's hand. When Charles said that, Darrell let Sarah's hand go and looked at her with panicky eyes.

Sarah said. "Papa, how can you say that without asking me what I think and feel for Darrell?"

"Because I know what's best for you."

"Is that what Mama's father told you when you asked him for her hand in marriage?" Kate covered her mouth to hide her laughter, Charles cleared his voice.

"Okay. I have that coming. How do you know you love Darrell? You just met each other."

"I admit it hasn't been a long time, but if we had known each other a year or two it wouldn't have made any difference. If we didn't love each other, we would know," Sarah said. "And I know I love Darrell." He held her hand again.

Charles looked at Kate, and she smiled at him. "Okay Darrell, we'll take into consideration that Kate and I have the same difference in our ages. I knew at the time, the reason they let me marry Kate is because since her family is Hispanic, they usually let older men marry younger women. You can date with our blessings, but you better take it easy with Sarah. The first time that Sarah comes over here crying for one of your tricks, you're gone."

"Understood, Mr. Hamilton, you don't have to worry about Sarah, I love her more than I can bear; I told her we would take things at her own pace."

"Darrell, I'm sure you know that I'm much older than my wife, and you have that in your favor, in a way. Because I know how much you can love her, I also know how jealous you can get, how protective you can be when there is no reason for it. How unreasonable you can get. I know you can make her suffer with all of that stuff and don't even know you're doing that."

"Thank you, Mr. Hamilton, for telling me that, I appreciate it."

"Sarah," Kate said, "Darrell is going to be hard to love because he is going to be jealous of everything do, who you talk to, what you see and what you touch and you can't convince him that you love him, only because it is him: the more he loves you, the more he makes you suffer." Then she turned to Charles and told him. "I'm sorry, darling, but I had to tell Sarah, how hard, how difficult it's going to be to love Darrell. Because first, he has to believe that Sarah truly loves him. You didn't believe me, . . . not for a long time." Tears rolled down her face."

Charles' eyes were misty. "Kate, I never thought for one minute...." He buried his face on her chest and told her. "Please forgive me, my only excuse is that I loved you so much I couldn't bear your leaving me; and I couldn't believe you could love me."

"Darrell, Sarah, I'm sorry for this display of emotions, but this is the best school you could have gotten to show you to trust your spouse. If she or he is telling you how much you're being loved, **believe** and **trust** each other."

Brent stood up and walked to Darrell and shook his hand. "Darrell, you have the luck of the Irish with a future Bride like Sarah."

"You don't have to tell me that. I never thought she would love me."

Sarah clinched herself to Darrell and said, "I do. I don't know that I fell in love so fast, I'm beginning to think I fell in love when you first came and I just didn't know it."

The conversation strayed and Irene took the opportunity to talk to Brent, Darrell and Sarah. "Listen, we don't have time to throw a bridal shower and a bachelor party for Carlos and Christina, so we can get some kind of gag gift for them and give it to them after the dinner tomorrow, what do you think?"

"What can we get for them?"

"A gag gift, I was thinking of a pair of fancy underwear for each one of them.

"I love it." said Brent.

"So do I," said Darrell.

"Brent, do you want to go shopping tomorrow? Or should I?"

"You know I love to go, but I never know if I'm going to have a call from ER."

"Me too," said Darrell.

"Okay, Sarah, do you want to meet me at the Mall? There is a Lingerie store by the entrance."

"Yes, that's on our way home and it won't take too long to do it."

"You don't have to come if you have plans, you know."

"No, no, I do want to come."

Irene and Sarah were rushing to their cars so they could meet at the Mall. "Do you know where the lingerie store is, Sarah?" She nodded.

"See you there in about fifteen minutes."

Some one came to offer their help. It was Sean, Irene's old boy friend. "Sean, it's nice seeing you again; are you working at the Mall now?"

"I'm in a different department. I'll get someone to help you."

"It has been nice seeing you, Sean. Did you know I'm getting married?"

"When?" he asked Irene.

"Sometime in November."

"No date yet?"

"No, we're waiting for the Priest to confirm which day is free for us. Well, bye."

"It has been nice seeing you again, Irene. You too, Sarah."

Irene entered the lingerie department and asked for her chosen item. The clerk smiled and came back with two pair of beautiful lacy panties. "I think these are to your specifications, Miss. We also carry some fancy underwear for men since we cater it for parties. Is this what you had in mind?"

"Some friends of ours are getting married and we thought that would be kind of funny, don't you think?"

"Yes, as long as they don't wear them outdoors." The clerk said smiling.

"Please wrap them for a bridal shower."

When they walked out, Irene expelled a big breathe of relief.

"I'm so glad we walked out of that store Sarah."

"Were you scared of Sean?"

"Not really, but he wasn't very happy when I ended our relationship. But like I told him, we weren't really anything but good college friends."

"Maybe not for him, Irene. Have you thought about that?"

"Oh yes, please don't mention to anyone we ran into him."

"Let's hurry up, it's time for Carlos' parents to come home, I still need to change."

Where can we hide these packages, Irene?'

"I think the library is a good place; no one will be going in there tonight."

When they arrived, everybody was dressed and waiting, Irene and Sarah rushed upstairs to get ready. On the way up, they met Christina.

"Are you nervous, Christina?" Irene asked her.

"A little, but I know them and they're very good people."

Christina went into the living room as her futures in-laws walked in.

Kate walked to Angelita and hugged her, and then she turned around and made the proper introductions with everybody. Carlos kissed Christina.

"Call me, Kate;" she told Angelita.

"Call me, Angelita."

Charles had taken Cristobal to pour them a drink.

Charles looked for Irene, when he saw her walking in, he said to her.

"Irene, do you know at what time Brent and Darrell are coming over?"

"I don't know Papa,"

"Well, get on the phone and tell them to hurry up."

"Hello everybody, I'm Irene, excuse me."

She went to the phone and called Brent.

"Brent, Dad wants to know at what time you and Darrell are going to get here for dinner?"

"Irene, I didn't know we had been invited."

"Brent, you were here when the arrangements were made, hurry up and come over, is Darrell there with you?"

"Yes, he is in the shower."

"Tell him to hurry up."

"Papa, they're on their way."

Sarah asked Irene. "Are they really on their way?"

"He'll never know they are not.

Sarah laughed, "Irene, you're terrible."

"Where is Laura, I haven't seen her in days."

"Mama said she is taking some kind of extra credits, so next year, she doesn't have too many classes to take."

"That's one way to do it; she can't see Benny any way because he is busy all the time. Do you know what he is studying?"

"He is going to be a Defense Lawyer."

"That's a good career."

"Yes, and here she comes now."

They both went to hug their sister.

"What kind of reception is this?" she said.

"We haven't seen you in day's sister."

"I come home, but you're never here."

"Mr. and Mrs. Lopez, this is our baby sister, Laura."

"It's very nice meeting you, Mr. and Mrs. Lopez."

"You're just as pretty as your sisters, I wasn't lucky enough to get daughters; the Lord only blessed me with sons."

Kate answered her, "And he blessed me with daughters, not sons. But now, we're getting sons from our daughter's marriages and you're getting your daughter from your son."

"You're right, but I wasn't complaining."

"I know, they're all healthy, that's what I prayed for when I was having my babies, healthy babies not the sex I wanted."

"We did the same; we didn't care what they were as long as they were healthy."

Irene said, "Laura, is Benny coming?"

"No, he is working late tonight; he has several jobs you know."

"No, I didn't know. Okay, we can eat if everyone is ready."

Kate asked Irene, "Why don't you let Clare know we're ready for dinner?"

"Because she is behind the curtain; waiting to announce dinner; Mama."

Everyone laughed as they got up and walked to the dining room.

"Are we late? Brent and Darrell said as they entered the house.

Laughs and loud voices were heard from the dining room table throughout the house. "This cornbread dressing is out of this world; Kate, it's delicious."

"Thank you Angelita, I'll tell Clare. She is great with everything she does."

"I'm so thankful for the cook we have, I don't even have to tell her any morewhat to cook, only how many are coming."

"I feel the same way with our servants, only Clare is more like family, she has been with us since Charles and I got married."

"Kate, I don't want to appear intrusive but is your other daughter also engaged to be married? They look so in love with each other, it's so obvious."

"Kind of engaged. We have given them permission to date, but they have to take it easy because she is so young you know, she just turned eighteen."

"Really? She looks a lot older; I guessed her twenty-three."

"That's what Darrell said; he is a Cardiologist and has a partnership with Irene's fiancé."

"I don't know him of course, but he looks so in love with your daughter."

They heard kind of a bell sound. It was Charles banging onto a glass.

"If everybody is finished with dinner, I want to offer a toast to our several couples. Clare, let's bring the champagne."

After the champagne was served, Charles raised his glass, "to Carlos and Christina, may their union last forever. For Brent and Irene; may their love be as strong throughout their lives as it is today, and for Darrell and Sarah; they're on trial: I wish them the best the Lord has in store for them. Everyone raised their glasses and said. "**Cheers!**."

Don Cristobal stood up and raised his own glass, "My wishes are the same as Charles for all the newlyweds to be; that their union last forever. **Salud!**" He said.

Laura stood up. "Benny, she said. I'm glad you could make it for dessert. Have you eaten dinner yet?"

Charles said, "Clare, please, a place for Benny."

"I'm sorry, I wanted to come earlier, but I had to go home and shower first."

"We appreciate that," Brent told him smiling at them.

Benny and Laura held hands as soon as he was able to get close to her.

"I would say no to dinner, but I haven't eaten since breakfast, I'm starved."

Charles told him, "Eat son, there is plenty, we're not finished, yet. I heard Kate has baked my favorite cake."

"In two more days we'll have the wedding. Could you draw us a map Cristobal?" Charles laughed "She has asked everybody to draw a map I guess she'll end up with one at the end."

"I said it before I thought. We'll have the Bride with us, and then I remembered she knows the way."

"I didn't know where I was half the time Mrs. Hamilton; I don't think I'm the best guide."

"You'll get a map, Mrs. Hamilton, but Mr. Moran knows the way himself."

"Of course, I can't rely on my memory," Kate said laughing.

Chapter Nine

"Christina, do you plan to dress here when you get married or are you going to dress after you get there?" Irene asked Christina.

"I've been thinking a lot about it, Irene; I think I'll be more comfortable dressing here, but the ride to the ranch is long I don't even remember how long it takes to get there."

"We better ask Carlos because we need to know how much time we need."

"I know we need to dress the children over there."

"Christina, you take care of yourself, and I'll help you. Cindy is going to dress the children and if she needs help Laura can help her."

"I can't believe my wedding day is tomorrow, I'm so nervous, Irene."

"That's understandable, I'm nervous for you and for myself, it is only a few more weeks and it'll be my turn," Irene said smiling.

"We better go to bed, it's getting late."

Irene heard someone knocking at her door. She got out of bed half sleep; it was Christina. "What's the matter? Is there something wrong?"

"It's six o'clock; you said you can help me with my hair."

"It is still early, Christina, let's have a cup of coffee and we will work on your hair."

"I'm sorry; maybe I shouldn't have awakened you."

"No, I want to be up with you, I just need to be awake."

When they arrived at the kitchen, Clare was sitting at the table sipping a cup of coffee.

"Good morning, this fresh coffee smells great."

"Let me pour you a cup right quick girls." Clare said.

"Keep your seat, Clare, we will pour our own."

"Clare, are you coming to my wedding?" Christina asked Clare.

"Am I invited?"

Christina hugged her neck. "You know we didn't have printed invitations. I don't know how many cars we are taking but I know there is plenty of space for you, we would love for you to be there, Clare."

"Okay, we're not eating here today, so I can give myself a day off."

"I think we're reasonably awake now, Christina; let's go do your hair."

"I washed my hair last night so we wouldn't have to wait until it dried today."

"Very clever."

"What time is it now, Irene?"

"It is not seven yet, Christina."

"I thought Carlos was going to call me early today."

"He can still call you and be early," Irene told her laughing.

"Don't make fun of me, Irene; I'm so nervous."

Irene hugged Christina, "I don't mean to tease you, Christina, it's so cute to see you so nervous. You're acting like a seventeen year old girl with her first love."

"I realize that Carlos <u>is</u> my first love Irene. Mike was someone in a nightmare. And Carlos, Carlos is my life. The only reason I don't curse those years is because of my children."

"Do you know how you want your hair, Christina? How about if we get the hat and try it on, then we'll have a better idea. We should've done this before now you know."

"I know, but no one had the time in the ten days we set to get married."

"I think I can roll your hair and comb it in, I can brush it and curl the ends and then put the hat on. I think it is the only way to do it Christina. I'll call Mama and ask her what she thinks, okay?"

"Have you decided to dress here, Christina?"

"Yes, I don't think I want to arrive running to get dress for the wedding."

"I agree with you, did you find out how long it is going to take us to get there?"

"About two hours, it depends on the traffic. **Irene,** I don't have a bouquet!"

Irene closed her eyes, "Good Lord, I remember Doris asking about it but I don't think we answered her."

"Today is Saturday; let me call our florist and ask her for a bouquet of fresh flowers. Do you want mixed colors or white?"

"I think mixed colors; I can just imagine them beautiful like a rainbow."

"Let me go make the call and maybe you can check on the children now."

"Good idea." Christina replied.

"Mama, good morning," Irene said knocking on her parent's bedroom door, "it's almost eight o'clock Mama. Are you up yet?"

Kate came to the door and opened it "Irene, I was in the shower and now your father is in, what's going on?"

"I want you to see Christina's hair. We never practice a hairdo; so now we're guessing what to do with her hair. It takes about two hours to get there so we don't have much time."

"Let me dress first, Irene. She can dress, as well and then I will come over." Irene stood there and then decided what she had to do. "Oh yes; the flowers."

She went to the phone and ordered what Christina wanted to carry. Then she went to the kitchen. "Clare, where are you?"

"Here I am, Irene."

"I guess I'll get dressed first; then will you please drive to Nita's Flower Shop, she'll be waiting for you with Christina's bouquet. Please bring it here. We have to leave the house no later than ten."

On the way back she met Mr. Moran. "Miss Irene, please don't tell Miss Christina; we don't want her more nervous than she already is."

"Is something happening Mr. Moran.?"

"Mike escaped last night."

"My Lord, I wonder if he knows Christina is getting married today."

"It's been in the newspaper, Miss Irene."

"Who put it there?"

"When people buy their marriage license, they put it in the paper.

"Don't tell anyone Mr. Moran, I'll tell Dr. Miller when he gets here, but no one else. We don't want to show concern at the wedding." It was time to leave; Mr. Moran had left the house. He had told Irene he would be watching the house. Irene told Christina to get in the car in the garage, so no one would see her. She didn't suspect anything, why should she suspect anything was going on? It was the normal thing to do. Irene looked at Christina; she looked so pretty in her bridal gown, her beauty was beyond words, probably because she didn't believe she was pretty at all, and that always makes a person look even better. Sophisticated and classy. Yes, you can say that about Christina.

Brent walked in, "Irene, I've been looking for you, I didn't know you were on your way out."

"Hi sweetheart, I'm waiting for my parents, did you see Lorenzo in the house?"

"No, do you need him?" Brent asked Irene.

"He is driving the bride, and my parents are riding with Christina. I'll ride with you; maybe Clare, and Laura and Benny are riding with Darrell and Sarah."

"Where are you putting the children?" Brent asked.

"I had forgotten about them, can you believe it?"

"We can put them with us and Cindy, Okay?"

"Sounds perfect. There are your parents now with Lorenzo, let's go."

"Is everybody else here?"

"Let's count heads, come' on Brent."

When they were out of sight, Irene told Brent, "Sweetheart, Mike escaped from prison." she said swallowing her tears.

Brent stopped. His eyes were full of shock when he imagined what could happen.

"Does Christina know?"

"Only you and me, and Mr. Moran; he is the one who told me."

"Yes, that's best; we don't want a panic on our hands. Is Mr. Betancourt sending anyone?"

"I didn't ask Mr. Moran."

"The first chance you have, ask him. No uniforms or everybody will know."

"There are Darrell and Sarah and Benny and Laura."

"Have you seen Clare?"

"Yes, she just went to give Christina her bouquet."

"Cindy is coming with the children, let's go." Brent said.

"Has anyone talked to Carlos today?"

"I imagine Christina has, she was expecting his call about six this morning."

Lorenzo came over to talk to Brent, "Mr. Moran told me for the other cars to go ahead, then our car and he will drive behind us."

"That sounds good. Let's go Irene. Who has the map?"

"I think Daddy has it; I'll go get it Brent."

Irene came back and Cindy was sitting in the back with the children.

I haven't told you, you look beautiful in green." Brent told Irene.

"Thank you; I like this shade of green. It's called forest green," Her eyes were teary and Brent noticed her hands were shaky, he held her hands, "Everything will be all right." He said to Irene.

She looked down and nodded.

You start studying the map so when we get closer you can tell me the way," said Brent.

She started to study the map and studying the name of the streets. Then she began to tell Brent where they were and how far they had to go. Brent noticed Mr. Moran was trying to call him on his cell phone, "Hello, Mr. Moran, is there something happening?"

"No, but I want to know if you see anything in front."

"Nothing, but we are wondering if the police is sending people to the ranch."

"I asked Betancourt; but he said it's not his jurisdiction."

"Can he ask for help? Surely he can tell the police in that area the circumstances of this case."

"He said unless we see something suspicious they can't send anyone."

"Cindy, if you want to dress the children on the way it is all right, it's still a long way. I heard about two hours. We're about half-way." Irene told Cindy.

"Yes, I think it is a good idea, Miss Irene. I will start now. Can you hold Amy while I dress Linda?" Cindy replied.

"By the way, I haven't seen you with a white tuxedo on, it looks great on you," said Irene.

"Thank you, we really haven't known each other long enough to see all we own."

"Keep talking to me, Brent, please, I can't stop shaking and I want to cry so badly."

"I know. I don't know what I can say to keep you from being so nervous."

"We can talk about our own wedding plans, our home."

"Maybe as soon as Christina and Carlos go on their honeymoon we can start looking for a house. If we can't find something we're happy with, we will stay at the apartment until we find something we're sure we like."

"It's a good idea, Brent. Brent, I want us to get married but I no longer want a big wedding, I'm so scared." she said crying.

"Sweetheart, you're caught up with the moment and you're scared for Christina, but there is no reason for you to be scared about anything."

"I know; I know I only want to be with you, I don't want to wait."

"It's all right with me Irene. Whatever you want to do, you talk it over with your parents and make your decision, just let me know."

"Brent turn right on the next road, we shouldn't be too far now. Oh my God! That looks like a castle." Irene said.

"That's my buddy, Carlos. You'd never know by talking to him; his family is loaded."

"Let me run in first and tell Carlos to hide so he won't see Christina."

"Carlos, Carlos," Irene shouted, "Go into the church or something, Christina is dressed already and you shouldn't see her now."

Mrs. Lopez was coming out and told Carlos "Son, go to the Chapel. Your father and I will take care of the guests."

Everybody started getting out of the cars and walking into the Chapel.

"Christina, you look beautiful." Mrs. Lopez said.

"Thank you, Angelita, you look great yourself."

"How are you Mr. and Mrs. Hamilton?"

"Fine, we have been admiring your Mansion, Angelita."

"It's pretty big, it's from the 19th Century and it has been remodeled a number of times."

"Well, we have been admiring it for miles until we stopped here."

"Thank you Kate. Let's go in. I sent Carlos to the Chapel. Christina, we arranged a small basket of petals for Linda to carry into the Chapel."

"It's a beautiful basket, Angelita, thank you very much."

"These are my sons Martin and Alvaro, with the short warning; they were the only two who could come." Mrs. Lopez said.

"What a shame, do you have any more children?" Kate asked

"Yes, they live on the East Coast, they are both Marine biologists, and it's very difficult to get in touch with them."

They had all gone inside of the luxurious home, from last Century Spanish Decor, lavish everywhere you looked. The Chapel was located inside the mansion.

"Mr. Hamilton, take your place next to Christina; Kate, since you are the only Matron Of Honor you walk ahead of the Bride. Linda, walk in front of the Bride."

Mrs. Lopez walked in and signaled someone to start the wedding march.

Linda looked beautiful with the basket of petals as she walked in all smiles, then, Kate looked beautiful, years didn't show on her, her dress was a Champagne shade lace over a heavy silk; a fine pearl necklace and small hat and high heels.

Charles walked in with Christina on his arm, and very proudly went down the aisle, Christina looked ravishing, with her cream color silk and lace dress and that big brim hat made her look like a high fashion model. She smiled at Carlos and he could barely believe his eyes; he knew Christina was a pretty woman, but after all, she was in bandages for so long. The change was drastic. A high fashion model had nothing on Christina.

They finally got through the ceremony and they were married.

"We have the dining room ready for the reception and later on, if you wish, we can go to the garden and have a drink or coffee and cake." Angelita announced.

When they entered the dining room, it was like in the movies, long beautiful embroidered white tablecloths, fine dishes, long base crystal wine glasses, crystal candelabras; the Hamilton's were used to very expensive Social Events, but this was like royalty.

There were a lot of people there besides them. "I thought Christina said it was only the family," Kate said.

"Maybe they are all their family," Charles replied.

"We might be introduced later on." Dinner started being served; starting from the soup, they were told it was called "Gazpacho" a Spanish soup; then several different vegetable dishes, Spanish rice and delicious roast beef. They must have cooked at least twenty roasts beef, and a servant was placed behind every other guest. The cake was a huge cake. They had two cakes, one chocolate for the Groom and the Bride's cake was a butter cake with almond filling that turned out to be the most delicious cake any one had ever tasted.

"Where do you want to eat dessert ladies and gentlemen? Would you like to remain in here or go outside in the garden?" Everybody chose to remain in the dining room, so they were served there.

"Carlos, when are we supposed to leave, and where are we going?"
"I may be wrong, but I thought I told you, we're going to Acapulco."
"It's great, darling, but I don't remember a thing. Let's mingle a little bit and then I'll throw my bouquet so we can leave."

In the meantime, both of Carlos' brothers, Brent and Darrell gathered cans and ropes and proceeded to tie them behind the car. "This will be enough because they are only going to the airport and someone else is going to have to drive the car back. Okay, let's go in."

Christina threw the bouquet and Sarah caught it. Darrell said to her,
"I'm ready baby, whenever you are." She blushed and smiled.
Irene came over to ask Christina if she wanted her to help her change clothes.
"Irene, in all the mixed up dealing I never arranged an outfit for the trip, Carlos said he told me we're going to Acapulco, but I don't remember."
"Everything you have is beautiful, Christina, and when you get there, buy more clothes," said Irene.

"Let's go Irene; I'll signal Carlos that I'm going upstairs."
"Do you know in which bedroom you're going to change?"
"Mrs. Lopez told me the same bedroom I was in before," Christina said.

"Here we are, Irene." Christina opened the door. Mrs. Lopez was in there.

"Mrs. Lopez!" Christina said surprised to find her mother-in-law in her bedroom.

"I'm sorry dear; I didn't think you'd be leaving so soon, I brought you a suit for the trip and a Mantilla we brought from Mexico the last time we were there."

"It's beautiful, how did you know it was going to fit me?

"Perhaps you have forgotten; I'm the one who did some shopping for you when you were here before," Said Mrs. Lopez.

"I'm sorry; I guess I don't have too much recollection from those days. The suit is beautiful and a beautiful color, thank you very much. With all the confusion I didn't buy a suit for the trip so it couldn't have been more opportune."

"Welcome to the family, Christina, we all love you and the children very much. Well, I better leave so you can get changed."

"Christina, she is darling and a very warm person," Irene told her.

"Yes, and I was getting upset to find her in here on my wedding day, I didn't know what to think about it."

"To tell you the truth, it surprised me too. But it ended up a good surprise."

"Christina, you'll find a small package, that is a gift from Brent, Darrell, Sarah and I, since there was no time for a bridal shower we thought that would replace it."

"Thank you, whatever it is, I'll always treasure it."

Christina and Irene went downstairs; Carlos was waiting for her at the bottom of the steps. "Hi, darling," he said kissing her. "Let's go."

Chapter Ten

Everyone gathered around the newlyweds to wish them good luck, they hugged everyone and finally they turned around to get in the car. When Christina got in the car, Carlos straightened up to say his final good-bye. A shot was heard and Carlos fell to the ground, a chilling scream came from Christina. She immediately put her hand over her mouth. Carlos was lying on his back. Brent and Darrell were there in a second. Christina couldn't get out on that side of the car; "He is alive," someone said.

Mr. Moran was running towards the hill in front of the house, Christina followed him. "Go back, Miss Christina," Moran told her.

Christina was wild. "You go to hell! I'm going to kill that Son-of-a-Bitch; I'm going to kill him if it's the last thing I do," She said so enraged that she could hardly speak. "Where do you think he went?"

But when Moran was going to answer, Mike came out from behind a tree.

"Hi baby, did I interrupt anything?" Mike said laughing.

Moran had a gun on Mike, but Christina knew Moran carried another gun tucked in his belt behind his right hand. She was very quiet, feeling frozen, and dead; her eyes were dazed as she pulled the gun from Moran's belt and shot Mike, two, three, four, five, six times. Then she stood there. "Is he dead?" she asked Moran.

"Yes, Miss Christina, he is dead," replied Moran while taking the gun from her.

She started to run back, "Carlos, Carlos" she shouted, "How is he?"

"They are taking him to our hospital, Christina. Brent and Darrell are with him, he is in good hands, and in the hands of the Lord," Irene told her.

"I want to go see him; I need to go to him. I'm sorry Mrs. Lopez, I'm sorry, if I had thought Mike would attack Carlos I would never have married your son. I always thought he would attack me, only me. But he won't be back, Mrs. Lopez. I killed him! I killed him!" she repeated again and again, "He won't ever be back." She said with a nervous laugh, with no feelings whatsoever.

Everybody was still. The air had frozen everyone looking at Christina with unbelieving and surprised eyes; but Christina didn't seem to be worried she had just killed a man. All she wanted to do was: to go after Carlos. Christina's eyes and reflections seemed to be confused, a faint note of hysteria and confusion were back in her voice.

"Let's go, Christina." Irene told her.

"I'll go with you; I need to be there myself," Mrs. Lopez said. "Everyone else left already."

Somebody had already pulled off the "decorations" from the honeymooners' car, and they went to the hospital in it.

When they arrived at the hospital they were told they were performing surgery on Carlos. It was only one bullet, but badly placed close to his heart. Fortunately, the best surgeons in the area were working on him.

As carefully as she could, Irene pulled her parents aside and told them:

"Papa, Mama. Please don't show that I'm telling you anything out of the ordinary, we don't want Christina to know what I'm saying. Do you remember Christina ran up the hill with Mr. Moran? Her parents nodded their heads. "Well, Christina killed Mike."

Charles said, "I can't say I'm sorry."

"Of course, Papa, but Christina probably is going to be charged with capital murder," Irene said.

"There is no court in this country that would convict her," Charles said.

"When they investigate the facts, I don't think she's going to be charged; her husband had been shot by him; she was almost killed by the same man twice and there were many other offenses, Betancourt can testify on her behalf, so can Mr. Moran. In fact, when they ask him if Christina was paying him, he can say, yes. The police couldn't protect her until she was killed. According to what the police said."

Hours went by; Irene went to check on Christina. She had been sitting by Mrs. Lopez waiting on news from the surgery, just then the double doors opened and Brent came out in his greens. He held Christina's hands, "Christina, Carlos' life is still in danger, but we're here with him. Darrell and I are taking turns to stay with Carlos, and we won't leave him Christina. All that can be done has been done. Mr. and Mrs. Lopez, you heard what I said. The bullet was in a very delicate place, that's why it took us so long to operate. We had to be very careful."

Christina said in a cold, emotionless voice. "Thank you Brent, Darrell; thank you for everything. But I want to tell you something, it was Mike who shot Carlos, and I killed him. He won't be back."

Brent looked toward Irene; she nodded her head and hugged Christina.

Chapter Eleven

Chief of Police, Mr. Betancourt, walked into the hospital; two officers had come with him. He spotted the Hamilton's and walked towards them. "Mr. Hamilton," he said shaking Charles hand, "what happened here?"

Irene spoke slowly and with, a trembling voice asked, "Didn't you guess Mr. Betancourt? Mike found out Christina was getting married. We asked for help but according to the law, it appears that the person has to be dead to get any help; even if Christina almost was killed, Carlos is fighting for his life. They were getting in the car to go to the airport when he was shot. Mr. Moran ran after him and Christina followed him, when they were looking for the shooter, Mike got out from behind a tree and asked Christina if he had interrupted anything. Christina pulled a gun from Mr. Moran's belt and unloaded the gun on Mike."

"Has the Sheriff been over?" Betancourt asked.

"No," Irene said, "He's probably issuing a warrant for Christina's arrest, I imagine this time they will make it stick so she can learn her lesson."

"I can understand how bitter you are, Irene; I'll have a talk with the Sheriff and brief him about this case."

Irene walked to Christina and Mrs. Lopez to let them know about Mr. Betancourt's visit.

"Has Brent or Darrell been out again, Christina?" asked Mrs. Lopez.

"No, Brent said the progress will be very slow; they won't come out too often."

"Mrs. Lopez, why don't you and your husband go home? I'll try to get my parents to go home as well," Irene suggested.

"I imagine it is smart for us to rest at different times so we won't get so tired at the same time. Ask your parents if they would like to spend the night at our house. I can provide bed clothes and send blankets and pillows back over here."

"Let's wait for the next time that Brent or Darrell come out and we'll see who goes and who stays."

Irene started going around where everybody had formed a group and let them know what had been said. Carlos' brothers, Martin and Alvaro, didn't want to leave. Charles and Kate accepted spending the night invitation to stay at the Lopez' home; Cindy and the children had already been sent to their home. Sarah said she better leave because she should go to the office the next day, Benny would drive her and Laura. Irene would stay with Christina. Clare decided she would stay in case Kate needed her.

Another hour had passed when the double doors to the operating room opened up again. Everybody walked to Brent. "Well, so far, so good. His blood pressure is almost normal and it has been only ten hours; it seems the surgery has been a success. We're not out of hot water yet, hold your breath. All I'm saying is: it looks good, but he is not out of danger."

Christina took a step to hug Brent, but instead, she suddenly collapsed. "Christina!" Irene said. "She has just fainted;" Brent knelt down to check her pulse.

"Christina is pale and weak from all that happened today; she is in distress from the shock, someone should have thought about her and given her something for her nerves. Not only what happened to Carlos, but because she killed a man! Even if he is the worse crumb in this earth, you still don't want to be the one who pulled the trigger. I'm going to admit her for stress and give her a sedative," said Brent feeling deep concern.

"You're right, everybody was so upset with Carlos, no one thought about Christina, I'm sorry," Irene said.

"Sarah is going home to be at the office Monday morning, which is tomorrow, now it's so late, what do you want to do about the office?"

"I think Darrell can cover my appointments and I'll stay here with Carlos until I think he is out of danger," responded Brent.

"Okay, I'll get the ball rolling with the plans for tonight."

Brent went back in to be with Carlos. "Darrell, any changes?"

"No, but his blood pressure is stable, that's good."

"Yes, it is. Boy, Darrell, I don't mind telling you I didn't think we could save him, did you?"

"No one would have bet a nickel for his life, but now, you can bet a buck."

"Listen buddy, I don't want to leave the nurses alone here, I want one of us here all the time, do you want the first guard?"

"No, you go ahead and lay down. I'll call you after a while," said Darrell.

"Two hours, Darrell." Brent told him.

"Okay."

Brent, half asleep looked at his watch. He thought "It's five thirty;" He opened his eyes, five thirty! Darrell didn't call me! I'll get him, he thought. He ran out of the room they had let him use and ran to the recovery room. "Darrell, how is Carlos?"

"He is fine, Brent; there was no need for you to miss your sleep."

"But you stayed here all night," Brent admonished.

"And you did the surgery, Brent, I only assisted you. I know how traumatic a surgery can be; you needed your sleep worse than I did."

"Okay. Nothing can be done now. Listen, you go back to the city today and go to work tomorrow and cover for me, please."

"I can do that," Darrell said smiling.

"It feels good to smile, doesn't it?" replied Brent.

A nurse walked in, "Dr. Miller, Christina Lopez from room 210 wants to know what she is doing in the hospital."

Darrell and Brent looked at each other, "Oh brother, I don't like the sound of it. Lets' go," Brent told the nurse.

When Brent arrived to Christina's room he greeted her very casually. "Good morning, how do you feel this morning?"

"I'm fine, Doctor, I want to know what I'm doing here. I'm not hurting anywhere, I want to go home," replied Christina vaguely.

"You were in a minor wreck and we don't know your name and your address to notify anyone of the accident. Just give the nurse the information and you can go home." Brent said.

Christina looked at Brent with an empty stare and said. "My name is…I don't remember my name, why? Why don't I remember?"

Brent looked down and closed his eyes before he responded. "You were in a car accident, Ma'am; sometimes you can lose your memory for a few days and then you remember everything. Don't you worry about it."

He signaled the nurse to come out of the room with him. "Please don't leave Mrs. Lopez alone. Everybody who goes in has to be told of her condition. Do you understand?" Brent told her.

"Yes, sir," she answered him.

Brent left Christina's room quickly, he started walking slowly down the hall, "Lord," he began to pray, "What else do you have for this girl's plate? It's so full already, it is overflowing. Please give her a break. He felt his eyes filling with tears; he wasn't used to feeling like that. He went looking for Irene; he didn't want her to find out from anyone else.

Brent found Irene in the cafeteria. "Good morning, sweetheart, do you want a cup of coffee?"

Irene greeted him, "Yes, I guess I need a cup."

"Have you been to see Christina?"

"That's why I was looking for you," replied Brent.

"Hey, that sounds serious, what happened to her?"

"You have to promise to remain calm, Irene. Christina doesn't know who she is. She has amnesia; it could last a few days, weeks, or longer."

"My God, what else is going to happen to this kid? Irene said crying.

"Carlos is stable this morning; he had a remarkably good night. Let's get the family together and let them know at the same time about Christina."

"Darrell," said Brent, "because Irene needs to stay here with Christina, when you get to the office ask Lourdes to get two more clerks. One to help Sarah, and the other one to take care of Irene's duties. After we get married she might not go back to work. Lourdes knows I don't like to advertise. Tell her to ask her friends and family if they know someone qualified."

Both families gathered in one of the hospital's lobbies. Brent started explaining about Carlos progress, how his youth, strength and health, helped him recover so fast. Then he started, "About Christina...

"Yes, I was about to ask how she was, and where is she?" Mrs. Lopez asked.

"Christina has amnesia. When she woke up this morning she had no idea who she was or what she was doing here. I told her she had been in a car accident and that she would regain her memory soon."

Everyone was quiet. Kate just cried and Irene went over to comfort her.

"Dear Lord, how much more grief are you sending this poor soul? Please help her get out of this." Kate prayed.

Mrs. Lopez said, "You know the children will be all right at the ranch, but we need to enroll Linda in school very soon."

"We also need to think about when Christina wakes up, because I know in my heart it will be soon. We need to know what to tell her, if she wakes up and she doesn't remember her children; we need to decide what to tell the children." Irene said.

"I have been thinking about that; we can tell her they belong to Carlos and he can hire Christina as a Nanny. That way she can be close to her children." Angelita said.

"That's a great idea, we can tell her Carlos is divorced, I don't think we can talk Amy into not calling her Mama, but that's easy to explain." Irene added.

"Also, since she doesn't know her name, she could be called Nanny by everybody."

"One thing which hasn't been discussed: the police charges."

"Mr. Betancourt spoke to the Police over here; they are not going to press charges."

"What are they going to do about it?"

"Paper work, it all can be done on paper."

"Has Mr. Moran come back?"

"I haven't seen him."

Brent stood up "Well, this is longer than I intended to stay away from Carlos."

Chapter Twelve

Brent was in one of the rooms next to the ICU where the hospital provides the Doctors to rest, Irene walked to him, "Brent is everything all right?"

"I guess so; Carlos asked why Christina hasn't been to see him."

"Oh brother, what did you tell him?"

"I told him the whole thing. I warned him so he could get hold of himself. It was a big shock to him."

"Could I go in to see him?"

"I'll go in with you, sweetheart."

Carlos had his eyes closed. Irene walked up to him and held his hand.

"It'll get better Carlos." She said to him.

"We keep saying that; but not today. One of these days it might happen."

"Have you seen Christina; Irene?"

"I try to go everyday; but she doesn't know who I am either, I told her we were working together when she had the wreck. It's hard to make conversation when there are so many things you can't discuss with her. She asked me what her name was; I told her I was told she was going to remember it on her own. She seemed to like my answer."

"I can't get into my mind that she shot Mike. Where did she find the strength to do it?" asked Carlos.

"When she saw you on the ground, Carlos." Irene said. "It enraged her and when she followed Mr. Moran; she was no longer reasoning. She had had enough of Mike taking over her life; she had enough and she had to end it; that's why she took the gun from Moran's belt and shot Mike, six times, Carlos! She unloaded the gun! If the Police weren't going to do it, she had to get it done herself."

Luis Moran walked into the hospital and asked where he could find Christina.

"One moment, please." the nurse said. Leaving her post, she went looking for Irene.

"Miss Irene, there is a man looking for Mrs. Christina."

"Did you get his name?"

"Luis Moran."

"Oh good, please take me to him."

"It's good seeing you, Mr. Moran, do you have any news."

"As a matter of fact, yes, I do. Where is Mrs. Christina?"

"I know you have not been back, Mr. Moran, but with all that happened; when Christina was going to ask about Carlos, she collapsed. When she woke up, she had lost her memory; she still doesn't know who she is." Irene informed Mr. Moran.

"What a shame, I think I know where her parents are. They went to Australia. They're still there, they bought a cattle station. That is an Australian ranch.

"We don't know what Christina's condition is going to be for a while. A condition like hers is one of those, about which a Doctor can't give you a concrete answer; it depends on her mind. We're hoping she comes out of it very soon.

"Do you want to speak with Carlos; Mr. Moran?"

"Can I see him?"

"I'll ask Brent, but I don't think it will be a problem."

"Brent, Mr. Moran thinks he found Christina's parents, he is outside waiting to speak with Carlos; is it all right?"

"I'll ask Carlos, he is still recovering, you know."

"Carlos, how are you feeling? Do you think you want to have company?"

"I guess it depends on who it is."

"Mr. Moran just came back from a trip he was on; he'd like to talk to you."

"It's all right, Brent," Carlos said without any enthusiasm.

Brent walked out with Irene.

"Well, we're facing another problem."

"Why?" Irene asked Brent.

"Carlos is falling into a depression. No good for his condition."

"Brent, wouldn't it be beneficial to Christina and Carlos if they saw each other? Carlos knows what not to say, he can just say he is in the hospital and is taking a walk."

"I knew there was a reason for me to love you so much." Brent told Irene.

They both almost ran to Carlos's room.

"Carlos, how strong do you feel?"

"I feel all right, Brent, a little weak. When I try to walk I can't go too far."

"If I put you in a wheel chair and take you to Christina's room, could you talk to her very casual? Just go into her room and say hello explain you're just taking a walk? Remember she doesn't know who you are. This is just a test to see how she reacts to your presence."

Carlos smiled big and said, "What are we waiting for?"

"Sometimes they start regaining their memory a little at a time. Tomorrow, maybe we can bring the children."

Slowly, Brent and Irene helped Carlos out of bed into a wheelchair and started to Christina's room. Carlos said. "Brent, my heart is racing."

Brent pulled the stethoscope off his neck and started checking Carlos' heart. "It's only anticipation, buddy, It'll slow down, I guess I was running myself; you ought to hear my heart," Brent told him. "But if you feel anything else, please, tell me."

"Okay, here we are, Carlos; I'll go in with you in case something goes wrong. I don't think you need to go in now, Irene, when we leave, you go in to see what she thought, if anything, of the visit."

They found Christina sitting by the window looking at the garden. Slowly, Carlos walked in and smiled at Christina. "Hello, how are you?"

"I'm fine; I don't know what I'm doing here. What happened to you?"

"I had minor surgery; I'll be out of here pretty soon." Replied Carlos. "May I sit down? Today is my first walk and I'm tired."

Christina thought for a second and answered him, "it will be all right."

Carlos sat next to Christina and introduced himself, "Carlos Lopez," he said. extending his hand to Christina. She shook hands with him. For a second there; there was electricity in their hands, she retrieved her hand and said.

"Carlos Lopez?" She repeated. "I don't know why I remember that name. Have we met somewhere before?"

"It's possible," Carlos said. "I am a physician."

"Well, maybe I went to you sometime or maybe for one of my children."

"Do you have children?" Carlos asked hopefully to as where the conversation was taking them.

"I don't remember, I probably do or I wouldn't have said it."

Brent walked outside and signaled Irene. She came running. "Call for the children, Irene." He didn't explain anything else; he went back into Christina's room.

"When you leave the hospital," said Carlos, "I'd like to see you, but I don't know your name."

"I'll tell you when I remember, and I think I'd like to see you too," replied Christina.

Pretty soon; Irene was back with the children. Brent said, "Carlos, your children came to visit you." Carlos tried to pick up Amy, but Brent was there to pick her up,

"Not yet, Buddy," and he put Amy on his lap.

Amy said, "Mammy?" Linda was by Christina's bed holding her hand.

Christina's eyes filled with tears. "What is this?" She said.

Brent interfered, "Maybe Carlos' family reminded you of your own."

"Would you like for us to leave? Maybe you're tired." Carlos asked her.

Christina had closed her eyes, tears slipped through her eyelids, but she said,

"No, I don't know why, but I don't want you to leave."

Irene, who had been standing by the door, remained silent; but obviously very emotional.

They were there for over an hour before Brent and Irene left, but Carlos and the children remained with Christina.

"Brent, what does it mean?"

"It has to be good. I'll get Carlos dinner to be brought here and for the children."

"Don't you think Carlos needs to rest? He is very tired now."

"Are you going to tell him to go back to his room? You saw him how depressed he was over there. This is the best medicine for his ailments." Brent told a nurse to keep a constant check on Carlos and the children.

An hour later; Brent and Irene went back into Christina's room. "Well, it has been a long visit, aren't your children sleepy, Carlos?"

"Brent; Christina has remember me **and** the children," he said with tears he could not hide, hugging Amy. "She remembered, I love her."

Brent and Irene were speechless. "I'll get Dr. Segura to come tomorrow for an evaluation, Carlos. Do you remember anyone else Christina?"

"I remember Irene and her family; and I remember you." She told him smiling.

"May I hug you, Christina?" Irene asked.

Christina opened her arms and Irene fell into them, they both sobbed.

"Mama, I'm sorry it's so late, but I just had to call you. I don't know how much I can tell you, but Christina has recovered her memory."

"My God, how did it happen?"

"Well, I won't go into details now, but it started, I think because Carlos was so depressed that Brent took him in a wheelchair to Christina's room. They started to talk and I'll tell you the rest when I see you some time tomorrow. I think I can leave her now."

"Irene, I'm glad you woke me up with such good news," Kate said.

Irene had gone to Carlos' house to visit the children and talk to Carlos' mother about Christina.

"Irene, welcome; I received a call from Carlos. It's such good news to hear about Christina recovering her memory."

"She is not all there yet; I imagine it is going to take her some time. She might not recognize us all at once; it might take her a while, we don't know," Irene said.

"In any case," Angelita said," it's a good start, I know Carlos was devastated."

"Yes, he was, listen Mrs. Lopez; I have to go back to town and stop by the office;

So I need to leave, it has been a pleasure even in this circumstances; to see you again."

The drive to town was a long way. Irene was tired. "What I need to do is go to bed," she thought," not go to the office." Oh, there is the office now, good." She walked into the office. "Hello, everybody." she said.

"Irene," Sarah ran out to the waiting room, "How are Christina and Carlos?"

"Carlos is recovering nicely," she said, "Christina is getting better, and she recognized Carlos and her children. She also recognized our family and Brent."

Darrell walked out of his office; "Irene how is Carlos? And, of course, Christina?"

"Well enough now, Darrell." And Irene went more into detail explaining what Brent had told Irene to tell Darrell. "I really need to go home and relax in the bath tub."

"Mama, Dad, I'm home," Irene hollered entering the house. "Where are you?"

"Irene," Kate said," it's so good to have you home again. How are things over there?"

"Much better, Mama, thank the Lord."

"Irene, have you even thought about your own wedding?"

"To tell you the truth, Mama, no; I haven't. But Brent and I talked about it, and we have decided to just get married without all the trimmings. I can't return my wedding dress Mama, but we'll go to Mass and get married as planned, then, we'll just have a simple meal at home. We'll invite Carlos and his family I believe by then, Carlos is going to be able to come here. It'll be too many to have a sit down dinner, but we can have it buffet style. No fuss, Mama, I really don't want any."

"Whatever you and Brent want to do, Irene." Kate said.

"Your father will be happier he doesn't have to wear a tuxedo."

Irene smiled. "Yes, I had forgotten about it. I think we'll all be happier, Mama, all we want to remember is getting married not anything else."

"If it's a pretty day we can set a table outside, Irene."

"Right. That way, we can have a sit down dinner. Mama, I'm going to soak a couple of hours in the tub; bye." She told her smilingly, but obviously very tired.

Kate and Charles were in the garden, Kate was reading and Charles was playing with the dog.

"Kate, dinner is ready, who is coming to dinner, do you know? I don't see anybody." Clare announced.

"I haven't heard from Sarah; and Irene left hours ago to take a bath, Clare, best you look in Irene's room, see what is keeping her."

KATE, KATE! CHARLES! Clare shouted from upstairs. They both ran upstairs to see about Clare's call.

"Clare; what in the world? What happened with Irene?"

"I guess she went to sleep in the tub, she is freezing and I can't get her out of the tub by myself. She passed out."

Between Charles, Kate and Clare; they got Irene out of the tub. Clare had brought an extra large towel and covered Irene up. Carefully they put her on the floor and started giving her a massage all over her body. Irene started moving around and moaning, she opened her eyes. "Mama? What are you doing here? **PAPA, WHAT ARE YOU DOING HERE?** She said.

"Clare came to call you for dinner and she found you asleep in the tub full of water; I guess you could have drowned soon enough if it hadn't been for her."

"I'm so cold, she said, "let me put some clothes on." Charles and Kate left, Clare remained with Irene. Clare pulled some clothes out for Irene to dress.

"Don't say anything, Clare."

"I haven't said anything."

"I know you; you're just waiting for the best angle to hit me with," smiled Irene.

"I wasn't going to hit you with anything. But I bet Brent will."

"And who is going to tell him?" mumbled Irene.

"Not me, no Sireee, not me," said Clare.

"Clare; if you tell Brent I won't speak to you again." She said smiling.

"Do you want to drink something hot first; Irene?" asked Kate.

"If it's not going to delay dinner, Mama. Yes, I would like a cup of coffee."

"No, you're not delaying anything, Sarah just went upstairs, and she'll be down in a few minutes. Laura called, she is on her way."

"It'll give us time to relax a little."

"About how long did you stay at the hospital with Christina, Irene?"

"I believe three weeks."

"I knew it was a long time; has Brent come back at all?"

"No, he will come back now, but he is leaving Carlos in the hospital."

Clare and Joanna came to the dining room with several platters.

"I know I didn't announce it but I'm so tired; my feet wouldn't want to go back again. Besides that, I know you were ready to eat dinner."

"Hello Sarah, where did your shadow go?" Irene asked Sarah smiling.

"Darrell, my shadow, like you call him, has been working so hard he forgot to invite me to dinner."

"I'm sorry Sarah, Brent told me he'll try to come back tomorrow."

"Oh no, he is fine with it; the reason more than justifies the fact. It will pass. The important thing is that Christina and Carlos are both alive and well."

"Isn't that the truth?"

"Laura, it's so late, why did it take you so long to come home?" Kate asked.

"I'm sorry, Mama, but the classes I'm taking are late classes, I showed you my schedule, remember? You commented on the times,"

"I'm sorry baby; it's not the same to read a schedule than when you are actually coming late at night. Can you change your classes to a different time?"

"Not if I want to take the same classes, Mama."

"Well, I hope it doesn't take too long."

"Brent! When did you come back?" Irene asked Brent who was walking into the dining room.

"I haven't stopped anywhere, honey, I came straight over here."

"How are things with Carlos and Christina?"

"Carlos is out of danger; that's why I felt I could leave. I hate I have left the practice's load on Darrell, but I couldn't leave Carlos any earlier."

"He knows, sweetheart, Sarah was just telling me he was so tired he didn't invite her to dinner tonight. But tell me about Christina's progress."

"I'm afraid the progress is slow, Irene. About the only thing she clings to, is Carlos and her children; which in itself is very good for her."

"Moran went over and visited with Carlos several times, Christina didn't recognize him at all. Moran told Christina's her parents bought a cattle station in Australia; now that they know about Christina, they might try to sell it to come back over here again. Maybe that will be another high point. Christina can react when she sees her parents again and may make her recognize most everything and everyone."

"I wonder why they went so far not knowing anything about Christina."

"Who knows, Irene; we'll get answers about everything when they come back."

"Do you want to go for a ride after dinner Irene?" Brent asked her.

"I would, Brent; but you must be exhausted. Why don't we go to the garden and sit on a bench?"

"It sounds marvelous, Irene."

"I've wanted to be alone with you for so long," Brent told Irene.

"Me too darling." she said. They embraced for a long time and remained enfolded within each other arms.

"I told mama I didn't want a big wedding any longer, Brent."

"Are you sure? You're just still feeling bad for Christina. But aren't you going to resent it later that you didn't have a big wedding like you had planned?

"No, I don't think so; I believe a big wedding is so impersonal. I want my family and yours as well as my closest friends, that's all."

"Well, whatever you say. If you invite Christina, she has a big family now; you're going to have you to rent tables to seat them all; you know," He said laughing.

"Isn't that wonderful? We're going to need a long table just for her family."

They both laughed out loud. "It feels so good to be able to laugh like that again."

When Brent and Darrell arrived at the office. It was full, "Good Lord, I'm so glad we didn't have any surgeries today."

"Okay, let's get to it, maybe we can eat lunch." Darrell said smiling. Hours went by, Sarah announced the last patient, "Mrs. Fuller," she called out.

"Mrs. Velvia Fuller." she walked to the only lady in the waiting room and asked her, "are you not Mrs. Velvia Fuller?"

Startled by Sarah's presence; the lady stood up and started walking fast. "I have been waiting for so long," she said, "I had forgotten what my name was." the little lady said walking into Darrell's office with a smile.

Sarah went to the examination covering her mouth trying to prevent anyone hearing her laughter. But Darrell walked in on her; he looked at her with curious eyes. Smiling at her he said, "Sarah, what's the matter?"

"I promise I'll tell you, but not now, go on and finish with Mrs. Fuller."

"Irene, how long is it until we get married?" asked Brent.

"Do you mean to tell me; you don't know?"

"It's only three weeks until Thanksgiving, Irene, and we haven't done a thing towards our wedding. Do you still want to get married?"

"Darling, I don't want anything else but to marry you. Don't you know?"

"I think I do, Irene. But I don't see signs of anything being prepared towards our wedding."

"I already have the invitations, only now there are going to be announcements, we have a guest list; my dress and my sisters' dresses are ready; food is going to be catered, the amount is the only thing that has varied. I don't have to order a tuxedo for my father nor you. We have the rings. We do need to address the announcements but we both just came back, Brent darling."

"Okay, I won't be nervous any more, you can slap me now."

"I'd rather kiss you," Irene said leaning towards him kissing him.

"One thing we haven't done is gone to the church. I don't think anyone has notified Father Gabriel about what has happened in our family."

"Don't you think we need to go in person?"

"Yes, I do. He may have decided we're not going to get married."

"We'll go tomorrow, okay?"

"By the way, what is that I heard about you passing out in the bath tub?"

"And who do I have to kill?" Irene asked Brent.

"Irene, were you that exhausted?"

"I knew I was tired, Brent; enough that I went to sleep in the tub and it wasn't any more than that."

"We don't know that because you were alone; besides that you were freezing. That means you were in the tub for a long time," Brent told Irene. "You need to have a physical, Irene; who is your medical doctor?"

"You're kidding, aren't you?" Irene asked Brent with an incredible look in her eyes.

"No, Irene, you had a rough time after Christina's wedding. God knows what you ate and probably not enough times a day. Then the stress you're under with the wedding and all."

"I can't believe you, Brent." She said aggravated at Brent.

"Baby, before you get mad at me, do you remember when your mother collapsed? You agreed with me then."

"Surely; you're not comparing me with my mother; are you?" Irene said totally scandalized.

"Irene, do you really think illnesses are exclusive for the elderly?"

"I'm going to shoot Clare." She said fuming.

"And before you start that. It wasn't Clare who told me, it was your father. Go scream at him."

"But why did he do it?" Irene asked Brent.

"Irene, when he was in trouble, you called me; when your mother was in trouble, again, you called me. You did it because you cared; now, it was their time to show you how much they cared for you."

"What can be wrong with me Brent? I felt great as soon as I warmed up."

"You are young, Irene, it may be nothing in your system, but I can't count the times I have found something wrong with people and have had to tell them, their life would have been saved if the problem had been found sooner. For example, a valve that goes into the heart could stop working; when you got so cold. When you warmed up it started working again; if you have a faulty valve, it can be replaced without any trouble now, but not twenty or thirty years from now."

"Brent, if it's a valve, I need to see a cardiologist, why are you sending me to my medical doctor?"

"I didn't think you wanted me or Darrell to examine you."

"It's all right; Sarah has to be in the room, doesn't she? All right Brent; we play it your way. Are there any other tests to be done?" Irene asked.

"You know the routine Irene, blood tests and EKG, EEG for now."

Irene looked down; Brent couldn't tell whether she was mad or worried. He got closer to her and said. "Darling, you know I don't want anything to happen to you; you know that, don't you? It might be nothing at all. But then we'll know; we don't have to worry about anything, okay?" he said kissing her tenderly.

"Okay, as soon as we have time tomorrow, we'll do it," Irene said.

"You can make yourself an appointment Irene; I want to have enough time for your examination, not a rush up job." He was very serious.

Chapter Thirteen

The examination had started, Irene was pleasantly surprised at Sarah's professionalism; she followed Brent's instructions to the letter. She just didn't act like her little sister any longer.

Without a word, Brent left the examining room; Sarah proceeded to tell Irene to dress.

"What will happen now, Sarah?"

"You'll go to Brent's office now, Irene." She did so and entered his office.

"Brent, do you have to wait for any tests now?"

"No, I already received them, Irene. Since you went to the hospital so early to get them done. I appreciate that."

"Well, are you going to tell me what's wrong with me?" a concerned Irene asked.

"You have a pretty faulty Mitral valve that has prolapsed; Irene. It has to be replace."

"What? What does it mean? Do I have to have heart surgery?" Irene asked.

"It is not a serious surgery, Irene. But yes, its heart surgery, I'll recommend you don't wait long." He told her.

"Do we have to postpone our wedding?"

"I recommend we do just that."

Irene didn't answer; she looked down; covered her face and began to cry.

"Irene, I would like to bring Darrell in as a second opinion, do you agree?"

"I don't need a second opinion to your diagnosis, Brent."

"I do. I want more than anything to bring him into your case Irene. Something else Irene, I can't do your surgery, I want Darrell to do it."

"**No!** I want you to do it, Brent." She said.

"We're not permitted to perform surgery on our loved ones." Brent held both of Irene's hands. "I can't imagine not considering you as my loved one." Brent was visibly tense and emotional. He then held her in his arms; they remained embraced for a long time.

"Brent, I want you to be with me when I tell my parents."

"Of course, baby."

"Mama, Papa," Irene started, "we need to talk with you."

"What is it; Irene?" Charles asked fearing what it was about since he had spoken with Brent about Irene collapsing in the bathtub.

"Brent examined me this morning and the tests showed I have a faulty valve that goes into my heart." She said with as strong a voice as she could managed.

"What about the wedding?" Kate asked.

"It has to be postponed." She said.

"Since we spoke earlier today," Brent said. "I reconsidered; I believe we should get married sooner, just us; then do the surgery. That way, I can take care of Irene better."

Kate said. "I don't want to appear indelicate but I assume you can't go on a honeymoon."

"**Mother!**" Irene said.

"Your mother is right; we need to speak about it. There will be no honeymoon until Irene recovers, but I think it's important for her to have high spirits. I think she will be happier being married than if she has to cancel her wedding."

"Brent, would you do that for me?"

"That and more sweetheart. I wish I could have the surgery for you."

"Now, someone needs to talk to Father Gabriel, we'll get married tomorrow, even if we have to do it at midnight." Brent said.

"Clare, Clare, where are you running to? I need to speak to you," called Charles. Clare turned her face; a messy film cover closed her mouth tightly. She said pointing to her mouth. "Mmmhhh, mmmhhh," while she ran.

"What in the devil happened to you?" Charles asked her.

Brent went immediately to check her mouth. He found her lips stuck together.

He dragged her to the kitchen, soaped her mouth good and rinsed it; then he rubbed her mouth with his hands until her lips were loose.

"Now," Charles said, "What in the devil happened to you?"

"Well, I have been having so much trouble with my dentures lately; I couldn't keep them in my mouth. I was so mad; I was in a hurry so I squeezed enough of that glue to do a good job! I thought the teeth would just glue to my gums, I was running to the door when you saw me, and I found out I had glued my mouth shut when I tried to answer you."

Charles laughed out loud, followed by Kate, Brent and Irene.

"Clare, you couldn't have done that at a better time, we all needed a good laugh."

Charles told Clare about Irene's surgery and getting married the next day.

"What time is it?" Kate said. "I think we better call Father Gabriel tonight."

"Let's call everyone we want there." Irene said. "I want to call Doris; I need to ask her about my wedding dress."

"Brent, do you think Christina and Carlos will be able to come to the wedding?"

"The only question is Carlos; Irene,"

"I have another idea," Kate said. "Why don't you get married now? And have another ceremony after Irene gets well?"

"Do you mean a big wedding?" Irene asked.

"Yes, we have the wedding when you recover."

"No, Papa, like I said, all I want is be married to Brent."

"Well then; is it too late to call father Gabriel?"

"No, we can call him now. I think Brent and I should make the call."

They went to Charles's office to call father Gabriel.

"Charles, were you the one who told Brent about Irene?" Kate asked.

"Yes Kate, the more I thought about it, the more worried I became. There was no reason for Irene to collapse and then she was freezing; that told me she had been there a long time for her to get that cold. So I decided to call Brent. I'm glad I did."

"So am I, dear, I don't want to think about what could have happened otherwise."

Brent was at the Hamilton's before seven in the morning. Before he could knock at the front door; Charles was there to open it.

"Brent, have you drank coffee yet?"

"No, Charles, I only got ready and came over to find out if you have any news for me."

"Brent, haven't you bought your marriage license? Father Gabriel said he can perform a wedding ceremony, later on, he'll do another one. Is that okay?"

"What did Irene say?"

"She nodded her head. Listen, I know her, she is really worried about it."

"I know, it'll be better than nothing. Is she up?"

"Yes, I'm up." Called Irene. "How are they going to manage at the clinic, Brent?"

"We hired several people since you were gone with Christina and Carlos."

"How about you'll be missing several days?"

"Darrell will take care of it, Irene. The appointments that he can't take care of; will be postponed."

"At what time should we go to the church?"

"Father Gabriel said whenever we're ready. Brent, have you scheduled my surgery?"

"Four o'clock, Irene."

"Let's go to the dining room and have something to eat, then we'll go to Church." Irene said.

"I'm glad is this early, eat something very light."

Brent held Irene in his arms. They walked like that all the way to the dining room. Sarah and Laura were there.

"Sarah!" Irene said. "You are not ready for work"

"I'm taking the day off. With only one Doctor there, they have plenty people to cover for me, I talked to Lourdes, it's all right."

"And how about you, Laura?"

"I don't have to go today either, there is nothing more important today than what's happening with my big sister," Laura told Irene.

Irene's head dropped; her eyes full of tears.

"No, no," Laura told her, "tears on your wedding day?"

Irene smiled. "That's better," Laura told her.

"By the way, did your wedding gown arrive?"

"I left a message at the dress shop; but I haven't heard anything. To tell you the truth, I don't feel like wearing my wedding dress; and since the wedding ceremony is going to be temporary, so is the dress."

The telephone rang, it was Darrell. "Brent, I thought we only opened this morning. Because neither one of us is going to be here, maybe we can leave Lourdes here and one of the other girls just to take care of people who want to know how come we're not open."

"Yes, it'll be okay. Thanks buddy. Can you be at the hospital at three p.m.?"

"You know I will, I wish I could be with you at the church."

"That's all right, but you can be at the real ceremony later on."

Irene dressed in a light blue silk suit, she wasn't wearing any flowers. Clare gave her a rose from the garden to carry with her. Both of her sisters were Maid of Honor. Charles was Brent's Best Man.

Father Gabriel waited for Irene with Brent and Kate. They all walked together. No music. Irene's eyes were full of tears. Charles squeezed her hand, "You'll be all right, Irene. We'll do this again and you're going to wear your wedding gown that day."

They arrived at the Altar. Father gave her a brief blessing before he started the ceremony.

He began, "Today I'm honored to unite Irene and Brent in holy matrimony". . .

Irene collapsed, Brent held her in his arms, with his eyes full of tears. He told Sarah, "Call Darrell," "Laura, call an ambulance."

Then all his attention was on Irene; he put his ear against her chest.

"Her heart is pretty strong, but without my stethoscope it's hard to say."

"Irene, Irene, darling can you open your eyes?" He asked her. Looking at Charles and Kate, he said, she probably had symptoms for a long time and didn't know what it was, she only dismissed them."

Father knelt by Irene's head and prayed for her health and blessed her.

The ambulance and their staff arrived at the Church; Brent began to work on Irene, Brent grabbed one of the medic's stethoscopes and started listening on her chest and began to tell the nurse what to give Irene. Once she was settled; they carefully picked her up and began to take her out of church. Brent was holding her hand. Charles, Kate and their daughters slowly walked outside with them. Father Gabriel walked behind them all.

Father Gabriel said. "Why don't you let me drive all of you?" And running around the back, he brought his car around to the front of the church.

When they arrived at the hospital; they walked to the Emergency entrance and asked where the person in the ambulance had been taken. The nurse looked in her list and said: "Dr. Miller said it was Irene Hamilton. They took her to Surgery, pavilion four on the fourth floor;" she said.

They all rushed there. No one was in the lobby. One of the nurses came out soon after they arrived and told them to be comfortable, it would probably take them about an hour before they came back out.

Chapter Fourteen

It had been just over one hour when Darrell came out in his greens. He looked exhausted.

He said, "She is very weak, Mr. and Mrs. Hamilton. It seems she held out on every one of us. The artery was very thin and hard to work with. I had to take a vein from her leg. She is very frail now; I think she'll recover well, but it's going to take a long time for her to do so. I'm sorry I don't have better news." Charles and Kate nodded and remained silent; they couldn't have spoken, had they tried.

"Can we go in to see her Darrell?" Charles asked.

"Of course; but she can't talk yet. Brent is with her now." Sarah and Laura were coming back from the chapel when they saw Darrell speaking to their parents. They ran towards them and asked. "Darrell, how is Irene?"

"I think there is no doubt she is going to make it."

"Tyke, I thought the surgery wasn't dangerous, what happened?"

"Her valves and surrounding area was in bad shape. No one could have expected it at her age. What we usually run into is someone with bad valves in their seventies; not Irene's age. Listen, Sarah, I need to go back, Brent is in no shape to be taking care of Irene."

"Darrell, do you have a thought about what caused Irene's problem?"

"We're going to study that, but if I was going to guess, I would say lack of oxygen."

"Mama, Papa, did you hear what Darrell told me about Irene?"

"Yes, sweetheart, I imagine it was a birth defect, I think that's what it's called in Irene's case. But I took care of myself; your father and I were always very healthy. We never smoked; your father only had a drink occasionally."

"Are they going to let us go in to see Irene, Mama?"

"Yes," Darrell said, "we are; someone will come to get you later."

"Well, I need to eat something; I haven't had anything since yesterday."

"Before you eat anything, Sarah, call Christina."

"Of course; the whole thing? Or just the fact she had surgery."

"I think the latter. Oh, call the house too, Clare must be very nervous."

"Charles, the fact that Irene collapsed in the bathtub turned out to be a blessing, don't you think so? There comes Father Gabriel now from the chapel." Kate said.

"Has the doctor been out of surgery, yet?" Father Gabriel asked.

"Yes, Father." And Charles filled him in with the details of the surgery.

Father said "Do you think they want to get married next month?"

"I don't think there is a chance; they said it's going to take a while for Irene to recover."

"Well, I think I need to go back to church now. I'll be coming by to check on Irene." Father Gabriel said. "Can I take anyone home?"

"No Father, we'll send for Lorenzo later on, thank you for everything."

Charles and Kate found Irene on a respirator, Brent was holding her hand.

"Brent, how do you see her?"

"Her blood pressure is improving and that is always a good sign."

"Could I talk to her?"

"Yes, you can, but even if she hears you; she can't answer you."

"Some people think when someone gets out of surgery they hear everything."

"Everybody has their own opinion about that."

"Irene," Kate called out to Irene, and then she put her hand over her mouth to suppress the sound of her cry. Charles had his arm over her shoulder. He could feel her whole body trembling. He held her tight. His own eyes were misty; he felt like screaming; only he didn't <u>dare</u>; He had to be strong for Kate. That's what he kept saying to himself. Kate turned around and walked back outside; "I can't see her like that, Charles. My baby. My baby. Is she going to make it, Charles?"

"She is, Kate; our prayers are going to give her the strength she needs."

Brent came outside to talk to them. "Kate, I think she can hear you. Compose yourself and go back in again. Talk to her and tell her she needs to open her eyes, tell her we're out here organizing her wedding and she needs to be in the middle of it." Kate kissed Brent and told him, "thank you."

Kate didn't know how long she had been watching Irene and every time she moved she hoped for her to speak; but she didn't. Hours went by and there was no change, Kate walked outside to take a breather, she was about to collapse herself when a voice surprised her.

"Mrs. Hamilton," when she turned around, she saw Carlos and Christina.

She fell into Christina's arms sobbing, "Christina, she doesn't want to wake up." She whispered.

"She will, Mrs. Hamilton, she will," Christina told her.

Sarah and Laura came to greet Christina and Carlos, "Are you both all right?"

"Yes, we are."

Let's get out to talk, then we can come back in."

"Could we go in and talk to Irene?"

"I'm sure it will be all right. You go in; I'll be in, in a little while."

Carlos and Christina went in to see Irene and found Brent by her side.

"Brent, how is she?" Brent, with disoriented eyes, said, "I don't know. I honestly don't know. We don't even know who to call for a second opinion. Between Darrell and I; we have the knowledge needed and more for this type of surgery."

"Did something go wrong, Brent?"

"Darrell did the surgery, but I was there, we both have done this surgery more times than we can count, It is not a complicated surgery; but it **was** in Irene's case."

You wouldn't have believed how damaged her valve was; in time, the other valve is going to have to be changed as well, but it was impossible to do it now."

"How did you find out she had a problem?" Carlos asked Brent.

Brent told him what had happened since she went home from the hospital. Carlos kept shaking his head in disbelief.

Darrell walked into the ICU room to check Irene. He checked all the monitors, checked her blood pressure again and again. Then he said. "Brent, buddy,". . .

Brent interrupted him. "I know Darrell, I know." He looked at Christina and said, "Irene's blood pressure is stronger." Irene is recovering," Brent caressed her face with both hands and cried. "I'm on my way to talk to the family." Brent stood up and left.

They all went to him for news. "Mr. and Mrs. Hamilton, Irene is coming out; she opened her eyes." He sat on the first chair he found and cried uncontrollably. Then he spoke: "I'm very sorry, that is not how I'm supposed to behave. But you know I don't see Irene as my patient; I see her as my wife."

Charles told him. "I'm glad I saw how you feel about my daughter, son."

Christina and Carlos looked at each other. Brent answered their question.

"We tried to get married this morning; Irene collapsed before Father Gabriel could finish the ceremony." Brent said. "What we can do now is: we take turns talking to Irene, no displays such as mine; when we are with her. Talk to her about school, work, about her wedding and yours, Sarah. Any arrangements you and Darrell have done, tell her, absolutely everything you can think of that is pleasant."

After an hour, Charles went into the ICU room where Irene had been placed. Kate was holding Irene's hand, and she was talking to her with so much love. "Charles," Kate said. "she moves her fingers, her eyelids move; like as she is trying to open them. Tell Brent to come in, I think it's his turn."

"Brent, come and check on Irene."

"Is there something new happening?"

"Kate thinks she is trying to open her eyes and she is moving her fingers."

Brent checked her heart. "Still the same Kate, it does sound a bit stronger; I don't want to give you false hope. We'll keep doing what we're doing now; no operation could do more than what this one already has."

"Okay Brent, I thought she was coming out of it."

"Of course, any little change we notice, we have to check it, Kate. Every time we see something; you have to tell someone to check her out."

Charles walked Kate outside of Irene's room. Brent stayed with Irene.

Sarah and Darrell were talking. "Tyke, I'm so scared for Irene; I was afraid for Papa when he had his surgery. But Irene. She is so young; she was going to get married."

"Sarah, she is not dead. Be positive. Talk to her when it is your turn to go in, write down stuff you have been wanting to tell her but haven't; pour your thoughts into her. We believe people in a trance can hear. Believe it!" Darrell held her. Sarah closed her eyes and stayed in his arms.

Everyone walked in different directions, not wanting to talk to anyone else.

Clare arrived at the hospital looking for Kate. When she found her, she wanted to know the latest news.

"All we can do is pray, Clare; we're taking turns going in and talking to Irene."

"Kate, do you remember the time she got so sick? One of the doctors who saw her said he thought it was rheumatic fever; but no one else agreed with him; so it was dismissed. Have you told Brent?"

"I'll talk to Brent. What are you going to tell Irene?"

"I thought I'll remind her she has to come back to make biscuits for Brent."

"That was so funny," Kate said with a sad smile. "Well, do you want to go in now?"

Kate went to Christina and Carlos, "Why don't you go to the house and lay down, Carlos?" You're just coming out from a very serious surgery you need your rest."

"You forget I have my own apartment, Mrs. Hamilton.

"All you have is an apartment, Carlos; go to my home; whenever you're hungry, You can tell somebody you want to eat. I'm offering you my home, so you won't make Christina go shopping and cook. Now, will you please go to my house?"

"Mrs. Hamilton, you're a hard person to say 'no' to, we'll be delighted to go."

Christina leaned down to Carlos, "Sweetheart, can I call someone to bring you a wheelchair?"

"No, I'm fine."

"Carlos Lopez, you're not your own Doctor, do you want me to have to call Brent?" He smiled and sat in the first wheelchair he found."

Kate went looking for Brent; and when she found him, she told him what Clare had reminded her about Irene possibly having had rheumatic fever.

"Thank you Kate, I don't think we can do anything else at this time, but maybe it will give us other ways to fight this thing that has gotten hold of Irene."

Brent went into Irene's room. "How is my favorite patient?"

"Your favorite patient is going to walk out of here if you don't send me home. Brent, you know that this hospital can't give me better care than I can receive at home; don't you?"

"You got me there, baby, but first you need to get a series of tests to make sure everything is okay.

"Start the parade," Irene told Brent.

Sarah was very pensive at the office when Darrell saw her that morning. "What is this? Don't you have a smile for me?" Darrell asked.

Sarah looked down. "You know, you were telling me once that you wished we could get married when Brent and Irene did. And now, they can't get married when they had planned. Isn't that ironic?"

"Yeah, maybe we can still make it a double wedding when Irene is able to get married. It's going to take a while for her to be able to, Sarah. Maybe we can talk to your parents, they'll be so happy Irene is out of the hospital. They have to say yes to us."

"You crazy thing, I love you even if you're crazy," Sarah told him laughing.

"That sounds like music to my ears, Sarah; I was going crazy thinking you were so out of reach for me."

"Why? Just because I'm a few years younger than you are?"

"Baby, when you were born, I was already in high school; with girlfriends and everything."

"Well, first of all, you are now, prohibited to call me <u>baby</u>. I'm only the woman you're in love with."

In the meantime at the office, Lourdes walked in, purse in hand. "Will it be all right if I left?"

"It would have been better if you had left without saying a word." Darrell answered her smiling.

"I wanted to ask you if I could go to the hospital."

"I would advise you to call the hospital first. Irene was trying to talk Brent into letting her go home. Let us know where she is Lourdes; we don't want to waste a trip to the hospital."

When Lourdes came back, she told Darrell, "You're right, she is home."

"We'll see you there Lourdes."

"Do you think it's all right for me to go?"

"You know she'll love to see you, Lourdes. Will Maureen go with you?"

"She has gone home already."

Sarah told Darrell. "I wish I could think about what I could bring Irene; I know she has enough flowers."

"Maybe something new to wear."

"She'll stay home now, maybe something to do."

"Yeah, that's a good idea."

"Not a cookbook."

"She'll probably get mad at you and throw it at your head."

.

"I remember Irene taking painting classes once; I think I'll bring her the whole thing. From oil paints to brushes, easel, and a couple of smocks to paint in so she won't get her good clothes dirty."

"Sarah, that is from the mind of a genius I know she'll love it."

"Do you really think so?"

"Sure I do. Now, where can we go for that big order?"

"I know where we can go, come' on. Let's meet at the World's Department store."

Sarah told Darrell how to get there. "I have been there lots of times."

"Well, I didn't know; you could have saved me the trouble to tell you how to get there," She said with a wink in her eye.

As they started walking through the store, several people came over to greet Sarah. Some of them kissed her on the cheek and hugged her.

"Boy, I didn't know how popular you were."

"Well, most of them have known me since I was little."

"And that hasn't been too long ago."

"We said we wouldn't talk about that any more. Remember?"

Then Bonny saw her, "Sarah! What a happy occasion! I don't know how long it has been since I saw you last, you were this tall." She extended her hand to a much smaller size.

"Bonny! I'm going to be so mad at you. Bonny meet my fiancé, Darrell, who is not too happy with you at this time."

"Oh. I'm sorry, Sir, I have known Sarah since always. I'm very happy to meet you."

"Likewise; I guess." He said laughing.

"Why do they all know you so much, Sarah?"

"Well, the store belongs to my Dad and we kids always came and spent time over here; lots of the workers kept their jobs here. There it is where I think, we can find what we're looking for." Sarah told Darrell.

Darrell had stopped on his heels before he continued following her amused at the way she was explaining owning such a large department store.

"Come on, you have to help me choose the right stuff for Irene. And don't let me forget to get a couple of smocks to go over her dresses."

"I'll help you here, but you can forget me going to the women's department."

"Chicken," She said.

Darrell and Sarah arrived at her house, both of them carrying lots of packages. "My God, Sarah; we were all wondering where you were."

"Well, wonder no more. Oh Irene, I do hope you like this. Darrell and I got to thinking you're going to have lots of free time on your hands and you are going to need a good hobby." Pulling the wrapping from the easel, she said. "How about painting?"

"Oh Sarah, baby." She opened her arms and Sarah went into them.

"I haven't even thought about it, but yes! Absolutely! This is the answer to use my time, I'll paint everybody." Everybody had a good laugh. "I'll start in the garden; I'll paint the roses first; while I'll get used to painting again.

Brent walked to Sarah and told her: "That was a very good thing, Sarah." Then he went to Irene, "This is the best therapy for you, darling. We might have to open a shop to sell your paintings."

"I remember she used to be very good at it. I don't really know why she stopped painting," Kate said thinking about it.

Irene said, "Maybe because I wasn't getting very good grades in art."

"Where is that teacher?" Brent said showing his fist.

Clare walked in and announced dinner was served.

"Irene." Sarah said. "I brought you a couple of smocks to put over your dresses so you won't get paint on your good clothes."

"How thoughtful little sister,"

Sarah cleared her throat. "We no longer call each other *that word.*"

"Oh, Oh, I'm sorry Darrell; will you forgive me this time?"

"Only because it's you. By the way, did Lourdes ever come? She said she was coming over to visit with you. She is the reason we knew you were at home after she called the hospital."

"She did come, and we visited, but that's how long you were gone."

"You know; my head is going around trying to get an idea what to paint first," Irene said.

Brent told her, "Flowers is a good idea, maybe the dog will be a good subject. My mother used to paint as a hobby. She would start something, she might get tired of painting that subject and leave it for a while and start a different project; later on, she'd go back to one of her paintings from earlier time." Brent said.

Clare said as she walked by, "That's a good idea Brent, neither the dog nor the flowers are able to complaint of the results of Irene's paintings." She said laughing.

"I'll get you yet, Clare."

"That's a very good idea Brent, thank you." Clare, who had been around serving said, "You can come to the kitchen and paint me. Maybe you can take a few pointers from me."

"I had enough of your ideas, Clare."

"Do you want to drink your coffee here or in the living room?" Clare asked.

"I think here, Clare, thank you," Kate answered her. "Who wants cake?"

"Everybody!"

"Irene, it will be a good thing for you to paint, but when you decide to move, wherever you want to go, do not carry anything, Irene, not one thing heavier than your paint brush. Is that understood?" Brent said.

Irene, put her hand on her forehead as mocking a military salute.
"Yes, Sir," she said.
"I'm not kidding Irene, we are not through; we're still going to have to do more surgery."
Her expression changed to a painful look.
"Brent." she said. "I didn't know, when did you decide that?"
"I'm sorry, baby, I told you, and maybe you blocked that out of your mind, but everybody does that, we're going to wait until you're fully recovered from this surgery, then we have to go in again. There is still more repair to be made, Irene."
Irene looked at her parents, as if they could provide her with an answer. "The only answer is to repair it, sweetheart. Darrell and I think you must have had symptoms a number of times, and you dismissed them because you couldn't have imagined having heart problems. The next time, you'll have a warning. The first time you feel something you're not supposed to feel, you let us know. Or we'll schedule the surgery, that's a better plan."

"Right now, Sarah came up with the best prescription for your ailment. Painting is going to be at the top of our schedule, besides eating."
"Has anyone talked to Christina or Carlos?" Brent asked. "I thought they were going to be here longer."
Kate said. "Christina called and said Carlos didn't feel like going out so they decided to stay in his apartment." Darrell and Brent exchanged looks.
"What time is it?"
"It's only after eight o'clock." Charles said.

"I think we're going to pay them a visit. May I have their home number?"
"Do you think something could be wrong?"

"Maybe nothing, but he is still my patient."

"Carlos, how are you buddy? Listen; are you ready for bed? Darrell and I would like to come over, is that okay by you?"

"Listen I hate to eat and run, but we would like to check on Carlos," Brent said.

Charles asked him. "Would you give us a call after you leave them, please?"

"Of course." They said goodbye and kissed their fiancés.

"I'm so proud they care so much for their patients. Even if Carlos is also a friend, I hope he is all right, but he made that trip earlier than he was supposed to leave the hospital." Charles said.

Sarah went to Irene and told her, "How about if we open these packages while we wait for the guys to call, okay?"

"You read my mind, kiddo." So Sarah started to open packages; and the others started to get closer to see everything.

"You thought of everything Sarah, thank you."

"Well, I can't take all the credit, Darrell helped me a lot. The only thing he refused to do was to go inside the women's department." Sarah said laughing.

"I don't blame him." Charles quipped.

Chapter Fifteen

"Hello strangers," Christina greeted Brent and Darrell. Brent whispered in Christina's ear. "How is Carlos, Christina?"

"Tired, he is always tired, Brent," she said with a gloomy face. He nodded to her.

"Carlos, how about if you come by the hospital tomorrow, I'm going to send a series of tests for you to take."

"I'm all right, Brent."

"I'll be happy to confirm it, Carlos. When you send an order to a patient; what do you expect from them? I'm not talking to you as your friend, but as your Doctor."

"Christina, can you drive yet?" Brent asked.

"I guess I could, but I still don't remember where I am Brent, I'm sorry, but we can take a taxi."

"Kate would skin me alive if I don't let her know you need transportation."

"Darrell, how is your relationship with Sarah? You know that was a surprise for me! I didn't know anything about it until I came back;

there are so many things that happened to me that, if I knew it before, I don't remember. But I'm very happy for both of you."

"I was the first one to be surprised; I never imagined Sarah would ever love me. I'm so much older than her years, but it so happens; her parents have the same difference in their ages. And that helped me a lot. I'm not ashamed to tell you I fell in love with her and she didn't know it for a long time."

"Yeah, he didn't even know how old she was, until I told him and then. He still didn't believe me. I told him he would be arrested if he pursue her."

Carlos started to laugh, a very strong laugh. At first it was fine but suddenly; he turned very pale and fell onto the floor. "Call an ambulance." Brent told Darrell.

"And call Charles and let them know. Get someone to go to the hospital; Christina can come to the hospital with us. Maybe Clare can go to the hospital and stay with Christina."

By that time, the ambulance had arrived. Brent listened to his heart, "Darrell, we're going in, I'm sure. Call the hospital and tell them that. I'm riding in the ambulance." They placed Carlos on the stretcher and wheeled him out.

"Christina, he'll be all right; try not to be so worried, I'll see you at the hospital."

She arrived at the hospital. And what she saw made her cry without limits, she was so moved that Charles, Kate, Sarah and Laura were there. They told her, "We couldn't let Irene come, Clare stayed with her, but she sent her love."

Brent and Darrell had been in surgery with Carlos for over one hour before they came back to talk to them. "Christina," Brent said holding her hands. "We repaired the damage; there was a leak that was too small to see before, but it's well sealed now, he is not in danger of any kind and he'll recover completely."

"Can I go in to see him Brent?"

"Of course; but no tears."

Christina turned around to Kate and the others. "Thank you for staying with me, I couldn't have lived through another nightmare without you." She kissed Kate and Charles and the girls, "Tell Irene I love her. Please, go home I'll call you tomorrow. I don't think I'll come back out tonight."

"Christina, someone can help you stay with Carlos, you can't stay here by yourself. You're not alone, Christina. Give me Mrs. Lopez phone number; she needs to be notified that Carlos had surgery again."

"Oh my God, I'm so used to being alone I've forgotten there is someone to notify. Here Mrs. Hamilton, here is their number. I'm sorry."

Kate and family watched Christina leave. "Poor Christina, I don't know when happiness is going to catch up with her."

Irene was waiting for them in the living room with Clare at her side.

"Mama, how is Carlos?"

"Good grief, Irene! What are you doing still up?"

"Mama, I couldn't go to sleep with Christina maybe losing her husband."

"He is going to be fine, baby. There was a leak where the bullet had been lodged; probably because they worked in such a rush; the leak was very small, they just didn't see it. Go to bed Irene, don't get too tired yourself."

"Thank you, Clare, for staying here with me."

"Any time, baby."

Next thing they knew, the phone rang, it was Darrell for Sarah. "Baby," he said to her, "when you get to the office in the morning cancel all the morning appointments, I hope you can stop everybody before they leave for the office."

"Don't worry Tyke I'll get ready to go to work earlier and call them early enough; I'll probably stop them all. I'll tell them you had to cancel because you're taking care of your patients. That is the truth."

"I love you, Sarah."

"I love you, too."

"Lourdes, I'm sorry I had to call you so late tonight."

"Don't worry, what happened Sarah, is Irene all right?"

"Yes, but there was an emergency with Carlos. Both doctors had to do surgery on Carlos. We need to close the office in the morning. If you could help me cancel the appointments, maybe Maureen could come, as well."

"We'll be there Sarah. See you in the morning."

It was just getting daylight when Sarah appeared in the kitchen. Clare said. "Sarah, you're about to give me a heart attack. What are you doing up so early in the morning?"

"I want to drink some orange juice, I guess, and go to work."

"Why so early, baby?"

"Because Brent and Darrell were up most of the night with Carlos. Don't you remember?"

"I wasn't there; I don't know who was there."

"Anyway, I have to call and cancel the appointments we had made for this morning. Lourdes and Maureen are going to help me," said Sarah.

"How many phones do you have?"

"Everybody has a phone."

"Okay, how many lines?"

"I don't know."

"Okay, not everybody can talk if you don't have but one line, you know."

"I know there is more than one line because we can put them on hold."

"Okay. You have a good day, baby."

"And don't call me baby!"

Kate was coming into the kitchen. "Clare, what did you do to my baby?"

"I called her baby. But she didn't hear you or she would have been mad at you too."

"Well, it was too early for her to be up. But Darrell asked her to call the patients and these days Darrell is king."

"I pray to the Lord he stays that way."

"And I pray she stays queen, I know how difficult that can be."

"Amen."

"I need to check on Irene before she wakes up. I'll bring her coffee." Kate went in very quietly.

"I'm up, Mama. Have you heard from anyone?"

"No, I told Sarah to call with any news."

"Sarah? Isn't she still in bed?"

"No, Darrell asked her last night to cancel this morning's appointments."

"And she got up?"

"Nobody had to wake her up either."

"I'm impressed!"

"Let's not make fun of her tonight when she comes home, okay?"

"Mama, it's so good."

"I wouldn't let anyone pester you about the biscuits."

"You win."

"Irene, I'm going to get ready and go to the hospital to see about Christina."

"I wish I could go, Mama."

"She wouldn't want you to go, Irene. But I'll try to send her your way. I'll try to stay with Carlos today, but I imagine all of his family is there by now."

"Let me call, maybe they'll bring the children over here so Christina will be more at ease."

"This is good coffee, Clare. I'm going to get ready and go downstairs; maybe I can start with my painting career."

"I'll help you dress, baby."

"Clare, I'm not an invalid."

"No Irene, you just don't need to overexert yourself. How about if you tell me what you want to wear and I bring it to the bed,"

Clare didn't go downstairs until Irene was with her. "Now you sit down here and I'll bring you coffee and you tell me what you want to eat."

"Clare! Are you going to treat me like that the whole time?"

"Irene, when you told Brent you wanted to come home, did you think we weren't going to baby you?"

"Boy, you and Mama are winning all my points."

"Christina," Irene got up and went to embrace Christina. "How is Carlos?"

"He is really doing fine; it was a blessing Brent and Darrell came in the nick of time. He started to laugh so hard when Darrell began to tell us about being so crazy about Sarah; he said he was crazy about her and she didn't even know he existed. Carlos started to laugh and before we knew, he was on the floor. What made them come over so late?"

Irene explained to Christina. "Brent asked if anyone had heard from either one of you. Someone said you had called and said Carlos was very tired. They immediately got up and left. They didn't like the symptoms."

"Well, they were right."

"How about if we eat breakfast together and then you get yourself a nap? Then I'll go paint."

"Are you painting now?"

"Sarah and Darrell got me all I need to paint with, and what to do with my time, and I love it."

"By the way, how about Sarah and Darrell? They look great together." Christina said.

"It hasn't been easy for me to see them together because he is so much older than she is. He and Brent are the same age, and I'm six years older that Sarah."

"Irene, fifteen years is nothing if you really love each other and I can tell they do."

"I know fifteen years is nothing when you're older but she is so young,"

"Changing the subject, have Mr. and Mrs. Lopez arrived yet?"

"No, but I spoke with Angelita; they're bringing the children."

"I called her and asked her to bring the children over here."

"Is she bringing the children over here before she goes to the hospital?"

"Yes, she said they're coming over here first."

"Well, Christina, don't wait for her, we'll be down here somewhere. She'll understand you need to rest."

"Yes, I can hardly stay awake now."

"I'll see you later. Clare, thank you, it was a good breakfast."

Kate asked Carlos. "How are you feeling?"

"I'm okay Mrs. Hamilton, Where is Christina?"

"She stayed with you all night Carlos. I sent her home when I got here. Your parents are on their way. You rest, everything seems to be okay." Carlos nodded his head and closed his eyes.

Darrell walked in and asked Carlos. "How are you, buddy? Sore anywhere?"

"I'm not going to forget you made me laugh last night and made me collapse."

"If it hasn't been because of me; you'd still be walking around with a hole in your heart."

Kate had to leave the room to laugh; it was so funny to see grown men picking on each other like little kids. When Kate came back, she asked Darrell, "Where is Brent?"

"He went to the office, we flipped coins and I lost." He said smiling. "No, I'm on my way there now, we had to see patients and we had a full house at the office. We both had to step on it. Mrs. Hamilton, would you mind waiting outside?"

"I'm sorry I was just visiting." Kate said leaving the room.

"Oh, is not me, it's Carlos; he is shy," He said laughing at Carlos.

When Kate walked outside of Carlos' room, his parents were there. "Hello, Angelita, Mr. Lopez, how are you?"

"That depends on how my son is."

"Well, I think I can tell you he feels fine. I was with him a few minutes ago and I had to leave because Darrell was about to examine him. But they were teasing each other; he was feeling good."

"We didn't get any details, Mrs. Hamilton, what happened that Carlos had to have another surgery?"

"I'll tell you what I know, Mr. Lopez. Brent asked if anyone had heard from Carlos and Christina, and we had, but when we asked Christina how Carlos was, she said he had been very tired. Darrell was there with Brent. They just looked at each other and got up from the table and said they had to go see Carlos. Next thing we knew, they called that they were on their way to the hospital. We all came to be with Christina."

"I wish we would have been able to come last night, but because of our health we didn't want to add that to the problem."

"That was very wise."

"I talked Charles into staying with Irene to keep him from coming with me for the same reason. Charles had open heart surgery not too long ago. That is how we met Brent."

"There is Darrell now," Kate said.

"Dr. Moore, I heard what happened last night. My wife and I want to thank you and Dr. Miller about being so prompt with Carlos," Cristobal told Darrell. "Can you tell me what the problem was?"

"Of course, Mr. Lopez, it was a very small leak. Because of the emergency of the first surgery, it was a wonder it was only one leak in the whole area. This time, Brent had more time to check everything, last time; there was no time."

"Could my wife and I go in now Dr. Moore?" Cristobal asked.

"Certainly, go ahead."

"Mrs. Hamilton would you like to come in with us?"

"No, you enjoy your visit, I already visited with Carlos. Did you bring the children?"

"Yes, our driver took them to your home, we trust him with our lives."

"Why don't you plan to eat dinner with us?"

"We'll see how our day goes. Is that all right?"

Kate rushed home. When she arrived, she found everyone out in the garden with Irene and the children playing. "This is a beautiful scene, but you don't need to exert yourself, sweetheart. Sit down and paint them, they'd love that."

"Mama I'm doing fine, truly I am."

"I hope so, but we need to take care of you so they don't have to perform the next surgery in a rush."

"You take the fun out of playing with the children."

"Only because I love you."

She leaned close to Charles and kissed him. "Am I going to get scolded?"

"No, darling."

"Listen, I invited Cristobal and Angelita Lopez to come for dinner, but they're not sure they're going to be able to come."

"Well, tell Clare that. Maybe we won't have to eat the same food for a week."

Clare came to the garden to talk to them. "Kate," she said."Mrs. Lopez is on the phone for you."

"I'm coming, Clare."

"I guess that it's a 'no'."

"Kate, how are you?" Angelita greeted Kate. "Listen, Cristobal and I were talking and we need to do some shopping badly, because we come to the city very seldom. So I think that's what we'll do today, but we are staying over here for a few days. So if it's convenient for you we'll come another day."

"Of course! You let me know which day and we'll get ready. We'll be happy to have you eat with us. Listen, Angelita, why don't you and Cristobal stay with us? You know we can accommodate you comfortably."

"No, I thank you for your invitation, but we have so many things we'd like to do, it's easier to be in the city anyway."

"All right then, I'll expect to hear from you."

"Christina, that was more like a nap. You lost many more hours of sleep last night," Kate told her.

"I heard the children laughing and I had to get up to take a shower and come to play with them myself. I have lost so much time with them you know."

"I know, dear."

Irene had a camera with her and had taken several pictures of everybody, her father and mother, the dog. Kate saw her and said to her. "Irene, I thought you were going to paint us not take pictures of us," she said laughing.

"Very funny, who is going to pose for hours at the time for me?"

"You win, but you better take a photo of Clare, she has already hinted she wonders if you're going to paint her too."

"I was thinking I better start with flowers and the dog, like Clare said, because they don't complain."

"I've known all along you're very smart."

"I'm hungry," Irene said. "I wonder if lunch is about to be ready, what time is it any way?"

"I guess it's time to eat because here is Brent." He kissed her and sat on the grass next to her. "I couldn't take you to lunch so I thought I'd 'bum' lunch from you."

"Do you know if Darrell and Sarah are coming over here for lunch?"

"I escaped, no one saw me leave," He said smiling.

Christina asked Brent. "When do you think Carlos is going to be able to go home?"

"If he keeps doing as well as he responded to everything so far, maybe he can come home in a couple of days. Not for working, you know. Everybody is helping out with his office and he has a full schedule for surgeries. I'm going to advise him to find himself a partner; like I did with Darrell."

"Yes, that would be great, Brent."

Clare came to announce lunch. "Irene, come on, let's go together." Brent held her hand. Kate had the camera and took their photo. "Let's take another one in case that one doesn't turn out good," Kate took many more photos.

Christina asked Brent. "Do you think I could take the children to see Carlos? He'll love that."

"Sure, but if you want to stay any time with Carlos; the children couldn't stay that long."

"I thought I'd ask Lorenzo to take us and wait for the children, maybe Cindy could come with me."

"That's a great idea."

Chapter Sixteen

Christina went quietly into Carlos's room. Angelita smiled at her.

"How are you dear?" Angelita asked.

"I'm doing fine. Sometimes I still have problems with my memory, there are people I'm supposed to know and I don't remember them; it bothers me a lot. Like they have been telling me about Mr. Luis Moran. He was marvelous with me throughout the ordeal with Mike; and in fact, he saved my life several times. And I can't remember him."

"Well, he did all that, but he still was not a close person to you, that may be the difference in your mind."

"I hope you're right. He found my parents in Australia. They're on their way here now, as we speak. I hope I can remember them."

"Christina, even if you hadn't had the problem with your memory, please take into consideration that you haven't seen them in many years. They won't look the same; you'll remember their younger years. They also will have the same problem with you, darling."

"Thank you, Angelita, you're right."

"Do you know how long it is going to take for Carlos to go back to work?"

"I only asked when Carlos could go home. He said, if he keeps up the way he has been feeling it might be two or three days. But I didn't ask about work. I understand every doctor in the hospital is helping with his office patients and with his surgeries. Isn't that great?"

"I had no idea they were doing that. Yes, I think it's marvelous." Carlos said,

"Neither did I. I have to think about how to thank everyone for that."

"We didn't know you woke up son; how are you feeling?"

"Pretty good Mama. I should be out of here pretty soon. Earlier, I had a good laugh with Darrell; I blamed him for putting me in the hospital because he made me laugh so hard and that's when I collapsed. And he told me I ought to thank him because he is the reason I'm not running around with a hole in my heart."

Mr. and Mrs. Lopez laughed at the idea of them teasing each other like that; with a problem as serious as that was. "But you have to recognize that Darrell is a very funny person with a marvelous sense of humor," Carlos said.

"Carlos, I was going to bring the children and then I thought I should wait another day to give you time to be stronger."

"I want to see them so bad, but maybe we should wait so I'll be more able to play and talk with them."

"Christina, did you know that my office has been kept open and my surgeries done for me by the other doctors?" asked Carlos.

"No baby, I guess I should have, but I don't think I've ever been told. I know a nurse and someone else from your office has been by asking about you."

"Christina, I don't want to make the call from my room, with so many people coming in, if you would, please call my office and talk to Kelly. Let her know of my progress and ask her if she needs anything to come here and I could sign papers or something like that. I guess she is capable to handle the office without me, but I know I'm always signing papers. Never the less, I would like to know what's going on at the office."

"Well, I guess our patient is getting better," Mrs. Lopez said.

"Mrs. Lopez, I'm going to make that call Carlos wants me to make to his office, did you say her name is Kelly?"

"Yes, sweetheart."

"I won't be long." Christina came back to Carlos's room. "Carlos, I hate to have to ask you, but I don't remember how to look for a phone number, or where do I go to find a phone? I'm so sorry." She said with teary eyes.

"No, I'm sorry I didn't think. Mama, go with Christina, I'll be all right. After all; I'm in the hospital. I'm sorry, but Brent doesn't want me to be making business calls yet."

"Christina, let's stop at this desk and let them know we're both leaving. I hate to admit it, but I'm kind of superstitious."

"Of course, I'm a little superstitious myself. Where are we going?"

"We're going to the nurses' station to let them know about Carlos being by himself. Good morning, could you look in on Dr. Lopez' room 412 for a while? He is going to be alone and had surgery last night. And please don't let him know we told you about it. Can you direct us to a public phone?"

"Angelita, I do hope you know Carlos' office number, I don't. I'm such a mess, I'm so sorry I don't seem to know anything anymore."

"Perhaps we're expecting too much from you dear. Let me look in the directory, let me check. . . . here it is."

"Angelita, what is the name of his clinic?"

"Internal Medicine. Try not to let it worry you dear, it will all come back in time. You'll see."

Christina called Kelly, she talked to her for a long time and then, they went back to see Carlos.

"Well, I was thinking you had left me here on my lonesome. Where did you go anyway?"

"Since the wave of cell phones, companies are taking phones out of public places, Dad and I don't leave home to warrant one for us."

"Christina, what did Kelly say?"

"You have been gone for so long, but because you were prepared to go on our honeymoon; you did leave many blank checks signed, she has managed so far, paying everything that needed to be paid. She'll be here this afternoon to talk to you.

"Kelly, how nice it is seeing you again," Carlos greeted his secretary.

"I'm the one that for a while didn't think I would see you again."

"Oh, that? That was nothing." He told her.

"I'm not going to argue with you."

"Kelly, have you met my wife?"

"No, I never had the pleasure."

"Darling, this is Kelly; this is Christina, the love of my life. And this is my mother. The other love of my life." Carlos said.

"It's very nice meeting you, Kelly."

"Christina, since Kelly is here to visit with Carlos, why don't you and I go to the Cafeteria and eat dinner. I don't think either one of us have eaten since breakfast."

"I'll wait for you ladies," Kelly said.

"Angelita, do you like me?" Christina asked Angelita in a quick turn of thought. Angelita looked at Christina. "Dear, I hope I haven't done anything that makes you think I don't. In fact, the fact you killed for Carlos is the ultimate gift of love, as far as I'm concerned. But tell me, what made you say that? I'd like to know what you were thinking."

"When Kelly came, I thought you wished Carlos would have married her. She is so pretty and I'm not pretty at all."

"Christina, Kelly is married; she has been married for a long time. I haven't met her before, but I knew of her. Carlos would say something every once in a while; she and her family went on vacation or something like that. And about you not being pretty: I can tell you, you're magnificent looking! The day you got married, no one could see anyone else but you; you are a looker, Christina."

Christina dropped her head and began to cry. "I'm so sorry, that was so petty for me to say. I was just so jealous of her. She looks so good, and Carlos wanted her to stay with him; not me, Angelita." Angelita walked to her and hugged her.

"You are whom he loves Christina, he never brought a girl to us, I'm sure he had girlfriends before you came along his path. But you, my dear, you had his number from the beginning."

"Don't tell Carlos I was so ungrateful to you, please."

"This stays between you and me, how about that?" Angelita told Christina.

"I love you, Angelita." Cristina told her mother-in-law.

"And I love you too, Christina. One thing, do you remember why Kelly came to the hospital? Do you remember calling her yourself to speak to Carlos?"

"Like I said, I'm just crazy." Christina said.

"Here is the cafeteria now; I hope they're bringing Carlos his dinner."

"Angelita, could we bring our dinner and eat with Carlos?"

"That is a great idea, Christina." Angelita didn't put anything on her tray and Christina asked her.

"Angelita, I thought you said you were hungry, what happened?"

"You inspired me, Christina; I'm going to the hotel and eat dinner with my own man."

When Christina arrived at Carlos' room they were bringing his own tray.

"Oh, great honey, we can eat together." Christina said.

"Where is my Mother?" Carlos asked.

"She went to eat dinner with your father. Anyway, tell me what Kelly had to say?"

"Well, there is a Doctor who Dr. Walters recommended, a very good friend of mine," Carlos said. "Anyway, he came to look up our town and maybe set his office up here; he talked to several of the doctors to get information and ran into my practice. He has been taking care of my patients and is waiting to talk to me about whether I want an associate. What do you think, Mrs. Lopez?"

"Do you know that Brent told me he was going to suggest to you to try to get someone to join you in your practice? As he and Darrell are in one practice together."

"I can see how useful that can be; I would like to see what kind of experience this doctor has and everything about him. Kelly said she thought he had to go to the hospital; but I'm so glad my patients didn't feel neglected."

"Good afternoon," Someone said by the door. It was a tall man with a nice smile standing at the door.

"Hello," Carlos said. "Come in, how can I help you?"

"My name is Keith Simon, at your service. We have been a kind of partners for the last several weeks."

"Oh, you are my savior for the last few weeks. I don't know how to thank you. I had everything arranged for one week of honeymoon, but what happened couldn't have been anticipated. Listen, what is your specialty?"

"Internal Medicine, like yourself. And I love it here! If you accept me joining your practice, Dr. Walters and I have been good friends all of our lives, he tells me he knows you quite well. We can see a CPA or whoever you choose, and give me a price to be a partner."

"I like everything about it. Tell Kelly to call me in the morning, so we can make arrangements. This was such a surprise, I have been told all my friends were pitching in trying to take care of my patients."

"Yes, they were, but when I came over; I scouted around to set up an office here and Dr. Walters, filled me in about your practice. He brought in several of your friends for consultation before I was turned in your office. I want you to know my credentials were well checked by everyone, you have many good friends."

"I'm just surprised Brent and Darrell don't know anything about it. They haven't mentioned it at all."

"If you're talking about Drs. Miller and Moore; they were with you. No one could get a return call from them because they were 100% with you. I heard one of them stayed with you the whole time or you wouldn't have made it."

"I have so much to be grateful for," Carlos said. "Oh, excuse me, meet my wife, Christina Lopez. I'm sorry; I just got involved and neglected my manners."

"I'll forgive you only because I've forgotten myself," Christina told Carlos smiling.

"It's a pleasure, Mrs. Lopez."

"Do you have a family Dr. Simon?" Christina asked him.

"Yes, I've been married for at least twenty years and have two teenage terrors." He said laughing.

Brent and Irene walked in. "Irene, how are you?" Christina ran to embrace Irene. "I've been thinking about you, I've been trying to call you but it's so hard to find a phone in the ICU area since the wave of cell phone invaded us."

"Irene, how about if you and Christina get yourselves a cell phone? Oh, excuse me; meet Dr. Simon who will probably be my new partner."

"Brent Miller, it's nice meeting you. I'm glad to hear Carlos is going to have an associate in his practice. We learned the hard way you can't do it alone." Brent said. "What made you decide to settle in Los Caminos?

"It didn't matter to me if it was Los Caminos, although I like the city. We were living in Chicago and my wife is from California and she threatened me to leave me if I didn't move to California. So here we are. Are you married already? Or you are about to?" Dr. Simon asked Brent.

Irene looked at Brent, waiting to see how he was going to answer. "We were about to get married, but for medical reasons we had to postpone the date."

Dr. Simon apologized to them. "I'm so sorry I let myself ask what I thought was a casual question."

"There was no way for you to know, don't give it another thought." Brent said. Irene walked out the door and Christina followed her.

"Dr. Miller I don't know what to say to express my regret about what I said."

"But that's it; you don't even know what you said. Please don't worry. Carlos, buddy. I have to leave; I'll come back sometime tomorrow." Brent ran outside looking frantically for Irene. He found her with Christina. He slowed down so she wouldn't see how distressed he was. "Irene, are you all right?" Brent asked her.

"Yes, darling, I'm so sorry. I'm going back and apologize to Dr. Simon."

"It is not necessary darling. Some other time."

"Brent, I think I'd rather do it now when it happened than some other time. Like you said. Let's go back." And she walked back between Brent and Christina.

They walked like that into Carlos' room. "Miss Hamilton, Dr. Simon started. . ."

"Please, you don't owe me an apology, I owe you one. But you see, this is the first time I got out of the house and I didn't prepare myself..." She obviously was having trouble saying anything.

"Irene, would you please let me explain? Dr. Simon, in a few words: We were ready to get married, after Carlos and Christina's wedding and everything that happened there. Irene stayed in the hospital for about three weeks, taking care of everybody, including me." He said, while he briefly kissed her. "She drove herself to Los Caminos and went to take a bath; she was found hours later still in the tub freezing. Her father told me about it, and against her better judgment, I checked her out and we found she had a badly damaged heart valve which was replaced in an emergency surgery, and now we are waiting for the other heart valve to be replaced before we can get married."

Dr. Simon took a step towards Irene. "I don't know what to say, besides that: I wish I had known." Irene nodded and looked down.

Christina hugged Irene, "Carlos and I didn't know all of that, Irene."

"Well so much for my first outing."

"Irene, have you started painting yet?"

"Only the sketching part of it."

"And what are you going to paint first."

"Tiger, he gets the honor to be my first project. After all, he didn't object when I told him."

"Very smart of Tiger." Christina told her smiling.

Brent told Irene, "We better leave; this is the first time you have gone out."

When they got to the car, Brent said to Irene. "Darling, people are going to ask for one reason or another. I wish you could practice a comeback. Don't let it bother you so much. It's just one of those things."

"I know Brent. I just wasn't prepared for it; it took me by surprise. Let's not say anything at home tonight. I'll tell Mama some other time."

"Baby, do you feel like going out to eat? It is still early. Only if you feel like it."

"I would love to go darling, we didn't say anything at home, but we can call, don't you think? I'll call so they won't wait for us," Brent made his call and told Irene. "Everything is all right darling. Our place?" he asked her.

"Where else? There is no other place for us."

So Brent headed for their favorite place. "Irene, are you all right, baby?"

"No, Brent. I don't want to feel bad, but I do. We have to go to the hospital."

On the way, Brent called the hospital and gave instructions to call Darrell STAT and call Irene's home. "I wouldn't take you in my car baby, but I don't want to wait for the ambulance. What do you feel, darling?"

"I can't breathe, I just can't breathe. And some chest pains."

"Irene, how long have you been feeling this way?"

"I don't know Brent. Most of the day, I think. I knew I should have told you earlier but I was so happy. I didn't want to spoil it."

Brent called the hospital and gave instructions to meet him outside with a stretcher and equipment. Brent turned his beam lights on and started to blow his horn and his foot pressed the gas pedal to go faster.

"I'm sorry Brent, I love you so much."

"I love you too, Irene." Finally, the hospital, he told himself.

Brent parked by the Emergency entrance and hurried out of the car. Darrell and a few nurses came out to meet him. "Brent, what happened?"

"She didn't want to tell me she felt bad. Darrell, we have to find someone to assist you in the surgery. I can't do it."

"Okay, let me see who is in here."

Brent went in with them. But he went out again. Darrell found a good Surgeon and asked him to assist him. In the meantime Brent went into the Doctors room next to the Operating room. He lay down on the bed and buried his head in the pillow.

"Lord, I have never talked to you much, but I promise you if you spare Irene's life, I will always go to Church with Irene, I don't even care if we don't have any children, we can adopt. There are so many abandoned children we can adopt. Only save her life. If she doesn't make it, I'll die, too. Please, please save Irene."

Brent stayed there for a long time. Then very slowly, he got up, washed his face, and walked out of the room and dressed to go into the operating room. The surgery was still in progress. But Darrell looked up at him and nodded his head. Brent took a breath of relief. "Dear Lord, thank you for this miracle, I pledge to you I will do what I promised."

Brent went outside where he knew all of Irene's family was waiting. Everybody surrounded him to find out about Irene. "Brent, how is she?"

Brent went to sit down and everyone followed him. "How come you're not wearing your greens?" Kate asked him.

"Kate, I wasn't in shape to assist anyone, much less Irene. But I went back in the operating room. Darrell gave me thumbs up."

"How did it happen, Brent?"

"She said she didn't want to tell me she was feeling bad, I had invited her for dinner, but I said only if you feel like it. We were about to enter the restaurant when she told me. I thought we would die together coming to the hospital. That's why I couldn't even dress to assist Darrell. I was afraid they couldn't find him. I knew I couldn't operate, I would have killed her."

The double doors opened and Darrell came out all smiles. "This was a breeze compared to the other job," He said. "She'll be all right. She has to take it slow. Two surgeries so close together."

Kate remained seated; Sarah and Clare sat with her when Laura came in running. "Mama, what happened now?"

"At least you didn't get the full strength of the news."

"Brent and Irene came to the hospital to visit Carlos, that's all I know."

Brent had a short laugh and shook his head. "What is it?"

"Well, when we went to visit Carlos, there was a new doctor there who is going to go in with him; anyway he innocently asked us if we were going to get married or were we already married?"

"Oh my God!"

"What did you say?"

"Irene tried to say something, and then she just walked out. She was very upset. Christina followed her and I tried to explain to Dr. Simon why Irene was so upset. I followed Irene and she decided to go back and apologize to Dr. Simon. The poor man was so embarrassed; he didn't know what to say. I guess Irene squared everything before we left."

"Did anyone notify Christina and Carlos?

"No, she'll find out when she goes home." Christina walked in about that time. "What happened with Irene?" So she got the whole story again from everybody.

Darrell came out again. "Brent; come on in, buddy." He turned around and looked at Kate.

"Would you like to come now, Kate?"

"I know it is one at a time;"

"You go first, Brent."

"Thank you, Kate." He followed Darrell. When he went into the recovery room, Irene had her eyes open. "Irene darling, don't you ever scare me like that again." She smiled at him and he knew she was going to make it.

Chapter Seventeen

Irene had been in the hospital for two days and she had just been assigned a room; she was happy. Then a couple walked in, it was Dr. Simon and a lady, probably his wife. He was carrying the biggest bouquet of flowers Irene had ever seen.

"Miss. Hamilton, this is my wife, Cary, and I humbly came to ask you to forgive me for all the anguish I put you through."

"Dr. Simon, Cary. Please, you didn't do anything to me. I'd been feeling bad all day, I should had told Brent sooner to bring me to the hospital, but instead, I chose to keep holding onto my discomfort. Thank you for the flowers, they're beautiful."

Brent walked in all smiles. "How is my favorite patient?" he asked.

"Sweetheart, meet Mrs. Cary Simon. And of course you already know Dr. Simon."

"It's a pleasure, Mrs. Simon."

"Likewise, but call me, Cary."

"Have you and Carlos had time to work out anything about the practice, Dr. Simon?"

"Well, not yet, since he just came out of surgery again, we'll wait until he goes back to the office; but I think it is going to work out fine. Well, we must leave, but I wanted to come by and introduce my wife to you and apologize again."

"I'm happy to have met you, Cary. No more apologies, please."

Kate came in with Charles. "I'm sorry we're so late, would you believe I overslept? I couldn't believe it when Clare told me what time it was. Charles just walked out of the bedroom and didn't wake me up."

"It was obvious she needed her rest. Don't you think?"

"I'm glad you slept, Mama." Irene told her.

"You look great, baby."

"Mama, I don't have any makeup on."

"That means you don't need makeup."

"Good morning." Christina said. "Good morning to you, Brent. Carlos has already started to get dressed to go home. I told him he had to behave himself."

"I'll go see him next."

"Is there a chance he can leave today?"

"I can't say anything until I see his vital signs."

"Yeah, that's what he was doing."

Brent laughed. He waved and kissed Irene before he left.

When everybody had left, except Christina and Kate, Irene motioned to them with her hand so they would get closer to her. "When Brent was bringing me to the hospital; he turned the hazard lights on and began to blow the horn and he sped up very fast."

Kate said. "He looked very frightened when he came out after you were in surgery, he didn't come out until he saw for himself you were all right. You know, he didn't even assist Darrell in the surgery? Don't tell him Irene, but you need to know how much that man loves you; the first surgery you had, he broke down in front of everybody. Then he apologized for doing it. I guess he had to be so strong to assist in the surgery, he knew he couldn't do it."

"You know, I didn't want Darrell to do the surgery, Brent told me," "we are not allowed to do surgery on our loves ones; I can't imagine you not being my loved one." Irene's tears ran all over her face. "I love him so much, mother."

Carlos came in, all smiles, "I have been abandoned!" he said. Christina immediately stood up and walked up to him, embraced him and kissed him.

"You're dressed!" she said. "Are we going home? Wait, let me think. I need to go shopping and pick up the children." Christina told Carlos.

Carlos said. "Christina, let me talk to Keith. I need to ask him about the office. Maybe we can go to 'Las Palmas' so you can rest too." In a few minutes, Carlos came back. "Okay, he said he has things now where he can handle it by himself. They're booking less people and he is not doing as many surgeries now, so he said to enjoy myself and take it easy. And I'm going to."

"Call Cindy, Christina, ask her to gather the children's things and we can come later on, don't let me forget to call my mother as well."

When Cristina left to make her call,

Carlos asked Brent. "Brent, who can you recommend for Christina? She can't remember many things like, yesterday; how to call my office or how to ask where a public phone was? She can't remember the streets. She remembered my parents, but she still can't remember Mr. Moran."

"Carlos, I think she needs more confidence in herself. Give her more time and wait for her parents to come back. I think that, in itself, will be a big shake for her mind and probably bring a lot of things back to her that are still inside."

"Of course you're right, I just feel so bad for her because it upsets her and I want to help her."

When Christina came back, Carlos held her and kissed her. "So, what are we going to do, Mrs. Lopez?"

"We're going by the Hamilton's and pick up our kids and go to your parent's house. Is that a good plan?"

"Perfect."

When they were gone, Irene said, "Well, maybe this is the end of Carlos and Christina's problems. Hopefully we are working towards the same ending."

"Yes, we are." Brent replied. "Irene, I made a promise to the Lord that you are going to have to help me fulfill"

"Yeah;" and what is that?"

"You were a very sick little lady. I promised I will start going to church with you, and that I don't care if we don't have natural children. We will adopt abandoned children."

"Brent, don't you want us to have our own children?"

"Irene, I don't want to see you, ever again in the hospital under anesthesia for any reason."

"I'm sorry if I scared you, darling."

Brent embraced her, closing his eyes. "Irene Hamilton, would you marry me in the spring?"

Irene looked at him and smiled, "Would I? Yes, Brent Miller, I will."

"Now we can plan slowly, we can look for a house and furnish it as we think we want. We can add a room for you to paint when you don't want to be outside; we'll call it the art room. We'll find the sunniest side of the house," said Brent dreamily.

"Oh, Brent, I love you so much. Do you know how much I love you?"

"I do, but I better leave because I know that door has opened and closed so many times, next time they're going to come on in."

"Let them come in, I'll tell them I'm taking the best medicine for my ailment."

"How long am I going to be in the hospital, Brent?"

"Maybe another two or three days. But your physician is Darrell; you know that, don't you?"

"Yes, I wish you would have done my surgery."

"No, my dear, you don't. I couldn't do anything, Irene; I don't mind telling you, I was afraid I couldn't make it to the hospital with you in one piece. That day, it was all I could do for you," Brent kissed Irene and waved good bye to her..

As Brent walked out, Darrell was leaning against the wall in front of Irene's door. He smiled at Brent. "You owe me buddy, you owe me big."

"Why?" Brent responded.

"I've been here twenty minutes waiting for you to visit in peace; I waived everybody off so you wouldn't be disturbed."

"I owe you big," Brent told Darrell smiling.

"How is she feeling today, Brent?"

"She is in high spirits, Darrell; I proposed marriage for the spring."

"That's great! Maybe they will let me and Sarah get married the same day."

"Oh, wait a minute, that's a big step, I don't know if the Hamilton's will go for that Darrell."

"Sarah and I have been planning it for a while, we're going to ask."

"Well, not too soon, let Irene recover some before you throw that bomb loose."

"Don't you believe they'll let us get married, Brent?

"In a few years, Darrell. I don't think they want her to marry now."

"Brent, I wouldn't want to marry Sarah if she didn't want to marry me, but she does."

"Well, I don't doubt it; but I'm just telling you for what I hear," responded Brent.

"We are not going to give up. If you remember, they didn't want us to be engaged either. But Sarah convinced her father. Because I don't think she'll have any objections from her mother."

That evening, Darrell told Sarah: "When we leave the office, Sarah, let's go have a cup of coffee. I want to discuss something with you."

"Good news?"

"I think it is."

"Let's go, everybody has been taken care of and its five now."

Darrell kissed Sarah as soon as she got into his car. "Okay, you have me in stitches, come out with it," Sarah told Darrell.

"Brent told me he proposed to Irene again to get married in the spring. I think we can make our own plans, don't you think?"

"Oh Darrell, if only we could! I don't know if Papa would let us."

"Do you know how old your Mama was when she married your father?"

"I'm not sure."

"Well, make sure and ask her. Count how old she is and how old Irene is. Was she born soon after they were married or did they wait?"

"Let's see, Irene is twenty four, Mama is, I think she is forty two. Mama was eighteen, Darrell! Oh Darrell, we can get married in the spring!

"Plus, I can promise your father, you can go to the University and wait until you're finished before we have children."

"No, you don't make promises for me, I'm not sure I want to go to college anymore. And I might want children sooner."

"Sarah, I better tell you Irene might not be able to have children. Not ever. So we might want to wait a little while so she won't feel so bad."

"I never thought about that; poor Irene, she has always wanted children. Never the less, no promises to Papa, Darrell."

"Okay, no promises. Brent thought we shouldn't ask your parents too soon; also for Irene's benefit."

"You know Darrell, I feel so differently inside of me; kind of nervous inside my stomach, I'm so happy."

"Me too, baby, but don't tell anybody else you feel like that, all right?"

"Why?"

"They might misinterpret your words." Darrell embraced Sarah. "I love you, Sarah, whatever happens when we ask your Dad's permission to get married; don't ever forget I love you."

"Dad won't deny us to be married, Darrell. If Mama was eighteen when they got married, he won't dare to say no to us." With a very serious face, she said. "He hates hypocrites."

"Sarah, you won't call your father a hypocrite!" Darrell said scandalized at her.

"Oh no. I will say I thought he hated them, he can't be one."

"Sarah, let's not plan to insult your father just yet, when he doesn't even know what we're planning. I know we're going to catch them by surprise."

"Oh, how much I'm going to enjoy that."

"Sarah. I do believe you're turning into a little witch!"

"Not really, Darrell, it's just that Papa approves something if it's his or Mamas' idea; but if one of us girls wants the very same thing, it turns absolutely prohibited. It gets old, you know."

"Okay, I'm taking notes." He said laughing, acting like he was taking notes on his hand.

"We better go back so you can go home, but I couldn't wait to tell you about it. It was good news, wasn't it?"

"Yeah, I didn't expect Brent to propose again. Maybe Irene didn't expect it either and he did it to make her happy. Let's go, we have to go by the office and pick up my car."

"Are we going to dinner tonight?"

"Eight o'clock sharp."

Sarah got home and she was on her way upstairs to shower when she saw Laura coming home crying. "Wasn't that Benny with you, Laura?"

"Yes, Sarah, he just dropped me off."

"Did you have a fight?"

"Sarah, come to my bedroom."

They both went to Laura's bedroom. "Sarah, I'm pregnant!"

"**What?** Oh, my God! What are you going to do?"

"Benny said we can get married."

"How did you let that happened Laura?"

"We didn't plan it; it just got out of hand, we haven't even kissed for a long time."

"Laura, you can't wait long to tell Mama and Papa about this, you have to get married at once. You haven't even finished high school."

"I don't know how to tell them, Sarah."

"Laura, you are not going to tell them by yourself, Benny has to come and be the one to tell Papa. Maybe Benny's father, Mr. Betancourt will come also, but the main thing is that Benny will be here with you."

"Yes, Sarah. Thank you. You are right. I'll call Benny and tell him."

"Listen Laura, I'm going out with Darrell, I think it's better if you're here just with Benny when that's going on, don't you think? Call him now!"

"Yes, I'll call him now."

"Tell him he has to come tonight."

Sarah went to her bedroom and said a prayer for Laura. "Boy, I thought I had problems," She thought to herself. "It's almost time for Tyke to get here. She got ready in a rush and went downstairs.

Sarah's' parents were waiting for dinner to be served. "Hi Sarah, are you and Darrell going out tonight?"

"Yes, Mama, if it's all right, we also want to go by the hospital and say hello to Irene."

"Have you seen Laura?"

"Yes, Mama, she is in her bedroom. Well, Darrell is here now, let me run. I'll see you later."

Darrell was by the door to say hello.

"Aren't you going to let me say hello to your parents, Sarah?"

"Oh, I'm sorry."

"We won't be very late Mr. and Mrs. Hamilton."

When they were outside, Darrell asked Sarah. "What's the matter with you darling? I've never seen you like this."

"I wanted to leave the house before Benny gets here."

Darrell looked at Sarah with inquisitive eyes. "Why? I always thought you liked Benny."

"So did I."

"Okay spit it out, what's going on?"

"Laura is pregnant." Sarah told Darrell.

"No! Darrell said. "Those kids?"

"I guess they're not kids anymore."

"I feel so sorry for Laura; she said they have never even kissed before."

"Good Lord!" Then he started to laugh.

"Darrell it isn't funny."

"I'm sorry Sarah, but it <u>is</u> funny! They have never kissed before and come out pregnant?"

"Well, I believed her. They kissed lightly like a goodnight kiss, and held hands but that was all. . . Listen, when we go to see Irene . . ."

"I know, don't say anything about Laura."

"Well, she'll find out, but not right now, she'd have a heart attack."

Laura went downstairs about the same time Benny and his father walked in. "Laura, are you and Benny going out to dinner?" Kate asked her.

"No, Mama."

"Mr. Betancourt! What a surprise. Is Benny riding with you?"

"No, Mr. and Mrs. Hamilton, there is no other way to come out and notify you that my son has misbehaved with your daughter. As the result, Laura has become pregnant." Charles and Kate both stood up in disbelief of what Mr. Betancourt had said.

"Laura? We had always trusted you and Benny," Charles and Kate said to her.

"I'm sorry, I'm sorry, we didn't know what was happening to us. We just didn't know." Laura said sobbing. Kate sat down,

"Well, it's too late for regrets now, what are we going to do?"

Charles said, "They're going to get married and Laura is going to have that child. And she is going to finish school."

"I'm glad you said that, Mr. Hamilton, we don't believe in abortions either. Also, if you don't mind, they need to live somewhere. I'm offering our home for them until Benny finishes school. He needs to finish so he can make something of himself. I'm sure you agree with that."

"I do, Mr. Betancourt."

"Tomorrow, they can get their marriage license. One of you has to go with her since she is a minor, and they can get their blood test tomorrow. Will they have only a ceremony at the courthouse or do you want them to be married in the church?"

Kate said. "I think that is a question that only they can answer by themselves."

Benny for the first time spoke. "I want to apologize for what has happened, but believe it or not we didn't know. I know I'm older than Laura, but I had never been with anyone else. We didn't know what was happening to us. I'm sorry. I do want to marry Laura in her Church. I intent to stay with Laura forever; we love each other, we don't need to be thirty years old to know that." He knelt in front of Laura and asked her to marry him and pulled a ring from his pocket. Benny had tears in his eyes. Laura smiled and gave him her hand,

"Yes Benny, I love you and I want to marry you."

Kate stood up and hugged her daughter, "Well, if this had to happen now, I'm glad it was Benny." And Kate hugged him too. Charles walked over and shook Benny's hand,

"I agree with my wife. Love my daughter, that is the only thing I ask of anyone who wants to marry any of my daughters," Charles told Benny.

Mr. Betancourt said. "Thank you for being so understanding towards my son. Laura, welcome to my family. If at any time you need my help on anything, you only need to let us know."

"Thank you, Sir." Laura said.

"Mama, can we go to Father Gabriel tomorrow and maybe he can marry us one day next week? It goes without saying we only want the ceremony, nothing else; you don't even need to walk me down the aisle, Papa."

Charles looked at Kate, "No, I'll walk you."

"We'll have a dinner at home. Mr. Betancourt, is there any reason why your wife didn't come with you?"

"Yes, she is out of town with the children out of school. We still have two daughters, a twelve and fourteen years old."

"All right Laura, you can wear a nice dress, and like I said we will have a dinner here at home, maybe Buffet style. We have to count Christina now, and the Betancourt family, I don't know how many they are. Kate said.

"As soon as my wife comes back. She will call you Mrs. Hamilton. Thank you and good night."

"Irene is going to come home from the hospital in a couple of days. I think we'll wait until then to tell her. Maybe we'll ask Brent ahead of time as a warning, in case she has any health problems with the news."

Laura looked down, "I'm so sorry."

"Laura, we know. I don't want to hear again how sorry you are, in fact if you say it in public; people are going to ask you why you are so sorry. Are you prepared to spill your guts to any one for the asking?"

"Does anyone remember we haven't eaten dinner yet? We were about to when Benny came home. Are you hungry Laura?"

"Mama, you don't know how good you are. You too Papa."

"Well, thank you for that, Laura; go tell Clare we're ready to eat."

Clare came in with Joanna and several platters of food. "Excuse me I'm not bringing one at a time, but I don't think this food can be warmed up again."

Kate said. "Clare, I'm telling you this now so you can start planning. Laura is going to get married next week. We're having a buffet dinner here at home. We're not sure if it's going to be daytime or night time."

"Anyone have a feather?" Clare said.

"No, why?"

"So you can knock me over."

Charles was trying not to laugh; he had been trying to act mad the whole time. He was so aggravated at things, but when Clare said that, he roared with laughter. "Clare, I swear, you come up with such sayings at the most appropriate time. When we really need it!"

Kate told Clare. "We'll talk in the morning, Clare."

"You know, Mama, the worst thing that is going to happen to me?" asked Laura.

"No darling, what is it?"

"That I'm moving out. That is going to be hard for me. Am I going to be able to come home, Mama?"

"Any time, sweetheart. Laura, this doesn't change anything between us, you're still our daughter and your sisters are still your sisters. You're only changing your address. Since you don't drive, if no one can bring you, you call and somebody will pick you up, just make sure you let someone know you're coming over here. Unless it is an emergency."

Darrell and Sarah walked in, "Hi, have you eaten dinner yet?"

"Sure, we went out for dinner, Papa; I told you, don't you remember?"

"Well, sit down any way. Clare, please bring some coffee and cake. Sarah, I think I can guess you know everything about Laura."

"I only found out tonight, Papa."

"Well, they're getting married next week."

"Papa, and you don't want Darrell and I to get married. I'm two years older than Laura."

Charles put his head between his hands "Sarah, please don't dare me."

"Mama was eighteen when you married her."

Darrell said, "Mr. Hamilton, I promise you it won't be the same case. It won't happen with us, I'm not a kid, Sir."

"Papa, I know Brent is going to try to marry Irene in the spring. Will you let us get married with them? You know, a double ceremony?"

"We'll see Sarah, please let me digest what is happening to us now."

"Oh Papa, thank you! I knew you would give us permission." And she got up from her chair and ran to Charles and hugged his neck. Darrell couldn't compose himself; he started to laugh, and laugh so much Charles started, and then Kate. Sarah, straightened herself up and said,

"Did I say something funny?"

Chapter Eighteen

"I'm so glad you're finally home, darling. Anything you need, please don't get up, ask whoever is with you," Kate told Irene.

Clare walked in with a bell. "Here, Irene, look what I found. When you need something, you ring the bell and someone will come over."

"Clare, how do you manage to always say or do something funny?"

"I guess it's just a gift. I used to think people were just laughing at me. But a friend of mine told me, no Clare, we're not laughing at you; we're laughing at what you say. Do you know what the difference is?"

"Irene, do you know if Brent is coming for dinner tonight?"

"I assume he is, Mama, why."

"I want to plan a nice dinner. When you talk to him, ask him if he can make it a little earlier."

"I'm getting interested in your inquiry Mama, what is it?"

"Nothing very important, I have a question for him sweetie."

"Brent, I'm so glad you came early." Kate told Brent as she greeted him.

"Hello, Kate, where is Irene?"

"We put a sofa in the library and I think she is resting there now. Brent, the reason I asked Irene to ask you to come earlier is because I need to let you know something about Laura that I believe is going to upset Irene a great deal. A few days ago, we found out that Laura is pregnant." Brent look was of disbelief, but he didn't say anything. "We know is going to be very upsetting for Irene, and I wanted to tell you first in case you should have to give her something for nerves or her emotions."

"Yes Kate, I can see why you're being concerned. It might be better if you and I; and Charles, if he wishes to, let her know in private." Brent said.

"Yes, that's what I had in mind. Let me see if I can locate Charles."

Kate came back with Charles. "Brent, let's go to the library, I don't think Irene is asleep. We can talk to her before dinner." They went in and they found Irene drawing something on the large pad.

"Brent darling, how did I miss you when you arrived?" They kissed. "Irene, we need to tell you something."

Brent started. "In the first place your parents want you to know they're all right with it. Benny and Laura are getting married in a couple of days." Irene's eyes got bigger and bigger, and then she said. "Mama, not Laura! Is she pregnant?"

"Yes baby, we told them if it had to happen, we are glad it was Benny."

Kate told them both what Benny had said that night. And it was so moving, it took the edge off the anger they both felt. "I felt so bad for Laura when she told Charles that he didn't have to walk her down the aisle to get married."

"Did he answer?" Irene asked Kate.

"Yes, of course." He said, "I'll walk you."

Clare came to announce dinner was ready. Charles told her.

"Clare, I brought a feather for you today."

"Ah, are you going to call my bluff? I'll show you." And without a word, she threw herself onto the floor. Irene and Kate were more than surprised, but Charles and Brent laughed hard at Clare.

"Mama, that needs an explanation."

"The night we found out about Laura," Kate told Irene, "I told Clare; Laura and Benny were getting married next week and to start making arrangements for a buffet style dinner we're going to serve.

She quickly said, "Who has a feather?

Charles said, "What for?"

Clare answered him, "So you can knock me over."

"So of course, your father had to have a comeback for her today."

As soon as they sat at the table, Sarah started.

"Well it is not fair Laura is getting married before me and even Irene."

"Well, it wasn't planned," Kate told her.

"I wonder if I can be her Maid of Honor?" Sarah said.

"Why don't you ask her? Here she comes."

"Laura, can I be your Maid of Honor?"

"Sarah, my wedding is very small, I wish you could."

"Laura, if you want your sister to be your Maid of Honor, there is no reason why not, unless you have someone else in mind."

"You know I don't, but under the circumstances, I don't want anything but to get married." Laura said.

"I can wear that pretty pink dress Mama bought me for Christmas." Sarah replied.

"Laura, did you get your blood test today?

"Yes Mama; right after we went to get our Marriage License." Laura said.

"Oh Darrell, how exciting." Sarah said.

Kate smiled and shook her head.

"Well, what do you think of me wearing my Christmas dress to be married in?

Sarah said, "Yes, I think I'll also wear the dress you bought me for Christmas, Mama."

"Yes, that's very pretty."

"You can be my Maid of Honor if you like Sarah, thank you."

A very shy Benny walked into the dining room, "Hello everybody, May I come in?" Benny asked.

"Of course Benny, sit down. We just started eating dinner. Sit down and eat with us," Charles told him.

Brent and Darrell told him. "Congratulations on your upcoming nuptials."

"Thank you, for treating me so well after I was so ungrateful with Mr. and Mrs. Hamilton, after they had placed their trust in me." Benny's eyes were teary and he could hardly speak.

Brent said "Benny, after any of us make a mistake, all we can do is repair it, and you are trying. So, let's be happy about it, okay?"

"Do you know when the wedding is going to take place?" Irene asked.

"Friday at Noon that was the only time Father Gabriel had free for us."

"Irene, Sarah is going to be my Bride Maid; do you feel well enough to be one yourself?" Irene looked at Brent.

"Well, am I well enough Doctor Miller?" Irene asked Brent.

"There is nothing exhausting about it. I believe you're allowed to."

"Thank you, Benny and I both felt we would be excluded from the family as a punishment for our stupidity." Laura said,

"We knew there was no sense in punishing you more than you were doing to yourself," Charles said.

Clare came in with their coffee. "Oh, coffee! I knew I was waiting for something good, it smells delicious Clare; but where is my cake?"

"There is cake, but you can't eat it; its not on your diet."

Charles said. "Brent, put that cake on my diet." Everyone laughed.

Charles stood up. "It has been customary to make a toast for the future bride and groom. And it can't be a difference because they started sooner than expected. May their life be very joyful, and when you don't know something, ASK." There was laughter but a lot of emotion as well.

Kate came in Laura's bedroom where she was getting dressed; she gave her a small arrangement to put in her hair. "Laura, I brought you these flowers for your hair, since they're all colors; I thought it would be right no matter which dress you wore today."

"They are beautiful, Mama, thank you." And she kissed her. Laura was wearing a pastel blue evening dress she had worn for the Country club Christmas Party last year; and she looked radiant.

"You look beautiful Laura, you really do," Charles said as he walked in.

"Ladies, it is getting late. Father Gabriel likes his Masses on time."

"Should I ride in the same car with you?" Kate asked Charles.

"Of course, I don't know why not?"

When they arrived at the church it was full. At the entrance, Linda, Christina's daughter was waiting with a basket full of petals. "Mama, look."

There were a lot of people in the church. It confused Laura, she didn't know why, they hadn't invited anyone but the family. She asked Charles and he told her. "Carlos' family is now Christina's family, Benny's family and all of us."

The wedding march began and Irene walked ahead of Sarah, they both looked fantastic, then Linda walked in full of smiles; dropping the petals.

Benny looked so good in his black suit. When Laura walked down the aisle on Charles's arm, Benny thought his heart had stop, Laura looked so beautiful. She stopped next to Benny, they both looked so happy. Mr. Betancourt stood next to his son, he was his Best Man. Laura had carried a bouquet that Clare had made for her from the flowers in their garden. She looked so pretty and so very happy.

When they arrived at the Hamilton's mansion, they had set the banquet in the garden and everything looked as pretty as a picture. There were even professional waiters. Kate looked for Clare and headed for her direction.

"Clare did you fix the buffet?"

"No, I couldn't do it in just a few days, you just told me to have it ready. That's just what I did. I called the caterer."

Benny and Laura arrived at home and everybody welcomed them with such a joy. Mr. and Mrs. Betancourt arrived and he looked for Kate to introduce her to his wife. "Mrs. Hamilton, this is my wife Antonia, we call her 'Toni'. She is Spanish, so is her name."

"A pleasure, my name is Kate."

"Everything looks beautiful, how did you have the time to do it all? I'm sorry I wasn't here to help."

"I thought I would handle it by telling my housekeeper to do it, but in the time they had to work, they decided to get a caterer and waiters. So they didn't have anything to do either." They all had a good laugh.

Benny told Laura, "I haven't had the time to tell you, you and I had talked about wanting to go to San Diego once. We're going there for our honeymoon. Why don't you run upstairs and pack for a few days vacation?"

"Are we going to drive Benny?"

"No, we're flying, San Diego it's too far to drive."

"I'll be right back."

Mr. Betancourt went to his son. "Benny, don't forget to carry your Marriage Certificate, you may not be able to get in anywhere without it. Give us a call when you need to be picked up at the airport, you don't need to leave your car there; how long do you plan to be there?"

"I was thinking a week."

"Laura, I think we can leave now, we cut the cake already."

"Yes, I only need to throw my bouquet." She went to Kate and asked her if it was time to do that. "Yes sweetheart, let me line up all the single girls." Kate called out all the single girls. Clare who was serving something, stopped on her heels and raised her arms as if to try to catch Laura's bouquet. Everyone cheered when they were all lined up, the bouquet landed in Clare's hands to her delight.

Laura had gone to change clothes for the trip to San Diego; and she was ready to leave. Benny told her. "I have to go by the house and pick up my suitcase, maybe I'll put on a clean shirt." Laura went to her parents to say good bye.

"Mama, Papa, we're leaving."

"Sweetheart, you know, when you come back to Los Caminos, you no longer will be living with us, so do you want me to pack your clothes?"

"No Mama, when I come back I'll do it. It serves a double purpose to let me visit you; I'll call you. Bye and thank you again for your understanding."

When the newlyweds left; everybody started leaving as well. Only Christina and her family and of course Darrell and Brent, stayed there to visit. "Is anyone game for a cup of coffee?" Charles asked.

"You know everybody is, Charles. I'll get Clare." Kate responded to him.

Mr. Moran and a couple of people started to the door. Clare came to let them know who was there. "Mr. and Mrs. Hamilton, Mr. Moran and…" Brent stood up and put his finger over his mouth as if to silence Clare.

"Mr. Moran; I'm glad you're back from your trip." All the eyes were on Christina. She stood up; not knowing what to do. Her mother made a few steps towards Christina, then Christina with a very low voice said. "Mother?" They both cried in each other arms, and then her father came over and embraced his daughter.

Christina walked to Carlos and he walked with her, "This is Carlos; my husband."

"Your husband?" her mother repeated.

"Yes, mother, I'll tell you all about it. Right now, all I want to know is why didn't you ever try to contact me?"

"We did, Christina, but we received a letter from Mike telling us you had been killed in a car wreck when you were going home after the honeymoon. He was leaving town to forget his tragedy."

"Yes, that sounds like Mike all right. We had two daughters. They are Carlos' and mine now Mama, I killed Mike."

"**What?**" Theresa, Christina's mother asked.

Christina looked up and Cindy was there with her children. "Mama, Papa, meet your grandchildren." Pete's eyes were full of tears when he knelt down on the floor and embraced Linda; and kissed his granddaughter; Theresa, his wife, picked Amy up and kissed her.

"So many lost years." Pete said.

"Yes, Papa, but we're going to regain all those years," Christina told her parents. "Now, I'm sure you remember Kate and Charles Hamilton; they have been my parents in so many ways. Irene, you remember her; and Sarah. Laura just got married and left on her honeymoon; this is Brent, Irene's fiancé, and Darrell, Sarah's fiancé. "Why did you go to Australia?"

"Without you, we didn't want to live here any longer, so we decided to leave the country. When we arrived and traveled over there, we chose to buy a cattle station, same difference as a ranch over here. Your father always wanted to live on a ranch and we loved it."

Clare walked in. "I hate to interrupt, but do you still want coffee, or does anyone want a drink?"

Everyone ordered what they wanted and Clare left. "Kate, I'm sorry I haven't had the chance to say hello, thank you for taking care of my child and my grandchildren."

"It has been a pleasure, Theresa."

Christina said, "Like I said, I'll fill you in later. But not all of it was a pleasure; when I came here it was because Mike had beaten me up. Irene and I had found each other at Brent's office where we both went to work on the same day. Mike beat me up that day because we met at a restaurant and he got mad at me because I stopped to say hello. But I promise I'll tell you all of that later."

Carlos said, "Since we're staying at my parents now, let me call home. They should be home by now, to let them know we're bringing your parents, they'll love that."

"Why don't we stay home in town, Carlos?"

"Because we don't have anything there yet. That was the reason we went to my parents, remember?"

"You know, I remembered! Isn't that wonderful? I do remember."

Christina's parents looked at each other with a curious look. "Well, I guess I have to tell you a little more of what has happened to me. Mike had shot me, and that's when I met Carlos. He did the surgery. Because I was still in danger, Irene's family hired a guard for me, Mr. Moran. Hey! I remembered him! And Carlos took me to his parents' home to hide me, along with the children and my body guard. Carlos and I fell in love and we wanted to get married. Mike was in prison, but the day we got married he escaped and found out where we were And when Carlos was getting into the car, he was shot in the chest by Mike." Christina had to stop because she had remembered for the first time since it happened. "I thought Carlos was dead, Mr. Moran ran to the hill in front of us, and I followed him, he told me to go back, but I was not going to let him kill Carlos," she held Carlos hand and kissed it.

"Don't you want to stop, Christina?", Brent suggested.

"No Brent, I really don't want to. I was one step behind Mr. Moran. Mike came out from behind a tree and asked me if he had interrupted anything, I didn't answer, I don't remember answering him, I only remember pulling the gun from Mr. Moran's belt and I fired until the gun was empty; I think I threw the gun down. I remember running back to find out how Carlos was."

Brent said; "I can take it from here. Darrell and I did the surgery on Carlos, Christina was exhausted. When the surgery ended, we went out to speak with the family, Christina collapsed and she was admitted into the hospital. The next day, she awakened with amnesia. That's why Christina was talking about her memory. She didn't know she would remember you or not."

"My God Christina, you have really been put to the test."

"Yes, Mama, but now the Lord has blessed me with a very good man. As soon as possible, Carlos is going to adopt my children. So they can become our children. But tell me Mama, where is your cattle station?"

"It's in Western Australia, about 200 Miles north of Perth."

"It sounds sophisticated."

"It has nothing about sophistication, only hard work and lots of sand. But we love it, we really do. The people are very warm and wonderful; we plan to go back, Christina."

"Well Mama, it's too soon for a decision like that. We'll talk about that later, now we need to re-acquaint ourselves let's not talk about leaving."

"Papa, you haven't said much."

"I haven't had the chance, baby. I have been reminiscing all this time; you haven't changed much. If I had to decide, I'll say you're much prettier now."

Carlos smiled and said, "I didn't know Christina then, but I think she is beautiful."

"Carlos, did you ever called your mother about my parents?"

"Yes, sweetheart, she is very happy for you; and she is expecting us tonight."

"We have an apartment in town," Christina told her parents. "But Carlos had another surgery because the first surgery had a small leak and had to be repaired. He just left the hospital. The doctors decided I shouldn't work at all, so Carlos's family have servants and I don't have to lift a finger."

Christina's mother said. "Our ranch is big, but there is work everywhere you look. I'll take a few days off. We're so far from everything that we wait four months or so to go to town. We make most everything that we use, just like old times. It's beautiful, Christina, the vegetation is so much different than over here, and the animals are so pretty. We have all kinds of kangaroos, birds, and many other animals; I enjoy seeing them about and playing."

"Mrs. Hamilton, we have to leave, we are two hours from the ranch."

"I know Christina, I want to invite all of you for dinner one day, but I know you have to rest before you come back to the city." Kate told Christina.

"Papa, let's go." Some of the men have made themselves a group away from the women.

"Now that I was enjoying myself so much," Pete said.

"You'll come back and we'll continue our conversation."

Charles told Pete, "I do remember you from years past."

"Yes, so do I."

"Do you still own that big department store in town?"

"I own the store, but now I have people that run the store for me. So I get to sit a lot."

When they had gone, Irene said, "I love Christina to death, but I couldn't wait for them to leave; I just needed to sit down."

"Irene, everybody knows you need to rest and if you just say so, and go sit down, nobody will get mad at you, baby."

"Brent; I need to go to bed. Really, I'm more tired than I thought."

"Mr. Hamilton may I take Irene to bed? Darrell, do you have a stethoscope with you?"

"I have a hospital bag with me, blood pressure pump and all, I'll be right back."

"Irene, even if it was your sister's wedding, you could have gone to rest a half hour so you wouldn't overtire yourself. Kate, if you want to come, I'm only going to check her vital signs before she goes to sleep."

Brent went upstairs with Irene, Darrell told Sarah. "When you go back to work on Monday, bring one of those kits home, so you can check Irene's vital signs before she goes to bed; every night."

Chapter Nineteen

After they left, Irene told her parents. "Brent and I haven't been able to visit at all with so many people around. Would it be all right if Brent stays over here so we can visit?" "Of course, Irene, it's only after eight o'clock, it's not late after all; the wedding was at noon."

"Good night, everybody."

"Brent took Irene by the arm, and very slowly started climbing the steps."

"It was a long day, sweetheart," Brent told Irene. And with louder a voice, he said,

"Sarah, bring me Irene's medication."

"All right, Brent."

"Mama, where are Irene's pills?" Sarah asked, "Tyke, is Irene's life in danger?"

"Take the pills upstairs, Sarah. And no. No more than anyone else's. Her life is frail right now; I guess you know that, that's why Brent said, she is not having natural children, but they might adopt," Darrell replied.

"I hope the Lord will allow me to leave this earth before any of my children," Kate said.

"And I." Charles answered.

Charles stood up and said, "I hope all of you understand that today has been a very difficult day for me. I need to go to bed myself." He kissed Kate, turned around and left the dining room.

"Darrell, I know you'll excuse me, I need to go to bed; you just visit with Sarah. Good night."

When Sarah came back downstairs, she found Darrell alone drinking a cup of coffee. "What happened with my parents, Darrell?"

"They're not feeling well, Sarah, they decided to go to bed; they said I could stay. I will if you want me to."

"Of course, I want you to stay, but not here; let's sit in the living room. Come 'on."

Sarah went to sit down on a large sofa and put her head on Darrell's chest. She started to kiss him. "Sarah, we're not going to make out on your father's furniture."

"We are not." Sarah said.

"Well, making out starts like this, Sarah."

"But I want to kiss you, Darrell."

"So do I, Sarah. But there is something that is called self-control, when you have to control your feelings, not vice-versa. And that's what we have to do, control our feelings, when you fail to do that, you end up like Laura and Benny." Sarah immediately sat up.

"I'm sorry Darrell, I didn't mean that."

Smiling, Darrell said, "I tell you what we can do, we can start planning our wedding; would you like to do that?"

"But we don't even have a date."

"It doesn't matter, baby, we can talk about whether you want us to buy a house when we get married, and we are, when we can. We'll buy and furnish the place. You can start planning what kind of dress you would like to wear to be married in. Who will be your Maids of Honor? There is a lot to talk about."

"Yeah, there is a lot to talk about. We can take rides around the city and look for the best location first. We always lived here, but I know there are more modern homes in different areas. You know, by the beach it's beautiful," And Sarah started to describe to Darrell what she has seen. He caressed her hair.

"I sure hope spring comes soon Sarah."

"It will Darrell." She quickly kissed him on the lips and stood up. "And I thank you." "What for, sweetheart?"

"For what you just did for me, I understand now what Laura said."

Brent came back downstairs. "How is Irene, Brent?" Sarah asked him.

"She was very tired, we have to help her remember to go and rest in the middle of the day. She's still not strong enough for a day like today. Darrell, I'm going ahead to the house. I'll come back tomorrow and check on Irene. Check on your sister, Sarah."

"I think I better leave myself, Sarah."

"But it is still early, Tyke."

Brent left. And then, Darrell held both of Sarah's hands, "Sarah, we just had a very close call, and we survived it, let me go home now." He kissed her briefly and left.

Brent was getting in his car when Darrell arrived at his car. "What was that all about, Darrell?"

"I'll tell you when we get home."

When Darrell got home Brent was getting ready to shower. "You ought to let me shower first," Darrell told Brent.

"I thought that was what was going on when I walked in on you."

"Sarah started getting too friendly on the couch and I had to work fast to stop her and then explain to her what would have happened if we continued. I said that was why Laura and Benny were in San Diego. She had no idea," she said "I'm sure Laura and Benny didn't know as well. You can't turn it on and off like a water faucet, I told her."

"I'm proud of you, buddy."

"Let me shower first so I can feel just as proud of me as you do."

In the morning, Irene was walking downstairs very carefully. Clare heard her and came out running. "Irene, what are you doing up so early?"

"Good morning, Clare. I went to bed about nine last night, believe me, I had my share of sleep. I tried to stay in bed, but I had to get up and do something," She said to Clare. "Well, in my book, that is a good sign of recovery." Clare said smiling.

"I believe I'll have a cup of coffee. Ask someone to bring my painting equipment to the garden and you and I will have some coffee; are you game?"

"I love the idea, Irene; we haven't had a cup of coffee together in a long time."

Kate came downstairs. "Irene, why are you up so early?"

"I slept a long time, Mama. In fact, I think I'll call Brent and invite him for breakfast. Is that all right?"

"Sure, he'll like that Irene."

"Can I tell him Darrell can come over, if he wishes to come?"

"Of course, should we tell Sarah?"

Brent and Darrell arrived together, in one car. "Hello, thank you for inviting us to breakfast."

"Neither one of us cooks, so we have to get out of the house to eat, any day we want to eat."

"When we get married; I can fry eggs, but no biscuits," Irene said smiling.

Darrell said. "Why, don't you like biscuits?"

"Brent, you can tell him, but not in front of me."

Charles came in then. "Did you think you could eat breakfast without me?"

Kate responded, "No dear, I was watching out for you."

Clare came to ask Charles what he wanted for breakfast.

It felt good to have the guys there eating breakfast with them, Charles thought, even if we don't have Laura now. Oh well.

"What are you thinking about Charles?" Kate asked him.

"I was thinking about Laura. I missed her at the table." Said Charles.

"I wonder what she is doing?" Sarah replied.

"They're cruising on the beach; she loves to go to the beach." Kate said.

"Yeah, she does."

"Last night, after everyone had gone to bed; Darrell and I started talking about planning for when we get married. We might buy a house. Since it is still a while before we get married, we can plan with plenty of time." Sarah said.

Irene said, "Funny you said that Sarah! Brent and I would like to do the same. I have my wedding dress; but we can start looking for a house. Don't you think? That way, time will pass quicker."

"Papa, are you going to let me and Tyke get married when Irene does?"

Charles looked at Kate. "As long as you don't pressure Irene into getting married too soon. Remember she needs to take her time."

Irene said. "Yes, I have to listen to my Doctor."

"Actually, Darrell came up with a plan to kill time while we wait."

"Is that right? I'd like to hear what it is."

"Well, basically what it is, is that while we're waiting, doing nothing, we can be planning how we'd like our house to be. Maybe sometimes we can drive around the city and look at homes."

"If I may intrude Darrell, what made you think of doing that?"

"Sarah thought it's a long time to wait until the spring and I simply listed things we can do while we wait." Darrell said.

"That was very smart, Darrell." Irene said.

"You don't know how smart." Sarah said. "We were alone in the living room and I started to kiss him, and he got away from me and stood up and told me that's how Laura and Benny got in trouble."

Darrell was blushing and trying not to laugh, (as was everybody else at the table.) Charles was speechless.

Irene said. "I'm proud of you, Darrell; but I can't say the same about you, Sarah."

"What? That's what happened."

"Sarah, remind me to give you a little talk when we go upstairs."

"About what?!"

"If I wanted to talk to you now, I wouldn't have said, later. Do you think you still want to marry Sarah, Darrell?" Irene quipped.

Kate said. "Let's go to the living room and drink our coffee there." That was a good move because it cut off Sarah's uncomfortable conversation.

"Have you heard anything about Carlos going back to work?"

"No, but I have the feeling he is taking his time doing it."

"Good for him! He and Christina have lost so much time together. And so have Christina and her parents."

"Did any of you hear Christina's mother talking about going back to Australia? On the day they arrived."

"I heard Christina telling her they couldn't do that now, it was too soon."

Kate said. "I believe once they found Christina, they would stay here and sell their property in Australia."

"They might yet, they have to get to know the children, their roots are here not in Australia."

"Irene, do you feel up to going to church tomorrow?"

"I might not feel like getting up early but why don't we go to eleven o'clock Mass and we can go to lunch after Mass. Doesn't it sound good?"

Sarah jumped at the chance. "Darrell; why don't we go to Mass together? Then we can go to lunch,"

Brent said. "Just a minute Irene, last time when we were about to go into the restaurant, we almost went in, and you couldn't tell me you were hurting because you had promised me we were going to eat. We can't have any nonsense like that again. Your life is on the line and I found myself blaming me for your state of health at the time. You shouldn't have the same problem again, because we didn't know you felt bad, understand?"

"I realize I scared everybody and I apologize; I thought it would go away. To tell you the truth, it scared me too," Irene said.

"Sweetheart, we call it a plan that means we don't <u>have</u> to do it regardless of the circumstances. That's why it's called 'plan', because is not a done deal."

"Okay, do you want to go to church?"

"I'll be here at 10:30 a.m. is that all right?"

"Darrell, are you taking me to church?"

"Under the circumstances, yes, I'd love to go to church with you."

"Mr. Hamilton, Mr. Lopez is on the phone for you." Charles went to answer the phone. When he came back he was all smiles.

"Well? Are we going to find out what all that was about?" Kate asked Charles.

"The Lopez family is throwing a big barbeque this evening."

"Couldn't they have called any later than this?"

"I told him it was kind of late. I didn't know if anyone had any plans for this evening. He said how many of us are able to come, they'll be happy to have us."

Brent said. "Irene, how do you feel about a trip like that? We can go slowly and it is like sitting at home. I would like to check on Carlos, but you can do that Darrell and I'll stay with Irene. Maybe Irene and can I go to church tonight. They'll understand it's a long trip for her."

They dressed for the trip. Brent and Irene decided to stay. The Hamilton's, Darrell and Sarah would go to 'Las Palmas.'

"I don't think I'll ever get over the first impression of this place; it's just out of this world, don't you think so?"

"It is, I don't know how Christina handled the children in this house when she first came and didn't even know them."

"Well, she didn't have to handle the children, it was done for her."

"Yeah, that was good. Anyway, I really love this place."

"Well, you can look at it, but you can't have one," Charles said laughing.

By the time the car had stopped, most of the family were there opening the car doors. "Welcome, where is Irene?" Christina asked.

"She didn't feel like making such a long trip, dear." Kate answered her. "Theresa, how do you like being back in the States?"

"It doesn't feel like I'm back, we haven't been anywhere."

"I'm sorry, Mama. We haven't been in the best of health." Kate said. "Listen, we're not far from town. If you like, why don't you come and stay a few days at our house?"

"Christina, would you mind if your father and I stayed a few days at the Hamilton's?"

"No, Mama, if that's what you would like to do, by all means."

"I'll be packed in five minutes."

"Mother! They haven't even said hello, and they're spending the day here,"

Christina was visibly shaken, a sign that her mother's visit was not a success. Kate walked to Christina and asked her. "How are you feeling, dear?"

"I think you can guess in the first five minutes you've been here. My mother has been so rude to the Lopez' family. She has embarrassed me every time she opens her mouth."

"Maybe she needs to go shopping. I'll take her around. Have you asked your father why she has changed? Was she like that before?"

"I don't remember her being like that. Dad said he is so used to her that he doesn't pay attention to her any longer."

"Kate, I was busy inside and didn't look at the time." Kate embraced Angelita, "It's so good seeing you again."

"How do you feel with a house full of people?"

"It's lovely," she said." I know Mr. Findley enjoys the horses."

"I've always loved horses, I can ride for hours." He said.

"And does," Theresa responded.

Angelita said. "Let's go inside and get something cool to drink."

"I want something with 'spirits' in it, not lemonade," Theresa said.

"I do want lemonade," Kate responded.

"Lemonade is the most refreshing drink to have."

"You can have your mixed drink Theresa, Kate and I'll have lemonade. Sarah, what do you like to drink?"

"I'll like lemonade, as well."

"I don't mind drinking alone." Theresa sneer.

"Christina, what are you drinking?"

"Lemonade, please."

"Theresa, how are you getting along with the children?"

"How do you think? They don't know me; they'd rather go to Mrs. Lopez than to come to me."

"You haven't been here, Theresa; they don't know you, when you've been here for a while they'll get used to you and your husband. Part of love is getting used to the person; learn to know them well so you can inspire trust, especially in a child."

"I guess so; I hope it happens before we leave the U.S."

"Are you still planning to leave soon?"

"We have a Visa for six months, that's all the time we have."

"Visa!? Why did you need a Visa to come into your own country?"

"Well, in order to buy the cattle station we had to become Australian citizens, so we did." Christina got up and walked outside; Carlos followed her.

"Christina, don't let it bother you so much, she has been so used to you being gone, she can't handle the idea that you are here."

"And two grandchildren. At least, I know where they are and what happened to them. I won't feel now like there is an empty space in my life. She is not staying because she doesn't want to. I just can't believe it," Christina said leaning on Carlos.

Chapter Twenty

"It's getting late;" Charles said, "Why don't we start back into the city? We don't go to work, but Darrell, Brent and Sarah will."

"Brent didn't come with us, Papa." Sarah said.

"But you know he's still with Irene." Kate stood up.

"We had a marvelous day Angelita, thank you for inviting us. Are you ready to leave, Theresa?"

"I've been ready since you arrived this morning." Everybody ignored her.

Charles said, "Well, Pete, if you are ready we can leave. Cristobal, Angelita, you are the best hosts I've known in a long time. You have to come for dinner to our home once you get ready for a drive into town."

When they left, Theresa took a breath of relief, "Oh, I thought we would never leave that place," She said.

"I don't know how you can say that Theresa, they're very gracious people and their home is beyond words. We have only come a few times, but it's a joy being here."

"For one thing, it's too far from town."

An aggravated Kate said, "I might be wrong, but I thought you said your ranch is 200 miles from town. And you love it, anyway."

"It probably is the excitement of being in Australia. It doesn't matter where I am there, I just love it."

"Do you feel the same way, Pete?" Charles asked him.

"No, I love Australia, but not over my country." He responded. "I used to love it over there. Theresa, when I thought Christina was dead, I didn't care where we lived, but now that she is back in our lives and two grandchildren; I have to tell you, I don't care in the least to move away from here ever again."

Theresa looked at him with angry eyes; "We'll see about that." She told him.

"What are you going to do to me, fire me?" he said laughing.

"I think that is grounds for divorce," She said. "Would you let me go back alone?"

"We don't have to go back, you know." He told her.

"Yes, we do."

"All we have there are things, Theresa; here, we have a <u>family</u>."

"Christina has a family now; she doesn't need us anymore."

"Maybe not, but I know in my heart they would love to have us around; and I would love to stay here."

"I'm not going to argue about it; I'll stay here six months, but at the end of that time, I am leaving for Australia. In the meantime, we can use that time to file for divorce."

"Theresa! What are you saying? Are you serious?"

"I have never been so serious in my life."

Kate said, "Why don't you wait for tomorrow, you have been upset all day, Theresa."

"Tomorrow I want to visit an attorney; I need to know how long this is going to take."

"Theresa, since you're so determined to get a divorce, I want you to know, you can have the ranch in Australia; all I want is half of the cash."

"You know this trip just about cleaned us out."

"When you get there, you can sell part of the stock and send me the money, I'll try to find a job somewhere over here."

"Anything to stay away from me," she told him.

"No, Theresa, I have been trying to convince you to stay here with me; but if you insist on leaving, I am not going to leave my daughter and grandchildren," He told her, as he turned his face away from her.

The next morning when Charles went downstairs; he found Pete in the garden drinking a cup of coffee. "Pete, how are you doing this morning?"

"Very sore, I'm not complaining. Your sofa is beautiful but not very comfortable," Pete replied smiling to Charles.

"Kate and I thought about offering another bedroom for you, but if there was a hope for reconciliation between you guys, that would have put a damper on it. I'm sorry."

"Charles, this has been developing for a long time, it didn't just happen last night. There were many times I felt like coming back to the States. But I didn't have the heart to leave her alone over there; obviously she felt the same way I did."

"Well, Pete, if you're serious about getting a job here, I still have my store. I'm sure we have something you'd like to do; and you are more than welcome to stay with us right here at home."

"Charles, it seems I'm going to have to do something and your offer is very generous. I accept. But for now, let's keep it between us, okay?"

"It's fine with me, Pete."

"Good morning," Kate said. "Are you the only ones up?"

"Yes, let's enjoy the peace," Pete said smiling.

"I guess Theresa has been away for so long, she is confused with her priorities."

"We'll find out soon enough,"

"Oh, I see I'm the only sleepyhead here." Theresa said as she walked in.

"Good morning, Theresa, I just walked in. Didn't you see me?

"I probably wasn't looking."

"How about a cup of coffee?"

"I stopped drinking it a long time ago."

"Not everyone drinks coffee, Theresa."

"If we have what you drink in the morning, I'll be glad to offer it to you."

"In that case, I'd like a beer."

"I don't know if we have a beer, Theresa."

"I'll get it for you, Theresa," Charles told her.

Pete said, "Don't leave the impression people drink beer for breakfast in Australia. Most of the time, they drink tea, more than coffee, but it's usually either one; not beer."

"Yes, I guess I'm the one with the bad habits." Theresa said.

"Theresa, please, we're supposed to visit with the Hamilton's, I feel we need to apologize to them for this display of ill manners. I'm sorry Kate and Charles." apologized Pete.

"No," Theresa said, "I'm the one who needs to apologize. All I can say is that I can't handle being away from home. Now, I know my home is Australia, not here. And before anyone feels sorry for me, I can tell you now, that Ken Sadowoski loves me, and I love him. He told me once that if I was free he would marry me. I believe I'll wire him."

Pete stood up, "Theresa, I never thought I'd hear you say that. But it's good to know you recognized what you want."

"Yes, I think tomorrow, I'll look for an attorney and find the fastest way to get a divorce and leave," And she turned around and walked away.

"Don't you want to take your beer with you?" Pete asked her.

Pete spoke up. "I'm left without words; all I can say is that I am sorry you had to witness Theresa's worst display of bad manners."

"Don't worry about it for our benefit, Pete. We only feel bad for you. Now you have to worry about telling Christina because, under the circumstances, I don't think you should allow Theresa to talk to Christina about it."

"Kate, I hate to impose on you any more than we already have, but since Theresa wants to see a lawyer tomorrow, would you mind taking her yourself? I don't think I need to go since I'm not contesting the divorce. And if you would do that, Charles, maybe you could go with me to talk to Christina. I don't want Theresa to come along."

"Yes, maybe we can arrange that. Irene's car is parked. She won't mind me driving her car. Kate, do you know a lawyer you can take Theresa to?" Charles asked.

"I really don't, Charles, I was going to ask you if you could recommend one."

"Kate, how about the one that Christina used?"

"Pete, we don't know this attorney personally, but Christina used him. That ought to be enough recommendation, don't you think?" Charles told Pete.

"Listen, we don't say anything, Kate. You invite Theresa on this trip and maybe lunch. I do hate to involve either one of you in this, but you heard her from her own lips."

"Yes, there is no going back for her."

"I know what you're saying, but going back is the answer for her. In any case, I guess she has been unhappy for a long time, and I didn't even know about it. To me, I was satisfied; I thought that was the way it was supposed to be."

Kate said, "Well, I think I better go see about Theresa and make some arrangements for tomorrow." Kate found Theresa in the garden, drinking her beer.

"Well Kate, I guess I'll try to find an attorney now, do you happen to know one?"

"As a matter of fact, I do. Christina divorced recently and maybe you want to use the same attorney."

Theresa stood up and said, "I think I'll give her a call and ask her for the lawyer's number."

"Don't you think you need to give her some time to tell her news like that? After all, she's just adjusting to having you here, Theresa. You have no idea how much that child suffered not knowing where you were or if she ever would see you again."

"The other alternative is; you call her and tell her someone you know is planning to divorce and needs a lawyer."

"Yes, that's an answer. I believe I'll do that later."

"What's wrong with now?"

"It's too early, not even ten in the morning. You can make the appointment for tomorrow and you and I can have lunch either before or after you see the lawyer."

"It sounds good to me."

"Yes, that way, you don't have to be in a rush to tell Christina."

"Wait to spread the bad news, huh? But we were very unhappy Katy. The way I see it, it's good news. Before we get any older, we can be happy again."

"I guess you're right, Theresa. I know not everybody has a good marriage. Look, tomorrow, after you call the lawyer, we'll get ready and leave, and we can make a day of it. There is a new shopping mall by the beach, I heard it's beautiful, but I have never been to it yet."

"I think it's a great plan, thank you, Kate. The way things are with Pete, I can't even talk to him anymore."

"I think you need to try to be civil to each other. You know, you have to eat at the same table every day."

"Just don't seat us together."

"Oh, you want to be seated across the table from him so you can see his face, huh?" Kate told her.

"You're terrible Kate; this is not a win situation.

"Pete," I think you need to go by the immigration office and let them know your situation, because if you intend to go to work, you need to have some kind of papers to do it with."

"Since I was a citizen before, it might help me and it might not," stated Pete.

"One thing about it; you're not in a rush to go to work."

"I don't know, Charles, I don't have a clue as to when Theresa is planning to go back to Australia. I have to keep fluent so I can live here."

"Charles, I don't know where the morning has gone," Kate said coming in where Charles and Pete were visiting. "I swear it's almost lunch time."

"Kate, are you ready to leave?" Theresa asked Kate, "Don't tell me you forgot you're supposed to go to town with me today and have lunch somewhere in town."

"I'm so sorry, Theresa, I did forget. Have you called the attorney yet?

"Yes, I did. He said he could see me after lunch, at two o'clock."

"I won't be long at all. Charles, will you let Lorenzo know, please?"

"Of course, Dear," replied Charles.

After both of the women had left, Charles asked Pete." Have you had the chance to call Christina, Pete?"

"I probably would have, but I don't have her phone number."

"I'm sorry, Pete, let me find it somewhere. Kate is the one who makes the calls in this house."

"Let me tell Clare to let Kate know when she gets back that we went to town. Maybe to our store."

"That's probably a good idea if I'm going to be working there. Well, I only told Christina I wanted to see them again. I told her Theresa and Kate went to lunch and she was satisfied with that."

"I think we better leave now, Las Palmas is a long way."

"Papa! It's so good seeing you again, and you too Mr. Hamilton. How come Mama didn't want to come with you?" Christina asked Pete when she greeted him.

"Well, Christina, that's the reason we're are here. Your mother and I are divorcing. As we are speaking, she is filing divorce papers. I didn't want to give you this kind of news over the phone."

"I'm sorry, Papa, but I can't say I'm surprised with what I saw. Mother was so unhappy over here. I couldn't get one civil conversation with her, and it saddened me."

"It happened on the way back to the city. She finally exploded and asked me for the divorce right there in front of the Hamilton's. She said as soon as the divorce is final; she is going to leave for Australia. She told me someone asked her to marry him."

"Well, Papa, it seems to me, she was ready to leave you. I'm glad you are here with us."

Carlos said. "Mr...."

"Carlos, please call me Pete."

"I want to tell you, Pete; you are very welcome here and at our home and in the city."

"Thank you, but Charles has offered me a job at his store and the guest room in his home. I have accepted his offer until I'm able to get an apartment of my own."

Christina hugged her father. "I don't remember mother the way she acts now, Papa. I hope she is happy wherever she goes. Obviously, she doesn't want to stay here."

"Let's go inside, we started our visit outside, but we can finish it inside. We'll have lunch together."

They had a good visit, Christina told Pete. "I'm glad to know you're staying Dad, I'm going to learn Mama is not here because she didn't want to stay, it won't hurt as much."

"I'm glad you're taking it that way, sweetheart."

"Dad, I'm ashamed to admit I don't like the person that Mama has become. How long has she been like that?"

"I don't know, I think it must have happened when we learned you had gotten killed. It was a bad experience for both of us."

"The list keeps piling against Mike. How cruel can a person be to even think up something like that?"

"We better leave Christina; we didn't want to tell your mother we were coming over here. Honestly, I didn't want your mother to come with such news. She went to talk to an attorney today. I believe the one you used when you divorced Mike."

"Tell your in-laws good-bye for me, it was nice to see them again."

"I'm sure they were trying to give us some space for us to visit."

"Do you know when mother is leaving?"

"I'll let you know as soon as I find out something. I imagine it will be a few weeks before a divorce can be final."

On the way back, Pete told Charles. "If everything is where we can, Charles, could we go to your store tomorrow?"

"Of course, I don't think Theresa would mind. Pete, do you think the divorce will be over pretty soon?"

"I have no idea, Charles, but I think when it is not contested it has to be quicker. I would like to start working as soon as possible, but like you told me the other day; I have to go to the immigration office first and get some papers."

"I think it's a working permit. I don't know where we need to go, but I'm sure they're the ones to ask about it. We can look it up in the telephone directory."

"I appreciate all your help, Charles."

Kate met them at the front entrance. "Charles, I was getting worried, sweetheart."

"I thought you knew where we were; I told Clare we would be gone all day. Where is Theresa?"

"I think she is in her bedroom."

"Okay, we went to see Christina. Tomorrow, Pete wants to go to the immigration office to find out what he needs to do to obtain a working permit. Also, (between us), he wants to work in our store. But he doesn't want Theresa to know, since she is supposed to sell part of the cattle. She might not send him the amount of money she should."

"I'm sure Theresa has a plan designed to bore me to tears; but I won't send her back to Christina and poor Angelita again. It's kind of late, Charles, I'm sure Clare has dinner ready."

"Clare, what have you planned for dinner?"

"Your friend came to the kitchen and asked me if I could fix a roast Australian style. I offered her the kitchen; I told her, I barely can find the country on the map, much less know what they eat."

"Well? Is she going to cook?"

"I haven't seen her again."

"What are you going to cook?"

"This late? Steaks."

"Who is in the house, Clare? How is Irene? I haven't seen her today, you know"

"She is fine, Kate. She has been in the garden most of the day. Brent came over to eat lunch with her. Sarah and her better-half didn't have lunch at home."

On her way back to the living room, Kate met with Theresa. "Kate, I need to ask you. Since all of you know I'm divorcing Pete, I don't see any reason to be in the same bedroom with him. Could you make arrangements to move him out? Or do you want me to move out of that room?"

"Let me see which bedroom we have available, Theresa. Is it more convenient for you to just stay there?"

"To tell you the truth, I'd rather that he moves out," Kate left.

"What are you thinking, Pete?" Kate asked him.

"I know you have servants' quarters, why don't I sleep there? It will be far enough from the enemy, I believe." Pete said with a grimace on his face.

"Well, to tell you the truth, that will solve some of the sleeping problems I have arranged for you and Theresa."

"Well, I'll let Theresa know I'm going in to pack. Just let me know where my new accommodations are."

"Clare, show Pete one of the vacant bedrooms, will you?"

Pete and Clare went to the servants' quarters. "This is nice, Clare,"
"Just as nice as the rest of the house."

"Are all the rooms, the same size?"

"No, some are bigger, come on in and I'll show you." Clare took Pete around the rest of the rooms available to him.

"Well Clare, if there is a room with a view of the garden, that's the one I want."

Pete left to pack his suitcase. He knocked. Theresa opened the door. "Theresa, may I come in to pack my clothes?"

"Of course, I'm sorry we ended up this way, Pete," She said.

"Well, if you're happier this way, that's the best way. We only live once. What did the attorney say?"

"He said it might take a little longer because we have to wait for an attorney based in Australia. He knows someone in Perth," She said. "When I know more, I'll let you know." Pete nodded and left with his suitcase.

He walked to the kitchen. "Clare, do I need a key to get in my bedroom?"

"Of course you do. I just didn't think about it, sorry." She gave him a key.

"I'll see you around, Clare."

Clare watched him leave and shook her head.

"Kate, Charles, dinner is ready; I'm going around to see who I find." When she came back, she said. "Irene, Sarah and their fiancés are in the living room, so I guess we can eat."

"Clare, did you look for Theresa?"

"Do I have to?"

"You are terrible, Clare. Also, you have to look for Pete," Kate told her.

"Are we all here?" Kate asked.

"I believe so, Mama." Irene said.

"Charles, do you want to say the prayer? Clare, we're ready to eat now."

"Kate, I want to thank you for getting Pete out of my bedroom." Theresa said. Everyone was silenced.

Irene said. "Theresa, we all know of your problems, but we don't need to know. We're talking about a wedding here, not funerals; so, please, I ask you not to speak in that manner again."

"Well, I'm sorry; if you don't want me in your house, you can just say so. I'll go to my daughter's in-laws."

"And what make you think they want you there?"

Theresa stood up; her eyes had an incredibly angry look, "What did you say?" "I'm sure you heard me the first time, Theresa." Irene said.

"Who taught you manners?" Theresa asked Irene.

"I'm sure she is not as well skilled as whoever taught you."

Pete stood up. "I'm sorry, Theresa. You are still carrying my name; you have to stop insulting people every time you open your mouth. I want to apologize to everyone for this. Theresa get up from the table, you don't deserve to sit with this family."

Pete walked to Theresa, held her by her arm and led her to her room. Once there, he told her, "Pack your things, Theresa, you have to stay somewhere else."

"But where?" She asked.

"I'm going to take you to a hotel. You have worn out your welcome with this family and with the Lopez family."

"With the Lopez family? What did I do to them?"

"If you don't know, Theresa, I can't tell you."

"Pete, I think I want to go back to Australia as soon as possible. Would you come with me tomorrow to the attorney's office? Maybe I can sign something and you can take care of the divorce papers after I leave."

"Under the circumstances, I think it's for the best."

Pete returned to the table. "I don't know what else I can say. I sent Theresa to a hotel. We'll go to her attorney tomorrow."

"That was not necessary, she can stay here. I just didn't think what she said was appropriate," Irene said.

"Nothing she says is appropriate, Irene."

"No," Kate said, "if you'll both go to the attorney tomorrow. The divorce can be handled and signed after she leaves."

"Well, that's the most intelligent thing she has done since she arrived!" Irene said. "Irene! What's wrong with you?" Kate said.

"I guess I'm getting senile in my young age, Mama." Irene smiled big.

Brent asked Irene, "I want to know if you have started my portrait."

"Believe it or not, I have. I'm just playing with it now. The best posture I want to use. Maybe you will pose for a picture sometime, are you game?"

"You know I am, baby; whenever you're ready, let me know, I'll bring my portrait costume."

"That's right; we have to agree on what you want to wear for it."

"I think something very casual, like you're at the beach or something like that.

"You know. Irene, I have my sailboat out on the coast of Maine. It's in storage now, but I used to ride it every chance I had when I went to school in New York. I would love it if you painted me on my boat. In fact, I think I'll get my boat shipped to South Carolina."

"Pete, do you want to go to the store tomorrow? We need to give them a warning to get a position ready for you," Charles told Pete.

"You bet I do, Charles. But don't forget I have to go with Theresa's to visit with her lawyer tomorrow. I'll check at what time I need to go with her."

"Like I said, they need time to find a position for you, don't you think so?" Charles said. "What kind of work did you do before?"

"I sold insurance, Life, Home, different kinds."

"I think you can get acquainted with several of the departments in the store."

"Great, Charles!"

"Sarah, is there anything new in your daily routine?" Kate asked her daughter. "No, Mama, we're still doing the same thing."

"Clare, since Theresa didn't have a chance to eat dinner, would you please ask her if you can take something to her?"

"I thought she had left."

"Not until tomorrow."

"Would it be all right if I brought her a tray to her room? It'd save me a trip upstairs."

"That will be fine, Clare." And talking to everyone else, she said, "Why don't we move to the living room to drink our coffee?"

Once there, Brent and Irene remained standing and said: "We said several months ago, we would announce when we thought Irene and I could get married; we have thought about it and we think, we can safely say we could marry in June." Brent said.

"Irene," Sarah said, "Oh, Irene, can Darrell and I be married on the same day?"

"I think you're asking the wrong person, Sarah." Sarah turned around and asked Charles.

"Papa, could Tyke and I get married when Irene and Brent do?" Charles hugged his daughter and said,

"How can I say no to you?" She went to Darrell and embraced him,

"Did you hear honey? We can get married in June."

"Thank you, Mr. Hamilton." Darrell said to Charles.

"Laura! Benny! Hello, we haven't seen you for a while; would you like a cup of coffee?" Kate came over to welcome her daughter, "How are you feeling? How much longer are you going to wait on this baby to come?"

"I think it's a matter of days, Mama."

"Oh, I hope the baby is not going to come at the same time as the weddings!"

"What weddings?" Laura asked.

And Sarah answered her at the top of her voice. "**We are getting married, Irene and Brent and Tyke and I; are finally getting married!**

"When is the wedding going to be?"

"In June." Sarah answered.

"Is anyone getting married besides Sarah?" Laura asked amused at her sister's excitement. Everyone laughed.

Irene said. "Sarah, I'd like to know what kind of fantasies you dreamed for your wedding."

"Honestly, Irene, I just want to get married, I don't care about a big wedding."

"I'm so glad you said that, Sarah. Because Brent and I decided a long time ago; we're not having a big wedding, family and close friends only."

Pete and Clare came into the living room, "Charles and family, as you all know, my divorce became final last month; Clare and I came to notify you that we are getting married next week." Everyone stood up and went to congratulate the new couple.

"Oh Pete, we're so happy for both of you. But when did this happen that we didn't notice?"

"We kind of knew we loved each other, we have been having coffee every morning for weeks now, so when I was brave enough to tell Clare how I felt, we decided we didn't have to wait for anything. I received the final divorce papers last week, so now; we're getting everything ready to be married."

Kate walked to Clare and hugged her. "Clare, I'm so happy for both of you. Pete, have you told Christina yet?"

"No, we plan to go there next Sunday, but I know she'll be happy for us."

"Yes, she will, she has always liked Clare," Kate said.

Charles said, "Brent, Darrell, Benny Pete, come with me; we're getting some champagne. This is a big celebration." The men went to the cellar to get the wine and Clare went to the kitchen. When she came back, she was carrying a big cake and Joanna was following her with saucers and everything else for their celebration.

Kate said. "Clare, did you know you were going to make your announcement today?"

"I had an idea, and a cake is never wasted in this house, anyway."

"Tell me Clare, how did this happen with Pete and you?"

"Well, we are neighbors you know? Every day, when he came back from work, we'd have a cup of coffee and lots of conversation. He is a very interesting man. I was hooked. It kind of scared me, because I never had boyfriends, you know, and I'm too old to be carrying on with someone. I told him so; he told me right away he wanted to marry me, so here we are."

"I'm so very happy for you Clare; you deserve to be happy, and Pete seems to be the one. He'll know how to treat you. He seems to be a good man who chose the wrong mate the first time."

"And he deserves to be happy as well," Clare said with a twinkle in her eye.

The men came back carrying the champagne and being jolly, laughing and dancing. "Well, it seems you already started celebrating in the cellar." Kate told them.

"And why not? We are happy, and we want everyone to know about it." The wine was poured, and the cake served.

Pete said, "Thank you, I want to thank everyone for my happiness. I honestly didn't even know I wasn't happy. It had been so many years of plain monotony; I thought that was all I was supposed to expect from life at this age. I didn't know there was this wonderful creature waiting for me. Thank you, Clare." Clare, clearly bashful, looked down at the floor, her face flushed.

Brent took the floor next. "I want to thank the Lord, for saving Irene twice for me, I love Irene beyond words, but she knows that." She kissed him; he smiled and kissed her back. "We'll have a good life."

Darrell was next. "What can I say? I made a fool of myself for a long time in front of everyone and I didn't care. I have been the ladies man for years, and this young princess put me down to size, and didn't know it. She didn't know for a long time that I was crazy for her. I am humbly thankful that she loves me, I hope, as I love her."

Everyone raised their glasses and drank champagne.

"Clare, are you going to be married in Church? Kate asked. "Pete, did you marry in Church?"

"No, we went to a Courthouse to got married."

"Well, Clare, you have never been married, why don't you do it right? Charles will give you away."

"Pete, have you talked about where you are going to live?" Charles asked.

"No, we haven't done much talking; it took me some time to convince Clare to marry me."

"Clare, do you think you want to continue working here after you get married?"

"Yes, I don't think of any reason why not. Pete will be working all day, so I can work as well."

"Pete, we have some rental houses not far from here, I think there is a vacant house now, I'll ask tomorrow and you can both go to look at them, see what you think." Charles said.

"That will be wonderful, but you're going let me pay rent, you have done so much for me."

"Clare, you and I are going shopping for your wedding, little lady. Irene, why don't you come along? Maybe we could do lunch together; wouldn't that be fun?" Kate said.

"Laura, what are your plans with school now that the baby is so close?"

"They're letting me do some courses at home, Mama, so I have been getting extra credits, and the ones I did before we married, I don't have that long to finish High School."

"Are you going to walk with your class when you finish school Laura?"

"Yes, I think I am, Mama."

"I'm glad, Laura. You have worked a lot for that, and you deserve to walk with your class."

"Thank you, Mama. I really came to ask you: I feel I'm ready to have the baby, I want to know if I can call you before Benny takes me to the hospital."

"Laura, you need to forget why you're having the baby so soon. You call me whenever you need something, same as Irene or Sarah. You better get Benny to call your Dad and I before he takes you to the hospital. Nothing has changed between us Laura, not one thing." Laura kissed her mother.

Chapter Twenty One

Kate said, "I'm so excited! We are bringing Christina such good news."

Clare said, "I'm glad you feel that way, Kate. But we don't know how she is going to feel when she hears the news."

"I can tell you, Christina was very happy when her mother left. She was only unhappy she turned out the way she did," Pete said.

When they arrived, everyone was waiting for them. "Papa, I'm so happy you came, and brought the whole family!"

"Yes, we all decided we needed a ride out of town," Charles said.

"Please, come in!" Christina went in hugging her Dad. "Christina, I have some news for you."

"Is it good news?"

"I think it is, I hope you think so too."

"Christina, Clare and I have fallen in love, and we are getting married next week."

"Oh Papa, I'm so happy," she hugged them both, and then she told Clare. "I always thought of you as if you were my mother, now I know why." She hugged her and kissed her.

"Wait a minute," Sarah said. "They are not the only one getting married; Irene and I are getting married in June." Mr. and Mrs. Lopez walked in, everyone was congratulating someone,

"Just a minute, Cristobal said, "We need to be in on this celebration." So they were told about all the weddings.

Don Cristobal walked away from the group towards the barracks. "Mario," he said. "Didn't you kill a cow yesterday?"

"Yes Sir."

"How many steaks did you get? Would it be enough for our company?"

"I'm sure, Sir."

"Go to the kitchen and tell them to cook steaks and enough of everything else for dinner. Tell the vaqueros to bring some music. We have company." He went back and told them. "You know you're staying for dinner, everything has been arranged. Pete, congratulations to you and your bride, welcome to our family."

Clare's eyes were tearful. Kate saw her. She held her hand. "Clare, it was past due for you to enjoy life. One thing: I don't think you should keep working with us. Did you hear Mr. Lopez? I didn't think about it, but you are part of their family now. You come any time you want to and visit with us, Lord knows Irene needs company all the time, but not to work anymore. Pete has a good job Clare, he is taking care of all the insurance business for all of Charles's businesses, and he gets paid well. Have you looked at the house Charles mentioned?"

"Yes, Pete and I went a couple of days ago. It's very nice, Kate. Kate, you know, nothing like this ever happened to me before, it was always someone else. I'm afraid I'm going to wake up and everything is going up in smoke."

"No, it's natural for you to feel that way. But didn't you hear Pete mentioning something similar about it? He didn't believe he'd ever be happy again, but it happened. Believe, Clare. It was about time it happened to you, too. We'll go shopping tomorrow. I'll tell Irene."

"Irene! Have you come to pick up your dress?" Doris greeted them as they came in the door.

"I can take it with me, but we came to get a dress for another bride."

"Of course you can take your gown whenever you like. But let's take care of the new bride first, shall we? What do you have in mind Miss.?"

"What color do you think would look good on me, Kate?" Clare asked.

"Irene, you have good taste, what do you think."

"I think she needs to wear what she likes, any color she likes. Let's see what they have, and choose a gown from that, Clare."

"I think that dress would look beautiful on you Clare. Why don't you try it on for size, after all, you have to start somewhere." It was a long gown, light grey with a pink shine to it, with heavy taffeta and over it, a beautiful lace that touched the floor. The blouse was high neckline with a turtle collar and long sleeves, the sleeves were also lace. A sash made out of taffeta with a corsage, an orchid, and a spray of tiny flowers and greenery was on the waist.

"Oh, Clare, it looks fantastic, and you look gorgeous in that gown!" Kate told her.

"If I were you, I wouldn't look any farther. It's a beautiful dress and the color is so unique. I love it." Irene told Clare. "Do you have any hats and shoes to complement the dress, Doris?"

"Of course, wait a minute,"

"I think we lucked out unless you want to see something else, Clare."

Clare said, "I'm totally in your hands, and if you said this is satisfactory for me to be married in, then I like it too."

"No, Clare, if you think this dress is "satisfactory" for your wedding, don't wear it. We'll find another dress. What Mama and I said was, we love the dress for your wedding, but not if you find it only 'satisfactory' Doris, show her more dresses."

"No, Irene, I'll take this one."

"Doris, why don't you walk with Clare, and let her see other dresses she might like."

"But Irene, I'm happy with this dress,"

"Mama and I are happy with your dress; we want you to be happy with it, Clare. So, go and look at other dresses; you need to be sure you love your wedding dress."

"All right, but I can wear this dress."

Clare left with Doris, and stayed gone for a long time. "I don't know how Clare wouldn't like the dress, I think it's beautiful, and it looks great on her," Irene told Kate.

They came back. Clare was still wearing the same dress. "Well, what does it mean that you're still wearing the same dress?" Irene asked Clare.

"It means that you were right the whole time. This is the prettiest dress I saw."

"Yes, but now, you know it, as well."

"Lorenzo, did you get bored waiting on us?"

"Oh no, Miss Irene,"

"All right, we want to go eat lunch now. Mama, do you want to go to the restaurant that Brent and I go to all the time?"

"Do you mean, you're going to take us to your private restaurant?"

"With all my heart."

"Great," Kate said.

"You have been telling me all about your restaurant, giving me their menus and now, I can order!" They all laughed.

The next day, Irene was awaked by a sharp pain in her heart. She opened her eyes, "Oh no," she thought to herself, "Nothing can happen to me, not again." She closed her eyes and kept them closed for a long time, she fell asleep. When she woke up again, she felt good. She didn't move, she didn't dare. "I won't say anything, I'll probably have to cancel the wedding again. I'll just be very careful from now on. Yes, that's what I'll do," she convinced herself.

Irene didn't shower, she felt tired. She dressed slowly and went downstairs. "Clare, I think I'll have a glass of orange juice; I won't eat breakfast this morning. I'm going to paint; I think I'll try to finish Brent's painting." When Clare went back with Irene's orange juice, she found her asleep on the couch. She quietly sat down the glass of juice on a table, and went out running to Kate.

"Kate, it might be nothing, but Irene came downstairs and asked for a glass of orange juice, no breakfast this morning, I went out to the kitchen to get it, and when I got back, she was asleep on the couch. It might be nothing, Kate, but under the circumstances, I thought I better let you know."

"You did right, Clare."

Kate and Clare went to the studio where Irene was sleeping. "When they arrived, Irene was drinking her orange juice."

"Good morning, Mama."

"Good morning, Irene."

"How do you feel this morning, dear?"

"A little tired, Mama, we had a long day with Clare yesterday. Remember?"

"Irene, if you feel bad. You would tell us, wouldn't you dear? Remember no one is able to know how you feel but yourself, alone."

"Don't worry about me so much, Mother."

Kate left Irene and went to Charles office so she could have more privacy in order to make a call to Brent.

"Brent, I don't like to interrupt you, but would you come to eat lunch with Irene today, please? Listen," and she told Brent of the incident as she knew it.

"You did right, Kate... No, I won't tell Irene you called me. I know she doesn't like to be watched, but we must, because she doesn't do it herself. Thank you for calling me, Kate."

Brent came in and went looking for Irene. He found her in her study painting his portrait by his sail boat. "Well, I see that is taking form, it looks great baby, considering you don't have much to work with." He said kissing her.

"Hey, what are you doing here?"

"I came to see if you would invite me to lunch. How about it?"

"You can have lunch with me any day." Brent took both of Irene's hands and gently pulled her towards him and kissed her, "Come here," he told her.

"Are you keeping any secrets from me?"

"What are you talking about?"

"Oh, nothing really. I just don't want you to keep any secrets from me."

"Brent, I know what you're not saying, I had a long day yesterday, and I'm a little tired today."

"Baby, you know we have to be very careful with you. Don't get me scared, if you have any strange feelings, please tell me so I can check you out."

"I will, when there is something to say, but now, there is nothing to say, really."

"All right, I'll leave you alone, as long as you're straight with me."

Clare came in, "Kids, lunch is ready."

"How much longer are you going to work, Clare?" Brent asked her.

"I understand Mama is trying to get her fired, but she won't let her." Irene joked with them. Arm in arm, Brent and Irene walked to the dining room.

Pete came in all smiles, "Clare, how long will it take you to get ready to come with me?"

"Where do you want to go?"

"We need to get our wedding bands." Pete told Clare.

"I told you to leave earlier, Clare. Go on and leave with Pete. When is the wedding going to be?" They looked at each other and said.

"We have to ask the Priest when he has a date for our wedding. Also, we need to get our marriage license."

"You need to take some time for your wedding; did you hear that, Clare?"

"Kate, I need some help, I can help, but I don't know how to be a leader."

"Well, tell me what you need to get done and between Irene and I, we'll organize it for you."

Clare and Pete left. Kate said, "I am so happy about Clare and Pete. I never thought she would marry anyone, and Pete is such a good man."

"I spoke with Christina the other day," Irene said. "And she is so happy about her Dad getting married again. She has always loved Clare and she knows she will be good for her Dad."

"And Clare needed someone so bad, she is so painfully shy. I think she is over 50 years old, and never had a boyfriend! Not that she couldn't have one but being so timid, kept her from it."

"Pete will take care of that." Kate said smiling.

"Mama, are we going to hold a reception at home for Clare and Pete?"

"Yes, I thought so; I talked it over with your Dad. He told me to find out how many people are coming, to decide to hold the reception here or at the club. I feel like my sister it's getting married," Kate said. "Let me call Christina, maybe she knows how many people are coming from the Lopez' home. Then, it's all of us, Benny and Laura; I think we should invite Mr. Betancourt and his wife as well.

"I think I'm going to ask Joanna, to substitute Clare with the house duties. What do you think?"

"Yes, she has been here almost as long as Clare. She knows your taste the same as Clare does."

"Let's go back to the living room, your Dad and Brent will think we left."

"Well, we thought you left the house." Kate looked at Irene, and they both laughed.

"No, we were making plans for Clare and Pete's wedding."

"Do you know when they're getting married?"

"No, that's the only detail we're waiting for."

"We have to hold a reception for them, Charles, either at home or at the club, according of the amount of people they're inviting. I'm guessing they only want the family. I'm also guessing she is going to ask you to give her away, Charles."

"Pete, Clare, I'm glad you came back. We have so many questions to ask you."

"Go ahead." Clare said.

"Do you know how many people you are inviting to your wedding?"

Pete and Clare looked at each other. "Just the family, Kate."

"That's twelve counting Laura, Benny and her in-laws. Carlos, Christina and his parents, four more, Mr. Moran is the only friend we know Pete has."

"Clare, how about if we cater the reception here at home?"

"Don't forget to invite Father Gabriel," Charles said. "Christina, Carlos, welcome!"

"What are you doing in the city?"

"I miss all of you. How are the wedding plans going?

That's what we are talking about this minute."

"We were counting heads, do you know if anyone besides Mr. and Mrs. Lopez are coming from Carlos's house?"

"No, that's all Mrs. Hamilton."

"Clare, do you have a date yet?"

"Pete, is there anything final for the wedding date?"

"We had to give a date for the rings," he pulled a piece of paper out of his pockets and reading it, said: "February 14th."

Everyone laughed. "You didn't remember that date?"

When everyone left, Kate told Clare, "I want to ask you, Clare, would you like to dress in my bedroom for your wedding? The reception is here and it might be better."

"Thank you, Kate, but it doesn't really matter, Pete knows where I live. Thank you for all the arrangements, Kate, I really appreciate that."

"Something else, Clare, I have asked Joanna to replace you." Kate hugged her. "Clare, I can't tell you how happy I am for you."

"Thank you, Kate. I don't know how I would have endured all these years without you."

Charles and Pete walked in. "Hey, Clare is not going away, she's just moving a few blocks from here." They said laughing.

"You can laugh if you want to; we're going to miss each other."

"Okay, can you decide now, who are you going to invite to your wedding? We can go ahead and reserve the caterer. Also, at what time is your wedding?"

"You're right Kate, those are things that have to be decided now, not next week." "How about Saturday evening?" Pete said. "No one has to work Sunday. I asked for a week off after the wedding. Where do you want to go on our honeymoon, Clare?"

"What are you talking about? Honeymoon, for us?"

Everyone tried to ignore Clare.

Carlos said. "My father and I want to give you the reception as our wedding gift. Being Saturday night, we need to offer some kind of liquor, wine and something stronger, several kinds of whiskey."

Charles said. "Yes and a driver for everyone who drinks. I say, offer wine, but nothing else."

"I agree." said Kate. "After all, it is going to be in our home."

"I have an idea," said Carlos, "Why don't you get married at our ranch? Unless you have already made arrangements with Father Gabriel, we have a Chapel at the ranch. The only thing, it really would be a lot better if you get married during the day time, because we live so far out of town."

Christina said. "Well, it would take away the bad taste of the last wedding."

"It was nothing wrong with the wedding, Christina." Carlos told her kissing her.

Clare said. "We haven't talked to Father Gabriel, so it's up to you Pete, where do you want to get married?"

"Since my daughter lives at the ranch, I believe we should marry there."

Charles said, "Do you mean there is nothing for us to do?"

"You can give me away." Clare said.

"Kate, would you, please, be my Matron of Honor?" And I would like for Christina, Sarah, and Irene to be Maidens of Honor. And Linda the flower girl."

Kate said. "Oh, Clare, that's so nice!" Christina said hugging her.

Carlos said. "Christina, we better go home and let my parents know we're having company."

"Don't they know it?"

"Oh yes, we talked about it, but now we know the details."

"Papa, my children can be the flower girls, Amy is old enough now to be Grandpa's flower girl." Christina said.

"That will be great, baby. I like that."

Christina went to Clare, "Thank you, Clare, for asking me to be you Maid of Honor, it means a lot to me, we need to clear the air about my mother, I love her because she is my mother, but I don't like her. I like you." Clare hugged Christina.

"Oh, thank you Christina, I've been so worried about you; I didn't want anything wrong to be in between Pete and I."

"It won't be me, Clare. I'm happy for both of you, but I am especially happy for my Dad, I didn't know how he was going to live alone, but now, I know I don't have to worry about him."

Pete and Clare had gone to the garden, "Clare," said Pete, "Do you want to go to Acapulco for our honeymoon?"

"Did Christina put you up to this?"

"Of course not, why do you say that?"

"Because that's where she and Carlos went. In fact, the first time, they couldn't go because of Carlos getting shot. When he recuperated, they tried it again and went."

"If you don't want to go to Acapulco, we can go to San Diego."

"Benny and Laura went there."

"Clare, any place I'd mention to you, someone has gone there. I tell you what, I'll surprise you, unless you have a place in mind and you can make the arrangements."

Christina asked Irene, "Do you want to wear the same color dress for my Dad's wedding, Irene? I was thinking of wearing a short dress, don't you think? It seems a long gown, always makes the wedding looks more formal and Clare doesn't want that. Isn't that right?"

"I will let my mother know, but since she's the Matron of Honor she can wear a long dress if she wants to because the bride is also wearing a long dress."

"I think we better ask them both, don't you think so?"

"You're right."

Christina went close to Brent, made sure Irene wasn't with him and said to him. "Brent, have you been watching Irene? Don't you think she's been very dry and ill tempered? She has never been like that, Brent I'm scared for her."

"I know Christina; I talked to her the other day, but I can't do anything else. There she comes. Hi baby, how are you?"

It was about nine in the morning; Kate went to the kitchen looking for Clare. "Clare, I knew I would find you here."

"I wanted a cup of coffee."

"Let's have a cup," Kate put her arm over Clare's shoulder and said.

"I need a cup, too," and went over to the stove to pour herself a cup.

"No, Kate, let me pour you a cup, it might be the last time I do that. I know I'll be coming for a visit, but it won't be the same." They sat there and visited, reminiscing over their years of friendship.

"Conversation is great, but we have to get ready, Clare."

"Can I tell you a secret, Kate? I'm scared to death."

"Don't be, Clare. Can I help you in any way, Clare? We don't have to rush. We still have several hours."

"When you're finished dressing, Kate, please come back. Check that this old bride didn't put her dress backwards."

Kate went upstairs and knocked on Irene's door. "Irene, are you dressing, dear?" She opened the door and found her asleep. "Irene, dear, are you all right?"

Irene opened her eyes and smiled at her mother. "Of course, Mama, I'm just lazy this morning."

"Do you want me to call someone to help you?"

"And what would they do, Mama?"

"Well, okay,"

"Mama? I want to get married sooner, I don't want to wait until June, I think next month, okay?"

"Whatever you want baby, you're the bride."

Kate closed Irene's bedroom door, she stood still against the door and closed her eyes tight. "No, dear Lord, don't take her away from us. Take me, I have lived a long life, she hasn't even gotten married." Slowly she walked to her own bedroom and dressed.

"I don't think I tell will Charles," she thought. "I might tell Brent, prepare him." She arrived at Clare's bedroom.

"Oh, Clare, you look marvelous!"

"You think so?"

"I do."

"Let's go to the living room and see if the others are ready to leave." Sarah was there, Brent and Darrell had just arrived. Kate motioned Brent to come with her.

"Brent, has Irene told you she wants to get married next month?"

"No Kate, do you know why she has changed her mind?"

"I think you know, Brent, she wants to get married, and she probably knows she doesn't have long..." her voice broke; Brent put his hand on her arm.

"Kate, I think we shouldn't act as if we know what she thinks; we'll get married when she wants to. Let her have the time she has left, the way she wants to spend it. Who knows, if she is happy, she might live a long time."

"Brent, let's not tell anyone about this, I don't want Charles to know."

"Of course not But whenever he finds out, it won't easier."

Brent and Kate went back, Irene was there. "Baby," Brent said to her. "You look fantastic."

"So do you." She told him smiling and kissing him. He embraced her tightly.

"Hey, what's that?"

"I haven't seen you all day, I missed you. Let's go." Brent said.

"You're right, if we don't leave now, we're going to be late. Where is the bride?"

Making her entrance, Clare said. "Here comes the bride with her walking cane." Everyone burst out in laughter.

Lorenzo had brought their car around; Kate said "I'll ride in one of the other cars."

"No," Clare said, "You ride with Charles, and I'll tag along with you two." I guess Laura and the Betancourt family will ride separately."

"I guess so, but if they don't know the way they would have asked."

"I know they know the way. Don't you remember Mr. Betancourt was over when Christina got married?"

"I hope she doesn't remember."

"I don't think she ever saw him."

"I guess Brent and Darrell and the girls decided to ride together."

"Good."

They started the long trip to Las Palmas, "What time is it?" Clare asked.

"It's eleven, Clare. We have plenty of time to get there. I imagine Pete is as nervous as you are."

"Charles, do you know if Theresa has gotten married yet? I thought if that guy didn't want to marry her, she might want to come back for Pete."

"Oh, Clare, where do you come out with stuff like that? If that would happen, she's going to waste her time and money, because Pete would never take her back, especially after he has you, as his wife."

"Charles, has Pete ever talked to you about me?"

"Only the best Clare. He is crazy about you, at first, he was afraid you would reject him. He talked to me about it, it was the fact that you had never been married, and he was worried you would be hesitant about marrying at this time in your life. He thought you might have had a bad experience, and wouldn't want to marry anyone. But he loves you, you can be sure of that."

"Thank you, Charles."

When they arrived to Las Palmas, there was music welcoming them. A beautiful band playing what Clare thought was music from heaven. "Oh, Kate, pinch me." she said. "All of this for me."

"You deserve every bit of it, Clare." Charles got out of the car, and gave his hand to Clare, Kate had ridden in the car up front with Lorenzo, Carlos offered his hand to her.

Christina came over and hugged Clare. "Dad is in the Church, Clare,"

"Thank you, dear." Irene and Christina wore a beautiful evening gown in different shades of blue, Kate wore a darker shade of blue and Clare wore a pearl dress that was so outstandingly beautiful, against the dresses of her bride's servers. Sarah was the first to walk down the aisle, then Irene and Brent and Christina and Carlos walked in as the wedding march began to play, then Darrell walked with Kate. Linda and Amy walked in front of the bride, scattering rose petals, they looked so pretty.

Everyone stood up when Charles walked in with Clare. No one had ever seen her so dressed up. Her dress looked great on her with the small hat that made her outstandingly beautiful. Pete was wearing a white tuxedo; he smiled at her. He looked so good. She thought her heart had stopped, but she kept walking, until they reached him. And the ceremony started.

Pete turned towards Clare and kissed her, she was too disturbed to respond to his kiss. Clare turned around and fell into Kate's embrace. "Clare, congratulations."

"Kate, did you see how he kissed me in front of everybody?"

"Clare! You're his wife now." Kate told her trying very hard not to burst out laughing at her.

"I knew he was going to kiss me, but not like that, in front of everybody."

"Clare, have you ever kissed each other like that before?"

"No, not like that."

"I guess that's why he did it. I say it was about time, Clare."

Kate went looking for Charles. "Charles, come over here. Listen, this is not funny, I want you to talk to Pete and tell him to be careful with Clare. She might be fifty years old, but she has never been with a man and he needs to anticipate that. If he is not careful with her, she is going to run away from him. I mean it."

"Kate, you're seeing things."

"No, Charles, I'm serious, she freaked out when he kissed her after the ceremony."

"Okay, I'll talk with him." Charles said.

Someone came over looking for Charles and Kate; they were waiting for them at the bride and groom's table along with the Lopez's, Irene and Brent and of course Christina and Carlos. Sarah, Laura, Darrell and Benny were together at another table.

"Laura, how much longer do you think you have to wait for the baby?"

"I think any time, Sarah."

"Well, if you go into labor, you have three doctors here."

"It's nice to know, but I'd rather go to my own doctor and to my hospital."

"Did you see the cake, Laura? It's beautiful." "Yes, I guess everything here is beautiful." Laura said, "I didn't know Christina's parents had divorced when Mama called about Clare's wedding to Christina's dad. It really took me by surprise."

"You're lucky you were not around the house when Christina's mother was carrying on wanting to go back to Australia the day they arrived or the day after."

"Didn't she want to visit with Christina?

"I guess not."

"How about the grandchildren?"

"It seems they didn't make an impression on Theresa."

"How sad." Laura said.

"Clare doesn't think so." They all laughed.

"Do you know where the newlyweds are going on their honeymoon?" Sarah asked.

"It seems it was a secret a few days ago." Laura answered her.

"Irene tried to find out, and she wasn't successful."

"Listen, I wasn't crazy about this beef stew, but when I tasted it, I changed my mind. It's delicious, it's beef in wine sauce, I heard. I'm going to ask for the recipe." Sarah said. Darrell, are you going to invite me to dance?"

"I didn't know there was going to be any dancing." He said.

"There is dancing if someone starts. That can be us."

"They're going to cut the cake, let's go get us a piece of cake before they run out. I guess there're not any single girls here for Clare to throw out her bouquet."

"Come on; let's ask Clare if she is going to leave on her honeymoon."

"You go ahead, Sarah."

"Mama said she was very sensitive about it."

"But, why? She got married."

"I guess she didn't expect all this fuss about it."

"And here I sit, waiting for all this fuss to start for me," Complained Sarah.

Clare came by and stopped at Sarah's and Laura's table to say good bye, "Clare, where are you going on your honeymoon?" Sarah asked her.

"We're going to Acapulco, baby."

"Clare, you're not supposed to call me baby any more, remember?"

"Sarah, you were not supposed to ask me where I was going on my honeymoon, remember? I have to change, so excuse me,"

"Clare, the airport is much closer from here. Do you have to go back home?"

"No, baby, I'm going to Christina's bedroom to change clothes. We also brought our luggage with us." Smiling, Clare left the party.

Chapter Twenty Two

The telephone rang, "Charles, the phone is ringing, what time is it?"

"It's almost four o'clock in the morning. Hello, who is this? Oh, Benny, what happened, Son? Did Laura have the baby already? Why didn't you call earlier? Is she all right? It was a boy! We're very happy; we'll come to the hospital later on."

"Well, how does it feel to be a grandmother? You heard it was a boy. Benny said they didn't have time to call any sooner; Laura had the baby in the ambulance. How do you like that?"

"Do you want to go to the kitchen and drink a cup of coffee?"

"I believe I do, Kate. I don't think I can go back to sleep, now"

"Neither can I."

They both put on their robes and started walking downstairs. They found Irene sipping on a cup of coffee. "Irene, what in the world are you doing up so early?" Kate asked her.

"I couldn't sleep. And what got you up so early?"

"Benny called; Laura had a boy in the ambulance."

"Oh, I'm so happy for them." She looked down; Kate saw a tear roll down her cheek.. She squeezed her hand.

"At least, she didn't have a bad time giving birth." Kate said.

"Mama, Papa, Brent and I want to get married next month. I really don't want Sarah to get married the same day. I want her to have her own day, more festivities than I want for my own wedding. Would you help me with that mama? I don't want her to have her feelings hurt. Tell her she'll want maids of honor and more celebrations that she deserves, and I don't want, please, help me make her understand."

"I will, Irene, don't worry about it."

"I think I'm going to bed again, Mama."

"Irene, I wish you would talk to me. Don't keep things from me, I'm your mother, I want to be able to comfort you, but I need for you to talk to me."

"Come to my bedroom with me, Mama."

"Charles, do you want to stay here? Or do you want to go back to bed?"

"I believe I'll stay in the kitchen, Kate. Why don't you take your coffee with you?

They sat in Irene's sitting room, separated from her bedroom. There were two beautiful, comfortable chairs across from each other. In between them was a beautiful, heavy coffee table over a round Arabian rug.

"Irene, what's troubling you sweetheart?" Kate asked Irene.

"Mama, I don't want this as a piece of conversation, I'm telling you something. I feel my heart problem is not cured. That's why I want to get married sooner than planned. I want to be with Brent before I leave this world. Is it too selfish of me, Mother?"

"Of course not, Irene. But I think you should tell Brent how you feel and give him the opportunity to find out if there is anything he can do for you."

"I don't want any more hospitals, Mama. And I don't want to tell Brent about this, promise me you won't tell him."

"I won't tell him if you don't want him to know, Irene."

"Thank you, Mama. I just want to be happy for a little while. Something else Mama, I need for you to talk to Sarah; I want her to have her own wedding day, not to think of mine."

Kate left Irene's bedroom; she wasn't able to stay any longer. She went to her bathroom because she didn't want Charles to see her cry. She didn't know how she was going to hide it from him. And now, she couldn't tell Brent. She had to go downstairs or Charles would start asking questions she couldn't answer.

"Well, I was beginning to think you had gone back to bed." Charles said.

"No, Irene wanted to tell me about her plans to get married next month."

"And what was her reason not to tell her plans in front of Papa?"

"Because she is planning such a small wedding. She thinks it's best if Sarah has her own wedding, on a different day. She wants me to talk to her."

"We need to get ready to go to the hospital and meet our first grandson."

"Mama, why didn't you wake me up? Laura had a boy!" Sarah said.

"Yes, baby, she did."

"Mama, now that we have a real baby in the family, could all of you quit calling me, baby?"

"I'm going to get dressed and go see my grandson, are you coming?"

"I will, but I think I want to call Darrell and we can go together."

"Sarah, come to my bedroom, there is something I want to talk to you about."

"Okay, what is it that you couldn't tell me downstairs?"

"Is not that I couldn't tell you downstairs; I need to get dressed at the same time. Sarah, for reasons I can't get into now, Irene, wants to get married next month, no bride maids, just the ceremony, she doesn't even want Dad to walk her to the altar. She only wants to get married. So, she believes you need a proper wedding with all the trimmings. Get your own day, Darrell and you, can get married whenever you want to; by yourself."

"Can we get married right after Irene?"

"What do you mean by, right after?"

"Maybe the following month, not too much fuss. But I want bride maids and I want Papa to walk me to the altar. We can have a reception here at home for the family, and we can have invitations, is that okay, mama?"

"Yes, sweetheart, you and Darrell can start making your arrangements; remember Irene will get married next month. Two weeks away."

"Brent," Kate greeted him at the entrance. "What brings you so early?"

"Irene called me and invited me for breakfast."

"Didn't Darrell come with you?"

"I left him asleep."

"Oh, sleepy head. I'll call him."

"I wouldn't if I were you. He was called to the hospital last night, I understand he did surgery, I know he doesn't want to get up, he went to bed as I was leaving home, Sarah, sorry."

"Do you mean he is not coming to see me today?"

"He probably set the clock for five hours of sleep, isn't that fair?"

"Yes Brent, it's very fair." Sarah said smiling.

"You know something Sarah, you have grown up."

"I hope so, Brent, I want to do it for Darrell, I love him very much. Did you know that?"

"No Sarah, but I hope you do. Because I know how much Darrell loves you."

"Thank you for telling me. Darrell tells me he loves me, but to hear it from you it takes a different angle. Brent, can I ask you a question?

"Of course Sarah, what is it?"

"Is Irene in any danger?"

"Not particularly, no, why do you ask?"

"You know we were supposed to have gotten married the same day. Now, she doesn't want us to get married on the same day."

"I talked to her about it, Sarah; she thinks when you think of your wedding day, she won't be in the middle of it. It will be your day only. I think it's very thoughtful, really."

"That's what I want to talk to Darrell about, you'll get married in about two weeks, I'll get married next month. Mama said its okay."

"Well, let me go upstairs and talk to Irene. I'll see you later."

Brent knocked on Irene's bedroom door. "It's open." She said.

Brent opened the door, Irene was lying down, "Hi sweetheart." she said. "Did I get you up too early?"

"You know you didn't, Darrell had to go on an emergency and wound up doing surgery. He was up all night. He came home as I was leaving to come over here."

"Brent, when are we getting married?"

"Do you want to go get our marriage license tomorrow? We can go by the hospital and get our blood tests."

"Yes, Brent. And we can get married in one week; will that be all right with you?"

"Yes, Irene. Where do you want to go on our honeymoon?"

"Could we just go to the beach, right here in Los Caminos?"

"Yes, Irene, that will be marvelous. Let's tell your parents. How about if we go downstairs now and eat breakfast. I think I'm hungry."

"I think I want to wait a little while on eating," Irene said.

"Irene, sweetheart. You know I'm doing everything you want to without a question, but you need to let me try to help you, baby."

"Brent, I don't want to go to the hospital, I don't want you to tell me I need another surgery I'm never coming out of."

"Irene, right now, that's what is consuming you. Let's go to breakfast. Then we'll go to my apartment. All right? I'll call Darrell and tell him to leave and stay out."

"Do you mean, what I think you mean."

"Why not? We're getting married in one week; we'll just anticipate the honeymoon."

"Yes, why not? It's a marvelous idea sweetheart. Don't tell mama, okay?"

"Not me," Brent said smiling.

They arrived at Brent's apartment. Brent opened the door. Darrell was gone.

"Irene, we have to go slow and stay in low key, all right?"

She smiled, "You're the driver." She said.

He took her to his bed, and left the bedroom, "I'll be back in a few minutes, darling."

When he came back, Irene was in bed with her eyes closed. He got into bed and kissed her very gently. He held her in his arms for a long time. Then he started kissing her, Irene kissed him back. . . .

"Irene, are you all right?" Brent asked her.

"I'm more than all right. This is better than any surgery you could have done."

He laughed. "I don't think your father would have approved."

"Brent, I don't have that awful feeling in my heart, like I am never going to be with you. That feeling is gone, darling. I think I can wait a week for you now."

"Well, if we behave ourselves, we can come back again."

"Could we, darling?"

"Any time you say, my love."

When Brent and Irene went back to her home, Kate said, "You had me worried"

"Why," Irene asked. "You knew I was with my doctor. We stopped somewhere on the beach and necked a little. Mama, we're having our blood tests done tomorrow and buying the license. We can get married next week."

"I say that's fast. Any reason?"

"We should have thought about it a long time ago." Irene said smiling.

Sarah said, "When can I get married?"

"Pick the day, sister." Irene told her.

"Really?"

"You're getting married about the first of March, can I get married a month after that?"

"You would pick April fool's day to get married." Irene said laughing.

"Oh, no! I'll look at the calendar and pick Saturday after that. I have to wait for Darrell." Sarah said.

Irene was sipping on a cup of coffee; Sarah came over to chat with her. "Irene, why do you want me to have my own wedding day, instead of holding the ceremony together?"

"Well, Sarah, I got to thinking. Any time either one of us think about our wedding; we'll see the other one's face as well. Besides that, I don't want anything at all, and I know you do. It's better. You'll see. Who is coming to see our nephew?"

"I'll come later Sarah; I think I want to rest some before I leave home again."

"I'll tell Laura." Sarah said.

Brent smiled at Irene. "How did you manage to convince Sarah so quickly?"

"I guess she must have been in a hurry."

"Brent, I'll lay down here in the study. Will you come with me?"

"Of course baby, I saw the morning newspaper somewhere, I'll look for it and meet you in the study." Brent got the newspaper, and followed Irene to the study.

Irene smiled at Brent when he went in; and still smiling, closed her eyes.

Brent looked at the paper, but he wasn't reading anything. He looked at Irene, how long did she have? How could he maintain this charade? At least, they were going to get married. Brent had to leave. He had to talk to Darrell in case Irene wants to go back to the apartment before they did. His heart ached, what if she died when they were making love? It would kill him, but that wasn't what she was thinking of, and he knew it. Brent dropped his head and went to sleep.

Something woke Brent up; it was Irene trying not to make noise, walking out of there.

"Well, are you escaping me?" Brent asked her.

"I'll be right back, darling." She told him. "Do you want to go to the hospital to see Laura?"

"Yes, I think we should go, everybody else is there. Clare we'll be mad that she wasn't here."

Irene went upstairs to shower and dress. Brent waited for her in her sitting room.

"Brent, don't you need to shower yourself?"

"I did that before we left my apartment dear; I guess you must have been asleep."

"Irene, as soon as we get married, I want you to go to a gynecologist and ask him to prescribe you birth control pills." Seeing her surprised face, he added. "We don't need another problem, Irene."

"You're right. The only thing, it could have already happened."

"Don't tell me that." He said with a faint smile.

"Brent. I'm so sorry I have made so many problems for you."

"No, Irene, I only wish I could solve them."

"I need to tell you something: you've given me more than anyone in the world, if I only live a few days. You have given them to me; remember that. I know my days are numbered Brent, but I don't want you to blame yourself for anything that might happen to me, Brent, I have been so selfish."

"No, Irene. Why do you say that?"

"Because I made you make love to me, knowing the danger I'd be in; and knowing what it will do to you. But darling, I couldn't leave this earth without loving you like that. I'm not sorry for that, but I want to make sure you know, that I know what I'm doing. And that's the way I want it, all right?"

"I don't want to tell you Irene, but I'd rather have you alive even if I'm never able to make love to you again."

"No, when I'm gone, I want you to have good memories of us. And Brent, when I'm gone, I don't want you to be alone, I want you to find someone to love, have a family."

"But I have good memories, Irene. And I don't want any advice about having another love. I only want you. I wish you'd work on my painting some more."

"I know, I'll get to work on that tomorrow."

"Sweetheart, tell me how do you feel?"

"I feel fine, Brent. I don't want you to worry about me so much, but I felt I had to tell you what was coming; because I wanted to change the wedding date, and that is the reason why I had to change it."

"I'm glad you told me, Irene, for many reasons. It also gives me the chance to check on you every day. As for now, your vital signs are normal."

"Kate, I'm back!" said Clare coming into the house.

"Oh, I'm so glad, Clare. When did you get in?" Kate asked her.

"It was kind of late last night. Of course, Pete wanted to go to work this morning, so I had to come and tell all of you, hello. How has Irene been, Kate?"

"She has been just fine, Clare. Tell me, was everything the way you hoped it would be?" Kate asked Clare.

"Kate, I didn't know what to expect, and you know that. But everything was great!"

"Let's have a cup of coffee, do you want to?"

"I want to visit with Irene first. Maybe she would want a cup herself," Clare said.

"You're right. She has been doing a lot of work on Brent's portrait."

"Irene, baby, how are you?" Clare hugged and kissed Irene.

"Clare!, it's nice seeing you again."

Kate came in saying, "I went to the kitchen to ask Joanne to bring us coffee over here, Irene, if you would like something ask her when she comes in. darling."

"Thank you, Mama. Come on, Clare;tell us how your trip was?" Irene asked Clare."It was great; you know I had never been out of the U. S. before now?"

"And what did you think of it?"

"It was a good experience. I had never danced before. And Pete made me dance every time there was music being played, and there was always music playing. Beautiful! I may add. The beaches were so lovely. I will never forget them. They would bring us drinks right there where we were by the water, and bring us drinks in a coconut. And I had to buy a bathing suit because I never thought about buying one before we left." Clare said with a happy tone in her voice.

"Clare, I hope you are as happy as you sound." Kate told her.

"I am very happy, Kate. I am so happy I met Pete," Kate and Irene hugged Clare.

Clare walked around to where Irene had been painting. "Irene, this is terrific, I didn't know you were so artistically inclined. Brent looks more handsome than he really is." She said with a twinkle in her eye.

"Now, just a minute, Brent is every bit as handsome as I portrayed him."

"Maybe, but you did him justice."

"Thank you Clare, it makes me feel good you think so."

Irene said. "Do you want to go to town to eat lunch? Or do you prefer to stay here."

"To tell you the truth, Pete is coming home for lunch today." She said blushing.

"Pardon me," Irene said winking an eye at her and her mother. "Mama, do you know if Brent said anything about coming for lunch today?"

"I believe he said he would come if he didn't have to go back to the hospital."

"We need to get our marriage license and get our blood test." Irene said.

"Is there something I don't know?" Clare said.

"Brent and I plan to get married next week, Clare."

"Just you? How about Sarah, isn't she having a heart attack over it?" Clare said.

"We talked about it; she's getting married in April."

"Clare, with the excitement of your arrival, I forgot to tell you Laura had a boy a few days ago." And she went on telling her all about it.

Chapter Twenty Three

"Irene, do you want me to help you dress, darling?" Kate asked Irene." It's almost time to be in church."

"I guess so, Mama." Irene responded.

"Oh, you decided not to wear your wedding dress" Irene was wearing a light pink dress, made out a silk fabric. Long sleeves, high neck, and on her waist, a sash made out of heavy satin. Very elegant and beautiful on Irene.

"Well, I thought it's very heavy, Mama, I don't feel like carrying such a heavy load today," Irene told her mother.

"Sarah has been waiting on a wedding date, and I don't think she has gone to pick out her dress, maybe she would want to wear your dress, do you think so?"

"I hope she likes it well enough to wear it, Mama, I hate it's going to waste."

"Mama, if Sarah doesn't want to wear my dress. When I go, that's what I want to wear." Irene said with teary eyes.

"Irene, please don't talk like that, especially today, your wedding day."

"I'm sorry Mama; it's that I have gotten accustomed to the idea. It's not scary to me any longer." She said half smiling.

"Let me see if Brent is here," Kate said trying to run out of Irene's bedroom.

"Mama, he should be at the church."

"You're right; I don't know what's the matter with me. Let me go get your Dad."

Kate stopped just outside of Irene's bedroom to take a deep breath before she talked to Charles. "Charles, dear, are you ready to leave? Irene is."

"Kate, just how is Irene, is she all right, sweetheart?" Charles asked Kate.

"Of course she is Charles, do you think Brent would continue with the wedding is she was not?" Kate said trying to swallow her tears.

"I guess I'm just so frightened for her, dear."

"It's natural for us to feel that way Charles, but if something is to happen to Irene, this is what she needs Charles. She needs to be married to Brent, and you know that."

When they arrived at the church, they saw Brent and Darrell's cars there. Benny's car was also there, along with several other cars. They guessed Carlos and his parents and Pete's car.

"Well, let's go in, baby." Charles told Irene. Kate walked ahead of them. Irene smiled when she saw Brent waiting for her at the Altar. All her family and close friends were there, no one else. That is plenty of people for me, she thought. No music. Charles walked Irene to the altar and Brent, the men shook hands, Charles kissed Irene, and stepped back.

Father Gabriel had always been very eloquent. But he excelled himself when he spoke to Irene and Brent; he called them to be very exceptional people. "And may the Lord give them a long life." When the ceremony was finished; they all went to their home, Irene didn't want any more than that.

Brent asked Irene, "Irene, darling, are you feeling all right? Will you be up to company the rest of the day?"

"Maybe not all day, Brent. We could go to the apartment as soon as we can. I'd rather not tell them that's where we're going."

"You're right. We don't need innuendoes." He said smiling.

When they entered the house, there had set a long table with everything under the sun. It looked delicious. "Mama, when did you have time to do that?"

"I only made a phone call, Irene. I called the caterers; aren't they great?"

"And look at the cake, Mama, is beautiful! Thank you, I didn't expect anything like this," She said. Brent held her in his arms constantly.

Everyone surrounded the newlyweds to congratulate them. And then it was time to eat. They had everything arranged for a Buffet style luncheon, and it was a generous one. After they ate, they cut the cake. Then they walked to Kate and told her.

"Mama, I'm going to change clothes, I think I need to rest some before we can go anywhere."

"Of course, darling. Please keep me informed, Brent; call me every day if at all possible." She said. Her voice broke in mid-sentence. After all, they all knew, she may not see her alive again. They embraced, Irene told Kate. "Mama, try not to worry too much, all right?" Kate smiled.

After they said goodbye, they left. They went to Brent's apartment. "Irene, taking a shower is also a lot of effort; I wish you'd just lay down and try to take a nap. I'll be here close to you."

"Don't you want to lay down next to me?" Irene asked Brent.

"Yes, but we don't want to start anything we can't finish." He said smiling. He kissed her briefly on the lips.

"All right, I think you're right. I better charge my energy some."

While Irene took a nap, Brent checked the medication kit he had put together in case Irene needed help while she was in his apartment. He sat on a big chair and leaned back, he closed his eyes. "Dear Lord." He prayed. "Don't take Irene yet, give us a little time."

"Brent, Brent," he heard Irene calling him. He ran to her. "Darling?" He said,

"I only wanted to ask you if I could take a shower now."

"I think it will be all right. May I join you?" he asked her.

"I thought you would never ask," She said smiling.

Brent was so scared, that something was going to happen to Irene; he wanted to be with her the whole time. He was so tender with her; he loved her so much, he couldn't stand the thought that she would be gone when he least expected it.

They embraced in the shower; they both had their eyes closed. As if they both wanted to keep that memory with them. He dried her hair, "I don't want you to exert yourself, darling." She smiled, but she didn't see Brent's tears in his eyes.

Slowly, they walked to the bed. "Remember Irene, we have to go slow." He said.

"You're the driver." She teased him, as she always did.

"Brent began to kiss her." Her eyes were closed.

"Irene, can you keep going?"

"Yes, Brent, I'm all right. Don't worry so much, darling." She said with a faint voice.

Their love flourished, the love they felt for a long time, at last was being carried out.

Brent stopped. He looked at Irene, her eyes were closed. "Irene, darling, talk to me," He said. Her body was flaccid. He ran to get his stethoscope; he checked her heart, she had a heart beat.

She opened her eyes. "Brent, darling? I'm all right; I was only enjoying the moment." She said.

"Don't do that to me, you scared me to death!" he said flopping onto the bed next to her, with a very relieved expression on his face. They embraced and went to sleep.

Brent woke up first. He tried to slip out of bed without awakening her; she just moved over and went back to sleep again. He went into the bathroom and took a shower. "I don't know," he thought, "how can I tell when she is in danger?" he dressed, I think I'll make some coffee, he thought.

"Brent, darling, why didn't you wake me up?" she said.

"I felt like taking a shower, there was no need in awakening you. How about a cup?"

"Yes, what time is it, anyway?" Irene asked.

Brent looked at his watch. "It's only 6:30 am," he said surprised at the time.

Irene said smiling at Brent. "It's too early for everything, Brent." And pulling him by the hand, she told him: "There is only one thing it's not too early for."

"Irene, please, you are not strong enough for this. You know we have to be very careful," He said trying to get loose from her grip.

"Is there anything more romantic than dying in your arms?" She said.

Brent stopped. He wasn't smiling. "Irene, is that what you're trying to do?"

"Not really. But if it happens that way, is it a better way?"

"What about me, Irene? Think about that. Why can you think I want to do that?"

Irene walked to Brent and rested her head on his chest. "I'm sorry, baby. I was trying to let you know that if it happens that way, not to feel bad for me, and not to feel guilty. We know it's going to happen sooner or later, it might as well happen when I'm happy." Irene said leaning on Brent's shoulder.

"All I know is that I'm going to die with you Irene, you know that," Brent said with his eyes full of tears.

"No, I want you to find someone else, make a family just the way we dreamed we would have a family some day," She said kissing him. He kissed her back. She led him to the bed, and he went with her. . . afterwards, they both went to sleep.

"Irene, Ireneee.....don't leave me yet, Irene, not yet." he said sobbing. He checked her heart, crying he listened to her heart. But there was no use, she was gone. Brent, lay down by Irene, and held her close to him. Every once in a while, he would kiss her. He did that for a long time. Then he stood up and made a phone call.

"Darrell? Yes, it's Brent. She is gone, Darrell. I don't know who I should call first. I don't know who to call, Darrell." He said between sobs for his dear Irene.

"I think we should notify the family first, Brent, I'm going to their house now, and you call the Police because you were alone with her. I think that's the norm. I'll come over as soon as I can Buddy, I am so sorry, Brent."

"I know. Hurry, Darrell." Brent told him.

Darrell arrived at the Hamilton's mansion. It was still very early and no one was downstairs yet. Lorenzo was in the garden. "Lorenzo, please go upstairs, or have someone go, and tell them I'm down here. I need to speak with them."

"Yes, Sir." Lorenzo told him. He ran upstairs; he probably sensed why he was there. In only a few minutes; Charles and Kate came back with Lorenzo.

"Mr. and Mrs. Hamilton, Brent called only a few minutes ago. It is Irene, something happened to her." Charles and Kate embraced each other crying. Sarah came downstairs.

"Darrell! What has happened! Is it Irene? Is she at the hospital?"

"No, dear, she is not." She threw herself into Darrell's arms. "Oh, my God! She didn't get a chance at her marriage. She only got married yesterday." She said crying.

Kate said, "She spoke with me about it. She knew what to expect and that's the way she wanted it. Brent knew it as well. She didn't want to leave this earth without marrying Brent. She knew her days were numbered, and she knew what she wanted to do with them."

Charles said, "Let's get dressed and go to Brent's apartment."

Darrell said, "Let me call Brent first. He had to call the Police; he might not be there himself now."

"The Police, why?" they all asked.

"I may be wrong, but I think when there is only one person with the deceased, the Police has to be called, so he was going to make the call when we hung up."

"Mr. Hamilton, allow me to go ahead and leave first, I don't think Brent should be alone too long," Darrell said.

"Of course." Charles said. "Sarah, call Laura, Christina and Clare."
"Yes, Papa."

"Brent, where are you?" Darrell asked Brent on the cell phone.
"I'm still at the apartment, Darrell. Aren't you coming?"
"That's why I'm calling you; I wanted to know where you were, Buddy. I'm on my way."
"Lorenzo, tell Mr. Hamilton we'll meet him at Brent's apartment."

Darrell rushed to Brent's place. He climbed the stairs, so he wouldn't have to wait on the elevator. When he went in, Brent was sitting on one of the sofas with his hands holding his head. Obviously crying. Brent said, "She is gone Darrell, she left in her sleep."
"Well, you know she didn't suffer, Brent."
"No, she didn't suffer. We talked at length about what was going to happen. She was resigned to it, and she was determined to do what she wanted to do in the time she had left."

Kate, Charles and Sarah came in, they all embraced Brent. "Where is she, Brent?"
"She is still in our bedroom, Kate. I haven't called anyone but the Police. I didn't know which funeral home you wanted, besides that, that's not what I wanted to do today."
Sarah went to Brent and hugged him. "I think that's why Irene didn't want us to get married the same day; don't you think so, Brent?"
"You got it; she didn't want you to carry her grief with your celebrations."
"She never wore her wedding gown. I might wear it myself."
"No, Sarah, you get your own wedding gown. Irene is going to wear hers." Tears rolled down Brent's face. Sarah hugged him and cried with him.

Laura and Benny came in. Then Pete and Clare. Kate said, "I think we best get out of here and leave Brent. Darrell can stay with him. "Has anyone called Christina and Carlos?"
"I did, Mama." Sarah responded.

"Charles, do you have any preference on a funeral home?"

"I was thinking about it, Kate. I guess the one we pass when we go to town from home; will be all right."

"I'll get her wedding gown; she wanted to wear it, Charles."

"Kate, did you and Irene talk about what it was happening to her?"

"Yes, Charles, she felt like she needed to when she wanted to get married sooner than what they had planned. And I know she spoke with Brent at length about it."

"I was the only one that didn't get into the conversation, huh?"

"We all wanted to spare you as long as possible of the reality and finality of the situation, dear."

"It is not helping, dear." Charles said hugging Kate.

The funeral home attendants came over to take Irene's body. Brent ran into the bedroom and closed the door. Darrell looked down; his face was red trying to force himself from showing what he really felt for his friend. After a while, Brent came back and sat on a sofa. "Darrell," he said. "I can't stay here with our practice, I couldn't practice here seeing the same people and working out of the same office that Irene decorated. I don't know where I'm going, but I have to get out of here. I hope you understand. When you get another partner, you can pay me what you think I have coming to me."

"I understand, Buddy, as much as I hate to see you leave, I know I couldn't stay here myself. Let me know where you're going, keep in touch."

"I will, but promise me, you'll give me a little time. You can leave now, Darrell."

Two days had passed, No one had seen Brent. Darrell went back to the apartment. He knocked, "Brent, Brent," he said, "its Darrell."

Brent came to the door. "Come in," he said.

Darrell said, "Brent, the funeral is tomorrow. You need to go to the funeral home tonight." Everybody is going to be there. There're several hundred flower arrangements and plants. "Irene is wearing her wedding dress."

Brent looked at Darrell. "And you want me to come to see her in that? When I promised her she would wear the wedding dress for our wedding? And she is wearing it for her funeral? I'm not going to the funeral, Darrell. One more thing, I want Irene to wear our wedding band and her engagement ring."

"I'll let them know, but don't you think the Hamilton's are grieving for their daughter? You have to come for them."

"No, Darrell. I'm going to see them at home. But no one, not you, not even them, can talk me into going to the funeral. I made a decision, I'm leaving on my sail boat, and I'm just going to get in my boat and set a destination and let the boat go."

"Where is your sail boat now?"

"It was in New York, that was the only thing that kept me sane when I lived there. But not long ago, I had the boat moved to Charleston, South Carolina. I thought it would be easier for me to go out there some time on a vacation. Now, I think I'm going to move in it and travel somewhere around there. I'm leaving tomorrow, Darrell."

"Brent, how can I get in touch with you to pay you?"

"I'm going to keep my account open over here; you can deposit the money there."

It was late that night, when Brent walked into the Hamilton home.

"Brent," said Kate, "How are you, son?"

He didn't answer. "I only came to say goodbye. I'm leaving in the morning."

"Brent, you shouldn't do that. Look what you're leaving behind."

"I'm not leaving anything behind, Kate; I couldn't work here any longer. Irene decorated the office, everything reminds me of her. No, it's best if I leave."

"Where would you go?"

"I really don't have any idea right now. All I know is, I'm going in my sail boat. By the way, do you know if Irene had the chance to finish the portrait of my boat?"

"Yes, Brent, and many photos that we took one day before lunch."

"I remember. I'll take any photos you can spare. Charles, how are you holding up?"

Charles didn't answer. He leaned his head on Brent's shoulder and sobbed.

Kate came back with an envelope; she pulled out the portrait of Brent on his boat. She also had many photos of everybody.

"Thank you Kate. I'll always remember you, all of you."

"Let us know where you are, Brent."

Brent hugged both of his friends and left.

Next day, on the day Irene was buried, Brent boarded a flight for Charleston, S.C. When he arrived, he took a taxi to the pier. He showed his papers at the gate where they let him in. They had a golf cart for transportation to the boats.

"I'm glad you came over Mr. Miller. I've tried to keep your boat clean ever since we got it."

"It's in good shape, thank you. I need to get supplies to keep me in there."

"My name is Bill and I can show you where you can get supplies. Everything you want. They even have maps to travel on the water."

"That's good to know. Well, I'll put my luggage in the boat and I'll go with you."

"Let me help you Mr. Miller."

"It's Brent, Brent Miller."

Both men went into town, and Brent bought everything he thought would need for his journey."

"Well, Brent, you certainly plan a long trip," Bill remarked.

"Yes, I had planned this trip for a long time. Just let the boat go and not worry about where I'm going to land."

"You still need to know where you are."

"That's why I have some maps."

That night, Brent studied the maps. Early in the morning, he started his journey. He eased through the hundreds of boats docked at the harbor until it was the open Atlantic Ocean. He went to sit behind the wheel. "Well, Irene, my darling, Here we are." He said with teary eyes. His body shook with grief. The wind started to get stronger and stronger, Brent checked his map and set the automatic pilot, and made sure the sails were secure. He went into the spacious cabin and went to the berth. In the meantime, the storm was now hurricane strength. But Brent didn't care. He poured himself a stiff drink and went to bed with a book, not that he was going to be able to read it.

"Nothing is going to bother us, Irene."

The boat was barely afloat and every turn was in danger to turn the boat over. The waves were higher and higher every minute. He heard Bill on the radio calling him to come back. He had been calling Brent number of times, but Brent didn't respond.

Brent felt such anguish in his whole body. It was saturated of grief. "Irene, stay with me, baby, I can't stand the thought that I won't ever see you again, or hear your voice, or feel your kisses, hear your laughter, ever again". . . He went to sleep. The pillow case was soaked with his tears.

The next morning it was calm. Brent went out of the cabin, everything was in a shamble. He started to pick things up, threw a few things over board. "Not bad," he thought. He went back into the cabin and went to the berth. "The pilot is still set. We'll see where it takes us. I'm hungry; let me see what I have that I want to eat." Brent ate crackers and a piece of cheese, and went back to the berth. It was open sea; but Brent didn't care any longer where his destiny was taking him.

Days had come and gone, Brent woke up. The boat wasn't moving. He got up and looked outside; the boat had hit the beach somewhere. He looked as far as he could see, there was nothing there. Good, he thought, I'll stay here.

The deck was still covered with debris from the storm. He noticed the sail was torn; maybe I'll sew it up later. He started to clean up the deck. There's no broom here. 'Can't remember everything', he thought. He went back into the cabin and drank a sip of water. He opened one of his suitcases and pulled out the picture Irene had painted of him on his boat. I need a picture of Irene. Her mama had given him some pictures. Here, here they are. He selected some pictures and pinned them on to a bulletin board.

"Brent," he said talking to himself. "Check for damage while you're on a bank. I'll do it later; I don't feel like getting into the water now." Brent lay down on the berth and went to sleep. When he woke up it was dark. Oh, I wonder how much I slept. I can't see anything; I have to find a lamp. I need to organize myself better, he thought as he was trying to find the lamp. Here it is! Maybe I can find something to eat. Tomorrow, I have to try to find out where I am. I've been at sea for ten days, just to the open sea without a course. There is no way for me to find out. I have to find out somehow where I am. Tomorrow. I'll do it tomorrow.

"I'm glad that old man talked me into bringing a fishing rod and tackle to fish with. Maybe I'll fish later for my dinner." He went into the cabin and got some maps and started to try to find his location. For the first time, he turned on the radio. He called. Not knowing to whom he should address his call. He said who he was and where he came from, he also told them he didn't know his location. All he knew was, he was on a small uninhabited island, somewhere in the Atlantic. He had had the automatic pilot set for almost ten days throughout the storm.

He heard an answer. "I am in San Juan, Puerto Rico, and your signal is strong, you might be close by," the man said.

"Thank you," Brent said, "that's good to know. I'll start out tomorrow morning and scout the area."

Chapter Twenty Four

For the first time, Brent tested the power of his boat. It works! He thought surprised it did. After all, the boat had not been used for a long time. But then he remembered the maintenance people at the dock had to keep with it. Anyway, I think I'm going to make me a cup of coffee. When coffee was made, he poured himself a cup and went out on the deck to drink it. He went over to sit by the wheel looking into space.

Several months had passed . . .

Brent with a full beard, walked along the beach carrying a sack full of fruit he had found of his regular trips to the jungle of the island, beautiful, fresh tropical fruit. Any more, that was all he had to eat, unless he could catch a fish, he also managed to build a trap to catch birds, and they fell in it every once in a while. So he didn't get hungry. But he still couldn't get Irene out of his mind; not that he would want to.

He arrived to his boat and started to search the ocean as he usually did. Then his attention was drawn to something floating on the water, .. He got his binoculars to get a better look, yes! Someone was floating on the water surface!

Brent took his shoes off and dived into the water, he swam towards the person in the water, fast. When he got there, he checked for the pulse, is he alive? He asked himself. Yes, he is, he turned him over to start taking him to his boat and.....it's a woman! He tossed away the piece of wood she had been laying on; it was a miracle it had kept her afloat.

Well, I can't leave her out here just because she is a woman. Let's go, Lady. Brent started to his boat swimming with one arm and carrying the woman with the other.

He put the woman in the boat and lifted himself into it. Okay, are you hurt? He asked her out loud, knowing she couldn't hear him. No apparent broken bones. Very gently, he started to call out to her, "Lady, lady, are you all right" The woman started to moan. And then she opened her eyes. She seemed to try to recognize him. When she didn't, she asked Brent. "Who are you? Water, water . . ."

"I'm Brent Miller, from California. Who are you?"

"I'm Isabel Saldaña, from Costa Rica."

"Costa Rica! What in the world are you doing so far away from home?"

"You might not know it, but Costa Rica is much closer than California."

Brent smiled. "You're right. I just didn't expect a woman floating on the water."

My fiancé and I were going to Puerto Rico on a boat ride, we were caught in the storm, our boat capsized, he didn't come out of the water. He didn't survive, he gave me the only lifesaver in the boat, there were two, we didn't find the other one, must have blown away. She was incoherent, she whispered, tears rolled down her face.

Brent looked down. If anyone knew how she felt, he did. He got up to get her a sip of water. When he came back, she drank the water fast, "no, drink slow, it's going to make you sick." Let me see if I have something for sunburn, you are burned to a crisped. Brent went over to his first aid kit to try to find something to help. He found some cream.

"Do you want me to put the cream on your face, lady?"

"My name is Isabel."

"Sorry, Isabel, do you want to put the cream on your face. Or do you want me to do it for you?"

"I don't know that I can find my face."

Brent started to put the cream on Isabel's face and shoulders. "How long have you been at sea, anyway?"

"We probably had been on the boat about one week, then the storm hit us, Carlos thought he could reach San Juan, Puerto Rico, but we never got there. She said crying profusely, "I'm sorry, but I'm just now being aware Carlos is gone. We were going to get married next month. And now he is gone forever." She said.

"I understand," Brent told Isabel.

"How can you understand? People always say that. But how can they understand?"

"Because tragedy is not exclusive to one person; tragedy belongs to many people."

"What happened to you?" Isabel asked point blank.

"I got married, my wife had a heart problem, and she died on our wedding night."

"I'm so sorry. You're right; tragedy spreads itself thin on many people."

"Listen, can you send a message for me? I know people are looking for us, asked Isabel.

"Of course, give me your name again and your fiancé name as well, also the name of the town you came from." "Oh, and the name of your boat."

"You know my name. His name was Carlos Seifert, and the name of the boat was Maria, the name of the town we came from is Tamarindo."

"Let me try to send this message, then, I'll try to catch a fish for our supper."

"If I wasn't so weak, I could catch a fish, I'm really a very good fisherman, but I don't think I could do it right now." Isabel said.

"Don't worry, I'll send this message and then I'll start fishing." Brent said.

Isabel walked to Brent and asked him, "Were you ever able to find someone to answer the radio?"

"Yes, it was the same man I spoke with many times before. He's still is in San Juan, Puerto Rico. He is going to ask around and call us back.

"Good, thank you. And thank you for saving my life. I'm sorry I didn't thank you sooner. I just didn't think about it. Can I do anything to help?"

"Well, if I catch a fish, can you cook it?"

"Yes, and I can catch it too." She said smiling.

"I'll take you up on that, here is the rod," Brent told her. "Ever since I arrived on this island, I have been eating mostly fruit, fish and birds when I can catch them." Brent told her.

Isabel took the rod, put bait on the hook and threw it in the water. Brent watched her handle the rod like a professional; "Hey" he said to her" you have been fishing before, haven't you?"

She smiled at Brent; "My family has a big fishing business in Costa Rica."

"You are a very strong lady. Here you are, fishing when you just came out of such an ordeal, and you lost your fiancé."

"My Priest raised us kids with a thought; don't remember the events of the past, the things that happened long ago. By doing something new, you spring forth. Do you understand it?"

"I think it's a great advice, but it's very hard to follow. I believe your loss is just as great as mine, and you're putting it together better and quicker than I have been able to. Your tragedy happened a few days ago, mine is not as recent, about a year ago."

"The fact that I am fishing doesn't mean I don't want to scream, fishing helps my mind to behave."

"You're right, I just can't do that, not for me, it's too soon for me."

"I grew up with that thought in my head, and I'm thankful for it now, I can see that is helping me at this time. I don't know how many days I was out after we lost our boat. I'm grateful you found me and rescued me."

"Well, you found me; you were only about thirty feet from my boat. I couldn't fail to rescue you, as you put it."

"Yes, you could have. Who would have known?

"I would have known," Brent said.

"Oh, a man with a conscience." Isabel told him.

"I guess, if you always do what is right, neither the devil nor the police are going to get you." Brent said.

"Hey! I believe we're going to eat fish for supper." She said pulling a big fish out of the water. "Does this boat have a place to clean fish on?" Isabel asked.

"It's out on the back of the boat." Brent replied.

Isabel reeled the fish in and Brent helped her bring it into the boat. Then he carried the fish there and proceeded to clean it up.

"Do you happen to have a bucket?" Isabel asked Brent.

"Yes, Bill, in Charleston, insisted I get one."

"Good for Bill! Get some water out of the ocean, Brent."

"Do you have a knife or something to clean the scales with?"

"Yes, I do, thanks to Bill, he insisted."

"I'm going have to meet Bill,"

Between them both, but with more thanks to Isabel, the fish got cleaned. Then she started to fillet the fish. "Brent, did you buy your groceries, or did Bill buy them for you?"

"Why do you asked?"

"I'm inclined to believe that you have grease to fry this fish if Bill bought the groceries for you. If you bought the groceries, we're going to have to boil it." She said laughing.

"We went together and he put in my basket what he thought I should have in a trip such as mine, don't forget, it has been about a year ago when I came to this island. But I've never fried anything."

"Let's go to find a skillet and hopefully grease. Let me see what kind of stove you have in your boat."

"It's gas." Brent said.

"Fine, I like to cook with gas."

"Do you know how to do everything?"

"You would be surprised, I run into things all the time, I can't do." she said laughing.

Brent shook his head. "You know? You have brought more sanity to my soul than I thought I would ever find, for that, I thank you."

"Isabel, this fish is delicious! What did you do to get it to taste like this?"

"I didn't do it alone, Bill helped a lot." She told Brent.

And before he knew, Brent was laughing out loud.

He looked at Isabel and shook his head. "I think I saw a bottle of wine."

He came back and proudly showed Isabel a bottle of white wine.

"The right kind of wine for fish. Next time you make this trip, bring Bill."

When they finished eating she started to clean up, he got up to help. She said, "Keep your seat, Brent, I'll clean it up. Why don't you study the maps, and tomorrow we may be able to find San Juan, Puerto Rico.

"All right, but I don't mind helping with the dishes. After all, you cooked a fantastic supper."

Brent went into the cabin and Isabel finished up with the dishes. Then she poured them another glass of wine and went to Brent with it. "Thank you," he said. She sat on the next bench and just looked at him studying the maps.

"I have never been in this area, are you familiar with this area, Isabel?"

"Some, I imagine my father's boats are scouting the area if they knew. But we were on our way to San Juan; they're not going to miss us for days. Unless they heard your call."

"I can try to call Costa Rica, I don't know if I will be successful until we try."

"What is your father's company name or some other identification for his company?"

"Let me write it down, so you won't forget it."

"Thank you, it may take me awhile until someone hears me."

Brent started to call, hoping someone who knew her father would hear him.

"How long have you been on this island, Brent?"

"I think about one year. That's why the groceries I brought with me are about gone, and I have accumulated so many different kinds of fruit here, I love them. Some of them I have never seen before. I learned to eat them because birds ate them."

"That's good to know."

"No luck, so Brent turned around to tell her he couldn't find anyone. She had fallen asleep. He looked for a blanket and went to put in on her. When she felt him next to her, she started to call him Carlos. Brent said, Isabel I'm not Carlos, I am Brent, remember? My wife is Irene. Remember? I told you all about her."

She had her arms around Brent's neck, "I can't see anything," she said. How do I know you're not Carlos?"

"Because I am Brent, and you are not Irene."

"But I can be, you call me Irene, and I'll call you Carlos. Just imagine I am Irene."

Brent looked, **it was darkness,** and she could be anyone, even Irene................

He leaned down and kissed Irene, **"Irene, Irene," he said, "Yes, my darling, I love you." "Irene, is it really you?" "Yes, it's me; you didn't think I would leave you, did you?"**

In the morning, they woke up in each other arms, Brent was up first, he started trying to get loose from her arms, and she woke up. "Don't leave me Carlos, she said..

"Just a minute, my name is not Carlos, its Brent Miller. And last night was a mistake that can't happen again."

"Why? I was asleep, I was still dreaming. I know who you are. I was dreaming. But last night you were dreaming as well, don't tell me you didn't get carried away with the moment."

"I did. Yes I did. That it's why that can't happen again."

"Brent, if all the lights are off, what is the harm of dreaming our loved one came back to love us? I don't love you Brent, I love Carlos, but last night I dreamed you were Carlos. And don't tell me you were not making love to Irene, last night; it was her you made love to."

Brent didn't reply. He left and he was mad that he let himself get carried away like that. That wasn't him at all. I bet Darrell would laugh, if he only knew.

Brent went into the water to survey the storm damage. He swam around and found nothing that could be dangerous for a trip as long as they didn't have another storm.

"Do you have anything else to eat for tonight?"

"Help yourself and look; I only bought what Bill told me to buy: and it has been a long time. I told you I've been living on fruit and bird meat, a fish every once in a while."

"Brent, do you like salmon croquettes?"

"I guess I'm going to love them today. Isabel, I want to apologize for talking to you the way I did. But I want to be very clear, that I don't want to be involved with anyone at this time."

"But you wouldn't be. When that happens, I am really Irene. You are not making love to Isabel, its Irene you're making love to."

"How can you believe that?"

"Because I feel her inside of me, in my soul and in my guts. She is using my body, because she couldn't use hers. But her soul, Brent, it's hers."

It was dark again, and no one tried to light a lamp, Isabel went to her bed and lay down. Brent went to his bed. Before he knew, Isabel was there. You still don't believe I am Irene, you have to believe, she has taken over my body, and she's using me to be next to you. Why do you think I ended up here? She brought me here, Brent.

Brent started to kiss Isabel, "Oh, Irene, I miss you so much, why did you leave me?"

"I didn't leave you, darling, here I am. And you don't have to be careful with me this time."

It was a night of passion, one that Brent had dreamed of before and knew it couldn't ever happen anymore, but it was happening, and he was happy he could still be with Irene."

In the morning, Brent was still smiling. He told Isabel. "I'm sorry I didn't believe you before, but I do believe you now. Thank you for what you're doing for us."

"Brent, you have to remember, during the day time, I am Isabel, and I can't not be Irene, so during the day time, we'll be friends only, at night, we are lovers. All right?"

"Sounds good to me." Brent replied. Then he started to talk to Irene within himself.

"Well, Irene, at least you found a pretty woman to replace you, not as pretty as you, but one that I can live with. Now, I feel more relaxed, thank you for what you did, I thought I was going crazy, this will help me not to go crazy. But I guess you knew that."

Brent was working on the boat, he didn't know what he was doing, he was checking under the boat, he went back up, Isabel walked over to him. "Do you need some help?"

"I would be lying to you if I didn't admit it; I don't know what I'm doing."

"Let me see if I can see anything wrong with the boat."

"Do you know anything about a sail boat?"

"Why not? The bottom of the boat shouldn't be any different than any other boat."

She pulled her pants and top off and a lovely bathing suit appeared on her beautiful body. She was wearing a black bikini that if other men besides Brent had been there, they would have been turning their heads. But Brent didn't turn his head. Isabel went into the water. Just then, Brent saw a shark, too close for comfort, and he yelled, **"Shark"**! He gave Isabel his hand and told her, "hold onto my hand, Isabel, get hold of my hand!" Isabel was trying to climb on the boat, and Brent caught Isabel's hand as she was trying to board the boat.

She hit the deck hard, she was breathing very hard, she sat and started to feel her legs as she thought she was injured, "Isabel, are you all right?" Brent asked her.

"Yes, I think so, but I thought I was a goner. That shark was closer to me than I would have liked," She was shaken; tears were running down her face. Brent got closer to her, and put his arm around her neck, "I know, it had to have been very frightening; we had been in the water a number of times, we throw food in the water all the time, that's probably what attracted the shark."

"Brent, it was more than one shark."

"Well, in the morning, we are leaving this place; I have been here long enough any way. Maybe you can help me with the maps, come' on."

They both entered the cabin and started to study the maps.

At sunrise, they were both up and working to get things ready to leave the beach. Brent unrolled the sail, and the flag he had brought with him.

"How beautiful, what a difference made the flag and the sail. Didn't it tear up in the storm?"

"Yes, it did, don't you see my stitches?"

"I can now, where did you learn to sew like that? Good Lord, it looks better than the factory stitching!"

Brent laughed. "I was being careful; I had all the time in the world."

By now, they were away from the beach.

"Sharks, you can have the beach, I don't think anyone will be here any time soon."

"Can you read the maps, Isabel?"

"I'm sure I can, Brent. Try to keep to your left; it should take us to San Juan, Puerto Rico. We are going through other islands, but we don't know which one we were on."

"Can you remember how far you were from San Juan when the storm hit you?"

"Carlos thought we were half way, when it happened."

"Okay, maybe that will give you an idea of where we are."

"No, not yet. Don't you have an idea where you were?"

"My storm it's a year old, and I put the boat on automatic pilot, and left it there. throughout the storm. I just didn't care if I made it somewhere or not, the storm brought me there, but like said, that was about one year ago. I guess five days went by after the latest storm before I saw you floating on the water, and you know the rest."

"I keep thinking I have to be very thankful the sharks didn't find me when I was out on that little inflatable raft. There was enough room for Carlos; I don't know why he didn't get on it."

"Have you thought that the storm was so violent that the wind didn't let him get on board? I was in the cabin and ended up lying down on the deck because I couldn't stay on the berth. I really can't imagine you staying in that little boat for three or four days, and passed out."

"I wasn't out the whole time; we didn't have hardly anything to eat in the boat. Between that and very little water, and just be in the exposure of the weather, I guess it contributed to make me lose consciousness."

"And all I thought to do; was offered you water."

"That's what I wanted. I remember, all I wanted was water."

"And when you ate, you had to cook it." Brent hit his forehead.

"I'm tough, I may not look it, but I guarantee you I'm tough."

"Well, we had a good day and it's almost dark, Isabel, I think I'll put the automatic pilot and try to find us something to eat. We still have a lot of fruit."

"No need for that, I found two cans of soup in your counter, we're having soup, and unless you can find something else I didn't see." "I hope we reach land somewhere so we can buy groceries."

"If we do, I'll do the shopping." Isabel said smiling at Brent.

They both went into the cabin to heat the soup. When they're finished, Isabel said, "I'll put things up. This might be our last night together."

Brent looked at her, but remained silent. He went to her and offered her his hand.

She took it and went with him. . .

"Do you really think we won't see each other again?" Brent asked Isabel.

"Brent, you told me you're staying here, and I have to call home and let them know I'm still alive."

"Something else you need to do, you need to go to the police and let them know about Carlos's drowning in the storm."

"When we arrive in San Juan, let's get separate rooms at the hotel, I'll go to the police station with you, after all, I rescued you. I also need to call home. I want them to send me Irene's death certificate."

"Finally!, I think that is San Juan." Isabel said.

"I have never seen it. It's a pretty city, but it could be any other island, I wouldn't know the difference." Brent answered.

Brent took the boat in and went in to register the boat to be able to leave it there.

"I've been meaning to thank you for the use of your clothes. They fit pretty well."

"I wouldn't have wanted you to run around with the same clothes. It should only take a minute; I need to register the boat."

"Let me make reservations for our rooms there. It looks like a nice hotel. Don't you think?"

"Yes, Brent. It's very nice."

"Come to think about it. I'll try to rent a car. We don't know how far the police station is."

"Maybe they can give us the information in there."

"I'll be right back."

"Okay, let's go rent a car, and then we go to the police station."

Brent came back with a very nice convertible car.

"Wow, I thought you had gone to get a hotel room."

"I did, but they rent cars in there, how about this baby?"

"It's beautiful!"

"I thought so; I love convertibles in this weather!"

"Do you know where are we going?"

"Yes, they said its a few blocks west."

"Good afternoon, Sirs." Brent told the policeman.

Isabel approached the police man.(she spoke Spanish to them) "I am from Costa Rica, my name is Isabel Saldaňa, I was coming to San Juan with my boyfriend, Carlos Seifert, in a boat, when the storm caught us by surprise. He put a life raft in the water and put me in it, but he couldn't make it himself, the waters were so rough. I hung on and called out to him, many times, but he never surfaced. I don't know how long I was in the water. I passed out, when I awakened; this gentleman had me in his boat."

"Let me look for the lists of calls of people looking for their family, a lot of people have been lost at sea. And you, Sir, what is your story?"

"I left the United States in the first few days of March of last year, my wife passed away a couple of days earlier, I was badly depressed and when I got to the open sea, I put the boat on automatic pilot and went to the cabin and laid down throughout the storm and all. The storm made my boat hit the beach on some deserted island, I just stayed there, didn't even look for a location, I think I have been there around one year, living on fruit I found in the island, when I saw a raft and a person in it, I thought it was a man, until I went to it to rescue him, and found out it was a she."

"Can you prove that you are; who you said you are?"

Brent pulled his passport out of his pocket and showed it to the policeman.

Isabel said. "I lost all my identification in our boat, how can I replace it?"

"We have an immigration office here; let me write down the address for you, Miss."

"Isabel," Brent told her when they left the police station, "Let's go to a ladies' store so you can get some clothes."

"Brent, I would love to get something to wear, I'll do it if I can re-pay you when I get in contact with my family. I need to call them next."

"It wouldn't be that much, Isabel. Besides, I owe you for all the cooking you did for me."

They went shopping and they went back to the hotel. Once there, Brent gave Isabel her key, and went to his room himself.

Brent pulled his address book from his pocket, "Darrell, should still be there." he thought. "Darrell, its Brent."

"**Brent, thank God.** How are you buddy?"

'I'm fine, considering, I'm in San Juan, Puerto Rico."

"We figured you were around there, did the storm hit you when you first left?"

"Yes, last year it threw me to a deserted island. I was there several months, I don't really know how many. I've been living on fruits lately; I managed to trapped birds and caught some fish. I spend all this time doing nothing, just walking by the beach. Then, we had another storm, very bad but they claimed it wasn't a hurricane. I discovered something floating on the water, when I got in the water to investigate, it was a woman, in pretty bad shape, I brought her into my boat. Later, she told me she was traveling with her fiancé, and he didn't make it in the storm. Anyway Darrell, I'm calling to get you to fax me Irene's death certificate. Did you give them cause of death?"

"Yes, I did. And I had to produce a lot of the tests to prove that she was that sick, because she was so young. Also, her parents had to testify to that effect. Brent, we want you to take whatever you need. I'm going to get Lourdes to deposit more money into your account tomorrow."

"The only thing, I don't know how much money I have in my account. I think there is a branch of our bank in Los Caminos here in Puerto Rico. And the girl I rescued doesn't even have a passport because everything she had, was in the boat. I feel obligated to do for her until she can reach her family. I had to get a room for her, meals or whatever; it has to come from me. I just rented a car. I needed to get the boat checked because after the storm something may have been broken under the boat, and when I was trying to get underneath we saw several sharks, so I decided it had to stay broken."

"Brent, I'll send Lourdes to the bank and deposit money in your account. And I'll go to the Hamilton's tonight and get Irene's death certificate. I'll fax it tomorrow."

"How was the wedding, Darrell?"

"Well, I don't have to tell you, it has been a nightmare over here. We are getting married, but just us. Even Sarah doesn't want to wear a wedding gown now."

"Is Sarah there with you? Let me talk to her." Brent told Darrell.

"Brent, Brent, how are you? How are you doing?" Sarah told Brent all excited.

"I'm doing fine, Sarah. I wanted to speak with you, because I know how Irene felt about you and your wedding. That's why she didn't want you to get married on the same day as she did. Get your wedding gown Sarah, do it in Irene's name. She would want you to do that. You shouldn't have waited this long to get married. Now, get everything ready. If you don't want to invite anyone, that's fine, but wear a wedding gown and have many photos taken, and you send one to me. Okay? And tell your parents I often think of them, of all of you. I love you. Let me speak with Darrell again."

"We'll get married right away, Brent. We just didn't want to be happy with Irene gone. Thank you for calling, Brent. We all wanted to hear from you, call back soon."

"Okay, buddy; this is the fax number they gave me at the hotel. It was nice talking to you. Don't worry about me, I'll be all right. I just couldn't stay there, Darrell. Everything reminds me of Irene, she decorated the office, I couldn't work in there, not ever again."

Brent went to Isabel's room. "I didn't think to tell you to go ahead and call your family, let them know you're all right. I don't think you can leave here until you have some kind of papers, also, until it's clear about your fiancé's death."

"Thank you for your help, can I give my parents your name? They might want to know who I am with."

"Of course you can, here is my business card, and a phone number where they can find out I'm not a killer," He said smiling at her.

"Thank you, Doctor Miller." She said, making a funny face to him.

It reminded him of Irene, that's what Irene would have done.

"When you finish with your call, come to my room and we can go to dinner."

"What is your room number? You left me here, remember?"

"We are neighbors; I'm on the next wall. I have never thought of asking you, how come you speak such excellent English?"

"I went to the University of Miami; I came back only last summer."

Chapter Twenty Five

"Well? Were you able to reach your parents?" Brent asked Isabel.

"They were so happy to hear from me. They thought I was dead! Of course they are sorry about Carlos drowning. I told them I have to wait for that to clear up before I can go home."

"I have driven around the front of all the big hotels; did you see a restaurant you think sounds good to you?" Brent asked Isabel.

"There are several steak houses, and they usually carry everything. I've always like to go to them."

"You know, Irene and I used to go to a steak house in Los Caminos for the same reason."

"I'm sorry; we don't have to go to one."

"Oh, no, we can go to the first one you locate. I just thought it was kind of funny."

"By the way, you have good taste; you picked a pretty dress." She was wearing an off white strapless dress with a 'bolero' fitted jacket and a flower design around the skirt hemline, simple but very appealing summer dress.

"Thank you."

When they went in, they were seated immediately.

They brought them the menu, Isabel started to read it. "Brent, they have roast beef in wine sauce! I love that, that's what I want. I used to eat it all the time when I lived in Miami; I thought I would never find it again."

Brent closed his eyes. "Brent, did I say something wrong?" He looked at her with teary eyes. "Brent, what did I say?"

"That restaurant I told you about Irene and I used to eat all the time? That's what we ate most of the time, roast beef in wine sauce."

Isabel covered her mouth in disbelief. "We don't have to eat that, Brent."

"No, I feel Irene is right here with me, and you are Irene. You said, yourself, you felt she was inside of you when we were making love. I couldn't believe something like this could ever happen. But ours was such a tragedy, that she found you for me, <u>we need to get married, Isabel.</u>"

"Brent, no, there are too many things against us. For one thing, I don't want to pack my things and live in the United States."

"I don't think I want to go back to the United States, Isabel. I can set up a Clinic where you live. We can go every once in a while for a vacation. That will be enough for me."

The waiter was there to get their order. Brent said. "Two orders of your roast beef in wine sauce. What do you want to drink?"

"Water, I don't want to get tipsy."

"Of course." Brent said with a sad smile thinking of Irene.

When they went back to the hotel, Brent left Isabel by her room, and then he went to his room. In just a couple of minutes, he opened the adjoining door, Isabel smiled, Brent said,

"I'll take a quick shower and I'll come back for a drink, is that all right?" She nodded.

When Brent came back, he had shaved his beard, and smiling at Isabel, he asked her, "How do you like the new Brent?

"Oh, I love it! To be honest with you, I have never liked beards. Thank you. You really are a very handsome fellow.""

The sunrise woke Brent up, he smiled at Isabel. "I'm sorry I haven't asked you about your relationship with Carlos, I don't know how you feel about getting married so soon after his death."

"Brent, it seems to me you and Irene, had a great love for each other, and you are ready to get married. Carlos and I, was a marriage that had been arranged by our parents when we were children. We liked each other, but we didn't love each other."

"Do you want to wait to go to Costa Rica to get married? Or do you want to do it here in San Juan, after you get your papers."

"Brent, I want you to know I wasn't going to say anything to you. But since you are proposing anyway, I think I will tell you. I believe I'm pregnant with your child."

"Isabel, what do you mean, you were not going to tell me?"

"I was the instigator, Brent, and I know that. Being together wasn't you idea. I didn't want you to think I did it to trap you, it was a supernatural force that pushed me towards you."

"I didn't think I would ever want to look at another woman, and it's just about over one year since Irene passed away, I wouldn't have ever believed it if someone would have told me this is what was going to happen. But it did. I can't say I love you, just yet. But I know I can learn to love you, if you take me like that."

"Like I said, Carlos and I were only friends, so I did fall in love with you. And I would like to wait until you fall in love with me." Said Isabel.

"Okay, let's get dressed and go out, I want to go shopping."

Brent saw a big shopping center and stopped. "Come on, let's go in this shopping center and do some walking."

Brent stopped in front of a jewelry store. "Here, here it's where we need to go in."

"Brent, are you sure?"

"Isabel, I am going to marry you. I don't think I would ever do it with anyone else. Besides that, you are carrying my child."

"All right, Brent."

They were standing by one of their display cases. While they were looking; someone asked them if they had made their selection. "No, give us a few minutes, please."

"I want you to pick one that you really like," He told her.

"I feel funny, I know Irene died not long ago, I don't want to be disrespectful to her memory."

"Thank you for saying that. You are not being disrespectful to her memory. I don't believe I am. I never lied to you about Irene, so, you see? Nothing was underhanded."

Isabel looked back in the jewelry case and picked out her ring. It had a small diamond; it was not a bulky ring. Brent liked it.

He took the ring and put it on her finger. "Isabel, I know this wouldn't have happened with anyone else, and I know the day will come when I can tell you I love you with honesty."

"I can tell you now, I love you. And I promise you I'll have a lot of patient with you."

He kissed her briefly on the lips. She smiled. Brent liked her smile.

When they entered the hotel, the clerk approached Brent; "Mr. Miller, there is a fax here for you, Sir." Brent took the envelope, he was grateful the clerk had put Irene's death certificate in it.

"I'll go to my room Brent. You go to your room and open the envelope."

He nodded. He couldn't have said anything at the time. He was glad Isabel understood. Brent went to his room, he sat on the bed and very slowly, started to open the envelope and got the certificate out. And he started to read it. "Irene, Irene," he said to himself. "Sometimes, I lie to myself and don't believe you are really gone, like with Isabel; she likes the same things you do. Now she is having my baby. How could that have happened? But I thought I was going crazy, and then she came into the boat, I found my sanity again. I'll always love you, Irene, no matter what. I will always love you." He wiped his tears and washed his face.

Brent showered, he felt like taking a very long shower. Then he got dressed and went to see Isabel. He knocked at her door. She opened it. "Hello, are you all right?" she said.

"Yes, thank you for giving a little time for myself."

"Any time, Brent, I'm very aware of your feelings, please don't feel at any time you need to hide your feelings from me. If I can help you, please let me know."

"You have helped me a lot. Ever since I met you, and you know that. We have never talked about it, but I thought I was going crazy, **when you came into my life**, my sanity came back, and my life started to make sense again."

"I'm glad, Brent. I often think what it would have happened to me; have not being you who found me. I'd like to go back to the police station tomorrow; maybe they have some news for me."

"Were your parents going to send your birth certificate? I don't know what else you might need to get married, but maybe they told you." Said Brent. "All right, we'll do that tomorrow, but tonight, we have to eat, where do you want to eat dinner?"

"How about if we order room service? I think their restaurant is pretty good. Don't you think so?"

Brent smiled. "What are you smiling about?" Isabel asked him.

"Because I dreaded the thought of having to go out again. This traffic is bad, you know."

"Brent, didn't I tell you when you don't want to do something, all you have to do is, ask me?"

"I know, do we have their menu in the room?

"Yes, we do. Let me get it." She rushed to the desk and came back and "threw" herself onto the couch.

Brent thought, Irene would have done that. He smiled. "Are you that hungry?"

"Not really. But I can eat."

"Do you still think you are pregnant?"

"I'm pretty sure. My 'friend' hasn't visited me ever since the first time we were together. If you know what I mean."

"I'm a Doctor, remember? Have you decided what you want for dinner?"

"Yes, this dish is typical of San Juan; I think we need to honor it."

"I don't know, I'm not too adventurous when it comes to something to eat."

"That's part of traveling, is the taste of where you are."

"All right, you order and I'll try to eat it." He said smiling. "What is it, anyway?"

"Its mashed green plantains, you can order it with beef, chicken or pork. The seasoning makes it unique to this country. It's cooked with olive oil. Plantains are used all over Latin America and cooked in different ways, this is the Portorican way. It's called simply, Puerto Rican Mofongo. And then, we can order a local drink, it's called Mavi. It's a tropical drink made out of fruit juice, very refreshing. I'm told you don't want to drink a lot of it. When you think of having been in Puerto Rico, you can add that to the scenic view of the country."

"It makes sense; yes, I'll be glad to try the food. I was thinking: tomorrow when we check on the boat, we can take a spin in it and go for a ride. Juan, the man who is looking after my boat, put a new sail on; I'd like to try it."

"That will be fun, you know I love sail boats, don't you?"

"I know you are used to boats since your family is in the fishing business, but I didn't know you went with them."

"Ever since I was old enough that my Dad wasn't afraid to leave me by myself while they fished. I must have been ten years old."

"I hope you get your birth certificate soon, we can get married then, unless you want to wait until we go back to Costa Rica."

"We can have the civil ceremony here, and we can get married in church when we go to Costa Rica, unless you don't want to get married in church. I'm Catholic, which religion do you belong to?"

"I haven't followed any religion for many years. When I was going to marry Irene; I received instructions in the Catholic Church and married there."

"Oh, good. That's the door, maybe they finally came with our dinner." Isabel said.

"I think next time we better go to it if we want to eat." Brent said laughing.

Brent looked at his plate and then he looked at Isabel. "Am I going to be able to eat all of this?

"Remember, this is part of your trip, come' on, be brave and try it."

"Okay, I like the pork in it. I like the plantains; actually, I think this is very good."

"Let's go to the police station first, that way, we don't have to worry about coming back sooner than we are ready to after a ride in the boat."

"You're the driver." Isabel told him smiling. She was wearing a short set very becoming to her slim figure.

"Good morning." They greeted the policemen. "We came to check if you have received any documentation for me from Costa Rica." Isabel asked.

"I believed I saw something came in for you yesterday, Miss. Saldaňa."

The man came back with a big envelope. "Here we are."

"It's from my father." She said. She opened the envelope and pulled out a lot of paper work. "Here is my birth certificate, Brent. Look, he sent me a credit card."

"Where is the Courthouse?" Brent asked the police man.

"We are at the back of it, so you can either walk around this street, or move your car."

"Isabel, what do you want to do?"

"Brent, I don't think I want to get married in shorts."

"I'm sorry, I also want to find a doctor and take you there, as soon as possible."

"Brent, we can come back tomorrow and get married, I can wear the dress you bought me the other day. Plus, we need to get our blood test and license."

"Of course, and we can go to a store first and get you a nice dress to be married in."

Isabel's eyes were tearful. "There is no need for that." Brent told her. "I'm going to take care of you, I hope you know that. "

"Give me time to put the top on the car and I'll be ready." They were at the dock; they got out and went looking for his boat.

Juan was in the boat cleaning it up. "You did a good job Juan, what color sail did you get me?"

"I only have white; we have to order anything special you want."

"I understand, well, do you think I can take the boat for a spin? Is . it safe?"

"It wasn't anything terribly wrong with the boat; the sail was the worst part of it. It just needed a good cleaning job after the storm."

"You should have seen it before you got it. Isabel and I cleaned it pretty good, we thought."

"Isabel, are you ready to go?"

"Yes, ready and waiting." She said smiling at Brent.

Brent started the motor and eased it out of the multitude of boats docked in the harbor. Once he was out in the open, he displayed the beautiful sails.

Isabel was sitting down close to the cabin. Brent was gearing the boat. "If I can do something to help out, let me know. I just don't want to be in your way."

"You wouldn't be, but I love to sail, you know."

"Me too." She told him. "Did you get the weather report?"

"You know, I was so happy to leave and in a rush to get out of there that I neglected to do it."

"I think we better get it Brent, do you see those clouds over there? They started getting worse as soon as we got into the open sea."

"I think we both have had enough bad weather for one year. Let me make the call and you steer the boat."

Brent came back. "I'm glad you were looking at the clouds, they told me to get back immediately."

"Do you think you can roll the big sail, Isabel?"

"Of course."

"Here we go."

Brent started to turn the boat around. Isabel rolled the largest sail in.

He could tell the sea was rougher, the waves higher. Brent wished he hadn't gone so far out. "Do you need me out here, Brent?"

"No, why?"

"I think I'm going into the cabin, I don't feel so good."

Brent watched Isabel go into the cabin. But he couldn't leave the helm.

After almost one hour of fighting what, by now, was a storm, they were almost in the harbor. He started in, there were many boats trying to go in just like himself; so the entrance was very slow. When he finally reached the deck, he went into the cabin to check on Isabel.

"Isabel, are you all right? What's wrong with you?"

"It was just the water was so rough, I couldn't stay on my feet."

"Let me take you to a hospital, Isabel. We don't want you to have any problem with the pregnancy, and you haven't seen a doctor at all."

"I was going to say no, Brent, but I better not. Let's go."

"I'm going to bring the car closer. Don't walk farther than necessary."

Brent started to run. It started to rain heavier and the wind was increasing.

When he reached the car, it was raining very hard. He started the car and went back as fast as it was possible and safe as well. He looked, and looked for Isabel, and then he saw her on the pier; she had fallen on the pier! "Good Lord!" he thought.

"Isabel, Isabel, are you all right?" He said kneeling by her side and taking her pulse. She had passed out. He carried her to the car. There was a man at the gate, Brent stopped and asked him to direct him to the nearest hospital.

When they arrived, Brent got out of the car at the Emergency entrance and went into the hospital to get service for Isabel. "Please, my fiancé is pregnant and we got caught in the storm in the middle of the Ocean, when I went back with the car, I found her on the jetty floor, unconscious."

He came out with several medics, nurses and a stretcher.

Brent waited outside, he decided he didn't want Isabel to lose their baby; he needed something like that to survive Irene and stay married to Isabel.

A doctor came out looking for Brent. "Well, your fiancé is going to be all right." He said. "I'm going to keep her overnight. She is in her first trimester and I want to make sure she is safe as well as her baby. I'm glad you brought her in."

"Yes, I'm glad I brought her in as well. Can I go in to see her now?"

"Yes, you can."

"Thank you, doctor."

Brent went in to see Isabel. "Isabel, how are you feeling?"

"I feel weak; otherwise, I'm all right."

"Could I bring you some clothes tomorrow?"

"Yes, I think you better, bring me long trousers and a top, and of course underwear."

"I feel terrible, it was my fault, I should have thought about your pregnancy and being more careful."

"I was just as eager as you were about going out for a spin in the boat."

"I think I better let you rest, I'll come back early tomorrow with your clothes. Do you have your key?"

"No, but you can go in from the adjacent door." Brent leaned over and kissed Isabel on the forehead.

She said. "Thank you." Brent squeezed her hand. She smiled.

When he arrived to the hotel, he went to his room and went into Isabel's room to get her clothes. He looked into the chest-of-drawers and got what she wanted. He went to the closet, not too many clothes. I have to buy some clothes for her, he thought to himself.

Next morning Brent woke up, showered and went to the restaurant to eat breakfast. Eagerly, he rushed to the car and drove to the hospital. He walked into Isabel's room, and no one was there! He felt 'his stomach went to his feet,' he looked around for a nurse.

"Nurse, can you tell me where Miss. Saldaňa is?

"Yes, Sir. She is in the shower."

"Of course, thank you." He said smiling. My imagination is running away from me. He thought. 'I actually thought she had died'. He was sitting by the bed waiting for Isabel, when she walked out of the bathroom wearing a hospital gown.

"Good morning, I brought you some clothes. I saw your closet. If you feel up to it, I'd like for us to do some shopping soon."

"I do want to go shopping, but now, I have my Dad's credit card. Thank you, anyway. I'm glad you came early; I'm anxious to leave the hospital. Of course we have to wait for the doctor."

"Good morning, Miss. Saldaňa, are you ready to go home?"

"Yes, Dr. Peňa, is there anything I should do?"

"I'm going to give you a prescription for vitamins; other than that, when you get home, go visit your doctor."

Brent asked Isabel, "Did you have breakfast?"

"Yes, I did, but they brought it when I was ready for my shower, so I ate it very fast. I don't think it stuck to my ribs. I'm hungry again."

"Good. I didn't eat it the first time. So let's go somewhere and have a very slow breakfast, okay?"

They found a place to stop and eat breakfast. "If you feel up to it Isabel, I want us to buy you a pretty dress to be married in. We need to get our license so we can get married. I'm glad all my papers were with my passport; otherwise I wouldn't have a birth certificate either. Isabel, do you feel up to getting our blood test today? We can go by the courthouse and buy our marriage license. I don't know if they allow us to get married on the same day, but if we do it today we can get married in a couple of days." Brent asked Isabel.

"Yes, I feel well enough for that, let's do it today." Isabel replied.

It was a very simply ceremony, Isabel wore the dress Brent had bought for her to be married in. They had for witnesses workers in the Judge's court. After the ceremony, they kissed briefly. Afterwards they went to a restaurant to eat dinner. "I know I will learn to love you Isabel, I just need some time."

"I know you do, Brent. Like I said before, I'll be patient."

"Isabel, it has been a couple of months and you had never let me know if you want to have the baby here, or do you want to go home?"

"I'm really not sure, Brent, I just want to be with you when the baby comes."

"It has been a long time since we arrived on the island, and I need to start thinking about opening a clinic somewhere. Puerto Rico is part of the United States, so I don't think I'd have a problem working here.

If we go to Costa Rica I don't know if I have to get a license to work over there. But it wouldn't be a major problem; all I need is for you to make up your mind now, before it's too late for you to travel in the boat."

"Okay, Brent, let's go to Costa Rica."

"Have you told your parents you're expecting a baby?"

"No, I haven't."

"I suspected as much. You can tell them we are married. Also, you can tell them we had to wait on your papers, all of it is true. Juan told me earlier, we should travel on a cruise, and have my boat shipped. He said it's too dangerous on my boat. He said lots of people perish in the water. It wouldn't be good for you, baby." He kissed her briefly and smiled.

"Brent!" she said holding his hand; referring to him calling her baby.

"I know, it just slipped, I guess I'm getting out of my shell." He smiled and hugged her close to him.

"I want to tell you I live in a small town. You are a cardiologist so I think we need to go to San Jose, Capital of Costa Rica. It's more for a cardiologist. I live in Tamarindo, a beautiful city on the Pacific side. You would have to send your boat anyway; your boat has to cross the Panama Canal."

"If you want to, we'll go ahead and go to a travel agency and book a trip to Costa Rica. I wish you call your parents and let them know you are married and expecting a baby."

"You are right; I'll call tonight and talk to them."

When they boarded the Cruiser, they were taken to a lavish suite with a beautiful view of the ocean.

"Oh Brent, this is absolutely breathtaking!"

"I hope so. Isabel. You never told me what your parents said about the little bomb you threw their way the other day."

"They said they would let me know later what they think about it. After they meet you." She said smiling. But I know they will love you. I'm glad you brought me a suitcase, I don't know what I was going to pack my clothes in."

"I didn't want you to leave the hotel with their plastic bags."

"Let's go for a walk, I have the feeling I'm going to love this trip."

Brent held Isabel's hand and they started their walk on the deck, she breathed deep.

"Oh, Brent, I love it here, I think this is a beautiful place. Its, kind of a honeymoon."

"Yes, I guess you can say that."

"Brent. Look at those tables covered with food, the platters with fruit to the top, it looks delicious!"

Brent smiled, "I'm glad you're enjoying everything, we can come back some other time. This is July; I guess you're about four or five months pregnant, I think you look quite big for that time. I'm not a Gynecologist, but I think you might have twins."

"Are you saying that to scare me? Because I am, you know."

"There is nothing anyone can do about it, if you have twins; I just thought I'd mention it so you won't be surprised."

"No, I actually think it would be neat to have twins. We have to think of two names, how about if we have two girls, or two boys, or one of each?"

"Yes, I would like that." Brent said. "Let's sit down; we have been walking a long way." The first bench they found, they sat on.

"Brent, if we have a boy and a girl. Let's name them Irene and Carlos."

Brent looked at Isabel with a very surprised stare. "Isabel! Would you do that?"

"We are together, only because they are not. You bet I will do it."

"Isabel, I think I'm getting to learn to love you, but I need to be honest with you; I still can't get rid of my feelings for Irene, they're still very deep in my heart."

"Brent, those feelings are probably going to be in your heart forever. I know that. But if I can get in your heart, just a little bit, I'll be happy. My love is enough for the two of us. Now, let's go get something to eat, I keep thinking that, that fruit is being eaten by someone else. And here we sit talking when we should be eating."

They both got up and starting walking holding hands, "Tell me a little more about what you eat in Costa Rica," Brent asked Isabel.

"We eat a lot of fish, probably because we are in the business. Mama cooks it sometimes with lemon and cilantro, marinates the fish in lemon and spices, and then stews it. I like it like that a lot. There are other ways with tomatoes and onions, peppers and cilantro. I think our main fish its Tilapia. We also grill a lot of our foods. Our food is really kind of bland if you compare it to the rest of Latin America."

"Which dining room do you want to go to?"

"I think I want to eat outside, so I can see the ocean."

Brent looked at Isabel and smiled. "I have to try to do better by Isabel. She it's really a wonderful person. I mean, to offer to name her child after Irene, it's beyond words." He thought.

I'm going to be sad to leave the ship, Brent." Isabel told him. "It has been a good trip. Don't you think so?"

"Oh, yes. Are we supposed to wait on someone to pick us up?"

"No, I didn't know how long it was going to take us to get here, so I told mama I would call when we got here."

"Good, how about if we go to a hotel, I need to call Darrell again."

They left the ship and took a taxi to a hotel.

"Darrell, its Brent." He said, and as soon as he said, "Darrell," Isabel left the room to give him some privacy. "Can you spare a few minutes? I need to tell you something that I'd like to explain. I don't have to tell you the shape I was in when I left you. I put the boat in pilot and went into the cabin; I don't remember steering the wheel on the way. After the hurricane, I started looking around, a few days passed before I found myself outside of the boat, walking on the beach, I found a lot of fruit to eat that kept me nourished all these months. Almost one year passed before I found Isabel floating on the water. After she got over the shock of her ordeal, she told me she had lost her fiancé in the storm. She was very upset by it. In the night, she proposed to make love, I would call her Irene, and she would call me Carlos, I was reluctant at first, but she kept telling me she was Irene, and it was dark, and I couldn't see anything. She kissed me telling me all the time she was Irene. This happened many nights, as soon as it got dark, I found myself waiting for the darkness so I could go to Irene again, and

I believed in my heart I was loving Irene. When we arrived in Puerto Rico, she told me that was the last night we would be together. And I found myself thinking I couldn't lose Irene again. I proposed marriage to her. Then she told me she was having my baby. Something else, she didn't tell me about her pregnancy until I proposed to her, she said she wasn't going to tell me, because she instigated the whole thing. I wanted to tell you first how it happened. And if it is a girl, her name is going to be, Irene."

"Brent, that is so fantastic! I'm happy for you, I know everybody will be. Are you ever coming back, Brent?"

"I told Isabel we may go to the States for a visit every once in a while. But I don't think I can go to Los Caminos, I will never get over Irene, Darrell. Going into the office she decorated, I close my eyes and see her in my office. Maybe you and Sarah can come over here for your honeymoon."

"Brent, there is a Cardiologist who wants to come over and join our Practice, I asked for $150.000.00 for his part, and that will be yours, you know that."

"If he pays that much, send one hundred, you keep fifty, do you think that's fair?"

"More than fair. I'll wait until you send me your new information." "Isabel thinks the best place for me to open a Clinic is, San Jose."

"That sounds good to me, call again; buddy, and congratulations! We will all feel better about you from now on. Isabel sounds as if she is a great lady."

"She really is, Darrell. But I needed someone like her so I could function at all. Now I'm planning to open a Clinic. Before she came into my life, medicine was out of the question for me."

"I can't express my delight to hear you're planning to live. When you left us. I wasn't sure you were."

"When I left you, Darrell, I don't mind to tell you I didn't care whether I lived or died. But now, especially with a baby coming, I hope it's a girl so I can call her Irene."

"That's grand, Brent;but is Isabel going to be able to live Irene down? After all, having your ex-wife's name mentioned all the time is going to be very hard on her. You need to think about this lady's feelings."

"You're right; but this was her idea, if it's a boy his name is going to be Carlos, her ex-fiancé, I thought, if it's a girl I'll propose for the middle name to be Isabel."

"You can suggest that, but the names don't go together, I'm already in Isabel's corner, buddy. She sounds just too good to be true! If I was in your shoes, let the baby be Isabel this time, if you have another girl, she can be Irene."

"You just poured cold water on my parade, Darrell. I was so happy I could say Irene all the time because it is my child, and in my dreams, Irene's also."

"Brent, I'm not going to pretend I know how you feel, I can't imagine that. I saw your anguish, but you need to imagine this woman's feelings, Brent. Make a life for her and you, don't have Irene in between you two."

"I know you're right. I'll give that a thought and I'll have a talk with Isabel. Maybe we shouldn't have Irene or Carlos in our family. Let them be Brent and Isabel. But, I still want you to explain to the Hamilton's about how this came about. I did call Isabel, Irene, for a long time. She told me to. When the lights were out; I felt the woman I was making love to, was Irene. I know I was going crazy and that probably had a lot to do with the situation."

"Don't worry about it, they know what condition you were in, we were all worried about you quite a bit. And we were very relieved when you finally called."

"Yes, and I'm going to open a clinic in San Jose, Costa Rica."

"Buddy, they don't know how lucky they are to have you there."

"Thank you, get Sarah to send me my Diplomas, without frames, it's easier to put them in a frame here than to ship them in one."

Epilogue

Brent walked out of their hotel room and started looking for Isabel. He found her in the hotel Chapel. He knelt by her.

"Isabel, I promise you I will love you forever, I had the time with Irene that the Lord wanted us to have. This is our time now, and if we have a girl, I want her name to be Isabel."

Isabel's tears rolled down her face."And if we have a boy, his name will be Brent." She said.

They kissed; it seemed, for the very first time. . . .